THE
ELOPEMENT

Also by Gill Hornby

The Hive
All Together Now
Miss Austen
Godmersham Park

THE
ELOPEMENT

GILL HORNBY

C
CENTURY

CENTURY

UK | USA | Canada | Ireland | Australia
India | New Zealand | South Africa

Century is part of the Penguin Random House group of companies
whose addresses can be found at global.penguinrandomhouse.com

Penguin Random House UK,
One Embassy Gardens, 8 Viaduct Gardens, London sw11 7bw

penguin.co.uk

First published 2025

001

Typeset in 12.5/16.5 pt Dante MT Std by Jouve (UK), Milton Keynes
Printed and bound in Great Britain by Clays Ltd, Elcograf S.p.A.

The authorised representative in the EEA is Penguin Random House Ireland,
Morrison Chambers, 32 Nassau Street, Dublin d02 yh68

A CIP catalogue record for this book is available from the British Library

isbn: 978–1–529–90333–1 (hardback)
isbn: 978–1–529–90334–8 (trade paperback)

For Charlie, Sam and George, with love

A Note about Names

Edward Austen, brother of Jane, was adopted in his teens by a childless couple, Thomas and Catherine Knight, and became their heir to Godmersham Park in Kent, as well as Chawton in Hampshire. When Thomas Knight died, Edward took over both estates, but it wasn't until Catherine Knight's death, in 1812, that he took full possession. And it was in that year, as he was obliged under the terms of the will, that he changed his name. From then on, he was known as Edward Austen Knight, and decided that his eleven children would drop the Austen altogether and became simply 'Knight'. *How I miss being dear old Austen,* his eldest daughter, Fanny, wrote in her journal.

This novel is based on the true story of the Knight family after that time, a period in which, by an unfortunate coincidence, three of the main actors share the name Edward. Though there is no record of his family ever using the diminutive, I have, for simplicity's sake, taken the liberty of renaming Edward Knight II: Ned.

I leave it to be settled, by whomsoever it may concern, whether the tendency of this work be altogether to recommend parental tyranny, or reward filial disobedience.

Jane Austen, *Northanger Abbey*

THE FAMILIES

The Knights of Godmersham Park

EDWARD AUSTEN KNIGHT, widowed father and elder brother of Jane

And his eleven children:

FANNY KNIGHT

EDWARD KNIGHT, 'NED', heir to the estate

GEORGE

HENRY

WILLIAM

LIZZIE

MARIANNE

CHARLES

LOUISA

CASSY

BROOK JOHN

SAYCE, Fanny's Maid

MR JOHNCOCK, the Butler

BOOKER, Maid to the children

MRS SALKELD, the Housekeeper

SACKREE, known to the children as 'CAKEY', the Head Nurse

The Knatchbulls of Mersham-le-Hatch

SIR EDWARD KNATCHBULL, widowed father

His aunt: LADY BANKS, widow of Sir Joseph Banks, the distinguished botanist

And his children:

MARY DOROTHEA

NORTON

EDWARD (died 1818)

CHARLES

WYNDHAM

JOHN

The Austens of Chawton Cottage

MRS AUSTEN, mother of Jane

MISS CASSANDRA AUSTEN, Jane's sister

PROLOGUE

On the morning of the 25th day of May, in the year 1826, Miss Cassandra Austen settled herself down at the corner window of her dear Chawton cottage, and waited. Though the light was just so – such pretty, spring weather they were blessed with this year! – her mind was too full for work. And, as this promised to be a significant day in her own personal history, she should preserve all her energies for later. So instead, she simply sat – this was quite out of character – with empty hands clasped in an empty lap, and eyes firmly trained on the Winchester Road. But rather like a watched kettle, the longer she stared, the sleepier it seemed to become.

The new lad from the farm, White's youngest boy, brought up her milk; Cassandra waved, mouthed her thanks and signalled to leave the pail at the kitchen so that she did not have to move. Ten minutes later, there came the sound of hooves; the first stirrings of dust. She stiffened, alert. But it was only a humble pony-and-trap and, of course, *that* could hardly be *them*.

At last, she lost patience. Really, she chided herself, what on earth was the matter with her? Miss Austen was, famously, never known to be idle, and there was a mound of darning yet to be done. She rose to retrieve it, caught the sight of her latest letters piled up on the table, and smiled.

These past two weeks, Cassandra had received more correspondence than she had in her youth! Even the post boy, by nature so sullen, had been provoked into raising a brow. Dear brother Edward, her many prurient sisters-in-law and Fanny, of course – poor girl, how she suffered – they had all taken the trouble to write often, at length. And though she should rightly be touched to be kept so closely informed – after all, she was hardly a principal in this particular drama – instead, Cassandra suspected their motives.

For were they not, in fact, trying to set the agenda? After an event such as this, a narrative quickly takes hold and turns into popular legend. Some wanted to see tragedy; a few preferred scandal, though was that not typical? The more sensible took the view that the best should be made of it. Well, she had no need of their guidance, though she thanked them very much. Cassandra Austen was perfectly able to make up her own mind. Indeed, she already had.

She marched to the work basket, took it back to the window, and let out a chuckle. Oh – was there ever a family such as her own! Though her life had not been without its misfortunes, in that particular moment Cassandra could see only the privileges. She held a stocking to the light, decreed it past saving, set it aside – it was bound to come in for some other purpose – and reached for the next. Certainly, her seat at the edge of this great, never-ending saga was never known to be boring: this was merely the latest instalment. The things this new generation got up to! One could scarcely have imagined it, back in that closed little world of the Steventon Rectory in which the Austens began . . .

As she chose the best thread for a jerkin, there came a sudden commotion. Cassandra tightened her grip; leaned forward: face pressed to the window. And yes! The coach-and-four in its unmistakeable livery. She must leave now – at once!

First, of course, she packed up the basket – any mess was abhorrent – then she went up the stairs to check on her mother. As ever, the poor lady was sleeping, but peaceful. Her moments of clarity were increasingly rare, but she knew no discomfort, which was a blessing, and the maid could be trusted to keep an eye. Those duties dispatched, Cassandra headed back down to the front door, grabbed a shawl and a bonnet and only then thought to remember her cane. She selected a good stick. One did not need a fall, on that day of all days. With a quick firm stride, she went out into the sunshine, turned right and set off for the Great House.

The route did have its challenges. There were significant hills to be taken both down and up and, lately, Cassandra found it a struggle. Of course, she could always find some good man in the village willing to take her by cart, but, on the whole, she preferred to stretch her old legs while she still could.

When her sister was alive, they had together been the most desperate walkers – that was their phrase. She passed the thatched cottages, crossed the lane, came to the top of the long drive – the first view of the mansion – and then paused. The blossom was heavy; the air purest green. The glorious vistas of Chawton, particularly at this time of the year – the cusp of the seasons – always brought Jane back to life in her mind.

And how she missed the dear one in that moment! They would have so much to discuss and would no doubt have done so late into the night. Feeling again the sharp pain of her absence – the loss was a wound that could never quite heal – Cassandra could not help but wonder: what would Jane have made of it all?

PART ONE

CHAPTER I

Fanny Knight of Godmersham Park was in the twenty-eighth year of her settled existence when she suddenly found her life changed.

It was 30 August 1820, and she was late to breakfast that morning, having spent a hot, difficult hour in the linen cupboard with Mrs Salkeld. Fanny always aimed to do the more tiresome tasks early in the day, and there was little more tiresome than the counting of pillowslips or the company of the housekeeper. By the time she got to the table, the rest of the family had already left to pursue their various sporting interests.

Fanny made herself comfortable, poured her own tea and glanced through the long window. It was the third week of infernal hot weather and even the impeccable Godmersham lawn was baked brown as a biscuit. She surrendered to worry – on the subject of younger children, the force of the sun and the wearing of hats – and then determined to enjoy her moment of solitude before the next duties beckoned.

With one hand, she stirred; the other rifled through that morning's post. A letter from Ned: no doubt a detailed account of some triumph against fish, fowl or Hampshire cricketer. Dear brother – few beings were safe. Fanny would save that to last. She raised the dish to her lips, saw the next was from her Aunt Cassandra, gave a tight little sigh and put that to one side. Fanny replaced dish upon saucer and, from what little had been left for her, selected something to eat.

The hand on the next packet was not immediately known to her. She turned it from front to back, decreed its author to be masculine – such strength and confidence in the stroke – and nibbled at the edge of a muffin. No doubt it would prove to be tedious; nevertheless, Fanny must own to some mild curiosity. After all, one simply never could tell. And in a deft balancing act of knife and bun, she sliced open the pages, skimmed the requisite address to her person, wishes for her health and read: *You are the only person in whose society I can find happiness* . . .

Good heavens! This seemed to be – *no*, it was surely impossible. And yet it *was*, categorically, so. Fanny held in her hand a declaration of love! The page started to tremble. Her heart thumped at her ribs. Again, doubt flooded in: oh, but she *must* be mistaken! Her eye raced on.

. . . and in whom I can trust the welfare of my children . . .

Fanny's pulse found its pace; the muffin began its descent. The words 'welfare' and 'children' were hardly in the lexicon of romance or high passion. And yet: *Your confidence, if given to me, will not I hope be misplaced.*

Was this, in fact, something yet more extraordinary? Indeed, was it not – might it possibly be – a *proposal of marriage?* Fanny read it again. It felt a little oblique, and certainly cautious – cautious in the extreme. Even after a third reading – it was really no more than a very brief note – she was forced to admit that at no point was the salient question directly asked of her.

Yet it was the work of mere seconds for Fanny's brain to declare that it was indeed a proposal and, as proposals went, this one was, quite simply, a marvel. And not just because it was the first she had received for a good many years.

Everything about it was perfect. Yes, it was more pragmatic than passionate, but then was not Fanny herself? So its language was sensible and serious, but was not the holy sacrament of marriage? One would certainly hope so. And beyond all of that, it also had one more, startling virtue: it was wildly, dramatically and utterly unexpected.

Sir Edward Knatchbull, the author of these astonishing words, was not completely unknown to her. He was now approaching his fortieth year and the families had been neighbours, in country terms – their estates were some distance apart, but no person of much consequence lived in between – for a few generations. The widower had come to dine with the Knights a few weeks before; had been, for the first time, seated beside Fanny and each had seemed pleased to discover in the other a like, sober mind. Then, the Tuesday before last, he had – rather curiously, now Fanny looked back on it: as if visiting a stables to examine a possible new pony – brought his thirteen-year-old daughter over to call.

So he was not a stranger exactly, but nor, by any stretch, could Sir Edward possibly be described as her lover, or even a friend. No touch or look or moment of even hesitant intimacy had ever passed between them. This declaration came quite out of the blue.

Yet at once, Fanny knew in her heart that it was a serious proposal, for Sir Edward was well known to be a deeply serious man: one of sound Christian faith and profound moral certainty. Though it was possible there was a more frivolous side to him, she very much doubted it. His name was never mentioned in connection with any sport or games or amusements – or any sort of fun whatsoever. Sir Edward Knatchbull, the world was agreed, did not do things lightly.

Which was why Fanny found this development so very touching. Perhaps another young lady might have thought it too abrupt or too formal; not this one. If Fanny Knight were the type for swooning – as it happened, she was very much not – but if she could, she would swoon right there in the breakfast room.

For the last three months, her mind had been consumed by nothing above or beyond the Godmersham summer. The season had tripped on with its cricket and boating and bathing and races; visits had been received and return visits made. All that time, Fanny had spent thinking about and working hard towards the provision of pleasure to others. And only now was it revealed: all that time – well, some of it, certainly – Sir Edward Knatchbull had been thinking about *her*.

Since the death of her mother twelve long years ago, Fanny – then just a girl, a mere fifteen years of age – had been in charge of the Godmersham world. *She* was the one plotting and scheming: the holidays, the schools; the doctors, the dentists; the guest lists, the menus. She was the secret intelligence that throbbed at the heart of every family, quite often unnoticed until it was gone. Half her young adult life had been spent behind the domestic scenery, every hour consumed with making other lives run smoothly. The welfare of her dearest papa, ten younger siblings and their nineteen servants was always uppermost in her mind. Try as she might, she could never rid herself of the notion that any insecurity they might feel was down to her laxness; the miseries they might suffer due only to her silly mistakes.

And now – it was quite dizzying to think of it – here was a whole other, previously un-thought-about person who seemed to harbour the desire to look after *her*! The secret intelligence of Sir Edward Knatchbull had formed an idea, taken a decision and propelled his physical self into action without her knowledge or say-so. He was offering to remove the heavy saddle of responsibility from Fanny's back and take control of the reins. So what did it matter that the couple had never been lovers? So what if they had never shared a dance or held hands?

This was, to Fanny, the most romantic thing in the world.

~

Fanny's first instinct was to find her father. Clutching the letter to her breast, she rushed from the breakfast room, across the hall and tapped at the door of the library.

'Ah yes,' came the voice from within. So he was already expecting her. 'Enter, dearest – do!'

Mr Austen Knight was seated at his desk, face to the door, back to the window, also holding a piece of paper. And as she hurried towards him, Fanny saw that this, too, had been blessed by the hand of Sir Edward Knatchbull.

Her father peered over the pages – his letter was the longer – and lifted one eyebrow. 'Well, Fanny?'

'Oh, Papa!' Fanny gasped and fell into the nearest armchair. 'I have *never* been so *astonished* by a thing in my life! Are *you* not astonished?'

Her father smiled benignly. If he felt any sort of surprise whatsoever, he was keeping it well under control.

'Papa, you already *knew*?' Fanny pressed her palms into

the pillows and sat up, ramrod. 'This is not the first you have heard of the matter?'

Her father coughed, stood, made as if to perambulate, before losing confidence in the whole scheme and sitting quickly back down again. Fanny sensed he was nervous.

'Perhaps, Fanny, if you cast your mind back' – he was now focused intently on straightening his blotter – 'you might remember the pleasant occasion upon which Sir Edward Knatchbull recently came here to dine?'

'But of course, Papa. It was only last month!' As if she wasn't stirred up enough, Fanny felt the stirrings of impatience.

'Quite so.' It was suddenly imperative that the left side of the blotter be exactly perpendicular to the inkwell. 'Then I can now explain that the arrangement followed a pleasant meeting between myself and the, er, the, um, gentleman in question.'

'Indeed?' Fanny felt rather affronted. She was, after all, the family's intelligence. 'And might I enquire where this meeting took place?'

Mr Knight looked up with the hangdog expression of a small boy admitting a crime. 'In Canterbury,' he replied miserably. 'At the last Quarter Sessions.' He cleared his throat. 'As you may know, it is now six years since Sir Edward was widowed and his aim was to bravely continue as the dutiful, only parent to his much loved children. Having followed the same pattern myself, I know only too well how lonely and difficult such a situation can sometimes prove to be.'

Fanny stiffened. She had presumed that the immaculate care and concern which she had quite showered upon her father had been enough – more than enough – for him. That he should now suggest otherwise, after so many years of devotion: it was too much! Tears sprang to the daughter's eyes. His confession struck Fanny as both terribly sad and a great personal slight. As they once used to say in the nursery: she *had* tried her *absolute* best.

Her father dropped his gaze. Perhaps after all it was the inkwell itself that was out of place? 'Of course, with the death of his father, his situation is changed. Sir Edward has assumed the baronetcy, is now due to move into the family seat over at Mersham-le-Hatch and, when the House sits again, he will – by rights, perforce, as is quite natural – become the next Member of Parliament for East Kent.'

Ah. As the causes of the proposal were clarified, so the romance began swiftly to dim. Fanny could hardly help feeling a little humiliated. She retrieved from within her habitual, practical self; regathered her poise; rose from the armchair and started a stroll about the library.

'So the responsibilities of his estate will be much more than those to which Sir Edward is so far accustomed.' Fanny was aware of a certain archness of tone, but rather thought the situation required it. 'I hear Hatch is a fine house indeed. The first *private* commission Robert Adam ever completed, I believe.' She turned to the bookshelves, grazed a long, delicate finger along the spines and casually flicked 'Much land?' over her shoulder, as if it were a fur tippet.

Her father seemed a little taken aback by this sudden change of approach. 'It is certainly substantial though I fear I cannot, at this very moment, provide the *exact* acreage.'

'Never mind.' With a quick swish of muslin, Fanny returned to the armchair. 'Now, the children.' She rested her hands in her lap and gazed steadily at her father. When first she came in, her cheeks had been warm; they were now returned to their more natural coolness. 'I had the pleasure of meeting his eldest, Mary Dorothea – a remarkably sweet child. Indeed, I have never before met one quite *so* keen to please.'

It had puzzled Fanny at the time. Of course, one wants the children to be biddable and courteous and so on and she was quite confident that she had raised her own siblings to be so. However, a little personality – individuality, certainly; even impudence, within reason – did add to their charms. But there had been something about Mary Dorothea's behavioural perfection that had caused some unease . . . Studying the plain, colourless creature, looking into her eyes perhaps hoping to see into her soul, Fanny had found nothing beyond her own self reflected back. But of course, she was being silly. The child had been nervous, no doubt, and might improve over time. 'And the rest are boys, if I am correct?'

'There were five sons when his wife died; four now remain.'

'That is unfortunate.' Fanny acknowledged the loss with a slight sombre nod, before moving on briskly: 'Then I quite understand that, all things considered, Sir Edward Knatchbull is, indeed' – she arched one fine eyebrow – 'very much in want of a wife.'

'Oh, my dear child!' Her father rose, came round to the chair, half sat on its arm and took both Fanny's hands. 'I fear I have got this all wrong and done both you and Sir Edward a terrible disservice. Yes, it would be as well for him and his family if he were to marry again now. But at the same time – coincidentally—'

'And conveniently!' Fanny cut in.

'It is, indisputably, convenient,' her papa conceded. 'But we must not let that distract from the fact that you, Miss Frances Knight, have captured his heart. Sir Edward spied you first last summer, at the Canterbury Races; then at the Fountain in the New Year. Our dinner here in July was more successful than you could possibly know. Yes, Sir Edward wants to get married, but he *also* very much desires to make *you* his wife. Both those things are true, and here' – he tapped the letter still clutched in her hand – 'on the record.

'The only unknown now, my dear, is' – he tipped Fanny's chin and looked into her eyes – 'what is your answer?'

CHAPTER II

On 1 September, Fanny sat at her dressing table and stared into the glass while Sayce, her maid, dressed her hair. It seemed extraordinary that, on this historic occasion, her reflection appeared to be completely unaltered. How could this be? Inside she was turmoil, yet there was her same physical self: eyes still shaped like an almond in the identical blue; nose long and yet slender; brow high and wide; hair of rich brown. The only evidence of change in her appearance was her colour. For the past twenty minutes, she had watched the blush on her face as she might watch the ebb and flow of the tide on their holidays in Sandgate.

Though she would always rather be pale, the first bloom to her cheeks she thought not unbecoming. But – alas – it did not stop there. The pink then built to a puce, spread to her neck and, all of a sudden, she appeared like a turkey in fear for its life. That was when Sayce came to the rescue with iced compress and lavender oil, which was all very well. But what, Fanny wanted to know, would happen at eleven o'clock in – oh goodness! – a mere half an hour, when she was due to be alone – entirely alone! – with Sir Edward in the library? There would be no Sayce then. With the dreadful weather – oh, when might it break? – she could hardly hope for even the slightest of breezes. Poor, kind Sir Edward: what would he make of his florid, hot, rather damp future bride?

Two long days had now passed since the interview in the library with her father, and Fanny felt she could look back with some pride on the composure she had mustered then. But, in truth, from the moment she left him – condemned to her own company; forced to confront her own future – she had fallen into the most terrible stew. And she so pragmatic and practical! The whole business was mortifying.

It was not even as if the decision to marry Sir Edward was anything other than straightforward. The proposal might have come as a shock, but it had also come at just the right moment. The catastrophe of her thirtieth birthday was not so very distant; one could hardly rely on another suitor discovering one *before* the event, and then after it . . . well, one might as well surrender all hope. Contented though she was, and much as she loathed all changes, Fanny *would* like one day to know what it was to be a wife and a mother in control of her own home, and not only and forever the single daughter of one's dear papa.

Furthermore, as an arrangement it was, if not a complete triumph, at least socially and economically sound. Fanny would be *Lady* Knatchbull – a promotion not to be sneezed at – in a mansion superior to her family's own. So the case *for* the union was really quite overwhelming.

Be that as it may, she was also keen to create the impression that the match was something more than the dramatic, last-minute rescue of a desperate spinster who could hardly say no. The world was already more than aware that there had been no courtship to speak of. If it were also to learn that she accepted at once, then face might be lost. Before the happy ending was announced, she had felt the need to put on an extravagant display of great indecision. Those around must be seen to persuade her. Fanny Knight was – at last – a young lady with a new proposal in her hand and she meant to enjoy it.

It had been a long while since she had found herself in this situation. Indeed, dear Aunt Jane had still been alive then, and they had worried away at the issues together. Such a happy time! The letters had flown between them: Fanny begging for guidance (should she or shouldn't she?); Aunt Jane returning with wise, loving counsel (but did he *deserve* her?). When it became clear that the young man in question had some other girl in his sights – was never, it transpired, even that keen on Fanny – the correspondence had rather petered out. Such a pity, when aunt and niece had been having such fun.

But she still remembered those few weeks of earnest romantic discussions with great fondness and it was perhaps in an attempt to recapture that earlier pleasure that Fanny fancied, for once in her life, to create a little drama. After all, once one was married, it seemed, one rarely got any attention ever again. So she had chosen a large straw hat from the shelf in the boot room and set out into the garden, where she intended to walk up and down with an anguished expression until somebody noticed her.

The back lawn was, traditionally, Fanny's favourite place for a perambulation, but as it happened to be three after noon and the heat close to unbearable, to venture out there would be foolish. So instead, she headed for the front of the house, between the drive and the ha-ha, where she might at least enjoy the shade of the cypress, beneath which she could play out her charade of heartsick indecision. She did not have to wait long to be seen.

'Sister of mine!' Ned blew across the grass as if propelled by a zephyr while a huge, scruffy hound bounded about him. 'Why on earth are you loitering out here?' He grabbed Fanny by the waist and spun her around. 'Lost your sheep, old girl?'

'Ned, *really!*' Fanny shrieked. 'Do put me down.' He all but dropped her. 'Why on earth are *you* here? You're supposed to be in Chawton.' Fanny straightened her skirts, patted her chignon and looked round to see him already heading back to the house. 'And now where are you going?' Her little tableau was not going to plan. 'Ned! You are *impossible!*'

The siblings had been born very closely together – she was the elder by just sixteen months – but ever since, experience had conspired to drive them some distance apart. Indeed, so wide was the gulf between their two lives that Fanny sometimes struggled to believe they were even from the same family. Ned lived in almost permanent motion – between Kent, London and Hampshire, plus the odd European capital – while Fanny remained rooted in Godmersham. His life was ruled by the sporting and social calendars; hers by duty and decorum. He was ravishingly handsome, madly athletic and a famous delight. Fanny was cross. 'Come here at *once!*'

Ned swivelled on his heels and bounced back towards her. The dog followed suit. 'Did write, old girl.' He returned to her side. 'Don't expect you to treasure my notes, but you could at least read them.'

Fanny had completely forgotten there had been other post that morning. It seemed a lifetime ago.

'Match. Dance.' He flicked the hair from his face with the palm of his hand. 'Rabbits. Shooting. Weather. I say, old girl—'

'I have asked you before: *pray*, do not call me that!' Fanny suddenly felt so drained she could cry. 'And *what* is that *thing* you have somehow acquired?' The dog approached her quite amiably, but Fanny recoiled.

'I say, how dare you?' Ned knelt down on the grass and, with devoted delight, buried his head in a coat that was possibly manged. 'This is Lord Byron, I'll have you know – so called for his looks, brilliance and breeding. You must see the resemblance?'

'And just like his namesake, he will *not* be crossing the Godmersham threshold.' Fanny shuddered. 'Pray, kindly lock him away.'

'Bit much, old girl.' Ned looked up with a mild frown. 'You're in a fine mood . . .' He drew back up to full height. 'Indeed, you look rather rum.' For the first time, he peered into her face and studied her. 'What is it, Fan? Don't tell me somebody died . . .'

Fanny pulled herself together, stood firm and upright. She simply could not cry now. It would send out quite the wrong signals. 'No. Actually, rather the opposite.' She cleared her throat and tilted her chin. 'In fact, it seems I may soon be engaged to be married.'

'And I've been away but a week! You *are* the sly one. Still, not before time, eh? I say, Fan: well *done*!' He pecked his sister's cheek, patted her head; turned to leave and only then thought to ask: 'Anyone one knows?'

'Yes, in fact. Well, a *little*. I believe *you* have made his acquaintance. It is . . .' Suddenly fearful of Ned's reaction, she declared the identity with a great, positive flourish: 'Sir Edward Knatchbull of Mersham-le-Hatch.'

Ned met the news with a level gaze. 'Ah, yes.' He nodded, suddenly quite still and thoughtful. 'Hatch.' He nodded, again. 'Fine place, Hatch.'

'I have heard.'

'Robert Adam, you know.'

'I gather.'

'Excellent cricket pitch.'

'So I believe.' Even to her own ears, she sounded half strangled.

'Bowled Bligh out there, last summer.' He put a strong arm around Fanny's shoulder and began to guide her back to the house, as if she were an invalid.

'Indeed.'

'Top strawberry sponge.' They reached the front door, which opened by the hand of an invisible footman. 'But then cricket's not your thing.' He guided her through.

'Not especially, no.'

'Such a shame.' Was that a reference to cricket or her engagement?

He turned her around to face him. 'You mean to accept him, of course?' The afternoon sun caught the gold in his hair.

Fanny nodded, biting her lip.

'Dear old Fan.' Ned took her face in both hands and planted a kiss on her forehead. 'What it is to be good.'

And with that, taking the stairs two at a time – the forbidden dog at his heels – he was gone.

Fanny staggered into the drawing room, closed the

blind on the corner window without calling for a maid, and collapsed into an armchair and deep despair.

It was all her own fault. Of all people to tell first, she could not have picked worse. Ned was the heir to the entire estate. Ned was due to get *everything.* Unsurprisingly, Ned loved the world and so in turn, perfectly reasonably, the world loved Ned back. He was the only Knight child who could ever really be sure of a life-long financial security; the only one who could marry whomsoever he liked. How on earth could he ever understand Fanny?

He had, at least, been far too sensitive and polite to acknowledge what he might see as any drawbacks to the match. But his shortlist of advantages spoke volumes. A house, a pitch and a half-decent cook: a harsh summary. Was it a fair one?

The truth was, there *were* disadvantages. Ned knew them at once; it was time for Fanny to acknowledge them, too. First, she had always been an inveterate enemy of second marriages: it was surely impossible to love truly, deeply and *twice*. Sir Edward *claimed* to believe that he did, or could, love her and, of course, she *might* one day love him back. But the idea brought with it no guarantee. And was Sir Edward even attractive? In her panic, she could not quite recall. All told, as a match, this fell far below her romantic ideal.

More worrying still was the matter of her replacement. Godmersham could not run itself; her siblings needed some sort of mother figure; her papa must be supported. What if *his* solution was to marry again, too – hand the house to a *stranger*, her beloved siblings to a *stepmother*, which was famously a fate worse than death?

As the sun started to sink on her momentous day, Fanny decided to brave the outdoors once again. She marched to the Gothic Seat in search of some sign; hid in the Temple, awaiting divine guidance.

At last, and as ever, Fanny sought out her father. They took a seat on the terraces and called for refreshment.

'Your *romantic ideal*?' Mr Knight's dish clattered back into its saucer as his hand shook. 'Oh, my dear.' He coughed gently, then patted her hair. 'Were you a girl of eighteen – as was your sister Lizzie on her engagement – then perhaps that might concern me more, but—'

'Oh, but of course!' Fanny exclaimed. The danger of their possible conversational direction suddenly lit up before her. She must arrest it – 'Forgive me! Foolish!' – and create a diversion. Some variant on the moral of beggars and choosers, however veiled, would not boost one's spirits. She moved the conversation briskly on to her principal worry: how would her papa cope without her? To her surprise, on this she found him complacent.

'My dear, we shall all be perfectly fine.' Her father patted her hand. 'How many sisters do you have, after all? Surely *one* of them will be only too happy to take over as my strength and stay. Perhaps I flatter myself to think it not so very *arduous* a position, possibly even a pleasure at times?' He issued a soothing smile. 'Indeed. Quite so. And you will have the whole period of your engagement to show her the way.'

'Ah yes. On that matter I think, Papa' – Fanny paused to bite on her lip – 'a *long* engagement might be the thing, in this instance, don't you?' Things were happening at a speed that did not quite suit her particular character. Fanny loathed all change, in particular change of the sudden variety. She simply must be given time to adapt.

'Hmm?' The cake was a fine date and walnut and Mr Austen Knight was selecting his slice with great care. 'Indeed, if you so wish.'

'And, sir, you would be so kind as to negotiate that when the whole business is—'

'Of course. And rest assured, sweet Fanny . . .' He sat back in his chair, brought his plate to his chest and lifted the cake to his lips. 'Once all is accomplished' – he was surely attempting to comfort, rather than wound – 'we shall barely notice you gone.'

And with that, the decision was taken. Fanny's nerves were by now shot completely to pieces. She could not possibly write to Sir Edward herself; her father kindly elected to do so on her behalf. This brought with it the added advantage that she could never now change her mind.

By the following day, the deal had been done.

∽

And now, as appointed, Sir Edward was waiting down-stairs to make his offer to Fanny in person.

'Thank you, Sayce.' She spoke firmly into the looking glass. She could delay things no longer. Her hair had been fussed at enough. 'I think that's the best we can do.'

CHAPTER III

As the clock in the hall chimed eleven, Fanny tapped, the door opened and the two men were revealed to her. Both stood on the rug in the heart of the library. She moved slowly towards them, eyes to the floor. At once, her father made his excuses and withdrew.

'Miss Knight.' The voice was a rich baritone.

'Sir Edward.' Fanny curtseyed, eyes still downcast even as she rose back to full height. Her horrible shyness had her well in its grip now. Her cheeks were warming at speed. She could not move; she could not speak: she may never do either again. It was a moment of pure torment – agony! Please, she thought – God, she beseeched – deliver me!

Then, as if by divine guidance, Sir Edward reached out to take her hand in his. And by that small and ordinary gesture, as a princess in a fairy tale, Fanny was released from her misery. He had touched her and she had, most unexpectedly, survived it! The blush beat a retreat. At last, she could look up and into the face of the man she was to marry.

Though he might not be the romantic ideal exactly, Sir Edward was a pleasant-enough-looking gentleman which Fanny, in her new joy and relief, decided was anyway much preferable to heroic when it came to husbands in general. Blue eyes twinkled back at her as she took in his round face and features. Despite the white at his temples, the beholder could still see the sweet small boy he once was. As a couple, the physical qualities of each seemed to complement the other. Fanny was spare, lean, long of feature and limb; Sir Edward, with his plump torso and full, ruddy cheeks, appeared as if nature had designed him as a hymn to the circle. He did, though, have the edge on her when it came to their height. Not much, perhaps not even an inch, but still Fanny delighted to see it. As an unusually tall girl, she had always lived with that *fear* . . .

'Miss Knight,' he said, again.

'Sir Edward,' she repeated.

And then he declared. The words that he spoke were no different to the ones he had written two days before. Fanny rather admired the economy. After all, he must have thought long and hard, chosen them with care in the first place. Why not use them again? It was really rather touching. Once more, he referred to his own happiness and the welfare of his children. He offered his 'most unremitting and constant attention'. But this time, it came with the all-important addition: 'Miss Knight, I would be most honoured if you would consent to be my wife.'

Of course, she accepted. Sir Edward gave a brief nod, a small smile, then made to bend his head towards Fanny, his mouth to hers. The air left the room. Fanny's heart stopped. Her whole body froze, screaming resistance. Stung, her fiancé drew back before he could touch her. The moment was lost ere it had begun. All that remained was Fanny's deep sense of shame.

~

It had been Fanny's idea to go out in the gig. Though they were now officially betrothed, her awkward shyness had not abated. Worse, it had proved contagious. The orphaned kiss lurked about them, full of reproach. Even the worldly Sir Edward seemed unsure where to look.

But that was the beauty of driving. Sir Edward himself took the reins; his fiancée sat beside him twirling her parasol: each fixed their gaze on the road ahead. It then occurred to Fanny that, thus uninhibited, any other engaged couple might thrill at the opportunities now afforded them. They would – what *would* they do? Gently touch, she supposed; discreetly make love; share any and all of the heart's hidden secrets. Oh, may the Good Lord protect her from so dreadful a prospect! Surely he would not now presume . . . ? She silently prayed: God, deliver us into good, plain conversation – on the subject of education perhaps, or the church . . .

Sir Edward tapped at a flank and the horses started to trot; they pulled away from the house. 'Now,' he began. 'Let us discuss the children.'

Fanny's whole being relaxed. She looked away from the driver, off to the side, and smiled at the view.

'As my firstborn child and only daughter, Mary Dorothea is *especially* important to me.' He paused to clear his throat, as if – could this be possible? – he was fighting back tears.

Fanny was moved. Such a kind and good man.

'In my estimation, and this is supported by many positive statements from other, less interested parties, the child is *particularly* blessed with all the gifts and talents for which a young lady could hope.'

Having met her quite recently, Fanny found this a little surprising.

'She has certainly suffered, though, from the absence of her dear mama. Therefore, it would please me, my dear – and I am sure it would *her* – if Mary Dorothea were to become your principal concern.'

'Oh, but of course,' Fanny replied earnestly. Nothing could delight her more. Girls she was sure she could do. She had brought out one sister and married her brilliantly; the other three were all set fair to follow and Sir

Edward's daughter was quite obviously the easiest and most biddable – even gifted, *apparently* – of them all. The carriage was now passing the stables. Fanny gave a happy wave to the groom. 'I must say Mary Dorothea struck me as a particularly' – she searched for a compliment which might also be genuine – '*dear* child.'

'But one never can count on it!' Sir Edward exclaimed with some passion. 'It is my firm belief – intractable, indeed – that when it comes to the children, one can *never* let up. They require *constant* reminders of their role.'

'Their role?' Fanny risked a glance at her fiancé's profile, while reaching up for the rim of her hat. They were out on the lane now, and the going was bumpy.

'To be a comfort and support to their parents.' Sir Edward's tone was that commonly used by those stating the obvious. 'The worry with dear Mary, though, is that with her living almost *entirely* at school in Ramsgate, the opportunities are rare.'

'Ah.' Fanny was almost too frightened to ask, but she did have to know. 'And at what age did the child first go to Ramsgate?'

'Let me see. Was it *on* the death of her mother, or just before?' He pulled at the reins and the carriage turned right to the bridge. 'I should say seven years of age. *Possibly* six.' The doves in the dovecote took sudden flight. 'I suppose it *could* have been five?'

No wonder poor Mary seemed so . . . unnatural! 'Sir Edward,' Fanny began, gingerly. 'Might I suggest—'

She broke off. It was crucial she did not cross the line. 'Well, it suddenly occurred: should Mary come home . . . after . . . soon?' She was simply too bashful to say the words *when we are married*, though that was her meaning. 'Of course, there is no need to decide now. However, my younger sisters are delightful young girls and—'

But Sir Edward seemed to have decided already. 'Capital idea!' In fact, had he decided some time ago? 'I took the liberty of enquiring and was told you have a sound schoolroom at Godmersham. The girls can all be taught and raised together. Mary will be delighted.'

So Fanny had said the right thing! The couple were of the same mind! She looked across to the parched Kentish hills and, for the first time, felt the small frisson that comes with wifely satisfaction. It was rather agreeable.

'As for the boys, madam, they should not trouble you much.' They were out now and on to the Ashford road. Due to the heat, there were no others around. 'For they *must* be educated out of the home. There is no other option.'

'Poor dears!' Fanny let go with her instant reaction; then, seeing the expression on the profile of her betrothed, she added: 'Of course, I have no quarrel with the decision, sir. It is just that I should have hated to go myself, and I can only feel for my brothers as we are packing their trunks.'

Sir Edward relaxed a little, smiled and patted the back of her gloved hand. 'That reveals within you a great reserve of kindness, Miss Knight, which is a pleasure to witness. And of course you are right. School can be a harsh environment for a boy and I know very well that my eldest son, Norton, suffers tremendously.'

'Then I am sorry for him,' said Fanny, with feeling.

'Now, now, my dear,' he admonished. ''Tis best not to feel sorry for *boys*. Does them no good at all. I was three years of age when my own mother died and, from that day on, knew not a moment of sympathy. Civility, yes; sympathy, no. And, madam, I am here to tell you that now I am glad of it! Grateful indeed. For it can hardly be said that it has held me back in life.'

Fanny struggled for a moment, and then took refuge in another question. 'So your own schooldays were not happy ones, sir?'

'Happy?' Sir Edward repeated the word as if he were sampling a new dish. 'No, I hardly think so but nor was that their aim, surely? I do, however, carry the burden of profound regret for the unfortunate manner of their ending.'

'It distressed you to leave, then?'

Again, he seemed to be at a loss. 'I have no memory of such a feeling.' He shrugged the enquiry away. 'But I did leave on extremely bad terms with the Master and *that* I would change if I could.'

'You quarrelled with the Master of Winchester College, sir?' That was akin to declaring war on the House of Hanover! Fanny could hardly contain her astonishment.

'We never quite saw eye to eye, throughout my entire school career. Then, in a final fit of undignified behaviour, he wrote such a letter to my father as to be almost defamatory.'

Fanny gasped in alarm; Sir Edward chuckled. 'Do not panic, my dear. He was a ridiculous creature who, mercifully, left College soon after I did. There is no need to go into the details but please rest assured that I can look back on the drama secure in the knowledge that Right was *entirely* on my own side.'

There were elements of his speech that disturbed her a little. A *master* being expected to see 'eye to eye' with a *boy*? Can he truly have meant what he said? But then she remembered: it no longer mattered. Any critical judgement could now be suspended. This was her future husband! She must believe and support him! From now on, Fanny, too, would always be there, with Right, on his side. She was visited by the sensation of a sudden lightness of being: how much less *thinking* would be required of her in this new future. How much *easier*, more straightforward life promised to be.

Sir Edward was dining at Hatch, so he turned the gig around and, sharing a companionable silence, they headed back to the Park.

Finally, he spoke: 'There is something I must confess,' he began. 'The timing is unfortunate and, madam, I beg you to believe that I would never have arranged things thus had I known that agreement between us would be made so very quickly.'

'Oh?' Fanny was instantly uneasy.

'I am mortified to announce that, in a matter of days, I must leave Kent on business for several weeks.'

She felt even lighter. 'Oh, sir! Please do not worry on *my* account.'

'But I must, my dear madam.' He gave a flick of the whip. 'You had the right to expect me to be by your side for the first weeks of our engagement. We should be going out in society; deepening our friendship. I am depriving you of all the excitement which is your rightful due, and I am sorry for it.'

'It is quite all right, sir.' Fanny tried to feel deprived as expected but simply could not. 'We will have plenty of time for all that in the future, God willing. It is to be a *long* engagement after all, is it not?' Her father had certainly reported that it was all agreed. Nevertheless, she saw no harm in mentioning it, just to make sure. 'Will this business be of interest, or pleasure?'

'I hope a little of both. First, I need to deliver my son to his first term at Winchester—'

'Indeed!' Fanny exclaimed. 'My younger brother is set to start there, too. And my eldest, Mr Ned Knight, is close to the College, at our estate in Chawton. I am sure, if I ask, he will keep an eye on your boy.'

The very idea brought her such happiness. Those two formidable tribes, the Knatchbulls and Knights, coming together, bringing added strength and security, increased opportunity, to each and every member – and all because of Fanny! Was that not the very definition of an excellent marriage? Would not the whole clan be grateful? She glowed with the anticipation of glory.

'That is an excellent offer, which I am delighted to accept.' Sir Edward gave a flick of the reins and continued. 'For the rest, I shall be acting on behalf of my dear aunt, who was recently widowed. Lady Banks has been important to me all my life, and takes a great interest in my dear family. She was aware that I intended to make you this offer and will, I believe, be pleased to hear of your acceptance. It is her wish that you call on her as soon as is reasonably possible.'

'I would be delighted,' she gushed, dreading it already. And with that they were home.

'Miss Knight,' Sir Edward began as he handed her down from the gig, 'that was a delightful day and, I believe, for us, an important one. While I am off on my travels, it will be of great comfort to know—'

Fanny alighted on the drive and stood quietly, waiting for the rest of what promised to be a romantic address.

'—that Mary will be living under your care, and being taught with your sisters. I shall inform her tonight and, if I may, deposit her with you tomorrow? And I might bring my boy Norton along also, to meet his new mama. Shall we say late morning again? Excellent.'

Fanny stood at the front door, watched the carriage retreat and pondered its passenger: a gentleman whom, it appeared, she knew well enough to marry and yet not to kiss. It was an odd situation and she determined to right it. If she did not love Sir Edward already, and all the evidence rather suggested that was, sadly, the case, then she must endeavour to do so as deeply and soon as she possibly could.

CHAPTER IV

The following morning, Fanny stood on the gravel in front of the house and watched the same carriage return. Though she could not have believed it possible, the agitation in her nerves was yet more acute. Admittedly, she had a mere day's experience, but it did rather seem that being engaged was just one ordeal after another. It led her to wonder: all those other affianced young ladies she had witnessed over the years, those pictures of perfect happiness – were they all pretending? In which case, she did wish someone had let her in on the secret. For the first time in a while, Fanny felt the sharp pang of want of a mother.

At least she was going into this latest great trial with full support. Her dear papa stood beside her, as close as could be – the front of his shoulder touching the back of her own. Her sister, Marianne, guarded the other flank, squeezing her hand. And when she looked left to right, all Fanny could see were members of her own family, arranged in a line – eleven of them all told, the twelfth due for dinner. She could not imagine a more splendid welcome. Or did it look more like an enemy rank? Perhaps they should break it up, relax a little . . . But then, surely Sir Edward would prefer the more formal approach . . .

It was already too late. The coach was before them and the footman down and opening its door. There followed a brief, eternal pause during which the entire Knight family held its collective breath and then there emerged one pretty pink slipper.

Mary Dorothea Knatchbull drifted down to the drive, more feather than person. It was clear she had left Hatch with a head full of dark ringlets – there were still just a few discernible kinks – but she was now peering out through a lank pair of curtains. What a pity, thought Fanny, straight hair being *such* a curse with the present styles. The child's appearance was met with a united, feminine silence, which Fanny regretted – her three youngest sisters were of the age that set far too much store by the mere superficial and nowhere near enough on spiritual depth – but could not completely condemn. Though Mary's complexion and poise were all beyond fault, her attire was regrettable. There stood before them a girl on the cusp of young womanhood, clad in the frills and flounces of a very small child. Fanny could see she had much work to do.

'Miss Knight.' Mary proffered her right hand to Fanny, took her skirt with her left, arranged her small feet into a balletic position and glided down into a bob. 'I am pleased to see you again.'

It was a most unexpected performance, of the class usually seen on stage in Drury Lane. Fanny was quite taken aback. Had the child spent hours with a dancing master practising for the moment? Knowing girls' schools – which Fanny did not particularly, though that did not stop her forming an opinion – this was the sort of lesson they were required to teach. *On Meeting Your Father's Next Wife . . .*

'It is a pleasure to see you back here, my dear.' Fanny took the little hand; Mary's face conveyed no expression at all. 'I do hope you enjoy your stay.' At some point during the interminable curtsey, Sir Edward had come up behind his daughter. Fanny fixed a bright smile. 'After all, we are all now to be family.'

Somehow, she dared not risk embracing the child, but then a curtsey seemed odd. Into the paralysis stepped Sir Edward.

'And this . . .' he proclaimed, pulling a boy from behind him and into the forefront. Had a shepherd's crook been at hand, there could be no doubt he would have employed it. '. . . is my eldest son, Norton.'

Oh dear, thought Fanny. Poor Norton. He was an

awkward youth – she gathered about twelve years of age – of sharp corners, high blushes and chronic embarrassment, who displayed no discernible immediate plans to turn into a swan. As she and the boy performed the necessary rituals, Fanny felt suddenly exhausted, not just from the morning so far – the heat was building again – but also the thought of the long days ahead of her.

It was as if her dear father could read Fanny's mind. 'It is a little warm out here, is it not?' Mr Knight seized control. 'Let us save the rest of the introductions for later. Pray – Sir Edward, children, do come in.'

~

Later that afternoon, Fanny stood, with her eyes closed, as the maid untied her lemon muslin and lifted it over her head.

'Thank you, Sayce.' She walked slowly to her bed, and gingerly sat down on the coverlet. 'Oh, perhaps you might unpin my hair.' Her hair was unpinned. 'And let us shut out the light.' The curtains were drawn; then, without being asked, Sayce lifted Fanny's feet and laid her down for her rest.

As the maid's footsteps retreated along the hall corridor, Fanny let out a deep breath. Though it had seemed fraught with peril, the day had, in fact, proceeded remarkably well. While the children were absorbed into the household, she and Sir Edward had enjoyed a peaceable walk through the Lime Avenue, during which she had found no cause for alarm and nothing at all had gone wrong. And now her fiancé and father were cloistered together in the library, at work on the settlement that would lead her to the altar at last.

Still, she was thoroughly done in by it.

'Darling!'

Fanny's bedroom door was flung open.

'Dearest!'

With some reluctance, Fanny removed the cool compress with which she had covered her eyes and propped herself up on her elbows.

'We *cannot* believe you could *do* such a thing!'

All of the Knights were good-looking, but Lizzie was, by some distance, the beauty of the family and took with her position the licence to behave without inhibition. Marianne, the next Knight sister down and Lizzie's soulmate, caught her as her legs buckled from under her. Gently, she led Lizzie to the bed, laid her upon it and sat at the end.

'Such a thing as to get married?' Fanny snuggled in beside Lizzie and took her hand. 'Do I not have your permission, my loves?'

'Of course, we're so happy—' began Marianne.

'No we are not!' Lizzie cut in. She sat bolt upright, her glorious face cross and scowling. 'You do *not* have *my* permission to marry *without love*, now or *forever*. Oh, *darlings*.' She laid a hand on her own heart and looked into the distance. 'When I remember my own engagement – the romance – the *passion* – I knew – the whole *world* knew that if Mr Rice could not marry *me*, he would simply lie down and *die*.'

Fanny certainly recalled that Mr Rice had fought hard for his bride, but still she retained doubts that he would have forced the matter too far beyond the limits of personal comfort.

'Which is what *I* want for *you*, Fan dear. What we *all* want for you. That is, if you *must* marry. We *did* rather – no, not *hope*, exactly, of course not—'

'Just *suspect*, perhaps?'

'Thank you, Marianne, yes, *suspect* that it *might* . . .' She grabbed both Fanny's shoulders. 'Because, of course, you absolutely *loathe* any sort of change—'

'And are so *devoted* to Godmersham—'

'But if it *must* happen, why—' She stopped herself, wriggled a little, began again. 'Darling. We just met Ned in the hall. He said this *Sir Edward* of yours' – her tone suggested some mythical being of Fanny's own invention – 'is positively *ancient*.'

'You all talk about it behind my back?' Fanny swallowed hard and was visited by that left-out sensation which was, to her, all too familiar.

'Oh no, *never*! Not at *all*!' Marianne's distress was quite evident. Her most heartfelt desire was complete happiness for all living beings, and the slightest dip brought her an almost physical pain. 'The merest, tiniest *mention*.'

Yet another unpleasantness about being engaged was the thought of becoming the subject of gossip. Fanny flushed even to think of it. And to find one's own siblings . . . The whole business was gruesome. 'He is not quite in his fortieth—'

'Goodness!' Lizzie flung herself back on to the bolster. 'Almost seventy years between you by the time you are wed. I can*not* find it *decent.*' She covered her eyes. 'My wedding present shall be a pair of old bath chairs and then I shall never see you again.'

Fanny gave a heavy sigh. 'Must even the bath chairs be old?' She laid back down, too, and studied the plaster-work on the high ceiling.

As Marianne stroked her feet, to no good effect, Lizzie wailed on. 'We are just so very *worried* you have not thought the scheme *through.*'

'Through?' Fanny stretched out a hand, groped for the compress in the hope of re-covering her eyes. 'Through to where exactly?'

'You know perfectly well, Fan,' Lizzie retorted. 'But if you must make me say it . . .' She lowered her voice, in case a servant was passing, and hissed, '*Marital love.*'

'Oh,' Fanny said dully. '*That.*'

'Believe me, it is *not* a mere trifle,' Lizzie declaimed with the full pomp of the married lady. 'And it is not *just* about the quest for more *babies,* you know . . .' She leaned in to her sisters, and whispered again. '*It goes on all the time,* and is not – so one *hears* – to *everyone's* taste.

Though, as it happens' – she licked at one finger and dampened a ringlet – 'I rather *like* it!'

The two girls squealed their signature squeals of delight – the sharp sound of wildlife being slaughtered at night – and fell back on the bed in fits of giggles.

Fanny felt faintly queasy, and turned on her side. 'Thank you for that, dear. Perhaps now I might rest?'

'Of *course*, darling!' Marianne stood up at once and, with a glance of warning, dragged Lizzie up to her feet. 'We will see you at dinner.'

'There is *one* other thing, though,' Lizzie insisted. 'We just wanted to make *absolutely* sure that you intend to do your duty by *Marianne* before you go?'

'My duty?' Fanny asked blankly.

'Indeed! Why, oh *why*, is she not officially *out* yet? It is the most *baffling* business. We talk about it *between us* all of the time. You did buy her the loveliest white dancing shoes—'

'I *do* love my dancing shoes,' Marianne put in. '*So* kind, Fan.'

'But a meagre two dances and that was that! Not even the *races* and why ever not? *No* one can understand it! Especially as we *all* remember the great fuss you made over *moi*, which I must say' – she held out a flattened palm – 'one neither wanted, nor did one require.'

'Oh, hardly at *all*.' Marianne was earnest.

'But then comes *her* turn, and almost nothing occurs. And will you look at the girl?' Lizzie placed a hand on each of Marianne's cheeks. 'The face of an *angel*. It's simply *too* cruel. But if you are not abandoning us all *yet*, you have plenty of time to bring her out *and* get her matched before it's too late. Do you not?'

Fanny seemed to remember Lizzie's engagement as one long holiday of trousseaus, dances and presents. Clearly, her own would be more on the arduous side. 'I am sure that will be possible.'

And after one more short burst of screaming – rabbit meets fox – they issued a joint promise to be on their absolute *best* for the dinner, and left Fanny in peace.

∾

The delicate green of the drawing room was burnished with gold by the evening sun; the long windows were open, and the babble of happy conversations floated through on the evening air. Fanny stepped out to join the rest of the party – the shadows were lengthening, the air starting to cool – and looked for the Knatchbulls.

There was Mary Dorothea, standing, awkward, beside the white wrought-iron bench, upon which sat the two youngest Knight girls, fresh as sweet peas in their simple pale dresses. Fanny could not help but let out a satisfied sigh. What a fetching pair they were, so decorously placed with the white rambling rose as their backdrop – as if Reynolds himself had arranged them. She paused for a moment to enjoy the tableau.

Louisa and Cassy held hands and laughed together – they could amuse each other endlessly, those particular two. Mary Dorothea lurked, with one ear bent down as if she were struggling to catch what the others were saying. Fanny thought that a little odd. She could not quite judge at that distance, but was quite sure *her* girls would not have been mumbling in an excluding sort of a fashion. That wouldn't be like *them* at all, although perhaps she ought to pop over just to check there'd been no sort of misunderstanding. But just as she began to approach, Ned burst through the garden door and strode to her side.

'My little friends not down yet?' He grabbed a glass from a tray and took a good draught of sherry. 'Not too surprised. Quite the day of it. Knocked out, shouldn't wonder. Ha!' He breathed out, tipped up his glass and drained it.

'Little friends?' Fanny asked, distracted – her eyes were still on Louisa and Cassy.

'The boys!' Ned put his empty glass down on one passing tray. 'Tickling trout, most of the day. Never tickled, poor little chap—' Then he grabbed a new drink from another. 'Time for some excellent bathing, too. Will did all his tricks and the poor fellow's eyes half popped from his head when he—'

Fanny blinked, came to, turned and focused on Ned for the first time. 'Sorry, dearest. I don't think I was quite listening. Forgive me. Who are we talking about exactly?

William did his *tricks*' – she chose not to enquire what these tricks might be. That was best left until later – 'for *whom*?'

Ned made a barking noise. 'What on earth is the matter, Fan? Standing there looking at me like I'm a turnip.' He waved one hand in front of her eyes, as if returning her from a trance. 'Your young Norton, of course!' He took another huge gulp. 'We all spent the whole day with him, showed him some fun. Must say, he seemed rather a stranger to it.' Fanny looked at him, baffled. 'Fun, I mean. As in: never had any. Warmed up eventually. I say.' He lowered his voice and tilted his head towards his big sister. 'That *was* the right thing, surely? Make the boy feel at home?'

'Oh, heavens! Yes, of course!' Fanny put her arm through his and laid her head on his shoulder. 'You are such a dear, kind soul.' This was getting rather awkward. Even Ned had devoted his day to the comfort of the Knatchbulls. It seemed everyone had, except Fanny.

'He was saying he has three younger brothers, too,' Ned rattled on cheerfully. 'They were not able to come today?'

'Sadly not,' replied Fanny, who, to her shame, had not even noticed their absence.

'You have met them elsewhere, I take it?' Ned raised an eyebrow, then shook his head. 'But of course! Sir Edward is hardly going to engage himself to a lady without his children's approval!'

Rather than admit the terrible truth – not only did Fanny not know the children, she was not even sure of their names – she simply smiled and said, 'Forgive me, I must just speak to little Mary.'

Now in a fog of great mortification, she moved towards the three girls. But at that very same moment, Sir Edward and her father stepped out on to the terrace, blocking her path. She looked around wildly for poor Norton, just as the second gong struck. She resolved to sit by them at dinner, but her papa insisted on placing her between him and her fiancé. Fanny could only sit down and hope for the best.

~

The Godmersham table was well known and generally loved for its gentle informality. Though the house was equipped well enough for grand entertainment – the hall was magnificent; the reception rooms plentiful; the dining room splendid – nothing of that kind ever occurred, for the simple reason that Mr Austen Knight did not want or require it. There were no dances, no balls, and should some dignitary pass through the locality, he would not be invited to dine. Their visitors were almost always just family or neighbours, and the resident children, generally being enough to form the majority of diners, were allowed to set the conversational tone.

Fanny not only loved the atmosphere of the family

home, she also took pride in it, which she was entitled to do. After all, it was, in the most part, her own creation, she having been the de facto lady of the house for so many years. This first dinner was, to her mind, her great opportunity to display the sort of relaxed conviviality that was her hallmark. Sir Edward would love her, his children might warm to her and, it was hoped, the bond between the two families would start to grow.

As the footmen moved around the table with the meat and fish, Fanny waited for one of her siblings to start up with some harmless prattle. Who would be first, she wondered, while selecting a delicate pink slice of salmon. Her brother, George, with some apocryphal Oxford lark, or Lizzie on the genius of her firstborn?

In fact, it was Sir Edward: 'An affectionate, large family around a large table is an excellent sight, I must say. One I hope we will recreate when we are established, my dear?'

Fanny preened and nodded. Not only had he noticed, he had appreciated! Her fiancé was a fine man indeed.

Her father, though, looked a little confused. 'You come from a great family yourself, Sir Edward, do you not?'

'We have the numbers, that is certainly true,' Sir Edward conceded. 'Harmony, however, has proven to be quite elusive.' He speared a great side of beef. 'Sadly, I did *not* enjoy good terms with my father, nor with the lady who is now his widow. And alas, also one or two of my brothers – four at a pinch – are not always the easiest company.' He picked up his cutlery and set to his plate. 'I find it simplest to have nothing to do with them.' Despite so much misfortune, Fanny could not help but notice his appetite was robust.

'Then I am sorry for it,' said Mr Austen Knight, with great feeling, 'and for the great unease such a fissure must cause you.' At the very thought of it, his kind face was cross-stitched with pain. 'Were I so afflicted, I cannot imagine ever enjoying even a moment's contentment.'

Sir Edward held up a finger while he cleared a particularly large mouthful. 'It could be distressing, if I so let it.' He swallowed. 'But having thought long and hard about each particular circumstance' – he dabbed napkin to chin – 'I can feel secure in the knowledge that, in every instance, Right has been on my own side.'

Despite the heat of the day, Fanny felt a sudden chill in the dining room. Goosebumps appeared on her bare arms. She beckoned a servant and bade him close all the windows, by which time Sir Edward had changed the conversational subject. Rather like a general inspecting his troops, he had begun to make his way around the table, with the clear intention of slowly – very, very slowly – interviewing each diner.

William Knight was the first to come under scrutiny, which was a relief: no one on earth could object to sweet William. Also, he was destined for the Church – what could be more satisfactory than that? But next up was Ned, and Fanny's heart sank. It was not that she was embarrassed by her brother or her husband-to-be – each man was excellent, *in his own way*. They were simply different, that was all. But still, surely for her sake, *some* commonality might *somewhere* be found . . .

'And what occupies *you*, Knight?' Sir Edward's voice seemed a little louder than usual. One might even call it a boom. She could hear the low, stifled giggles of her sisters.

Ned beamed. 'An *excellent* question, sir, at this time of year. On the cusp of the seasons, one never knows quite which way to turn, eh?' He put down his fork and leaned back in his chair. 'Still the weather for cricket, of course. Spot of bathing? Not yet out of the question, as this afternoon proved.' A hand through the hair. 'But then along come those infernal birds . . .' He brought a phantom gun to his shoulder, narrowed one eye, groped for an imaginary trigger. 'Irresistible, *obviously*. So . . .' He spread out his hands in an invitation of sympathy. 'Truly hard to *commit*, one way or the other.'

Sir Edward sat, flushed and speechless; Ned smiled his winning smile; Mr Austen Knight interceded as an innkeeper might at a brawl.

'On the *business* side,' Mr Austen Knight rushed to explain, 'my son has recently begun living on our Hampshire estate, over at Chawton. It is a happy arrangement that suits us both very well. Does it not, Ned?'

Ned, at last aware that he had somehow committed a rare social failure without quite putting his finger on how, nodded.

'I continue to run things here, while he learns the business of estate management over there, beneath my watchful eye. I must say'– Mr Austen Knight smiled – 'that, so far, I am delighted with the aptitude, diligence and skill he has shown. I am already confident that, in time, Ned will prove a worthy heir and head of the Knight family.'

Sir Edward gave a still-sceptical grunt.

'And of course' – Mr Austen Knight clearly felt yet more might be helpful – 'other options are being considered.'

Ned, mildly panicked, looked at his father, seemingly requiring a reminder as to what these options might be.

'Last evening,' Mr Austen Knight said, his eyes on his son, in the tones of a tutor coaching a pupil, 'we were discussing the seat in Hampshire and the possibility that Ned might stand for Parliament, were we not?'

Ned's face cleared. 'So we were, Father!' He was now happily reconnected with his strong social self-confidence. 'Splendid part of the world – know it at all? Excellent people – kind enough to suggest I might give it a whirl – thought it could be amusing – hustings do look rather fun. I say, sir, you are now in the same line, are you not? We could end up in Westminster together! Happy this, happy that, band of brothers, so on, so forth . . .' He was quite liberally spraying his unique charm around the Godmersham dining room.

Yet Sir Edward remained uncharmed. 'My dear young

Knight,' he intoned. 'Representing one's own community . . .'

There followed a short treatise on parliamentary democracy. Fanny put down her spoon. She had rather lost her appetite.

'And I wonder if you have even yet considered the huge *cost* of the endeavour?' Sir Edward went on.

There then came a merciful pause, during which Sir Edward recharged both his plate and his wine glass and Fanny dared hope he might drop the subject. But with strength reinforced, he returned to the fray.

'POLITICS' – his voice was pitched more for a county-wide open-air meeting than a family dinner – 'is neither a SPORT, nor a GAME, sir!'

And at that, Ned suddenly met with the end of his tether. 'And more is the pity!' His fist thumped down on to the table. 'The country might be a much better place if it were!'

As her brothers gave voice to their approval, Fanny's heart sank.

Tilting her head towards her plate, she peered around the table from under her lashes. She had so wanted Sir Edward to make a good first impression on her big family. Sadly, this was not a promising start. She knew Lizzie's hostility was set in well before dinner. One course down and it was clearly solidified. Even Marianne – the famous friend of all living things – looked a little concerned.

Curiously, the only person who seemed to be enjoying the evening was Mary Dorothea. The dead eyes now sparkled; those pale, invisible lips were rosy and host to a smile. Her pallid face was lit up with amusement and rapt admiration.

The child must love her father very much indeed, Fanny thought. And her anxiety duly increased.

CHAPTER V

Fanny's nerves were still raw on the following morning, when her fiancé drove her over to see Mersham-le-Hatch: the seat of the Knatchbulls and her future home.

'And here it is,' Sir Edward exclaimed as he steered the gig through the gate, pulled on the reins and the couple drew up in front of the mansion.

'Oh, Sir Edward!' Although her heart would always belong, first and forever, to her sweet Godmersham, Fanny could not help but be encouraged by the vision before her. 'It is indeed as fine as everyone says.'

The house comprised an impressive four-storey central building from which immense wings reached out on either side. This may well have been the first domestic residence which Adam designed, but Fanny could appreciate that it still stood as an almost perfect exemplar of the architect's style.

'And do look! All the servants assembled to meet us.' Indeed, the staff was so very enormous – well over twenty in uniform! – as to strike fear into Fanny's young heart. Having run Godmersham entirely alone, she had thought of herself as experienced. But here were many more than she was used to. How was she to cope?

The imposing façade of red brick was broken up with decorations of stucco. Either side of the great portico – and the wide flight of stone steps that led to it – were alcoves housing large, white, beautifully carved figures of marble. Fanny, whose once-favourite governess was almost over-fond of all things classical, was able to identify them at once. 'The Four Seasons!' she exclaimed.

Sir Edward alighted from the gig, walked around to offer Fanny his hand and said: 'The figures you see before you represent the Four Seasons.' As if he had not heard her, although Fanny could not see how that could be.

Sir Edward lowered her to the drive, tucked her hand under his arm, and proceeded to guide her. With her eyes on the central elevation, Fanny opened her mouth with the intention of speech.

'Although,' her fiancé cut in, 'this is the *first* such residence to be completed by the Great Architect.'

Fanny glanced at him sideways. Not only was this acceptably common knowledge among Kent's landed families, but Sir Edward had already mentioned the fact to her several times before. Might she remind him?

'. . . exemplar of Robert Adam's style.'

She decided she should very much not. 'Is that so?'

Sir Edward, she realised, was at his happiest when in the position of being able to explain.

They met every member of staff, with Fanny pursuing a short chat with each, at the same time as trying to memorise every name she was given, before Sir Edward could send them all back to work and the couple was once more alone. And for the next half an hour, they walked peaceably around the grounds to the front of the establishment, while Sir Edward explained, at length, to his kind heart's content.

'The brick wall that runs *around* the kitchen garden is in fact more than just an attractive feature . . .'

'Indeed?' Fanny obliged.

'It also performs the vital function . . .'

Her interested ignorance seemed to bring so much pleasure Fanny found it hard to begrudge. 'How very *clever* that is.

'And how is the accommodation arranged?' Fanny was looking back to the house now, and struck by the generosity of the size of each wing. 'East and west, for example: are all the rooms guest suites?' She rather hoped not. To have to entertain on quite such a scale could prove rather daunting.

'The west houses the library at ground level with

domestic offices beneath,' Sir Edward supplied. 'The east wing is entirely the nursery.'

'All of it?' Fanny could count at least ten windows.

'I believe so,' he replied. 'The general idea is that there is room for all the children to live there until their majority. I gather it works very well. Mrs Andrews has been running it for years.'

Fanny studied the section. Alone, it was something of the size of, say, a good rectory. 'And where does it connect with the main house?' She scoped the elevation. 'I cannot detect the join.'

Sir Edward furrowed his brow. 'I believe it is possible to travel from one to the other from somewhere on the first floor, possibly the second – or is it the basement, now one comes to think? I cannot say that I have often had cause to visit it. Remind me to ask someone for you.'

'And, sir – forgive me – but shall we be seeing your boys today? I have not yet had the pleasure of meeting the three youngest, and should very much like to.'

As Fanny was to be their new mother, the request was hardly over-assiduous. Indeed, now she thought, might it not have been preferable to meet children even before servants? Yet still, it prompted her fiancé to turn and gaze at her with a whole new affection.

'That *is* a kind thought, madam.' Sir Edward's dear face was awash with pleasure. '*Thank you* for your interest. I shall have them brought out to us later. Now, shall we continue?'

Mersham-le-Hatch – or simply Hatch, as it was commonly known – was unusual in having two principal entrances, of equal usage. They had arrived on the south side – looking over the stables and closest to the cricket field – which served its purpose best in the summer months. There, guests could arrive, clean and dry, and swan through the great door and into the reception hall.

The north, though, where the couple now headed, was blessed with the view. Fanny gasped. Beyond the carriage sweep and terrace, the land fell – swooping – away from them. At the bottom, a fine lake glittered and beyond it, rich and verdant, half of Kent draped itself – voluptuously spread out like an artist's model desperate to draw in the eye.

Fanny asked a few questions about visible landmarks which she already knew well, then turned to take in this other elevation and was surprised to discover it had a whole extra storey. This front door, large but essentially plain, opened on to the lower ground floor and offered a discreet vestibule in which one could shed one's damp, muddy clothing – deposit it all in the boot- or cloakroom – and repair oneself in private before one was received. This was favoured in winter.

Together they entered, took the marble stairs up to the ground floor, stood in the hall, the central point from which all the suites radiated. And there stood the four boys, all in a row.

Poor Norton she already knew and, sadly, he was

unchanged by being on home territory. Charles was nine years of age, Wyndham, eight: average-looking fellows, each much of a muchness, who bowed nicely enough. Then the youngest broke with the ranks and rushed up to her skirts.

'The new mama!' he cried out in excitement, while burying his face in her pale pink muslin. 'At *last*, the *mama*.'

Fanny put a hand on his fair head, and was overcome with a heady combination of sympathy and terror. This must be the one whose birth had brought on the demise of his mother. Poor little creature. He would need her to love him.

While she quailed at the challenge ahead of her, she lifted his face, said, 'So I take it you are John?' Saw his face wet with tears, worried he might have dampened her frock, and added, 'How lovely to meet you all!'

At which Sir Edward, beaming with satisfaction at her apparently touching performance, bade the nurse take them away and they went on with the tour.

There! That was behind her. No one could accuse her now of not knowing the children. They had all seemed perfectly manageable and, anyway, by the time of the long-distant wedding, would be several years older and closer to adulthood. Fanny felt greatly relieved.

Then she entered the drawing room, and there her heart fell. 'Oh.' Indeed, the situation was so extreme Fanny was at a loss as to how she might hide her true feelings.

'The architecture is simply magnificent.' This was inarguable. The drawing room was a large – in fact, it was enormous – semi-circle, its floor-to-ceiling windows leading out to a balcony which curved around the extent and provided a height which improved upon the already spectacular views.

'And the ceiling!' She stood in the centre and bent her long neck to study the gilding upon the stucco. 'Among the finest I have had the privilege to see.' But the glaringly obvious must, at some point, be mentioned. Though Fanny did try hard not to stare at the walls, it was like trying not to stare at a boil on a nose: the eye simply insisted on looking. 'Am I right in thinking that in *here*, some objects may have lately been *moved*?'

The financial affairs of Sir Edward's late father had been much discussed in local circles. His three wives, nineteen children and unfortunate liberal tendencies had inevitably combined to throw up the occasional crisis, to which London's sale rooms were the most common solution.

'It is true, there *were* one or two more' – Sir Edward cleared his throat – 'pictures in the rooms a few years ago.' He was clearly in some discomfort.

The panelling, which Fanny could not help but notice was some distance from clean, had huge gaps upon it – dark squares outlining where any pictures had been. She walked through the huge double doors that led into the dining room – the size of the cricket pitch, with long east-facing windows – where a very large mirror had once adorned the chimney breast and also left its strong mark. It was clear from the dust that there had once been carpets throughout. Now the scuffed boards were bare.

'And my man tells me,' Sir Edward confessed, 'that the ceiling in here is in some reasonable danger of – er – collapse.'

'Yes,' Fanny nodded. 'That I can see.'

'Shall I show you the library?' he offered. Then, on seeing Fanny's expression: 'Or have you—'

'I think, my dear sir,' she said gently, 'I have seen enough.'

'Quite so.' Sir Edward stood upright and clasped his hands behind his back. 'Improvements *are* to be made to both house and grounds and, madam, I would like to assure you, will start in the New Year.' It was clear that he was almost frightened by the thought of how Fanny might react.

'And what an exciting project that will prove to be.' Fanny smiled warmly. 'The house has its own great natural beauty.' She tucked her hand back under his arm and led him in the direction of the south door. 'As does the park.

'What pleasure you will have, sir, in restoring it to its rightful appearance.' They walked out on to the steps, and she looked around her. 'It will take a long time, of course, but I hope to be there, by your side, and doing my utmost to support you at every turn.'

They arrived back on the gravel, and Fanny smiled up at the Seasons. Nobody could possibly expect her to live here in its current condition!

'I am so delighted we came.'

Now she had seen it, she could be sure that there was no other viable option than to stay living at Godmersham for many months yet to come.

Her much-desired long engagement was quite guaranteed.

CHAPTER VI

It was a few weeks later, in the middle of September, that Fanny discovered she had been mistaken.

On this particular morning – though she was quite sure she had been as diligent as ever – discussions with Cook had proceeded at an excellent speed. And when the menus were settled and Fanny emerged into the hall, she saw from the clock she had won a few minutes to spare.

'Excellent!' She spoke over her shoulder. 'We just have time to pop into the schoolroom.' As she passed the hall table, Fanny noticed the second post laid out, and yet another letter from Sir Edward had arrived. Tucking it into her dress, she headed for the staircase and lifted her skirts to the ankle. 'Marianne. *Please.*'

Although Fanny knew she would not be leaving God-mersham for a long time yet, she was insistent that her younger sister, Marianne, shadow her throughout the day so as to be fully prepared when the difficult moment eventually came. 'Do hurry along.' If only Marianne showed just a *little* enthusiasm for the many tasks in hand.

'Oh yes, Fan.' There was a tone in Marianne's voice which sounded horribly like something close to bored. 'I am quite sure you are right.' She stopped, looked out of the window and immediately brightened. 'Do look! There goes Ned out for a canter.'

'My dear, if we stopped to watch every time a brother took to a saddle then nothing would get done at all.' Fanny reached back, grabbed Marianne's arm and marched her up the next flight.

'He has promised to take me to the Ashford Assembly while he is home,' Marianne chattered on. 'I thought I might wear my—'

'You really must at least *try* to concentrate.' They had now reached the attic. 'Running this house is very important work. The whole family depends on it.' They moved briskly down the corridor, and arrived at the door of the schoolroom.

'Think of these young girls, for example. I know it is hard to accept when you were so recently of their number, but they are soon to be *your* responsibility, and when Sir Edward has engaged a new governess, she will come under *your* jurisdiction.'

Fanny's hand went to turn the doorknob when Marianne's own came down to prevent her.

'If I may, Fanny' – Marianne's voice was as sweet as her dear, pretty face – 'there is one thing I do not yet quite understand.'

'Then do say, dear!' Fanny was so eager to teach, the question delighted her. 'Anything! You must always ask.'

'It is on this very matter of girls in the schoolroom – the *number* of girls, that is.' Marianne smiled prettily. 'Of course I would be happy to look after Louisa and Cassy – that is, *if* I am still here myself.'

Funny girl! Where on earth did she think she might be? 'And you shall do so splendidly, I'm sure of it.' Fanny did like to *encourage* wherever possible.

'Certainly until I am properly out – *remember?* – and my *situation* is changed,' Marianne shot back.

'Of course! Do not think I have forgotten my promise.' Fanny smiled, though she had forgotten it completely.

'Thank you, dearest. Now, to return to the girls.' Her eyes twinkled with the hint of an affection which her voice did not betray. 'I am happy to take them on while I can. After all, *they* are my sisters! Mary Dorothea, how-ever, is *not*.'

Fanny jumped back as if scalded.

Marianne continued. 'You say the three girls are to be taught together, even once you are wed. But, Fan, what does that *mean* exactly and have you discussed it with *them*? Do you intend to remove my sisters from *their* family home, here?' Her tone was one of genuine, con-cerned enquiry. 'Or Mary Dorothea from her own?'

As she had not quite thought all that through – was it not, now she remembered it, all Sir Edward's idea? – Fanny struggled to answer.

'Perhaps you *might* let me know when the matter is settled, as your decision will, naturally, have a significant effect upon us all.' Marianne opened the door then herself. 'Let us go in.' And swished into the schoolroom.

Fanny stood in the entrance, studied the girls at the table – heads bent over bibles – and pondered. It appeared that, unless she was madly mistaken, she had just received a significant reprimand. And from Marianne, of all people. She would like to be able to bristle with rage at the cheek of it, but the truth was it was quite well deserved.

Since the day she arrived in Godmersham, Mary Dorothea had received exquisite care – cook, governess and, she had to presume, all the Knight girls had made every effort to put the child at her ease. And with one maid in particular – dear Booker: a nice enough girl – Mary had formed a very strong bond, or so it was said. Yet, for some reason, Fanny – so famously good with children of all types and ages – felt some resistance to this girl in particular, which she was struggling to overcome.

What was it about her exactly? Mary Dorothea presented no difficulties and her behaviour was never less than impeccable. Fanny had been given no reason at all to dislike the poor child, but still she found herself going to some lengths to avoid her.

Would Mary *like* to continue living at Godmersham, or did she long to return to her own home? Fanny did not know her well enough to even guess at the answer. What she ought to do, she knew, was lead the girl out of the schoolroom and spend the morning with her quite alone. And she determined to do so, but before that, there was the small matter of the new letter from dear Sir Edward.

As was so often the way in life, for the Lord is kind, the unfortunate timing of Sir Edward's long business trip had turned out to be a great blessing. The terrible shyness which bedevilled Fanny when the couple met in person was no problem at all when she could hide behind her pen. Their correspondence had been honest from the beginning, and was now developing into something quite close to intimacy – romance, indeed. Her fiancé's letters were now the highlight of Fanny's long, busy days. She was beginning to approach something quite close to a version of a woman in love.

Fanny drifted into the familiar, friendly schoolroom, settled down in the nursing chair beneath the chart of the Kings and Queens of England and, with a warm glow of almost sensual anticipation, opened up the latest. The shock of its contents was such that she could not help but gasp out loud.

'Fan! What on earth?' It was Marianne who spoke, but all five pairs of startled, feminine eyes were upon her.

'Sir Edward!' gasped Fanny. 'He says—' She read it again. 'No, he cannot possibly mean it!'

'Has something happened to my papa?' Mary Dorothea enquired in her expressionless way. Her interest in
the matter seemed nothing beyond the mild or polite.

'Oh my dear! Not at all. Pray, forgive me. I am overreact-
ing. It is simply that' – she spoke to the room – 'Sir Edward
has expressed his wish to be married as soon as possible.'

'No!' shrieked Marianne. 'But *how* soon?'

Fanny went back to the letter, hands shaking as she
read on. 'Before Christmas, indeed.' She turned over the
page. 'Oh, possibly even next month!'

Fanny suddenly felt just a little unwell, as if she had
eaten something which now disagreed with her. Through
the new buzzing in her ears, she picked up the distant
sound of Louisa shouting: 'Smelling salts! Now!'

And Cassy calling: 'Nurse, someone fetch Nurse!'

And Fanny *was* about to protest that – No, no! – it was
nothing serious. She was just being silly. Truly, she was
perfectly fine.

Then she looked up and across. And saw Marianne,
completely passed out on the floor.

～

Fanny was sitting in the calming, pale blue silk surroundings of her own private dressing room, sewing his mono-
gram on to a cravat for Sir Edward, when Sayce stuck
her head around the door and announced, 'Madam, Miss
Knatchbull.'

'Ah, yes.' Fanny tucked in the needle, placed the silk down on the sofa beside her, rose, extended both hands and smiled her sweetest of smiles. 'Mary Dorothea.'

Mary curtseyed and stood, clutching her bag. Someone – perhaps Marianne? Fanny knew not – had provided a lawn day dress with a subtle sprig pattern of elegant simplicity, which rather suited the girl. Certainly, she appeared a *little* less plain.

'I thought we might work together this afternoon?' Fanny gestured towards the little pink plush armchair. 'I hope you would like that, my dear?'

'Thank you, madam.' Mary sat.

'Dear child!' Fanny sank back on to the chaise longue and smoothed down her day dress. 'Not *madam*, I beg of you! There is no need for such formality with *me*.'

'Then pray do forgive me.' Mary bit her lip, thought and then added, with a tentative up-lift: '*Step*mother?'

'Goodness.' The child might as well have run her through with a rapier. 'Stepmother is such a *formal* type of address, do you not think?' Fanny let out a light little laugh.

For over a decade, the word had been laden with doom for the Knight siblings – a fear; a threat; an object of dread. When employed either in fiction or anecdote, it – or she – was always a negative. Had Fanny ever heard tell of a *kind* stepmother? The idea was quite paradoxical. Monstrous was the default.

So how very odd of Mary Dorothea to use the term! Of course, Fanny saw that their relationship *could* be described thus – *officially*, as it were. But surely it was impossible for anyone to *really* use the hideous word against *her*? She was so good with children – ask anyone who knew her. Thoughtful, kind, diligent to a perfectly ridiculous degree. Look at the way she had raised her own siblings! They were all quite *devoted*. And while she and the child had not yet got off to the strongest of starts, there could be no doubt whatsoever that their future relationship would be anything less than exemplary. So to think of Fanny – of all people! – as a typical stepmother: well, it was patently absurd.

'My dear, it would please me if, from now on, you would call me "Mama".' So keen was Fanny to come across as warm and encouraging that she was starting to develop the face-ache. 'Do you think you might like that?'

Mary, who had chosen that very moment to rummage in her work bag with purpose, looked up. 'Thank you.' She held Fanny's gaze for a little longer than might be considered quite natural. '*Mama*.'

'There. It is good, is it not, to have that behind us?'

To demonstrate exactly how adept she was at conversing at a thirteen-year old level, Fanny then showed a keen interest in that which Mary was making – took a moment to advise on the perfection of satin stitch – before returning to the cravat and getting to the point.

'It has occurred to me that the suddenness of my engagement to your beloved papa might have come to you as something like, well, a shock, I suppose.' Already

Fanny erred on the side of dishonesty, for it had not occurred to her at all, until Marianne raised the matter.

Mary looked up from her work, betrayed no expression, then bent her head down again.

'And now, perhaps, the – well – again all the talk of the possible *immediacy* of a wedding might have compounded that feeling?'

It seemed Fanny had posed a question to which there was no possible right answer. 'I hope *you* are happy . . .' Mary paused, as if her words were a difficult melody and the next bar was a rest. '. . . Mama?'

It was all so horribly awkward that, on the spur of the moment, Fanny decided to take a huge risk. She dropped the silk into her lap. 'If I am to be completely honest – and as we are one day to live together, then I think that is what we should both try to be – it is not the way *I* would prefer it at all, and I have written to your father to say so.'

Fanny sighed. 'Getting married is a very big step for a lady, as you, my dear, will learn in good time.'

It was not always easy to see the adult in a child and in Mary Dorothea it was nigh impossible. The idea that she might one day be courted or wed seemed more than unusually far-fetched, but stranger things had been known. And, anyway, it felt to Fanny like a kindness to talk to the girl as if she might have some sort of potential romantic future.

'I do not take easily to change. It unsettles me rather – well, greatly indeed. And as we are not so very well acquainted, I would prefer more time for your father and me to get to know one another better.'

Mary gazed back at her, and slowly blinked.

'Furthermore, Hatch is not *quite* ready for—'

Mary, who had spent some months living there with her father and brothers and clearly survived it, cocked her head to one side.

'Altogether,' Fanny rushed on, 'it would be best for everybody if I could be present for one last Christmas in Godmersham. Marianne is not yet prepared, and—'

And when Fanny thought of her whole family coming together without her, she wanted to lie down and cry.

'—and so on. I am sure your kind father will quite understand my position.' Her voice was firm, to illustrate her confidence. 'Besides which, I am of the view that it would be advantageous if you and I *also* had the opportunity to deepen *our* relationship. To which end, I have had a little idea.'

Mary began a great display of checking her stitches. Fanny found she was directing her most winning of smiles on the parting to Mary's unfortunate hair.

'How would you like it if, before breakfast every morning – before I am dressed, even – you come to my room and we take tea in bed together? Just the two of us! I do think that would be rather cosy, don't you?'

Mary looked up. 'Oh.' Her attempt at a smile was less than half-hearted. 'Yes. Thank you.' A particularly long minim. 'Mama.'

CHAPTER VII

On the 24th day of October 1820 – seven short weeks from the surprising proposal – Fanny Knight suddenly found herself wed.

Unfortunately, her wish to delay the occasion for months – even years – did not coincide with Sir Edward's own plans. It seemed he expected to be busy in Parliament in January and therefore required that Fanny be installed before then to look after his children and his home. And if she were to insist on one last Godmersham Christmas, then he would have no choice but to go abroad for at least two years.

Fanny found the logic of this last a little confusing – surely if he *did* go abroad, he could hardly leave children, home or indeed Parliament to their own devices. But such was his passion on the matter – she had never before heard him quite so aroused – that she gave in almost at once. After all, announcing the engagement had been traumatic enough; the idea of calling it off was too much to bear.

It was a brief, plain service in her beloved little Godmersham church, quite as solemn and serious as its participants could have possibly desired. And though she might have hoped – in fact, quite often dreamed of – a glorious moment afterwards, in the pretty churchyard with bells and villagers and all eyes upon her, that was not to be.

Fanny was forced to wait in the porch while her brothers constructed a canopy with which to protect her. Then, hunching beneath it – clutching her dress to keep hem from mud – she was forced to make a mad dash. There were certainly cries of great jubilation, she was sure of it, though they were all but extinguished by the noise of the rain. Rose petals were definitely thrown – she had organised that herself – even if they did plunge straight to earth and melt into the puddles. Fanny was touched by the sight of the well-wishers crowding the path from church to gate, but her progress was too swift to be considered triumphal. Before she could even try to enjoy it, she was enclosed in the deafening quiet of the coach, her new husband beside her.

'That seemed to pass off very well.' Sir Edward leaned forward to rap on the front wall of the coach and, with a lurch and a sway, they started, very slowly, to move.

Fanny looked out of the window – through the

rivulets that coursed down the glass – and captured one final image of the witnesses. None of the Knatchbull children were present – for some reason, Sir Edward had thought it best that they were elsewhere. But the dear Godmersham family was, of course, all on parade. Ned and George – tall, broad and strong – wrapped their arms around each other and held up their handsome, laughing faces to drink in the rain. William leaped up and thrust through between them, and they both boxed his ears. Lizzie and her husband sheltered beneath the old elm, sharing some sweet conversation. Two of her three bridesmaids, Louisa and Cassy, picked up their skirts and ran to the gate, waving and calling her name. If Fanny was at all concerned for the future welfare of her Knight siblings, then this was a comforting sight. Each had his or her favourite; each was safe, folded into – forever protected by – a particular group. She could see, with a pang, that they did not desperately need her.

Only the third bridesmaid, Marianne, came alone, some distance behind them. Her tread was more careful – she was jumping from one island of grass to the next, and walking on tiptoe. What a curious performance, thought Fanny with slight irritation. Until she was close enough for Fanny to identify the chosen footwear.

She was wearing her lovely white dancing shoes! Oh, for heaven's sake. Only Marianne Knight could be so foolish as to wear silk in such weather. Fanny was half-minded to rap on the glass and tick her off. After all, *now* what would the girl put on her feet next time she went to a ball? And only then did she remember. The past month had been such a terrible rush. And really and truly her hands had been full. But still, she had promised and now did feel a slight stab of guilt. In all the bother, she had totally forgotten. Not that it mattered really, any more, given how things had turned out for her. But in the end, Marianne never had been officially brought 'out'.

Beside the happy couple waited a smaller coach, carrying the servants who were accompanying Fanny into her new life: Sayce – dear Sayce! What a comfort it would be to have her – and Booker, who took no persuasion to continue with Mary, once the girl returned to live at Hatch. She craned her neck to meet their eyes, and issued a small, encouraging wave. After all, Fanny understood how hard it could be for staff to change households; she knew how hard it was for herself.

Her husband leaned over her shoulder, rubbed at the steam on the window, created a spyhole and said: 'There, my dear. One last look at your family.' He patted her knee. 'Do they not look happy?'

And with that, Sir Edward and Lady Knatchbull set off for their new life at Mersham-le-Hatch.

~

The first months of married life passed with something quite close to ease. Fanny felt she had coped well enough with all of the various *novelties* that came with her new situation. Well, *almost* all – there was *one* in particular which still seemed a little unnatural. Still, even *that* turned out to be not quite as bad as one feared. And, for the rest, it was all starting to seem almost normal.

But there now rose up before her a whole new raft of challenges. In a matter of days would come Fanny's first Christmas at Hatch. The children were all home – or, at least, in the nursery – and her husband had invited the most august of visitors to join them for the season.

'Lady Banks.' Sir Edward Knatchbull stepped out of the receiving line crowded around the top of the stairs from the north entrance, took her ladyship's hand and bowed deeply. 'Welcome to—'

'Oh, *r-r-really*, Edward.' His aunt, puffing a little at the exertion, steadied herself on the banister, patted his bent head and then, signalling impatience, beckoned him up. 'I am your dearest aunt.' She placed one gloved finger upon her highly painted cheek; Sir Edward planted the kiss in the position suggested. 'Or I certainly should be, as you are my heir, eh?' Lady Banks peered over his shoulder and gave Fanny a somewhat vulgar wink. 'So, madam.' She looked Fanny up and down as she hobbled towards her with an amused sort of eye. 'I take it *you* are *the Bride*?'

This Lady Banks who stood before her was some distance from the Lady Banks whom Fanny had been expecting. She had been prepared for someone slightly grander, more forbidding than Marie-Antoinette. This person was – well – considerably less so. Her unusually short stature and uncommonly round form were both accentuated by a singular dress style. But no doubt the thick tweed, tied around the middle by something somewhat reminiscent of string, was selected for warmth. Fanny fell into a curtsey, too confounded to speak.

'Lovely, dear. Very pleasant, I'm sure.' Lady Banks was now tottering down the line of servants, flicking her hand in dismissal – 'Yes, yes. Very good. No doubt there is work to do. Off you go! Shoo!' – until she came to the end, whereupon she turned on her heel and barked at Sir Edward: 'And where is my *cher-r-rub*?'

'Ah. Perhaps in the nursery wing?' Fanny had never seen her husband look quite so discomfited. 'Possibly with her brother?'

'Norton?' Lady Banks gave a grunt. 'My need of Norton is less than urgent.'

Poor Norton, thought Fanny.

'However, *my* little girl: I suggest you r-r-root her out and bring her to me at once.' Lady Banks unpinned her hat. Wild white hair stood out on all sides like a dandelion meadow in seed. 'Mary Dorothea is why I am *here*, after all.' She peeled off her gloves. 'And in *my* view, it is as well, Edward' – she tossed a shawl from her shoulders and into the hands of a waiting maid – 'to have some *vague* idea of one's own children's whereabouts.' Leaning on her cane, she headed straight for the drawing room without being guided.

Fanny and Sir Edward exchanged glances of terror, before he took to the stairs and she picked up her skirts and trotted off in pursuit of their guest.

'Dear, oh dear.' Lady Banks limped towards the 'best' chair – Sir Edward's, indeed – and installed herself within it. 'Poor old Hatch. I have not been here since my late sister's day. Those ghastly *subsequent* wives did make a mess of it, did they not?' Her eye was caught by a length of silk peeling back from the wall. 'Do look!' She shook her head sadly. 'I regret to inform you, my dear Lady Knatchbull, that your late father-in-law – may God rest his soul, though He may have other priorities and no mortal could blame Him – was the most *terrible* rogue.

'Still, I have discussed it with your husband. What is wealth, after all, if one cannot help one's *young* when help is required?'

Was she referring to Fanny and Sir Edward? How very refreshing to be thought of as young.

'I suggest you sit there.' Lady Banks pointed her cane at a harder chair, a little further from the fire. 'You might find it a trifle more sanitary than the rest.

'Now. I have been very much looking forward to this little interview. I am sorry we have not met before now. It was sweet of you to ask me and my fault entirely, but on this matter my views are well known: there is only one thing worse than a funeral, and that is a wedding. Tell me, my dear, was it *completely* unbearable?' Her face twisted with sympathy. 'In my view, it is generally the poor *bride* who suffers the most.'

While Fanny merely stared at her blankly, her ladyship glanced around, saw the hovering footman and spoke up: 'Shall we take tea?'

'And here we are,' Lady Banks began as footmen and maids went into a flurry, 'gathering for Christmas: a time to r-r-reflect.' She gazed into the flames of the fire. 'We have had very different years, you and I – you having *gained* a husband, and I having lost one.'

'May I offer my deepest condolences,' Fanny began. These were the first words she had spoken since the great guest's arrival. 'I am so sorry to miss the honour of meeting Sir Joseph. He was a great man, so very distinguished—'

'Indeed, indeed.' When she nodded, Lady Banks's heavy jowls shook like blancmange. 'And the easiest of husbands, of course, for he was so often *away*, and for excessively long periods. Captain Cook could be *very* demanding, you know. And Australia' – Lady Banks leaned in, dropping her voice as if sharing a rare jewel of marital advice – 'really is the most exceptional distance from our own shores.'

Fanny played safe with an 'Ah'.

'To sum up: it was the very best sort of marriage, the like of which, I r-r-regret' – she looked up at Fanny, square in the eye – 'you are unlikely ever to know.' Her tone suggested something close to a death in the family.

'Unfortunately, we cannot hope that my nephew will be travelling much *without* you beside him. I know from the last marriage to dear Annabella – forgive the indelicate mention, my dear, but a spade simply will be a spade – it is not his *way*. Perhaps a few days in London, I suppose, when the House is sitting; the odd journey to Lincoln on my behalf – and if you ever want me to increase these, do' – she held up a gnarled hand – 'just say the word. It is hardly Australia; nonetheless, it is *something*... Otherwise...' She closed her eyes as she sighed: 'I fear he will be most often around.' Her whole head shook with pity. 'I do hope you are up to it? Not everyone would be, my dear. Not by a long chalk.'

Fanny, mute, fumbled with the cake stand.

'All of which brings me on to my next point.' Lady Banks sipped her tea and examined the pattern on the china with a small moue of disappointment. 'And that is your husband's character.'

She dismissed the sad dish back to its saucer, and lifted her gimlet eyes back to Fanny.

'Do not look so alarmed! Sir Edward is *essentially* a good man, of whom I am fond. But you should be aware that a hot streak of temper runs through that family. You are no doubt already aware of the *brother* in *gaol*—'

Fanny had heard, of course, but from other sources. The fact that Sir Edward himself never mentioned the man, she had chosen to take as a comfort. Surely it was just a trifling matter?

'The sooner they hang *him* the better, in my view.'

Oh good heavens! Fanny felt rather faint.

'Naturally, your dear *husband* is made of much finer stuff, and must not be tarred with the fraternal *br-r-ush*. Nevertheless, he will still require your *control*. Dear Annabella – God rest her soul – managed him very well, but then she was a *first* wife. They grew up together. She had some *power*.'

Fanny was not sure that she could bear much more of this. She glanced over at the door, and silently begged it to open. Meanwhile, Lady Banks settled further into her chair, with the air of one at last arriving at her salient point.

'My dear, I must declare my concern that you and Sir Edward may not proceed in the spirit of *equality*. While I am not entirely *against* second marriages, there is an *art* to them. You are the younger; he is established. He will expect your support, and you will no doubt provide it. Yet it is *imperative* that you do not surrender all sense. *He* will make mistakes; *you* must guide him to righteousness. *He* will let his passions o'errule his head; *you* must be the one to pour on the oil. And should you fail – oh, mark my words! – the *r-r-result* will be *r-r-regrettable* for all concerned.'

'Thank you for your advice, Lady Banks.' Though Fanny, who had so far been enjoying her new life of complete acquiescence, had no intention of heeding it. 'Now, perhaps if you will excuse me?' She started to rise, suddenly overwhelmed with the need for a little lie-down.

But it seemed Lady Banks was not finished with her yet. 'One other thing.' She held up her hand and flexed at the wrist to bid Fanny sit again, as if she were a poodle. 'All that being said, of course your *husband* should be merely your *secondary* concern. The children – poor, motherless darlings – must always be your absolute *highest* priority. Do you *pledge* to me, now that – Ah!' The door had finally opened. Lady Banks smiled for the first time. 'There she is!'

And Mary Dorothea almost skipped across the great threadbare carpet and stood, arms outstretched, before her great-aunt.

'Oh, what a joy!' exclaimed Lady Banks, pressing her head into Mary's neck and inhaling deeply. 'Is she not a joy, Edward?'

Sir Edward, who had brought his daughter in, could only watch on, too moved to speak.

Fanny could hardly believe it. She had been married for two months now, had known Mary since the summer, and had never before seen her show any affection. Now here she was, in an embrace with this quite – well – *unexpected* person, and seemed, of all things, to be giggling.

Lady Banks held out the child and smiled at her fondly. 'I think it is your *prattle* I miss most, my little darling. All your delicious little nothings. Do you not agree, Lady Knatchbull?'

Fanny, who was struggling to keep pace with events as

they unfolded and was yet to get used to her new, married moniker, failed to respond.

'Lady Knatchbull?' The jowls began to vibrate with impatience. 'Do you not find it *unnaturally* quiet when Mary is away?'

'Ah. Indeed!' The very idea of Mary Dorothea 'prattling' seemed to Fanny almost absurdly far-fetched. Indeed, she found it unnaturally quiet when the girl was around, as Mary spoke barely at all. But then, perhaps Fanny's experience was somewhat limited.

The awkward truth was that, by some stroke of misfortune, Fanny and Mary had been very little in each other's company. It seemed to be the child who was the busiest. She had been sent off, somewhere or other, while the wedding took place. And since then, of course, now Mary's lessons were at Godmersham, it made sense for her to sleep there, while Fanny's new life was with her husband in Hatch. In fact, with the four boys away, too, the young Knatchbulls were still, to Fanny, almost strangers.

'It is a pleasure to have all them at home for our first Christmas together,' Fanny said warmly. 'I am looking forward to spending more time with the dear little things.'

CHAPTER VIII

At last, Fanny was able to return to her beloved Godmer-sham, for the joys of Twelfth Night.

'Darling!' Lizzie flung her arms around Fanny's neck.

'Dearest!' Marianne took her hand and pulled her towards the blazing hearth in the great hall.

'How was your first Christmas without us?' Lizzie took her cloak and passed it over to Johncock. 'Were you so sad you could *die?*'

Fanny looked behind her to check that Sir Edward was not yet in earshot, but the front door was still open – there seemed to be some dispute about horses – and the coast was clear. 'It passed well enough,' Fanny whispered, while fiddling with the ribbons beneath her chin and removing her bonnet. 'The children behaved nicely.' They had barely said a word. 'Lady Banks was convivial.'

She did not stop talking. 'And we went twice to church!' She turned back to her sisters with a brave and bright smile, but could not help adding: 'It was nowhere near as *heavenly* as being here with you.' She patted her hair. 'Tell me honestly: how was *yours* without *me*?'

The girls exchanged glances.

'Honestly?'

'Of course!' Fanny stood up on tiptoe to catch herself in the glass. 'You know I want for nothing but you all to be happy.'

'In which case—'

'Our Christmas was glorious!' They both squealed at high pitch: a rat, say, on meeting a stoat.

'We all had the *loveliest* time.'

'Excellent.' Fanny turned her attention to the smoothing down of her skirts. 'That *is* good to know.'

'But, oh!' Marianne put her arm through Fanny's. 'We did so miss you, Fan.' She started to guide Fanny through to the library. 'Shall we go through and coze?'

'If you'll excuse me, I might have a rest before dinner.' Fanny instead headed through to the staircase. 'I take it, Marianne, I have my usual room?'

~

She was so lucky – that is what Fanny kept telling herself as she lay on her old bed, looked up at the silk drapes she once used to sleep under and blinked back the tears. Look at the difference in her position from last year to this! A solicitous husband – really, the *kindest* of men, at all the right moments. He might be irascible with others – she reached into her bodice and took out her handkerchief – but *never* with Fanny. He loved her! Already, Sir Edward loved her. And, in truth, she was becoming quite used to him; fond, indeed. Certainly, a sense of companionship had grown up between them.

And Mersham-le-Hatch was an excellent house. Yes, it might be a little tired in places, but, thanks to Lady Banks, the ceiling had been secured and renovations were due to begin in the New Year. It would soon return to its glory with Fanny as its mistress. And, most importantly, it was almost close by: just a horse ride away. How many brides get to stay so near to home, once they are wed?

Moreover, by some great quirk of good fortune, Fanny somehow seemed to have almost doubled her family, while halving her responsibilities. She was still in constant touch with all her darling Knights, but it was dear Marianne who ran the house and their lives now – and seemed to do so perfectly well. Certainly, Fanny was rarely asked for advice, or minded to offer it.

And as for the stepchildren – well, they barely impinged. Poor Norton had now followed his father to Winchester College – a sticky start, she gathered, but no doubt he would settle down there, in time; Wyndham was gone to prep school; the two little ones lodged out with a master and rarely came home. And now, Sir Edward had hired some splendid governess to take over Mary. Of course, Fanny would still be – to all intents and purposes – the girl's mother, and from now on they would be spending as much time together as they possibly could. The new governess would merely provide that little bit extra. Really, what could be more pleasant and easy? So why was she was so tired all the time, and generally feeble? There was no earthly excuse for it.

She rang for Sayce, and determined to pull herself together.

~

'Good morning, Marianne my dear.' Fanny placed dish back in saucer, and dabbed at her lips with a napkin. 'Of course, we two are the first down.' She smiled and rolled her eyes in a gesture of sympathy. 'No rest for us!'

'Do *you* have a busy day ahead, Fanny?' Marianne ran an eye over the breakfast provisions, lifted a dome to check the warmth of the pork. 'I hope you find some time to *relax*.' She sat down and flicked through her pile of letters.

Fanny felt nervous. There was nothing aggressive in Marianne's demeanour, but her words could – if one were so minded – be thought of as hostile. Of course, it was true that she was there as a guest and not, in fact, busy at all. No doubt it was annoying of her to pretend that she was. All the same, Fanny must acknowledge that something had happened to Marianne. Her sweetest little sister was definitely changed.

'I must thank you,' Fanny began in an exploratory fashion, 'for having Mary Dorothea here these past months. It has been a great help to me, while I find my feet over at Hatch. I hope she has not proved too difficult a presence and has settled in well?'

'We have found her a pleasant addition, and she seems to be as content here as could be hoped.' Marianne spoke into the letter she was currently reading. 'But perhaps she herself is the best person to ask?' She looked up and over at Fanny. 'Oh, but I am sure you already have.'

Had the maid provided sufficient hot water? Fanny made a great fuss of thumbing open silver lids and peering within.

'Being such a *talkative* child—'

'Mary Dorothea.' Ah, hot water a-plenty. 'Talkative.' But was the milk cool? 'Yes, of course.'

'Indeed.' Marianne put down her letter and turned her gaze on to her sister. 'As she is well known to chat on almost for ever, and seemingly quite uninhibited when it comes to her feelings – almost frank, I am minded to say – there can be no doubt she would be honest with *you*. After all, you *are* her mama, are you not? But if for some reason that doesn't suit, you might do worse than ask Cassy. The two girls are already the closest of friends.' She arched one fine eyebrow. 'As no doubt you are aware.'

So not only was Mary Dorothea famously garrulous,

somehow she had also found a new *friend* in one of her sisters? Fanny could barely imagine it. At that moment, the heavy door opened and she was rescued by the arrival of the younger ones.

'I do believe I love Twelfth Night even better than Christmas!' Cassy was yawning and rubbing at her eyes. 'I so wish Mary had been here, too. Do you know, her family has never celebrated it – is that not perfectly—' She looked around the table, eyes wide with pity, then noticed Fanny and stopped herself. 'Anyway, was I not quite the finest queen of all time?'

'To the palace born, my dear.' Marianne leaned over and put a dish of compote in front of her youngest sister. 'Now eat up and sit up, or no prince will marry you, and then where will you be?'

'And was I a good king?' Brook – the youngest, gentlest and most timid of all the Knight brothers – seemed genuinely fearful of the response.

Ned swung into the breakfast room. 'The complete Richard the Third, I would say.' He ruffled Brook's hair as he passed, before swooping down on a vast dish of ham.

'Truly?' Little Brook looked around, eyes alight: he was always quite desperate for any confirmation. 'Was he one of the good ones?'

'Marianne!' called Ned over the ensuing uproar. 'Care to remove this boy from his school at the earliest opportunity!' He drew up a chair and flicked back his jacket. 'It is somehow contriving to make him *more* stupid rather than less.'

All eleven of the Knight siblings reunited – was there a happier sight? Fanny looked around the table. Everyone, as ever, roaring with laughter at some joke of Ned's, apart from Marianne, that is, who was fiddling with her curls and looking down at her plate. Perhaps she was simply tired, for which Fanny could hardly blame her. The Christmas season was exhausting for the woman in charge, especially when one was new to it.

Whatever it was, Fanny refused to worry herself. This was the most cheerful of mornings, after the most splendid Twelfth Night before. Sir Edward was out taking his constitutional; their papa was down at the farm. The Knights had always been happiest in their own company. This was like the old days: just them.

'By the way.' Ned reached for a muffin, tossed and then caught it. 'Who is *that* waiting out in the hall? Sight for sore eyes, I must say. Rather a beauty. Thought of stopping for a quick flirt, until it suddenly occurred she might be someone's fiancée.' He practised a slow, overarm gesture. 'William?' He did a dummy throw. 'Have you proposed at all lately?' He then tossed the bun across the table. 'Would hate to get in your way, old boy.'

George leaped out of his seat and caught it. 'The Ashford Ball was quite the riot.' He took a hearty bite. 'It's perfectly possible our Will *did* get himself wed and has clean forgot.'

'Really, boys!' In just ten short weeks, Fanny had become so used to the quiet life, the Godmersham breakfast room was giving her a headache. 'I had forgotten how rowdy you get sometimes. Pipe down a little, I beg you.' More baked goods now flew through the air. 'Sir Edward will be joining us soon.'

The very mention was enough to bring silence to the table. Out of the corner of her eye, Fanny spied brothers exchanging glances and biting their lips. Ned's shoulders were shaking. Possibly for the first time in her life, she wondered if they might be somewhat childish, and if it was not high time they grew up.

'Anyway.' Fanny folded her napkin and placed it neatly down by her plate. 'You have reminded me.' Rising, she waited a beat for a footman to draw out her chair. 'The new governess is arriving at some point this morning. I must gather myself before the interview takes place.' She proceeded to the door, bade them all a good morning.

And, as she did so, wondered who might be this beauty who had caught Ned's eye?

PART TWO

CHAPTER IX

Mary Dorothea Knatchbull was still a very small child when she first formed the idea that she might be somewhat lacking. What exactly she lacked, she could not, at first, quite put her finger on. Being but five years of age, she had not yet acquired either the words or the experience which might enable the proper examination of self. But once she had grown up just a little more – indeed, only the following year, when she was first sent off to school – then it became horribly clear: she could not lay claim to the possession of any sort of distinguishing feature.

This absence did not form the basis of any great preoccupation – Mary sensed that would be unhealthy: God would, no doubt, disapprove. But it was certainly an awareness that she carried about with her, as a lady

might her reticule; and, from time to time, she rummaged within it, to see if there might not just be something which had been hiding thus far.

But though she worked hard at her lessons, any signs
of brilliance failed to present themselves. Her voice was
more suited to chorus than solo. In the absence of any
positive references to her appearance, Mary could only
presume herself plain – and anyway, she hastily reminded
herself, beauty was only skin deep. Ah, so might she be
distinguished by her exceptional goodness? She did try,
very hard, to be good at all times – even if only to please
her papa. But then, Christian obedience was hardly a
unique quality in her immediate world, and though she
prayed most terribly hard, still she remained stuck at
some distance from being a saint.

But if only, Mary thought later, she had not wondered
at all . . . Then the Lord might not have noticed her, or
marked her down as one who might benefit from punishment. And chosen to inflict a great wound upon her
small person that would scar her for life.

$\sim$

The last time that mother and daughter were together
was early in the spring of the year 1814. Though she was
by then heavy with child and approaching yet another
confinement, Annabella Knatchbull was perfectly well

and, in every way possible, her normal, affectionate, beautiful self.

As it was Mary's last day at home before she was returned to her boarding school, they were spending the entire day together in the mother's dressing room. Mary carried in her favourite toys, her mama rooted about in the basket of scraps and they embarked on the production of an entirely new summer wardrobe for the fortunate dolls who were chosen to accompany them on their annual holiday to Sandgate later that summer.

'I do believe that what this outfit requires,' her mother declared as she held up a navy-blue frock in the sailor style, 'is a straw just like your school hat. Now . . .' She twisted her mouth and pretended to think deeply, in that way she did when the plan was already conceived, hatched and close to unveiling. 'I wonder' – she leaned in to Mary, put a fingertip to the child's nose and wrinkled her own in excitement – 'if I were to write to my own milliner in London—'

But Mary was in no mood to hear it. 'Mama,' she began. The relationship between them was happy, honest and open. Though she would hesitate before talking in such terms to her father, her mother encouraged it. 'I have been thinking.' If some issue was on Mary's mind, she was expected to share it. 'And have now firmly decided that it would be very much for the best if I did *not* return to Mrs Grant's tomorrow.'

'Ha!' Annabella Knatchbull smiled at her fondly, turned back to the scrap basket, started to rummage and said in an absent sort of voice: 'My funny little darling.'

'But, Mama!' Mary rose. 'I am being most *serious*.' She knelt down and rested her head on the comforting bulk of her unborn sibling. 'Why can I not stay and be taught here at home? My Honywood cousins have that arrangement, as do the Finch-Hattons. And Great-Aunt Dorothea is worried that the whole idea of *schools* for *girls* is starting to look rather affected—'

Her languid mother gave a sudden jerk of alarm.

'Forgive me!' she cried then. 'I beg you, do not say I said so!' And then, in a very small, collapsed sort of voice added: 'Please, Mama dearest. Do let me stay.'

Her mother stroked her hair and gave a sad smile. 'You are worried, my love. And that is perfectly natural. I do believe I remember feeling something similar when your uncle was born. But that all ended happily, did it not? And this will, too. Mary?' She lifted the child's chin, the little replica of her own, and looked into the so-similar eyes. 'I *promise* you. I have done this five times before and never felt stronger than I do now, with this baby. All will be well. I feel it; I *know* it.

'And let me pledge here and now: when the baby is safely delivered, and the nursery is bustling, then I will send for you. Indeed, of *course* I will send for you. Heavens, now I think of it, how on earth can Nurse and I even begin to manage all those little boys without *you*, their important big sister! So, yes, my love. I am in full agreement. You can come home to us then.

'You have my word.'

~

By the expected time of the birth, Mary was back in the schoolroom in Albion Place, Ramsgate, where the wind whipped off the sea and the pupils kept their gloves on in lessons for fear of losing their fingers to frostbite. Though she had not particularly minded being there as a New Girl, Mary now found that the more established she became, the more passionately she loathed it. With an increasing and unhappy impatience, her every conscious and unconscious moment was consumed with longing for the moment her mother finally sent word to summon her home.

When, twice a day, the girls were dispatched to march up and down the promenade in crocodile formation, she alone kept her eyes on the school in case a carriage arrived. In lessons, her ear was permanently cocked towards the hall entrance, to catch that delightful, featherweight drop of paper packet upon pewter. By night, she sucked quietly on her little fingertip, recalling those heavenly sensations of napkins and muslins and milkiness and felt something quite close to soothed. Until at last, one cold Thursday morning, news arrived that the baby was born safely and to be called John. Curiously, the note was from Great-Aunt Dorothea, Lady Banks, rather than either parent. And although it was obvious there could be no good reason for that, with heroic self-control, Mary chose not to consider the matter too closely.

Officially, 'Letters' was an activity restricted to that Sunday afternoon lull between the many, *many* church services the girls were required to attend but, by the full force of her powers of persuasion, Mary obtained special dispensation to message her mother at once. She expressed her earnest love and good wishes and – though no one could expect her to be *too* excited about a fifth brother in five years – her conviction that she would adore him, in time. She closed with the assurance that no more than a moment's notice would be required for her to quit Mrs Grant's for ever, and waited, with her few possessions neatly assembled, for the blessed hour of deliverance.

The days dragged on; the nights stretched eternal. Though Mary could not lose faith in her mother's good word, it was hard not to feel a trifle put out by the lack of urgency being shown. Finally, on 8 April – more than a week into baby John's life – Mrs Grant herself appeared by her side at the breakfast table, to say that her father was waiting for her in the parlour.

Mary had never before been allowed into Mrs Grant's sanctuary, nor had any of the pupils with whom she was on terms. It was the most astonishing breach of the lady's defences and – sweetly, unthinkingly – Mary thrilled at her coup. For a minute, she stood in the cold, austere, tiled hall, pledging to remember every astonishing little domestic detail, before she knocked and then entered.

Her first thought was, Oh, my! as her eyes were assaulted by colour and softness. With the almost balmy warmth and chaos of chintz, it was as if she had walked straight out of winter into a garden in bloom. The sheer charm of the ambience – the discovery of this Eden within their grey prison – was nothing less than a revelation. Mary started, and smiled at it, and might even have giggled, had she not then noticed the one black stain in paradise.

'Papa?' Slowly, she approached the sofa as she might the gallows. Edward Knatchbull – sunken, crumpled – extended an arm without raising his gaze.

Mary slid in beside him; felt his hand tremble as he clutched at her shoulder. And then he began.

'My dear Mary Dorothea.' His voice was thick and damp and frighteningly unnatural. 'I regret to say that I am here with the most sorrowful news. I fear it has pleased God to inflict upon me the heaviest calamity that can befall the most loving of husbands.'

Mary felt horribly cold.

'Little did I know, when last we met, what cruel punishment then lay before me. The confinement went well; the child is a bonny one. In the very last minutes of her life, she seemed in better health than she had for a year. And then' – he stumbled and choked – 'and then—' He stopped to collect himself. 'At the eleventh hour of the morning, four long days ago – without any warning – she, my dearly beloved, was ripped from this world.'

He paused, sniffed; then he retrieved a large handkerchief, blew his nose loudly, and continued.

'As you are keenly aware, to me she was everything; as you could predict, without her I am nothing. And, as you would no doubt expect, my grief is deep and sincere.'

He paused, as if requiring an answer. 'Poor, dear Papa,' was all she could muster.

'Though it brings pain to admit it, true domestic happiness is now behind me forever. I have little more to look forward to – until I, too, am called up to heaven and by her side once again. I can only pray I will not be left long in my agonies.'

'Oh, Papa, no!'

'And, until that moment of blessed delivery, it falls to you, dear child, henceforth to devote yourself utterly to the comfort and succour of your afflicted parent.'

'Of course, Papa.'

'Your brothers are yet young, but then soon to be absorbed into their own lives and futures. You alone I can count on.' He laid his heavy head upon her crisp, white cap, and left it there. 'You are all I now have.'

'Thank you, Papa.'

'And you must always remember, the more you endeavour to be a good girl, so the prouder I shall become and the better I will love you.'

'I shall try my hardest, Papa.'

'Then that is the only source of contentment I can foresee.'

And with that, he abandoned himself to a loud and violent demonstration of his own misery.

Mary was gripped by paralysis. Her neck hurt with the weight of him. His tears spilled on to her pinafore, making her shoulder uncomfortably damp. Somewhere inside of her something was breaking, like a bone china teacup being dashed to the floor.

And yet even then, there grew in its place another sensation: the niggling feeling that she had some pressing commitment. What was it now? While her father sobbed, Mary worried away at it. She was *sure* there was something. Until gradually it dawned what was required, what was expected, indeed.

'There, there, Papa.' At first, Mary was tentative, shy even. After all, she was barely seven years of age, and had never had occasion to soothe anyone before, beyond a pet or a doll – or herself. But: 'There, there,' she said again, 'there, there.'

And then simply continued to repeat it like a mantra, while clasping his much larger hand.

∾

Though Mary was, from that moment, forever changed, she was no more than a mere member of a substantial herd while still at school. Even motherlessness – though new, livid and red raw – was not enough to set her apart from the rest of Mrs Grant's girls. A good number had been sent to Albion Place for that very reason. Many a mama was lost to childbirth, of course, and many a family the victim of those cruel, common diseases that stole into the home like a thief in the night. There was also a pupil whose mother had *run orf*, as Matron liked to put it in her scandalised whisper, but – as the woman could just as easily run back again at any moment – that pupil was more an object of envy.

For many, though, bereavement was a common condition and while, in the first hours and days, Mary did receive some sweet gestures of sympathy, the special attentions did not last long. No one around her wore mourning – they had never met Mrs Knatchbull, so why on earth would they? And because, presumably, everyone at home had other things to think about, no black was sent over for Mary, so even she had to go about life in her normal attire.

Mr Knatchbull had left without making mention of Mary returning back home; he did not even refer to their plans for the summer in Sandgate. She was left with no choice but to sink into school life – a paler, even plainer, more joyless version of her previous self.

By day, as per her instructions, little Mary endeavoured. Through long hours of labour, her embroidery became something close to exquisite; her curtsey astonishing; her demeanour and conduct never less than becoming:

she had her catechism down to a T. Every week, Mrs Grant dispatched glowing reports and Mary sent home, in her copperplate hand, endless tales of her honours and triumphs.

Her father's replies came perhaps once a month, but – although sometimes he suggested he hoped that he might – he never appeared.

Hot tears hung, scalding, at the backs of her eyes, waiting for the moment when they might gush forth and relieve her. But at night, in bed, however hard Mary willed it, they still would not come. How she longed to give vent to her misery – pour it all out; roll around and wallow, just as her father had done. But there had been something about that new and odd way he had addressed her. Somehow she had got the impression that true grief was a privilege she had not quite done enough to earn. It was not until 1818, when a letter arrived informing her that her sweet little brother Edward had died from a fever, that she could, at last, cry. He was but eight years of age! The sheer cruelty of that was overwhelming enough, but worse: it brought with it a new terror. Would the other boys stay safe? Could she trust *any* of her family to simply survive?

And as for her own future: Mary lay – lonely, fearful and sleepless – and pondered. Well, first she would stay at Mrs Grant's until such time as she was simply too old to stay. Thereafter, she would take up position by the side of her afflicted papa, where she would comfort and support him through his unending misery, until came the blessed moment when he was, at last, reunited with his beloved in heaven. And then what would become of Mary? Wither and die too, she supposed.

People like her – the great undistinguished – had no right to expect any more from their lives.

But, as Mary was beginning to learn, that was the thing about being a child: the exact moment one got used to one's own situation and learned to treat it as normal, was always the very same moment that the adults decided to throw all of it up in the air.

And at last, just on the cusp of her thirteenth birthday, came the moment when everything changed.

CHAPTER X

The Replacement Mother – or 'the Mother', as the Knatchbull children would say with a smirk once they mastered the great art of irony – was hardly the one they would have chosen. The differences between Annabella Knatchbull and Fanny Knight were so stark that to even consider the latter was to make a mockery of the maternal ideal. Where the first was plump and dimpled and laughing, the second was long, hard, pious – *so* pious – and bony. Where *Mrs* Knatchbull adored every one of her darlings; those very same darlings, as they were made only too aware, left the soon-to-be *Lady* Knatchbull a tiny bit cold.

So the idea that their father might wilfully choose to marry this creature struck his offspring as barely credible. And when it turned out that not only had she *interviewed* this Miss Knight for the very position, but she had actually given the appointment her blessing, Mary Dorothea could not have been more surprised.

~

Two weeks before that great revelation, the children were still at bliss in their ignorance, and allowed to run wild.

And on 15 August, they were flying across the lawn towards the slope that led down to the lake, with their feet bare and dirty, and clothing dishevelled.

'*Hurry!*' Norton cried in something between a yell and a whisper. '*You can't let them see us!*'

He was way out in front, the next two boys in age closing in from behind. Mary was struggling to keep up, to her shame. She passed the small ridge where the land fell away steeply – the point, they had established, at which they could no longer be seen from the windows – and stopped for a moment, to catch her sharp breath.

How were the boys so much faster than her, when she was the eldest? It could only be school, she supposed. Stupid school. At hers, running was forbidden; at theirs, encouraged. She bent over, put a hand on each knee, waited for her heart to stop banging, began to rage at the world. Then came a small voice from behind her: 'Wait for me, the Others! Oh, *do* wait for me!' And she turned just as John's little legs gave way beneath him and he fell to the ground.

Mary looked ahead of her – they were halfway to the boathouse – and back at the helpless, pitiful sight of the youngest. Oh, John, darling, she thought, do not ruin this glorious morning! They were all so excited. Still: more noble to die than desert him. 'Crawl to me!' she called quietly. 'Don't cry, dearest. I'm here. Crawl and keep low, mind. Don't let the grown-ups catch you.'

He wriggled on his belly until he was near enough for Mary to swoop down and grab him. 'I've got you, my precious.' She nuzzled into his neck as he sobbed on her shoulder. 'We've made it. Come on, I'll hold your hand.'

They were safe in that part of the grounds – invisible from their papa in the library – and able to take it more slowly. Mary thrilled at the spring of the turf beneath the pink skin on her soles, the dazzling light on her face – her brothers came out without hats and why should not she? The little one, cheerful now, skipped along by her side. Had she ever known a happiness like it?

'Look at this, Johnny.' The slope here was at its steepest – almost a hill. Mary lay on it, cross-wise, limbs stretched to their limits. 'Copy me!' And then, with a screech and a holler – what *would* Mrs Grant say? – they both rolled, over and over, down to the bulrushes.

Gingerly, she sat up, waiting for the dizziness to pass, let the grass stains on her pinafore come into focus, then sent her head back and laughed. So this was her life now! Her father had – quite unaccountably, and with no sort of notice – withdrawn her from school. And, for the summer at least, she could look forward to adventure after adventure; lark after lark; new sensation upon new, delicious sensation. She felt like one of Cook's best desserts, kept in the ice house all winter and now brought into the sunlight to thaw. If only little Edward had lived long enough to enjoy this with them all . . .

Though the estate of Mersham-le-Hatch had been in the family for some considerable time, it was all quite new to this generation of Knatchbulls. While their grandpapa had lived here, they had not been welcome, the last Lady K. having taken against their papa for some reason unknown. But now the grandfather was dead, his widow evicted and the whole place was theirs. And the sheer size of the mansion and extent of the park was truly the stuff of their dreams.

The last home had been extremely pleasant of course, but on a quite different scale. They knew every inch of it blindfold, and were never allowed to explore anywhere beyond it. The nurses and maids who had them in their charge had all known their late mother and, naturally, adored her as everyone had. Their chosen method of respecting her memory had been to wrap her poor offspring in cotton wool. The children were not once allowed out without supervision, and every cough, shiver and sniffle had them confined to their quarters. They had been finding it increasingly tiresome.

The servants at Hatch, though, could not be more different. As the housekeeper did not mind explaining to

Mary, the staff here had much preferred life under the previous incumbents – back when nobody asked to see 'the accounts' with the butcher or 'the key' for the wine cellar, and the nursery wing was just as it should be, shut up and dark. The last gentleman – God rest his soul – was not cold in his grave when, all of a sudden, they were expected to put up with the king in his counting house *and* his great rabble of children. Five of you devils! The servants, she said, had come to unanimous agreement: they would look after them as little as possible.

Mary Dorothea had never before known a minute's neglect and – oh! – how she relished it. It was not just the hours – endless hours, sun-drenched and warm – of true freedom that opened before her. It was also the time with her brothers. For most of their lives, she had either been away or just somehow separate – expected to do something other or be somewhere else. But now, here she was: one of their number; part of the pack.

At last, Mary and John arrived, breathless, at the back of the boathouse. When they saw Norton already at work – head bent over wires; brown paper and bottles assembled – John cried out in dismay.

'We missed it,' he wailed. 'They've done the a speriment!'

Norton, his brow low with concentration, looked up and snarled: 'Course I haven't, you fool. I've been wanting to electrocute you since the day you were born.'

Mary sank down to the earth, crossed her legs, patted

her lap, pulled John down into it and rested her chin on his golden head. Gosh, but were not boys *marvellous*? She loved that frank contempt with which they spoke to each other, when girls always pretended to friendship while inside they were beasts. And fancy knowing all about *electricity* and *galvanism*, when she had but the haziest idea of what the words even meant. And imagine – just imagine – having the sheer nerve to try it out on all of your siblings! Mary was completely in awe.

'Right, you lot.' Norton looked up. 'In a line with you. Now!'

Mary stood, held hands with her brothers, closed her eyes, bit her lip and awaited the thrill of her life. Could it really be true that her hair would stand on its ends? The maids might go wild, but that would come later. Right now, sheer anticipation was making her all over quivery . . .

And then it came:

'Miss Mary! Miss Mary? Where has that wretched girl got to?'

'Dash it!' Norton threw down the magnet in fury. 'Typical! You've gone and ruined my experiment. They've come to take you away.'

～

An hour and a half later, she was with her papa at an estate that called itself Godmersham, visiting some people by the name of Knight – though Mary had no idea what on earth she was doing there.

With her stockinged legs crossed at the ankle, white-gloved hands loose on her lap, Mary sat and – quietly, heroically; with the greatest politeness – started to melt.

Of course, their hostess had taken precautions against the worst of it. The table had been set in the shade of a cypress, Miss Knight had found Mary a Japanese fan and ices were served before cake. But still, the air was unusually stifling. One poor footman, in stiff Godmersham livery, was looking decidedly faint. Mary had a sudden vision of her brothers down by the lake or, more probably in it, and to her horror she heard herself sigh.

Thank heavens her papa did not notice and instead simply breezed on with his passionate views on the recent assizes. Mr Austen Knight, though, who Mary thought might be a very good sort of gentleman, looked over with sympathy.

'Quite so, Knatchbull. Quite so,' Mr Austen Knight cut in. Mary had noticed he agreed with her father on everything. Most people did. 'My dear' – he addressed his own daughter – 'are there no girls around to amuse our young visitor?'

'I fear not, Father.' Miss Knight's chest, exposed in a delicate muslin, started to flush with some violence. 'Please do forgive me.' The pink moved up to her cheeks and on to the roots of her hair. 'I could not—'

'Pray, Miss Knight, do not worry!' Sir Edward cried

with what seemed to Mary unnecessary vehemence. 'I assure you, my daughter could not be more happy.'

Mary essayed a smile, looked over at the house – a friendly sort of place, but not a patch on her Hatch – and then studied their hostess. Now, here was a curious creature – stiff as a poker and awkward with it; not *un*attractive, but what Mrs Grant used to call handsome-*ish*, which the whole school understood to be a fate worse than death. What age might she be? Not *ancient* exactly, yet there remained not a trace of her youth. Ah! Perhaps she was one of those 'poor spinsters' one heard so much about? How very interesting. As far as she was aware, Mary had never actually seen one in the flesh.

Her musings were interrupted then by a loud whoop travelling up from the direction of the river below them, followed by a sequence of splashes

'Forgive me,' Miss Knight repeated, leaning towards Mary. 'My brothers . . .'

Yet again, the lady started to flush – that long, goosey neck all red and mottling. What was the matter with her? Mary could not make it out.

And then came the unmistakeable sound of feminine squealing to add to the whoops from the water, and she formed an idea. So Miss Knight had asked those girls to look after her, and they had refused. These sisters were the excluding type, then . . . She knew them well from school. Still, on that afternoon, it was hard to lay blame. Who did not prefer being with their brothers? Mary certainly did.

Her mind drifted towards Hatch and to wondering: had Norton actually managed to create electricity? All that earlier, thwarted excitement thrummed through her veins, while Sir Edward opined on the latest Archbishop – 'hell in a handbasket' – and Miss Knight languidly enquired about her various accomplishments: 'Not *play*, my dear? Then surely you *sing*.'

And eventually – just at that crucial point when Mary felt she could bear it no longer – there was reached a general, unspoken agreement that the visit had come to its close.

On the carriage ride home, Mary sat, face fixed towards the window, as if she were actually interested in the passing, desiccated country, when really she just wanted to cry. Of course, she understood it should be an honour to accompany her papa on a visit, but really she could only resent it. If that was this 'calling' she had heard so much about, then they could keep it. Her papa and those Knights seemed close to strangers and clearly had little in common beyond a shared geography. On the basis of that experiment, Mary saw no earthly reason to meet them again.

Her father reached over and patted her leg. 'The most charming occasion I thought, did you not?'

'Yes, Papa.' Mary managed a smile through the side brim of her bonnet. 'Thank you so much for taking me.'

'You are a pleasure to take out, my dear,' he said warmly. 'I was most keen for you to meet *Miss* Knight in particular. I wonder, did you warm to the lady?'

'Oh, very much indeed, Papa.' She twisted her white-gloved hands in her lap. 'She could not have been kinder.'

At that, he fell into his thoughts and Mary turned her face to the window and pondered. Had she once, since the death of her mother, had an honest conversation with a single grown-up? Lady Banks, perhaps, but even her dear great-aunt – kind though she might be – set down limitations.

For the rest, she had long ago formed a habit of only ever telling adults what they wanted to hear. Having observed Norton's honesty and the trouble it brought him, it seemed obvious that her life would be easier if she did not follow his path.

Only now did she see that her own way had brought with it a whole other problem. There was not now an adult around her with any idea of who Mary truly was: not the feelings in her heart, nor the thoughts in her head.

⁓

On 31 August, straight after breakfast, the nursery maid lined up the children – wiped five eggy faces; scrubbed ten jammy hands – pronounced: 'It's as good as I can get 'em and 'e can like it or lump it,' and led them all into the library.

Like a chorus of angels, they chirruped: 'Good morning, Papa,' sounding so very unlike themselves, that Mary looked around. The fear in those little pink faces . . . So she was not alone, then. They all, even little John, could sense something afoot.

'Ah, yes.' Sir Edward cleared his throat. 'Children.' As if he had, until that moment, forgotten he had any. 'You are brought here today . . .' He studied the detail on the Aubusson with particular care. 'I wish it to be known . . .' he started again, rubbing at a knee with each hand. '*I am to be married!*' he blurted out in a rush.

This was met not with cheers, nor cries, but a paralysed silence. Sir Edward looked up, flushed, and looked down again. The library took on the quiet of the grave.

At last, as if this were his regiment and he was addressing the general on behalf of his men, Norton took a pace forward, stood crisp to attention, and said: 'Thank you, Papa. Then, of course, we all our offer our warmest good wishes. Might we now be informed as to *whom*?'

Sir Edward looked at his son and heir with barely suppressed fury, though that was not out of the ordinary. Norton's every word and deed provoked his father to fury, and had done for years. Still, Mary thought it a shame. Somehow, she sensed her papa had come to this interview fully determined to be kind – as kind as she alone believed him to be capable of being. Yet already – and as usual – things were going awry.

'My boy,' he thundered. 'You must concede that it is *not* in my nature to be wild or impetuous, and I *resent* the implication of your words. This is not a *wanton* decision, but one taken with great care. And I will have you know' – he half rose out of his chair, as if pulling a trump from a good hand and certain of victory – 'that not only has your sister *met* with the lady, but she has wholeheartedly *approved* of the match.'

Mary was stunned. All masculine eyes turned to her for some explanation. She was as baffled as they were.

'My *fiancée*, and your future *mother*,' Sir Edward went on, 'is Miss Frances Knight of Godmersham Park—'

Mary felt a dead weight in the pit of her stomach. Surely he *cannot* . . . he *did* not . . . not that strange, awkward . . . oh, dear, *good* Papa!

And they had all been so happy.

CHAPTER XI

Three weeks had passed since Mary's arrival in Godmersham, but still she felt nowhere near settled. Though she had, more or less, mastered the layout of both mansion and park, some corners of the family remained as yet uncharted. Of course, the daughters were all sorted out and straight in her head. Apart from the married one, Lizzie – gosh! The *scariest* creature! – the others all lived there, so Mary met with them daily.

When it came to the sons, though, she did still get into the most terrible muddle. Mary had formed the *idea* there were six of them (though she might yet be proved wrong), who, for most of their time, were apparently occupied somewhere other than Kent. But then at odd moments – generally just when the household had comfortably slumped into a period of peace – they would suddenly turn up in a pack: laughing and shouting at the top of their voices; taking pot shots at anything non-human that moved.

On those days, Mary tended to keep at a distance, intimidated – and yet not unintrigued. She preferred just to look on at a distance and, from there, try to dis-cern each from the other. But it was simply no good, like trying to pick threads from a box full of yarn: they all clumped together. Only one seemed to stand out apart from the rest. And *him* she found hard to forget.

Ned, the family called him but he was Mr Knight still to Mary, of course, and *young* Mr Knight to the world. It was he who had, at that very first family dinner, aston-ished the universe – or amazed Mary, at least – by starting an argument with her beloved papa. In all her thirteen long years, she had never before seen such a spectacle.

Later, in the privacy of their carriage, Sir Edward had denounced his opponent – an outrage! A blackguard! – and the dutiful daughter had, as ever, concurred. What else could she do, after all? Her papa was her world and his approval was everything. His enemy *must* be her enemy, or she would risk his displeasure – and therein lurked an evil that could never be borne.

And fortunately, Mr Knight had not been seen in God-mersham since then.

That afternoon found Mary tiptoeing along the first-floor landing of Godmersham, listening in doorways while appearing quite innocent. Of course, these were two conflicting activities – she wasn't the complete dunce everyone here seemed to think – but she was all out of ideas. Those girls had *said* they would meet her at two after noon when they had finished their riding, and that was *ages* ago. But there was no one downstairs, and the nursery was empty. Surely they had to be here, some-where or other.

The clock down in the hall struck three – late enough to merit concern – and then came the footsteps. At last, someone was . . . Yet this was a *masculine* tread! Strong, athletic, taking the stairs two at a time. Mary's blood quickened. Should she run, should she hide: why must she live in this perpetual state of horrible anguish? Now full in a panic, she made a run for the attic, her own room and safety – but it was too late.

'Hull-*o*!'

The early autumnal sun dazzled – danced – through the long, principal window and so blurred Mary's vision.

'And what have we here then?'

A halo of light obscured all physical details leaving nothing but a dark figure in outline. Mary could discern only an averagely tall sort of gentleman, broad enough in the shoulder, with a head like a mop that had met with a hurricane – though the weather was perfectly still.

'You make no reply, madam? Then I see through it at once. You intend to remain a figure of mystery.' The voice was something quite close to stern, though Mary felt, hoped, she could detect the hint of a chuckle – a bubble of air caught in a stream. 'Then it falls to me to unravel it.' The shape put its hand to its hair and made it yet wilder, said 'Hmm', stretched out an elbow, leaned on the banister, crossed its long legs at the ankles and thought for an instant. 'Quite so. There are but two explanations. The first being that you are a Burglar of the Master variety – in which case' – a muscular arm signalled her plain white day cap and starched schoolroom pinafore – 'the *perfect* disguise.

'Or – and this, I agree, is the more fantastic by far – you have got rather lost. Now.' With three long strides he crossed the corridor. 'Which is it to be?'

Mary, who had remained fixed to the same spot – a sapling transplanted – had until that moment stayed blind. And only now that the body had moved out of the shadows and the face was inches from hers, only now could she see who it was.

Mr Knight had returned. He was standing right there before her. But before either could speak, a great, shaggy dog bounded up the stairs, barrelled into Mary and rubbed his head in her hands, as if they were old friends. She bent down to pet him – it was a fine opportunity to hide her own blushing face and, anyway, he *was* rather a dear – while his owner let out a great laugh.

'So burglar it is!'

Though Mary was mortified, Mr Knight was, at least, amusing himself. 'I am proud to say that Lord Byron is not one of the world's more promising guard dogs. Far too noble a beast for so lowly a role. Any intruder would be in danger of being licked half to death.'

He was now begging her mercy, while his face – chiselled and fine; honeyed bronze rather than ruddy – cracked into a smile. 'Pray do forgive me,' he pleaded. 'I *have* had the pleasure and my manners are woeful. Miss Knatchbull, is it not? I had heard you were come to stay for a while. Enchanted.'

He tipped into a bow; Mary managed a nod.

'And yet, if I may, you seem somewhat at a loose end? Now, if it pleases you, do say where you *should* be and I will escort you.'

As if she could say a word!

He smiled, shrugged and went on. 'I was led to believe you are being taught with my youngest sisters but – if you will permit me the wildest of guesses – they have gone "missing". Might I be warm?' His voice softened. 'Miss Knatchbull, I *do* know the feeling. They would treat me ill, too, if I did not box their ears on a regular basis. Come, let us find them together.'

Mr Knight turned back to the staircase, began to climb the next flight and bade that she follow him. The dog stayed at her heels, as if she were his mistress. 'As you know, your father and brother came to stay with me a few weeks back.' He spoke over his shoulder as she and Lord Byron trotted behind. 'I very much enjoyed meeting *Norton*.'

Mary privately noted that her father's name was not mentioned – favourably or otherwise.

'Have you heard from him since he started at Winchester? I *hope* he is getting on well, though – as an old College man myself – I can quite see that might not be the case.'

A pause, in which Mary might have confided her brother's weekly accounts of his increasing misery. Of course she did not.

'Please know that my house at Chawton is but a short distance from there.' They were now up on the attic corridor, where Mr Knight proceeded to fling open one door and finding no one at home, march on to the next. 'I will endeavour to keep an eye on him when I can.'

Resolute, Mary maintained her silence, and yet she felt somewhere within – like the first shot of war in a far-distant land – the faint stirrings of conflict. Of course she could never show disloyalty to her dearest papa! The very thought was abhorrent. But then, what classed as loyalty? For example, were she, say, to wonder at Mr Knight's intuitive powers, or succumb to the warmth of his kindness, or let her heart sing with relief that Norton at last had an ally in life . . . would then she be thought of as wicked? It was so hard to know.

'Little beasts! So they *have* vanished. It is simply too bad,' he exclaimed, and signalled to the other end of the landing. 'They *could* be along there, but I fear I cannot brave the nursery yet a while. Dear Cakey – you have met Cakey, I take it – loves me considerably more than I could ever deserve and will detain me for hours.'

And so, with a light foot – he must make a fine

dancer! – Ned led her back down again and stopped at the door to a room overlooking the park. He then turned, smiled – said: 'Here at least, we shall find kindness' – knocked and went in.

'Ned, darling!' Miss Marianne Knight sat in a chair by the long casement window, a white silk slipper in one hand and soft brush in the other. 'I had no idea!' She laid her things down with great care, then rose to embrace him. 'And you have brought Mary.' Her tone was warm, but one of puzzled enquiry.

'I just had the pleasure of encountering Miss Knatch-bull on the stairs.' Ned stepped sideways and extended one hand. 'She seemed a little *lost*, Marianne . . .'

'My dear.' Marianne Knight approached and took Mary's hand. 'Pray, do forgive us.' And to her brother: 'Thank you, Ned. *I* will look after our guest from now on.'

'You are good.' Ned moved to the door, took the handle, then turned with a frown. 'But surely it is *Fan* who should—'

Marianne met his gaze, raised her brows and, pretty blue eyes full of meaning, replied: 'Mm . . .'

'I see,' Ned said, curtly. 'That is *most* – But if *you* would . . .'

'Yes of course, darling. No need to worry. I do *try* and step in as much as I can.'

He shook his head, gave way to a scowl and, just as quickly, altered his mood. 'Miss Knatchbull, it has been my *pleasure*.'

Then – this was to Marianne: 'Do look after those dancing shoes. I insist that you be my partner at the next Ashford Ball.'

And this to the room: 'And now, ladies, if you will forgive me, I must take myself off to be worshipped by Cakey until even I am bored of my wonders.'

And with that he was gone.

If she was honest, Mary, too, had had the impression that the eldest Miss Knight – whom they called Fanny – would be the one to take her under her wing. They were soon to be 'mother' and 'daughter', after all, and certainly her father, Sir Edward, had suggested that would be the arrangement. But somehow it had not quite come to pass.

'The Bride', as the young Knatchbulls referred to Fanny then – she was not yet 'the Mother' and somehow, given its connotations of romance and passion, 'the Bride' struck them as funnier still – seemed to be one of those very busy sorts of ladies. What exactly she was actually busy *with* was unclear, but Mary could see that this general busyness acted as a wedge or a stop in the relationship between them.

For Mary, life at Godmersham seemed to proceed at a gentle sort of pace, certainly compared to the rigours of Ramsgate; but the poor Bride sped around the place in the most terrible hurry. For example, the moment Mary entered one room was always the point at which Fanny remembered she was due in another. And should Fanny open a door and find Mary within, she would at once start and declare herself in the wrong place. Then if, through no fault of either, they found themselves on the same flight of stairs, Fanny's eyes seemed to darken with a mixture of guilt and regret, as if Mary were some chore – an untidy cupboard – which she ought not and yet somehow did keep putting off.

Mary did not mind any of it, particularly. Though she had learned next to nothing at school, she had developed a certain forbearance. And anyway, the longer she stayed at Godmersham, the more companionship she did seem to find there. Miss Marianne was the kindest of spirits, Booker, the maid, a complete darling and, soon after young Mr Knight's visit, Louisa and Cassy suddenly became her great friends. But when it came to her little brother John, she felt very differently. For John, Mary minded a lot.

Her youngest brother had been sent to Godmersham soon after Mary, though he had never been there before and was barely acquainted with the Bride. But still, his bags were packed, his papa bade him farewell and suddenly, there he was in a quite different nursery. He was so excited in the carriage from Hatch, chanting: 'We're off to see the new mama, the new mama, the new mama. Off to see the new mama . . .' over and over until Mary thought she might scream.

How she wished the new mama felt as excited about him.

~

'What do we think, then?' Booker was looking over Mary's head and into the glass. 'Hair up or down? Which will she prefer, do you suppose?'

Mary peered back at her own reflection and saw little to admire. 'Oh, Books, it doesn't much matter. I've got horrible hair. It's all – oh, I don't know.' What was that word again? 'That's it: lank.' Then the whole phrase came back to her: 'It's unfortunate and lank and a terrible *pity*.'

'*Lank*? And a *pity*?' Booker dropped the ribbon in outrage. 'Who on earth gave you that idea?' Their eyes met in reflection, but Mary did not reply. 'Oh, I see. Did she indeed. You've been listening in doorways. No good ever comes . . . Well, *I* never heard such nonsense.' She picked up a strand and let it run. 'Like silk, that is. Pure silk.'

Mary was not persuaded. 'Whatever you go for, it's going under a cap and anyway, she just doesn't like me. A bow isn't going to make any difference.'

'Owph, we'll have none of that, miss.' The maid took a swipe at her head with the brush. 'Why *wouldn't* she like you? I've not told you before – we don't want that head of yours too big for its bonnet – but all of downstairs says you're their particular favourite.'

'Oh, Booker!' Mary swung around in surprise. 'You

can't really mean it?' But of course, the maid's face shut up like a clam. It was never a good idea to question a compliment – one always ended up being punished, in some way or another. But imagine if it *were* true? She allowed herself a brief moment of silent fantasy. A rare accolade! And the good opinion of the servants was worth so much more than the Bride's. 'Ow!' How she hated those hairpins, and Booker was driving them in now with force.

'Stay still, now. Nearly done.' She measured out a ribbon, planted it on and conceded. 'It is indeed true, and not like there isn't stiff competition. They're all good sorts, here – the boys *and* the girls. Lovely family, the Knights. You couldn't have chosen better if you tried. There!' Booker stepped back, admired her own handi-work, then covered it all up with a cap.

'I hardly *chose* them,' Mary replied as she stood up. 'But I do agree: they *are* charming. All except—'

'That's enough!' Booker admonished. 'She may not have done much for you yet, grant you that, but it's all going to change now the wedding's upon us. Tea in her bedroom, indeed! What could be kinder? Now, let's have a look at you.'

Mary crossed the floor – it did not take long – over to the cheval, smoothed down her day dress and gave a little twirl. It was one of the three gowns that Marianne Knight had had made for her, to add to the new petticoats and nightgowns, and Mary was amazed at the magic wrought by a new wardrobe. She could almost pass as a Knight. But one knew better than to show pleasure in one's own reflection. 'I suppose I will do.' She turned and took the maid's hand. 'Wish me luck! Let's go and find John.'

It was not exactly hard finding John in those strange, early Godmersham days: find Cakey, and there he would be. It was Mary's one consolation that while the little one might not have been blessed with the mama of his dreams, he could not wish for a more loving nurse.

Cakey had been with the Knights since the Bride was a baby – now there was a curious image – and, though her services were no longer required, she was still there, in the attic. The idea of letting her go was quite out of the question. She was the Godmersham treasure! Cakey was touched, of course, but clearly, also, a little bit bored. So when this motherless bairn came into her nursery, she flung herself at the task.

They were still at the basin when Mary and Booker appeared. Was Cakey washing the boy or was she polishing him?

'Glory be!' exclaimed Booker. 'It's assault by a flannel.'

'Thank you, dear Cakey.' Mary tried not to laugh. 'I think that will do.'

'If you say so.' Reluctantly, the nurse let him out of her grip. 'Needs to be at his best, though . . .'

'For the mama!' John squealed as he ran to his sister

and buried himself in her skirts. 'We're going to see the new mama, the new . . .'

Cakey caught Booker's eye and shot a look of enquiry. Booker sent back a shrug, muttering: 'An attack of good conscience? Just hope it sticks.' And Mary pretended she had not seen or heard any of it.

Together, the two Knatchbull children – eldest and youngest – set off down the stairs and all the while, John prattled on. 'I want to climb into her bed! Will the New One let me climb into her bed? Like you used to do with the Real One?'

Mary privately fretted. For the truth was that she had told a little white lie. Miss Knight – the *mama* – had, in fact, only invited Mary to join her for tea. John she had somehow forgotten. But surely, if he came too, then it would be to everyone's benefit? The wedding was now but a fortnight away. They would soon be a family . . .

They arrived at the door; the maid knocked and announced them. Miss Knight – her head in a nightcap, rose silk shawl round her shoulders, tray across knees, looked up and cried: 'Dear children! You came.' Her lips smiled; her eyes flashed with fear. 'What a pleasure to see you. And yet, such a *pity*!' Now all in a fluster, she put the tray to one side – spilling tea on the bedcover – turned, put her feet into the nicely placed slippers. 'Today of all days!' She rang for the maid. 'So much to do, and so little time. Come, children.' She beckoned them both over, but only John approached. 'Do give me a kiss, dear. And are you not looking splendid? Ah, there you are, Sayce.' Her voice all relief. 'Time to dress now, too sad to say. But you are *so* sweet for coming, and we *will* try again soon.'

~

On the 20th day of October, Mary stood by her bags at the foot of the Godmersham steps and awaited the carriage. She was far too modest a girl to ever expect one of those great, grand farewells, although a fond one would have been pleasant. But the Wedding was now just a few days away and the household in absolute uproar. John had left a few days before, to live with a gentleman who would prepare him for school. And her own removal would inevitably be the last thing upon anyone's mind.

A kindly footman had been charged with seeing her off. They stood side by side, each endeavouring not to catch the eye of the other, though, when the worst did happen, they achieved a shy smile. But the carriage was late, their wait taking too long. Eventually, he was emboldened to speak.

'Weather set fair for your journey then, miss.'

In perfect unison, like partners in ballet, they raised their eyes up to the wide, Kentish sky and, necks stretched, traced the great arc of unbroken blue.

'Nothing like autumn for fine weather,' he declared.

'Oh, indeed,' Mary warmly replied, though she was not entirely convinced that was true.

'Mind, they do say it's soon on the turn. Rain from the east coming.' They both looked to their left. 'Always the worst. Shame, what with the Wedding and such. Poor Miss Knight. Waits all those long years and now in for a drenching.'

'Oh! I *am* sorry to hear that,' Mary exclaimed, with now genuine warmth. 'That *would* be a pity.'

In fact, her thoughts were less with the Bride and more with the bridesmaids: Miss Marianne in particular. She was so very determined to wear her white shoes. What if they were ruined? Mary found her eyes turning back to the house, and her thoughts to her friends.

Of course, Mary herself had been shocked that the marriage was to happen so soon. The Knatchbull children had, somehow or other, got the idea that they could enjoy a two-year grace, which in turn had provoked the hope that it might never happen, with the result that they were quite unprepared. And yet, somehow, for Marianne, the blow had seemed much more severe. In just a few weeks, she had become pale and thin, was moved quickly to tears: it was as if all the light had gone out of her person.

Though still too young to see clearly, Mary had just enough wisdom to judge that this wedding would affect so many lives – not just those of the Bride and the groom. Like elements in one of Norton's great chemical experiments, two families would be combined into one and the result could be, well – who could predict? Such a thing had never been tried with this particular set of ingredients. Suddenly, this new future – its changes and challenges – reared up before her. Though she could not expect to wield any control over, or say in, what might come next, she could not help but wonder . . .

There came the great rush of hooves, wheels, the roar of a coachman and with that her thought chain was broken. At once, her bags were stowed, her hand taken and small self settled. As the horses prepared, she turned for one last look at the mansion and, at that, the front door swung open.

'Miss Knatchbull! Miss Knatchbull!' Ned Knight skipped down the step and on to the gravel. 'Forgive me! I was not aware you were leaving us. How rude not to bid you farewell! ' He spoke through the window, kind face at the glass. 'Let me wish you safe travel.' The broad smile displayed near perfect teeth. 'And I do hope we see you here soon.'

Before Mary could reply – and how could she have spoken? What would she have said? – he issued two sharp slaps to the carriage, the man cracked his whip and the journey commenced.

As they turned on the gravel and took to the drive, Mary twisted round in her seat the better to study him. He first plunged his hands into his pockets, then had a word with the footman – flung his head back and laughed – drew a shape in the dust with the point of his boot. So it would be quite wrong of Mary to claim that Ned was watching her go.

But he certainly stayed there and waited, until she could no longer see him.

CHAPTER XII

In that particularly cold spring of 1821, one of the more popular attractions in all of London was Burford's Panorama. The *View of Naples and Surrounding Scenery* was housed in the specially constructed Rotunda in the Strand, and the great queue outside almost as famous as the spectacle within. Fanny was privately sure that, if she were to miss the experience, then she would survive. However, the young people had been begging to see it for weeks and, the happiness of others being her constant and guiding concern, here Fanny was.

'Stay close to me, Fan.' George, Fanny's brother, pressed her arm into his side as they emerged from Surrey Street and pushed through the crowd. Above the press of grim, filthy buildings there was a clear and bright sky. 'Keep in!' he called over his shoulder, where William

brought up the rear, with Mary Dorothea on one side and
the new governess, Miss Atkinson, on the other. 'Stick at
it!' The entrance was in their sights now. 'Watch it, Will!
Hold on to the ladies!'

A small crowd on the street was shouting abuse at the
top of its lungs. Honestly, Fanny would like very much
to be surprised to find such coarse people at an event
of such innocence, but she was now thoroughly used
to it. Everywhere one went in Town – the smartest of
places, the quietest of days; even once, heaven forbid, *on
a Sunday* – one could find a mob, quite out of its mind
about one thing or other.

'What are they protesting this time?' she shouted into
George's left ear. It was never easy to tell.

'They are against it!' George shouted back, grabbing
Miss Atkinson's arm and pulling the whole party towards
the enclosed entrance. He paid their one shilling per head.

'I gathered they were against *something*,' Fanny muttered and took a deep breath. They were now in a dark,
narrow corridor – utterly black, eerily quiet. 'They generally are.'

Fanny held George's coat-tails with one hand, and
Mary's muff with the other. The passage was so cramped,
they had no choice but to move single file, blind in the
darkness. 'Will?' she called out to her other brother, voice
regrettably shrill.

'Here, Fan,' William returned. 'Close to Miss Atkinson. All safe – bringing up the rear.'

Dear boy, Fanny thought as she cautiously edged her way forward with tiny steps. How he has matured lately. Even a few months ago, she could not possibly have imagined the young man he was now, so protective of Mary Dorothea – who, after all, was no relation of *his* – and quietly courteous to her governess.

'Up she rises!' George suddenly shouted. 'Ladies, beware!'

They were still in pitch black, and now forced to climb a steep flight of steps.

'Don't panic, girls!' Fanny's heart was thumping. She felt dizzy and sick. 'It is perfectly safe.' She heard a gasp, a little scream. And was that a giggle? Surely not. 'Miss Atkinson?' This place was so thoroughly unnatural. The poor young lady was quite possibly scared out of her wits.

'Thank you, madam.' Miss Atkinson's speaking voice had a pleasing musicality. 'Please do not concern yourself. I am perfectly well.'

'And we have made it!' George shouted in triumph. 'Here is the curtain. Ready, all?'

Their eyes were so shocked by the light flooding in through the glass roof that at first they were blinded. With all the grace and speed of a tortoise emerging from winter, Fanny groped her way to the central platform and clung to the railings in fear of her life.

'I say!' George exclaimed, spinning round on his heel like a dancer. 'Will you look at that?'

The five stood – suspended in space, bathed by the sunshine – surrounded on all sides by an enormous, painted replica of the Neapolitan region. William, bending his neck back to take in the sky, whistled in admiration. 'What an extraordinary sight!' He reached out and offered his arms again to Miss Atkinson and Mary. 'Ladies?' He smiled. 'A stroll through the Italian streets, if you will?'

Fanny hoped they were not wanting to spend too long here. Personally, she felt she had got the measure of it already. She had been once to Paris – *most* unenjoyable; the food made her ill – and formed there the firm opinion that one European city was much like another. She tucked her arm under George's and allowed him to walk her around.

'So what were they *against,* that crowd outside? While not doubting their passion, I could not quite make it out.'

'This very Panorama, apparently.' George spoke from the side of his mouth as he studied the painting. 'False representation . . . fakery . . . we mortal fools cannot be trusted to tell the difference between this and the real thing . . . all the usual.'

Fanny sighed. Londoners: give them all a day on horseback over the Weald or a full week of harvest, then let us see if they still hold these ridiculous views.

It was the middle of March. She and Sir Edward, with Mary Dorothea and her new governess, had been up in Town since January and, though she was trying her best to get used to it, London would persist in being so very different from everything she thought as the norm.

Take these other visitors, for example. Her eye had already slid from the 'astonishing spectacle'. She was now studying the people around them – that was the thing about these so-called attractions: one did rub up against all sorts – and seeing something she had lately noticed a lot: the staring. Was this a new custom? She had come to Town once or twice over the years, and had never previously been so aware. But now, wherever she went with Miss Atkinson and Mary, passers-by seemed to gawp and it was happening right there again, in the Panorama. The girls walked; the heads turned. Furthermore, some of these heads seemed then to whisper between themselves. It was deeply unpleasant. Fanny often found herself blushing and there was she, now a married lady. Her heart went out to Mary and Miss A. They simply were not used to such impertinence. It certainly did not happen in Ashford.

'I say, Fan.' William approached her. 'Will you look at that now?'

Fanny gave Naples a cursory glance. It appeared to be quite horribly hot, and frightfully busy. How did anyone live, all cramped together like that? 'At what exactly?'

'Oh!' Miss Atkinson clasped her hands into the position of prayer and raised them, as if the Holy Ghost were coming out of the wall. 'The quite wondrous basilica!'

'Ah, yes. Perfectly splendid.' None of it was quite Fanny's cup of tea – all rather *Catholic* – and she was beginning to wonder if the governess might not be just a little affected. 'Have we had enough, do we think?' she asked the young people brightly.

And soon they were back out on the streets.

As a London establishment, Number 57 Portland Place suited Fanny and Sir Edward exceedingly well. Within the towering white stucco mansion, the rooms were many and large, the amenities excellent and Lady Banks so delighted to host them that it felt almost as if the generosity were theirs.

It was now late afternoon, and the ladies were peaceably alone in the drawing room. 'How blessed I am to have you all under my roof.' Lady Banks was never to be found without her embroidery frame and, almost always, with a needle in hand. 'You chase away my old widow's sorrows, my dear, and keep me sprightly.' She gave a vague stab at the canvas, but did not pull the thread through.

'I was thinking the same thing only today.' Fanny directed her words around the person of the footman who poured her tisane. 'About my own blessings, I mean.' She stared into the fireplace and hoped that his next job might be another log. 'We were at that Panorama business—'

'Ah, yes. Of course, *my* views on that are well known. Did you not think it fr-r-rightful?'

The footman saw to the fire, which hissed and then flared.

'Perfectly dreadful, I'm afraid. I thought I might faint.' Fanny shuddered at the memory. 'But it did lead me to think how very lucky I am,' she said earnestly.

'Did it, my dear?' Lady Banks dropped her work in delight. 'Do tell me precisely *why*.' She snuggled into her armchair with anticipation.

'Well, just *imagine* if one had been born a *Continental*—' Lady Banks looked a little surprised.

'—and forced for *society's* sake to stay in somewhere like Naples. Lady Banks.' She leaned forward. 'I have *seen* it. Well, Mr Burford's representation, at least. The place is *impossible* Those poor, *benighted* Italians could not swing a *cat*.' She sat back again, and looked up at the great portrait that hung on the chimney piece. As well as being the most courageous explorer and quite brilliant botanist – or so it was said – Sir Joseph looked, too, as if he was rather gentle and kind. Had their paths crossed would he have approved of her? Fanny very much hoped so.

'So are we not lucky to be *British*, and gathered in London? And, of course, to have *you*, dear Lady Banks. You are so kind to us. Without you, I would have nowhere to stay while the House was in session: my husband would be in Town and I all alone at home in the country.' Fanny felt oddly moved. 'Well then, how sad.'

'Newlyweds.' Lady Banks winked like a pantomime dame. Fanny blushed. 'Anything else?'

'And, well.' In fact, something was on her mind. She decided to share it. After all, Lady Banks had softened a lot since the first time they met. 'I was worried, when I married my beloved husband, that I might lose touch with my dear siblings, whose lives would continue to travel down one avenue, so to speak, while mine took off on another. I was forced at a young age, you know, to be something more like a *mother* to them and have often worried that it had somehow prevented them from seeing me more as a sister, or *friend*.'

Privately, Fanny had feared that, once she was no longer looking after them – working, arranging, the general business of nurturing – they would have no further need of her whatsoever. They had often, when they were younger, played a game called the Most. Lizzie was always the Most Beautiful, William the Most Fun, and so on and so forth. Fanny had always longed to be the Most . . . well, she barely minded, as long as it was at least a *little* bit interesting. In fact, she was rarely mentioned. But that was too bleak to share.

'And now look! George and William have actually *chosen* to spend the whole of this week with me, which hasn't happened for *years*. They came with us to the Strand – and heavens knows how we would have survived it without them – even though they have no especial responsibility to us now. And they have just taken

Mary out to the park – fear not, Miss A is there as her chaperone – which seems to me so *enormously* kind. And on top of all that, we have *Ned* asking to join *us* for dinner . . . Is it not touching?

'I knew we were close, but had no idea until this season that they would, well . . .' She gave a little laugh which she hoped was suitably modest, and flicked her fingers. '. . . *flock* quite in the manner they have.'

Lady Banks opened her mouth to speak, then thought for a moment and closed it again. She stared into the fire, smiled to herself, shrugged.

Then up she spoke: 'And is there anything else you might like to mention? Anything at all?'

'I – no – I can't think—' Fanny looked nervous, and flushed.

'Then I shall say it myself.' Lady Banks returned to her embroidery. 'I hear your dear husband is somewhat unwell.' She reached for her thimble. 'Ague of the face this time, or something other?'

'Yes, the ague – or so I believe.' Fanny felt uneasy.

'Quite what that is exactly, I cannot possibly imagine, though I am sure it brings with it the most acute form of suffering, eh?' She picked at her stitching. 'But to my point: this is something you might want to make a note of, in future.' And groped for the thread. 'It will crop up every time, as it did with poor Annabella – do not be offended, my dear. Dead and buried, dead and buried.'

Now Lady Banks was warming to her subject, the embroidery was back in her lap.

'By the time she got to her third, of course, it was how she knew. Sir Edward's own health would suffer some hideous collapse and – lo! – the dear lady would discover she had started a baby.' The jowls wobbled in emphasis. 'Of course, we should still call Dr Maton here, to be on the safe side, but I think he will only confirm what we already know.

'Congratulations, my dear. It is the most excellent news. Another little Knatchbull! Let us hope it comes out just like our dear Mary Dorothea.'

~

Sir Edward and Fanny had planned to leave it some weeks before they told the children. They were all to be together for Easter in Kent, and that seemed the optimum moment, as the baby was due in the late summer. However, the business was not proving quite as straightforward as Fanny had hoped. Rather than blooming, as was expected, she felt, more often, indifferent and Dr Maton had ordered enforced rest. It was decided that Fanny should immediately return to Godmersham, where she could expect to be well looked after by dear Marianne. And of course, this had to be shared with Miss Atkinson, and Mary Dorothea.

Bearing in mind their particular closeness, Sir Edward was keen to be the one to tell his daughter. He later reported back with some pride that the child had wept tears of happiness and soaked his shoulder quite through. Fanny took Miss Atkinson alone.

'You asked to see me, madam?' The governess put her head around the door, smiled prettily, stepped in and then curtseyed.

She really does have the most perfect manner, thought Fanny. Respectful but easy – a combination quite hard to achieve. How remarkably clever of Sir Edward to hire her; what an excellent father he was. She bade Miss Atkinson sit, informed her of the interesting developments which Miss Atkinson politely pretended she did not already know and announced they'd be returning to Kent in the morning.

Somehow, she then felt more should be said: 'Now, of course, in the coming months – few years, indeed – I cannot see that I will be able to spend quite as much time with Mary as I would like.'

'Of course, madam,' Miss Atkinson replied with all possible warmth. 'You will have your hands full.'

'Quite so. Therefore, my dear husband and I would like some reassurance that you are happy in this situation and have no intention of leaving us before Mary is "out".'

'Madam, I could not be happier. Mary Dorothea is the most excellent pupil, as well as companion.'

As she spoke, Fanny studied Miss Atkinson's appearance

almost for the first time. Why had she not noticed before? It can only be that she had not truly been looking.

'She has such an *interested* mind, is so quick to learn and her facility for music has deeply impressed me,' Miss Atkinson went on.

The governess had about her an elegance rarely seen beyond the best drawing rooms. Her features were fine – her nose, in particular, slender and narrow. There, the skin appeared particularly thin and delicate so that, when she smiled, it stretched across the bridge, creating a flare in the nostril. Fanny could not deny that the whole effect was unusually winning.

'She has so many fine qualities – I am daily enchanted! – that in my experience are rarely to be found together. For example, she has a highly developed, innate sense of right and wrong – one might call it a moral clarity – unusual for a girl of her years. Yet at the same time, her sense of humour is simply delightful! Mary Dorothea is keen to work, pleased to play . . . Madam, I must say that, as a pupil, she is almost too good to be true.'

Her hair was not golden – more honey from heather – but her complexion was glowing, even on that dark, cold afternoon.

'And I hope – feel, indeed – that, while Mary Dorothea shows me all due respect as her teacher, she and I still manage to be, truly, very good friends.'

The fact was, Miss Atkinson was uncommonly pretty. So why on earth had Sir Edward taken her on? Once upon a time, Fanny herself had had a governess who was rather similar – charming and clever and all the rest. Naturally, it ended unpleasantly – does it not always? – and left her poor dear late mama badly shaken. If Fanny were to perform her stepmotherly duties properly, she should keep a good eye on this Miss Atkinson.

But for now, it was time for her afternoon sleep.

CHAPTER XIII

The loss of her first, precious baby almost broke Fanny's heart. For five long months he had nestled within her: her closest companion; the love of her life. All those spring afternoons, while the family was busy elsewhere, they had lain quietly together, she and her darling: mother and child. Completely contented while the sun poured through the window and filled both with strength.

It had seemed such a happy time, while she was living it. Fanny was back at her beloved Godmersham – Hatch being still uninhabitable – and dear old Cakey, who had been her nurse back when she herself was a child, was tending to her once again, with Marianne's assistance. The Knatchbull children were scattered around and about the South of England and were all perfectly happy – Fanny knew that from her most assiduous readings of their various guardians' reports. And so Fanny felt blessed anew, and vastly important: in a sublime state of grace. In her mind's eye, the small being inside her was born, growing and then grown: his whole future mapped out before him.

And then came the horror. What had she done to him? Why could she not keep him alive? How was she to live with the shame? Her own mama had delivered eleven perfect children in rapid succession. Though she was not around now for Fanny to ask – the 'success', so to speak, having led to her tragic demise – when one looked at the calendar of family birthdays, it did not seem possible that any were missing. And Lizzie, her much younger sister, was already popping them out, *comme il faut*, in that pea-from-pod fashion. Producing just one, living baby became Fanny's obsession.

Throughout that difficult time, Fanny tried hard not to forget her own good fortune in all other areas. The Lord was lavishly thanked, in her devout daily worship, for her kind, loving husband and large, prospering families spread around and about Kent. And she counted as a particular blessing the two treasures who were her strongest support.

First, the governess who devoted herself to the well-being of Mary Dorothea. Thanks to her, the girl seemed to be blossoming and that meant so much. Of course, Fanny's most fervent wish was to spend as much time as possible with her dear little stepdaughter, but with all this unexpected unpleasantness, she could not quite find it *in* her at that particular juncture. Though she did pride herself on being one of life's *copers*, even women like her did have their limit.

And then Marianne: *dear* Marianne. What a success she had made of running Godmersham since Fanny had left it. Their papa, the younger siblings and all the servants seemed completely contented under her management. Fanny had not heard a peep of complaint. It would be simply too much if she had to deal with her health *and* all those children and houses.

So as well as her Lord, Fanny thanked both her sister and the governess as often as the opportunity arose. She made sure they were both keenly aware how important they were to her in this difficult period. Neither could be under any illusion. And yet, and yet . . . even then, they could not be relied upon.

~

Marianne was the first to cause problems. It was early May 1822, Fanny had recently suffered a second, most unfortunate event and Dr Maton recommended some weeks in Leamington to take the waters. Of course, Sir Edward was too busy to accompany her – Fanny marvelled at Sir Edward's constant busyness. It was a privilege to be the support by his side – and therefore other companions had to be chosen.

At the time Leamington was one of the more fashionable spas and anyone would seize upon the opportunity of spending a few weeks there among the *beau monde*. So, for Fanny, the salient question was not who might be available, more which sibling truly deserved such a treat, and could be trusted to properly appreciate it. Fanny thought long and hard – she was never known to be flippant on any family issue – and made her decision.

'Oh, do look!' Fanny's sister, Louisa, pulled up her pony and took a moment to gaze upon the vista beyond Mersham-le-Hatch. 'A panorama of paradise in the finest of seasons.'

Fanny drew up beside her, and looked as she was bidden. It was indeed beautiful: a day on which to believe that, if you could stay still long enough, spring would dramatically transform into summer before your very eyes.

'I know you have been through the most terrible sadness, my dear,' Louisa began cautiously. Everyone was cautious around Fanny these days. They were almost too frightened to speak. 'But a day like today – surely that must give you hope?'

Hope! It was, indeed, all around her. The air was clear, the hawthorn pungent . . . but its presence was quite inappropriate. It made a mockery of the despair which lodged in Fanny's heart. She gave no reply. She felt completely inert: wanted to dismount, lie down and sleep for a week. But then Taffy whinnied and pawed at the ground and, for his sake alone, they resumed their ride.

Louisa spoke up again. 'You know, dearest, I would do anything to make you feel better. And am *thrilled* at the idea of taking the waters with you and George. You are so kind to ask me; we could have the loveliest time. But—'

But? Fanny sighed and rose to a canter. Listen to it! All that she did for them and still: not one ever satisfied.

'I feel,' Louisa continued, somewhat out of breath from the exertion of catching her up, 'it might be somewhat more *fair* if Marianne were to go in my place. She does do so much for all of us, and gets so little fun.'

Taffy, sensing the conversation had turned delicate, slowed to a trot; Fanny rubbed at his neck, prayed for some strength and then spoke up, firmly: 'Marianne has her hands full, my dear. She is desperately needed, both at Godmersham and by Lizzie and her new addition.' Why could nobody else grasp these arrangements? '*She* really cannot be spared, whereas *you*, Louisa, might see some benefit from being in new, different society.' Taffy picked her way carefully down to the lake's edge. 'This is your first season and we are all working hard to make it as pleasant as possible, so if you might be so kind as to try and enjoy it?'

'But I feel . . .' Louisa began.

Honestly, Fanny could scream.

'I feel that I have already had such a *lovely* debut,

and Marianne never did quite get one. Through no fault of anyone! Just,' she finished lamely, 'as things turned out.'

'My dear Louisa. I implore you. Be grateful for that which is given to *you*, and pray – understand that all people are different. Marianne is a kind, selfless soul,' proclaimed Fanny. 'Devoted to her family, lives to help others . . . She is perfectly content with this life God has given her. I am sure of it.' She pulled Taffy's head out of the water. 'And will hear no more on the subject.'

But when, the very next day, news came to Hatch of Marianne's sudden illness, such was the coincidence in timing that Fanny struggled to believe it. Although the details were rather dramatic and, it was true, might be hard to put on – several people had, it seemed, witnessed the most violent seizures – she still thought it a little suspicious that it should occur so soon after that very conversation.

Fanny made no changes to her travel arrangements, Marianne duly recovered and when the spa party returned they made every effort to include her in their week at the races. At the ball, Marianne enjoyed as many dances as all of her sisters, and, it was agreed by all onlookers, seemed to enjoy the whole festival more than anyone in Kent. Always a pretty girl, she was never lovelier than that glorious August, appearing to float through the week in her white silken slippers and on a cloud of euphoria.

Fanny looked on and did wonder . . . But it was not

until one morning in the middle of November that all was revealed.

~

The Knatchbulls were now properly ensconced in the family seat. Renovations were almost complete and, though her heart must always belong to Godmersham, even Fanny had to agree that – in principle, at least – Hatch was the superior house. Still, for all its spacious apartments and ornate decoration, the only room that offered true comfort was the one yet to receive any attention, and that was the library. So it was there, in the squashed, vermilion, book-lined gloaming, that she and Sir Edward tended to spend their few spare free hours. And there that her eldest brother rushed in on that day, without warning, demanding an interview.

'Ned, darling!' How Fanny loved it when one of her family turned up at her door. It made her feel she was still at the heart of all things; gave her a warm, happy sense of belonging. She moved to rise, intending to kiss, and then registered his unnatural demeanour: a little flushed, short slightly of breath; *almost* – a tiny bit – something like flustered. This was highly irregular.

Of course, when hunting or killing or hitting a thing, Ned moved like quicksilver. In the world beyond sport, though, he knew no sense of urgency and was rarely disturbed. Yet here he was, eschewing all greetings – Fanny prayed Sir Edward would opt, just on this one occasion, to *not* take offence – and – what was this? – spluttering about yet another drama of Marianne's making.

'A *proposal*?' Fanny fell back into the depths of the worn leather sofa. 'A *proposal* from *whom,* might one ask?'

It was to her eternal credit that Fanny's first thought was given not to Godmersham's domestic arrangements and her own convenience, but that the gentleman's identity did, in fact, take priority.

'Billington,' she repeated, once informed. '*Billington?*' Now she was thoroughly mystified. 'But, Ned dearest,' she explained in her patient voice, 'we have no knowledge of any *Mr Billington.*' As if that put an end to the matter.

To her husband, however, the name was familiar. Slowly, he rose; took position in the centre of the faded, elegant Aubusson; made fists like a fighter. '*BILLINGTON?*' When in the comfort of his family home, Sir Edward roared much less than might have been popularly imagined, but when he did, that roar came with significant effect. '*Your sister* has got herself mixed up with that fellow *Billington?*'

'Ah.' Ned looked worried and bit his lip. 'So you *do* know him, sir? We did wonder if you might have some information that would prove relevant. It is for that very reason my father urged me to come.'

'Know him?' Sir Edward marched to the tray and poured a stiff drink, even though, Fanny noted, it was yet to turn noon. 'Oh, yes. I *know* him.' He did not offer one to Ned. 'He has the living over at Kennington—'

'So he is a *clergyman*?' Fanny cut in. At last: this was hard, useful information, going some way to grounding her thoughts, which were, until that moment, spinning quite out of control.

'I fear so, my dear,' her husband supplied. 'A clergyman indeed, and' – an air of menace entered his tone – '*of the very worst kind.*' In the wobble of his jowl, Fanny marked a new likeness to dear Lady Banks.

'I *say*!' Ned, shocked and alarmed, ran his hand through his hair until it stood up on end. 'The rascal! What on earth is he up to?'

'He and I are in some dispute,' thundered Sir Edward as he stared first at his wife, then at her brother.

'A dispute?' Fanny echoed. Oh dear. Not another one . . .

'Yes, my dear. About *tithes.*' He swallowed the sherry, slammed down the glass, adding as an aside: 'Do not worry. I am convinced that Right is on my—'

'Oh, but of course,' his wife hastily cut in.

Meanwhile, Ned had sunk down into an armchair, placed an elegant foot over a shapely knee and was now smiling and returned to his habitual languor. 'So not the worst one might fear, eh, Fan?' He winked across at his sister, and clicked with his tongue. 'Thought for a minute there our May was giving herself up to an axe murderer. Ha!'

'Mr Knight!' Sir Edward roared.

'Hull-*o*?' Ned bolted straight up again.

'It is my considered opinion that this Billington is not a fit match for Miss Marianne, and his suit should be discouraged.'

'Ned, dearest.' At last, Fanny's caring, sororal nature ceded way to matters of her own convenience. 'What does Papa make of it? Is he minded to approve?'

It really would present difficulties if he did. Supposing Marianne and this 'Billington' were after a quick engagement? Godmersham had been running so well! As if she did not have her hands full already, no doubt the business of organising a replacement would devolve upon Fanny. Things generally did, after all.

'Can't say he is, old girl.' Fanny caught her husband's wince; Ned pressed on. 'Not so much to do with the tithes or whatever, though that' – he flung this in the direction of Sir Edward as one might a steak to a lion – 'is obviously of the highest importance. More the age-old story. No money. Not a bean. Love in a cottage and all that.' He opened both palms. 'Well, a rectory in this case, but I gather rather a mean one. Cold. Damp. Coming down round the old ears. She says she won't mind a bit, of course. But there we are. Such is love.'

'Love, you say?' Fanny repeated, puzzled. 'Marianne considers herself to be actually *in love*?' She felt oddly put out.

'She does rather. And do you know, old girl, I am beginning to think I believe her,' he replied. 'Something's up, that is for certain. Not exactly her usual sweet self. Charging around the place, drumming for supporters, stirring everything up into a terrible old rumpus. Dear Cakey' – he turned to Sir Edward – 'that's our old nanny, by the way' – then back to his sister – 'ready to block-ade herself into the nursery on the lovers' behalf. A less likely Robespierre one could barely imagine, but that is where we have got to.' He issued one last glance of regret towards the untroubled drinks tray.

'Sir, my father will be most interested to hear your views on the matter.' Ned smacked a hand on each thigh. 'As he is determined to put an end to the whole affair.'

He rose, stopped and, for a moment, stared out to the middle distance and plunged deep into thought. 'Must say, old Fan – quite *entre nous*, of course – I do find it all just a tiny bit odd. If Marianne really wants this Billington of hers, should she not have him? But then perhaps one is simply more of a live-and-let-live sort of fellow.' Ned gave a twist to his mouth and a shrug.

'Not that anyone has asked my advice, nor am I par-ticularly minded to give it, but seems to me there's only one possible move left in the game, and that is elope-ment. The young get their own way and the old have no choice but to get on with it, eh?

'Ah, well.' He snapped out of his musings and back to his natural ebullience. 'No doubt all will work out in the end.

'Tally ho, then, dear Knatchbulls, and back to the

163

battlements.' And, remembering to give a brisk bow, Ned took his leave.

Stunned, Fanny rose from the sofa, went to the window and watched his departure. *Elopement?* How could Ned throw that out in such a casual fashion when the very word brought her out in a rash? Once the gig had taken to the gravel and left her vision, she turned to her husband.

'Sir Edward.' She went to his side, and slipped her hand into his.

Her husband grunted.

'My darling. Though most reluctant to exploit your excellent nature—'

'No need, my dear.' Sir Edward raised her hand to his lips and kissed it. 'Our families are as one now. Our interests align.' He strode to the bell and rang for a servant. 'A spot of cold mutton and then I shall call on your dear father. I am quite sure that, between us, we can make the girl see some sense.'

'And if not?'

'There was a similar sort of business with a sister of mine a few years ago, and I must say that my late father – with whom, as you know, I did not generally see eye to eye – dealt with it admirably. The girl was simply closely guarded by maids, day and night, until the supposed passion abated, as all passion must. I shall be urging your own father to adopt similar measures.'

'Oh, Sir Edward,' breathed Fanny, feeling quite overcome. For – truly! – how lucky she was. Marianne might be 'in love' – or think herself so, silly creature – but Fanny already had the most excellent husband. One of those serious, solid sorts of husband who not only had all their best interests at heart but also pursued them, with vigour. In that moment, her own heart was brimful.

Fanny could never be entirely sure quite how much influence Sir Edward was able to wield. But what she did know for certain was that, within days, Mr Billington's plans had been thoroughly scuppered and Marianne's hopes utterly dashed. Moreover, the whole episode had been settled without any personal involvement from Fanny. Not once did she even have cause to voice an opinion. It really was most satisfactory.

CHAPTER XIV

'I beg you, no!' Miss Atkinson shrieked in her pretty and musical fashion. 'Leave the poor creature be.' She clasped her fine hands to her barely dressed bosom. 'Mr William, you are simply *too* cruel.'

'Got the blighter!' William Knight, handsome in shirt-sleeves and high postillion boots, knee-deep in the water, let out a great loud roar of triumph. 'My fair damsel,' he called in a courtly manner, 'I bring you my treasure' – he lifted his net, turned to the governess, issued a smile – 'as a token of my sincerest—'

And with that, he pulled his arm back, took aim, gave a flick of his wrist and a great, squirming, wet tench landed just by the hem of Miss Atkinson's best muslin. The shrill sound of *this* scream – more piercing, less decorous – brought the other girls rushing to her side.

'Oh, do look,' said Marianne.

'I say, Will. Well *done*,' put in Cassy.

'I call him a fine specimen,' Mary Dorothea agreed.

'How *could* you all?' Miss Atkinson, repulsed, took several steps back. 'He is in *agonies*.' They all watched as it writhed on the bank in the full glare of the sun. 'You girls are beasts. And *you* . . .' She turned to William who now, grinning and dripping, stood by her side. 'You, sir, are a monster.'

'Me?' He was all innocence. 'But *I* am his saviour. Watch!' As if by command, the fish leaped. 'There you are. Now is he or is he not jumping for joy?'

'Gasping for breath!' the governess shot back.

'Dear Miss Atkinson.' He took up her hand and bent as if to kiss it. 'I fear you show yourself up as one raised in the Town. We may be but poor, humble country folk' – he gestured to the large crowd of Knights and Knatch-bulls now gathered about him – 'but we know relief on a fish when we see it. The poor fellow was very near being drowned.'

'You are absurd.' She pulled back her hand and gave in to a smile. 'Now, pray, do put him back.'

'Your wish, madam.' With a flourish, William scooped it up and slipped it back in the water. 'Good old Tenchy . . .' A tail cut the surface and vanished. 'There he goes . . . And so' – he lifted both arms as if in surrender – 'must I. Miss Atkinson's displeasure has fair wounded my soul.' Still fully dressed, including the boots, William leaped into the air, turned head over heels; plunged into the water, issuing a long, plaintive 'Adieu'. And, because they none of them liked to do things by halves, all of the brothers followed them in.

Mary sank down on to the riverbank, watched them and smiled.

~

That glorious summer of 1823 was surely the loveliest yet of Mary's sixteen years. Sir Edward and Fanny were away and the entire Knatchbull offspring were removed for a few weeks to Godmersham. Hearing the call, the great flock of Knight boys swept in for the season and Ned, a singular kingfisher, flashed in and out. By day they all played; by evening they sang; a few danced more than a passable Highland Fling. The whole experience was delicious. And yet . . .

As if she could sense Mary's thoughts souring, Miss Atkinson – like a guardian angel – appeared, seated right by her side.

'Are you happy, my dear?' The governess's face was set towards the water, but her soft voice was all for Mary. 'It gives me great pleasure to see you have fun at last.' She reached up an arm and put it around her young charge. 'You were such a sad, lost little thing when first I came.' She turned to plant a kiss on a cheek. 'Your joy is my joy.'

Mary let her head drop on the dear lady's shoulder

and gave out a sigh. 'Oh, Miss A.' If only life could be *all* joy . . . Why must there always be darkness?

She was undoubtedly enjoying a heavenly stay, but Mary could not help but be troubled that it was born out of yet more unpleasant circumstances. Lady Knatchbull had now suffered two – or might it be three? – of her 'unfortunate events'. According to the doctors, the likelihood of another child was poor. Fanny's nerves (always delicate) were now totally shredded; her father's temper (never good) was particularly volatile. And Mary, too, was a little disturbed.

It was not that she had exactly *longed* for a baby at Hatch. Indeed, when her papa first told her one might arrive, she had found herself violently sobbing. He had presumed the tears to be happy ones; in truth, Mary had gone into shock. For a start, she had not understood theirs would be *that* sort of marriage. Imagine! Sir Edward and – Well, Mary would rather not. More than that, though, was the new and strange fear that her papa might yet have one more darling daughter. Was not *Mary* the Girl? Was *she* not 'his precious one'? He had told her so, constantly and – in their complicated, unwieldy, not-quite-happy family – she had come to rely on her fairer sex. Having failed to develop another as yet, it was still her only distinguishing feature.

So, certainly, the news had struck as a blow, but Mary was confident – in fact, positive – she had never wished the child any ill. Yet it was hard to deny that the matter of her sadness had come up in her prayers and, though she had only ever sought guidance and of the most general nature, she must now regret it. For when the latest poor baby died, Mary could only feel somehow responsible. After all, His ways were, quite famously, mysterious. Might He be taking these children unto Heaven just to please Mary? No, more likely to punish her, surely. Or was she confusing her private devotions with a contractual arrangement and, thereby, once again in danger of being thought wicked . . . Oh, weak, foolish creature! How she longed to follow, as taught, the path of a good Christian girl; with what ease was she pulled, by her wayward emotions, astray into sin.

But, as a short shock of cold water sprayed over her head, her troubled mind was brought back to more temporal matters. At once and as one body, the gentlemen were now done with the river and running on to the grass. Mary looked up and watched as they now sprayed all the spectators; soon laughed as the drenched ladies scattered, protesting. Cassy Knight – now firmly established as her best friend in the whole world – skipped over, held out both hands and drew Mary up to her feet.

'Archery now, on the lawn.'

The sodden menfolk led the way, with Miss Atkinson following them. As was their habit, the two girls dawdled behind.

'I am not *so* very bad with a bow,' Cassy began, 'though

my brothers are better, of course. How about you, dearest? I *bet* you're a shot. You are so good at *everything*, I do sometimes wonder how I can bear it.'

'Oh, darling, *do* stop.' Mary nudged her and laughed. 'I have never before even *seen* a bow, let alone held one. You must have noticed by now that my papa *"deplores all frivolity"*.' She had recently perfected a fair imitation of Sir Edward's excellent roar. 'We are never permitted any sort of fun whatsoever.' It felt a little disloyal to even admit that aloud, but the Knights had rather opened her eyes to a more cheerful way of living. 'How lucky I am to be staying here at Godmersham, with lovely *you*. And Emily A, of course.'

'Oh, *Emily A . . .*' Cassy mock-swooned. *'Did my heart love till now?'*

Their crush on the governess was one of the many joys that they shared.

'Forswear it sight!' Mary returned. *'For I ne'er saw—'*

'Soppy nonsense!' Norton, slower than the Knight boys and therefore considerably behind, came up and joined them. The girls felt obliged to stop and wait while he lifted his boots and emptied a gallon of river from each. 'Fancy quoting all that flowery stuff on a day like today. Look about you, for once.'

Mary did as she was bidden, saw the temple on the hill, the sheep in the meadow – the mansion ahead, sitting snug in its Park – and a few lines of Cowper swam into her mind:

'The sloping land recedes into the clouds;
Displaying on its varied side the grace
Of hedgerow beauties numberless . . .'

'The nonsense that governess has put in your heads is nothing short of a scandal.' He harrumphed with contempt. 'Far too much *literature* and too little *sense*. How can you stand here and dwell on the *picturesque*, when in *fact*, it is naught but a splendid arena for sporting and games? You see, that is how we *men* see things.' Norton was now fifteen years of age. 'Lord, but women are irrational creatures. And why must you go about holding hands all the time, as if you are *sisters*?' He wrenched them apart and forced himself in. 'You are not and nor can you ever be, so I don't know why you insist on pretending.'

'Darling!' Mary exclaimed. 'Are you *jealous*? You are! You're jealous!'

'What rot!' Norton muttered under his breath, but Mary could see that he blushed.

They started walking again. 'Anyway,' Cassy said, cheerful. 'We *are*. Fanny has been like a mother to me for most of my life, and now she is a mother to Mary – sort of.' The two girls shared a look. 'So that *almost* makes us sisters. And it makes not a jot of difference to me whether *you* mind it or not. I love Mary to bits and that is that.'

Oh! After those long years of loneliness . . . Mary's heart danced a jig.

Norton was now thoroughly put out. 'You remind me.' His tone was now one of serious business. 'I still have not yet electrified you. I must get around to it soon, for there is nothing on earth that could bring me greater delight. You two could both do with a *horrible* shock.'

The girls squealed together. 'Oh, yes please! We *long* for it! Do, Norton, do!'

But the three had now reached the lawn, the archers were already begun and Norton ran off to join them.

The two girls settled themselves down upon a tweed blanket. Being not yet of an age to join in with the men – but already too superior by far to be seen with mere boys – they instead adopted the position of two aged chaperones at the edge of the dance floor, from which better to observe the whole party. Their interest in the social behaviour of the Godmersham grown-ups was, anyway, mutual and keen, and that particular summer provided them every opportunity with which to indulge it.

'Oh, do look at poor Marianne,' Cassy began in tones of great anguish. 'I am sure she has not been the same since they banished her clergyman. It seems disappointment is so bad for one's *looks*.'

'A cautionary tale for us all,' Mary replied, as she watched Marianne drift distractedly about the lawn as if she were the harassed mother of multitudes, rather than a single woman approaching twenty-two years.

'I *fear*,' Cassy said darkly, 'there's not much to be done about it. Parents simply always get their own way, and even our tender hearts will, no doubt, one day be broken. Is that not what we have learned from our novels? First one finds love.' She ticked off each point. '*Then*, one is *horribly* thwarted. And it is only once one is in absolute *bits* that the happy ending arrives.'

'Oh, do stop! It's too gloomy!' Mary shuddered, suddenly chilled in the sunshine. Having already endured her fair share of misery, she was quite sure she would not survive any more. 'I simply *refuse* to be thwarted. Let us pledge, here and now, that will *not* happen to us.' She held up one little finger, and Cassy linked in her own, and together they vowed never to bow to authority. 'Now, darling, I beg you. Pray, change the subject.'

They turned their attentions to the handsome young couple currently enjoying tea on the terrace, displaying a closeness that bordered on intimate.

'Goodness.' Cassy's response was more moral guardian than younger sister. 'Papa should really keep more of an *eye*. I know he is bedevilled by gout, but *really*.'

'On William and *Emily*, you mean?' Mary sighed. They never passed up the opportunity to use the governess's Christian name. It always brought with it a delicious small frisson.

'Is she not the most *capital* flirt?' They shook their young heads in rich admiration. 'One can only look on in *awe*. Dear, funny Will – he does not stand an *earthly*.'

In the absence of her employer, Miss Atkinson had put

away all her governess's costumes and instead treated her admirers to a daily parade of fine summer fashions.

'Must they too be obstructed or do you think they could . . . ?'

'Oh!' Cassy held up a hand and gave a long blink of emphasis. '*Here* is our exception. *Emily* will always prevail. In fact . . .' She moved forward to a position of the utmost confidence. 'Mark my words, come the spring of next year, we shall be at *the wedding*.'

An unidentified Knight called out: 'A bullseye!'

'Ah! Are we not blessed?' Mary hugged herself with delight. 'To witness an actual *affair* . . .'

The warm air was rent by a scream. And, quite unlike the playing of earlier, this was a scream fit to curdle the blood. They both jumped to their feet.

'What – *who*—' Mary stood on her toes and saw the men gathered round, a small body beneath them. '*John!*'

She picked up her skirts and started to run, fast, towards the place where her little brother was fallen. 'Darling! I'm coming!' Her heart was pounding. Was it an arrow? Please God, let it not be an arrow. Oh, why had they sat at such a distance? She was nearly there. But her breath was failing. 'Hold on! I am coming!'

And then a large, barrelling obstacle ran into her path. Young Mr Knight? But he was not of the party! Where had he come from? He paid her no heed and propelled himself forward: stride, long; pace, thundering; dog lolloping on behind. Mary could only follow while the ground shook beneath her and the sheer force of his movement brought a wind to her face.

By the time she arrived, little John already lay cradled – lifeless – in the arms of Ned Knight.

~

Mary sat in the attic corridor, Norton on one side and Booker the other. With every shriek and sob that came from the nursery, they trembled – cried out – could bear it no longer. Together, the two Knatchbulls approached the locked door and knocked to gain entry, but were denied.

'Let's just sit here and wait.' Kind Booker sat them back down and took a hand from each. 'He's all right with Cakey and Mr Ned, I promise you that. They know what they're doing better than most. Oh, we've had that many accidents . . .' In an attempt to distract them, she reached back in her memory. 'There was that time when Master Will got into a fight with a bullock. Oh my days!' She had distracted herself enough to start chuckling. 'Never seen such a bloodbath. Eye hung by a thread—'

'Booker!' Mary could feel the tears building again. 'Please—'

The nursery door opened then, and Cakey beckoned them in. Mary and Norton entered, each clutching the other; both terrified of what they might find. The sight they beheld defied all expectations.

John was sitting in Ned's lap, with a long glass of milk. One arm was bandaged and in a sling, but – could it really be true? – by some extraordinary miracle, he was otherwise unharmed. Though the sweet face was still deathly pale, eyes pink with crying, at the sight of his Others, he looked up and beamed. Mary rushed over and knelt down before him. '*Dearest!*'

'Mr Knight saved my life,' he chirruped with triumph. 'I was quite dead, you know.' He took another, deep slurp of milk, smacked his lips and repeated: 'Perfectly dead. Dead as a dead thing. For *ages* and *ages*. Saved my life, yes he did.'

With one elegant foot, Ned rocked the chair; with a strong arm, he clutched the boy around his waist and with remarkable tenderness, kissed the top of the little blond head. 'Not quite mortal danger, old soldier.' He smiled. 'It may be that you fainted. But you've been in the wars, right enough.'

Cakey bustled over then, took away the cup and handed over a plate. 'There now, my chicken. Cook's cherry sponge is the best sort of medicine.' She turned back to Mary. 'Stroke of luck Mr Ned had just ridden in. Just the man you want in a crisis. Always knows what to do and when to do it.' She stroked the boy's cheek, which was bulging with cake. 'Poor little precious – arm quite out of its socket.'

'Pray, do not look so alarmed.' Ned half rose and passed the patient to Mary. 'Sling for a week or two.'

The transfer complete, he prepared to go. 'And when you're quite mended, we'll have a good game of cricket, eh?' He winked at the little one and left.

At last, the three Knatchbull children were alone in the nursery. The eldest two squashed into the rocker, John settled across both laps and together they wallowed in that sweet relief which descends in the wake of disaster averted.

Norton set the chair into its sway and, by some long latent instinct, Mary began quietly to hum – a tune she could no longer name, nor was she even aware that she knew . . . But, surely . . . was this not the lullaby once sung by their own lost mama? Yes! Long trapped by the years, now returned like a gift.

As if to compete, then, the sound of voices drifted up from the lawn: the ancient ritual of a hero receiving his accolade. Mary sighed, and gave a sad smile. So down there were the Knights, of whom she had grown so very fond. But *here* was her true family; *this* was her self. Mary Dorothea Knatchbull: thus she had been born; thus she would always be. And that she must take care to remember.

CHAPTER XV

Lady Banks was correct. Sir Edward did prefer to travel with his wife as much as was possible. Simply put, he was happier and more effective when she was by his side, and Fanny was touched by that. For, in truth, she now – nearly three years into their marriage – felt something similar. She might not be *in* love exactly. And she might never know the need to storm around the house protesting her passion – the memory of Marianne's recent behaviour was still somehow irksome. Still, as she had hoped, Fanny had come to love her husband.

Even her terrible luck with the baby business could cause no rift between them – indeed, quite the opposite. While she wept and grieved, Sir Edward was endlessly patient and kind: the sorrow seemed to bring them yet closer. They lived together in a mercifully peaceful spirit of gentle benevolence, and on every matter – the family, the estate, their country and their God – they were in harmony.

And so when Sir Edward was called to Town by business or politics, then of course, within reason, Fanny went, too. And if a particular trip looked to be inconvenient or tedious, then would it not be absurd to drag poor Mary along? She was so happy with clever and pretty Miss Atkinson; bolstered further by that precious friendship with Cassy Knight – and dear Booker, the maid, would lay down her life for the girl.

While the parents travelled, that little group was free to roam between Hatch and Godmersham – wherever the fun seemed to be at the time – and as a system, it seemed to work remarkably well. Certainly, Fanny never received any evidence to suggest cause for concern, and all the young people of both households seemed perfectly happy.

Therefore, when, in that summer of 1823, Lady Banks found an issue with Sir Joseph's estate requiring attention, Sir Edward and Fanny set off in the coach for the capital with nary a backward glance. Why on earth would the girls want to leave Kent in that glorious weather?

William Knight – he who was the Most Fun in that parlour game of old – had taken Orders in June, and was due to take up the curacy in Steventon in September. In the gap that remained, it was agreed that he would spend the summer based mainly at Hatch, while reading in for his position at St John the Baptist in Mersham. Fanny was delighted with this arrangement. Everyone would be happy with William about the place – how could they not? He was a purveyor of joy: it was as simple as that. Even Norton would surely have to cheer up just a bit. Poor Norton. It was a shame.

So on the Wednesday afternoon at the end of August when Fanny arrived home alone – her husband having been unfortunately detained up in Town – she rightfully expected to see signs of some sort of summer jollity. The coach swept in from the road, followed the drive past the cricket pitch – an incomprehensible score still displayed up on the board. Why *were* the numbers always so *high*? It seemed so unnecessary – and turned around the nursery wing. And all the while, her neck was craned for the sight of some fun: a boat trip; a picnic; the arc of a shuttlecock against a brilliant blue sky.

The place was deserted.

'Thank you, Daniel.' Fanny took the driver's hand and wobbled on to the top step. 'Where is everybody?' Five hours in that coach and her legs were like jelly. 'Surely they cannot be inside on a day like today?' Safely on the gravel, she paused for a moment for the blood to return and then tottered to the edge, where the grass began and the land fell away towards the lake in the valley. 'Ah, I see the girls!'

Halfway down the slope, Mary Dorothea and Cassy Knight were spread, lolling, on a tweed blanket – both stretched out with their legs on display, one using the stomach of the other as a pillow. Really, she thought to herself as she moved down towards them. They look practically debauched. She waved and trilled in a friendly fashion. They scrambled up, straightened their dresses and pulled down their straw hats. What on earth had been going on?

'My dears!' she said brightly while eyeing up evidence: lemonade and cake, they could not be minded. But the books . . . 'I see you are reading! How pleasant. Anything amusing?' Or yet more of those *novels* Miss Atkinson encouraged?

Cassy reached down, grabbed both volumes and clutched them to her chest. 'Not especially.' She stepped forward and kissed her eldest sister. 'How was the trip, Fan? I hope not too tiring.'

'Thank you.' Fanny peered around Cassy. 'Mary!' She held out her hand. 'You are well, child?'

Mary shuffled forward, and, as usual, they fumbled their greeting. 'Mama,' she said, with a slightly ironic grimace. It was ever thus – always that edge to things.

There seemed to be a general understanding that now Fanny was home, the fun must end. In her defence, Fanny had not intended it, and yet even she could detect that it prevailed and somehow must be obeyed. Together, they gathered up all their possessions and started to walk back to the house.

'I did not expect to find the two of you *alone*, dears.'

This was quite an understatement. 'Where is Miss Atkinson? William? The boys?' Even Booker, for heaven's sake, would be *some* sort of comfort.

They had now reached the front door; the girls were climbing the steps. From behind, Fanny could see the exchange of glances and intuited a sense of slight panic. 'Um,' said Cassy.

'I think—' Mary began.

And then they heard voices. It was a feature of the mansion that the stables were conveniently close to the entrance, and yet not visible from its door. Sound, though, did travel: the honeyed coaxing of a gentleman, for example – or a lady's delicate laughter, indeed – came across clear as a bell.

Fanny and the girls stood – staring at each other – until, hand in hand, the owners of those voices appeared around the corner.

'Miss Atkinson?'

The horror on the woman's face was a picture.

'William.'

'Ah.' William sidestepped away from the lady's side. 'Fanny,' and strode to his sister. 'We were not expecting—' He went in to kiss her, and was met with the side of her bonnet.

'Clearly.' She looked over her shoulder. 'Miss Atkinson, perhaps you might be prevailed upon to resume your duties, just until dinner? You are *too* kind.' She then took William's arm. 'My brother and I will now withdraw.

'Thank you, Graves.' She nodded at the footman as she passed him. 'I think tea in the library.'

~

'An *attachment*?' Fanny exclaimed. 'I suppose you must mean of the romantic variety?' Dimly, she hoped for some alternate definition; when William nodded, her spirits sank. Oh, how she missed her dear husband and his excellent roar. 'My dear boy . . .' She plunged into the sofa and closed her dry eyes. 'And how long has this' – she searched for a neutral word, one that might denote even a little respect, then quickly surrendered – '*nonsense* been going on?'

'It is not nonsense, Fanny, and I would be grateful if you did not demean us so.' William stood with his back to her, and chose to declare himself to the large window and the view of the Weald. 'We are in love.'

'In love.' Truly, all other words failed her. Did he not witness the Marianne saga? Apparently not, as it was all happening again with no lessons learned.

For there they were, faced with exactly the same issue. William was set for the church in Steventon. Their dear papa had recently spent five thousand pounds on improving the rectory. How now did William intend to furnish it, run it – live in it even – on the love of a governess, of all people? The boy was a fool.

'William,' Fanny began, 'I must confess to a feeling of

some disappointment. Both in you and, I am particularly sad to say, in Miss Atkinson. The woman is our *employee*, as you are *quite* well aware. And as such, her behaviour is truly depl—'

'Enough.' William, who had been prowling about like a beast in a trap, strode across the room and loomed over her. 'Forgive me, Lady Knatchbull, but perhaps your own behaviour might also be called into question.' Though his words were brutal, his tone was oddly mild. Still, Fanny shrank back into the sofa. 'Can you not find within you even an ounce of human sympathy? We *are* aware of the difficulties, as we are no longer children. Yes! We are in love. And I am sorry if this development might cause you some small inconvenience, but that does not entitle you to treat us unkindly. You are so harsh these days, Fan. And to be frank, it is not just me and Emily—'

Emily?

'We are all of us feeling it rather. Dearest . . .' He sat down beside her then, and took her hand. 'I do understand you have been having a rough time of it lately.'

Fanny froze. This was irrelevant to the topic under discussion and, furthermore, deeply intrusive.

'But it is making you—'

'Thank you, William.' Fanny stood, crossed to the bell and summoned a servant. 'That will be all.' Her whole body was trembling. 'Ah, Graves, Mr Knight is just leaving us.' She held a shaky hand out for William to kiss, and issued her final instruction. 'I suggest you go *at once* to see our esteemed father. He can always be trusted to supply the most excellent advice.'

Now alone, Fanny sank to her knees in the middle of the Aubusson, while there raged in her breast extremes of emotion: shock at all which had just occurred; cold dread of what was to come. But overhanging it all was the worst feeling possible, and that was her own, particular guilt.

William had been ten years of age when their mother died; Marianne not quite seven. Of course, Edward Knight had always been the most conscientious of parents, but he could not have raised all eleven of them entirely alone. Whatever the justice of the matter – after all, she had only been fifteen herself – Fanny, too, had been responsible for the upbringing of her younger siblings. She had been entrusted with their spiritual and moral education and had, she was sure, thrown herself into that challenge. Yet *now* look at how they were all turning out!

Lizzie – dear Lizzie – had managed to make an excellent match, but of the rest, only two had so far declared themselves and – unless Miss Atkinson surprised them all by producing a fortune – both with disastrous results. It was as if neither had ever learned the basic tenets of what was socially acceptable, or simply possible. Fanny must accept at least some of the blame, and could only fear what was to come. There were still seven more siblings yet to be matched. What more did fate have in store?

The one comfort was that, for these Knights at least,

the ramifications would be negligible. They would always know the protection of a good family. As happened with Marianne, William's affair would soon be over – possibly even by the end of that afternoon. As soon as he returned to Godmersham, her brother would be made fully aware of the facts of his situation and that would, perforce, be that.

For Miss Atkinson, however, the immediate future would not be so straightforward. And much as Fanny resented the governess's behaviour – and in so far as she fully approved of consequences for actions – it would be a shame, and moreover of great, personal inconvenience, if the punishment were to outweigh the crime.

The next morning, Fanny sat up in bed, reached for the lavender oil and applied drops to her temples. Such a pain in her head – as if she had been drinking gallons of wine, rather than dealing with the dramas of her dearest family. And what did this new day hold? She dared not even think of it.

'Madam.' Sayce popped her dear head around the door, and then walked into the bedroom. 'It's the Miss, ma'am.' And then she withdrew.

'Mary, dearest.' Fanny sat up straight and forced a huge smile, even though she could barely see straight. 'Do come in and sit on the 'pane here.' She tapped on the coverlet. 'Let us be cosy together.'

Mary Dorothea approached the bed slowly, as if fearing an ambush. 'Good morning' – a semi-quaver's pause – 'Mama.' Gingerly, she sat and passively allowed Fanny to take hold of her hand.

'Do you remember, child, back when your dear papa and I were first engaged to be married, that we planned to take our morning tea together whenever possible?'

Mary nodded and looked into her lap.

'We never quite got round to doing so as it turned out, did we?'

Almost imperceptibly, Mary's head shook.

'I fear events have rather conspired against us both, and that is unfortunate.' Fanny reached for the tray on the bedside table, placed the strainer on the dish, lifted the pot and started to pour. 'I am sorry that we haven't spent as much time together as I should have liked. But now, I should like to rectify that.' She passed Mary her tea, smiled – she hoped – winningly, and wrinkled her nose. 'And I think we could become the firmest of friends, you and—'

Mary had reached over and was placing her cup back on the tray. 'I am sorry. Perhaps, Mama, I should have informed you. I do not take tea, having not yet developed the taste for it.' She then looked up at Fanny. 'Thank you, though. *Most* sincerely.'

For a fraction of an instant, Fanny was quite sure that she caught an expression flash across Mary's face: the sort of expression Cook might find useful for the chilling of cream. It was not altogether attractive. Then: 'Ma-*ma*?' Just as suddenly, Mary's angelic demeanour was returned. 'Where *is* Miss Atkinson?'

A splash of tea suddenly left Fanny's cup and arrived on the bedlinen. In silence, both lady and child watched the stain slowly spread. Mary was the first one to speak.

'*Mama*?'

Fanny required a little time to collect her thoughts and prepare her answer. 'Well . . .' She isolated a few stray curls and tucked them back into her nightcap.

'Please do tell me, for it is most worrying. Has something awful befallen her?'

Of course, any sudden disappearance could be rather unnerving. The child deserved some explanation. Fanny looked across at the splendid bay window and predicted a fair sort of day.

'*Mama*?' Mary's once timid little voice had developed a sudden, new strength. 'Cassy and I are both deeply concerned. Yesterday, the lady did not seem herself and now, today, she does not seem to be here at all. Simply *vanished*, and without a word to us. *Dearest* Mama' – the fondest address, yet somehow laden with insolence – '*how can that be*?'

My dear, Fanny was tempted to say: it is perfectly straightforward. When a governess has got herself closely involved with a gentleman connected to the household, and the lady of that house has discovered the affair, and then the gentleman in question immediately lets that poor governess down . . . Well, *then* she is reduced to running to London to beg for an interview with her employer and plead that he overlook all her transgressions and keeps her in her job.

'Mm,' Fanny murmured as she took her first sip. 'Nothing out of the ordinary, my dear.' She dabbed at her lips and replaced cup upon saucer. 'Miss Atkinson left for London first thing this morning.'

'London,' Mary repeated, without any discernible expression.

'Mm.' Fanny grabbed at her teacup again and, in her panic, began to extemporise. 'She was needed . . . or *wanted* perhaps . . . by . . . by—' Sadly, the sheer depth and great fervour of her Christian faith rendered her a very poor liar.

'By *whom*, exactly?' Mary held out both hands. 'Since the death of her mother, Miss Atkinson is quite, quite alone. I am sure there is nobody in London for her to see.'

Was this turning into some sort of interrogation? Certainly, Fanny was starting to feel as if she were somehow the enemy, which was grossly unfair. The truth was that of course the governess should have been dismissed on the spot – and Lady Knatchbull was the one who should have carried it out. Instead, Fanny had written to Sir Edward, laid all the blame upon William – his reputation would survive it – and insisted – *insisted* – that the girls had been thoroughly shielded from all impropriety and at all times. They knew nothing of any illicit relationship! Of course, no lines had been crossed and no innocence compromised! She had then implored that her husband see his way to offering a reprieve, and find it somewhere within his generous heart to keep the governess on.

'I cannot say, as she was not explicit.' Fanny was starting to feel very uncomfortable. Was the child always this forthright? Fanny had not got the impression before. The shock of it reinforced the suspicion she had been harbouring that she still did not know Mary Dorothea as well as she ought.

'Mama.' Mary sat up at right angles to Fanny and spoke to the wall. 'I hope you will forgive me if I ask an indelicate question.'

'Oh. Yes. Of course. Please, dear.' Dread flooded through her. 'Do ask me *anything*.'

'Thank you, Mama. It is just that there is this *word* which I have heard much of just lately.' A turn of the head; a sweet smile. 'Actually, I do have to confess, I do not even quite understand its full meaning.' A blink of near-holy innocence. 'Yet somehow, it nags at me. I sense it may hold a clue to – a *key* to *unlocking* – these mysterious events.'

'Do go on.'

'*Thank* you, Mama. You are *so* very patient. My question is on the subject of your brother, Mr *William* Knight, and our own dear Miss Atkinson.'

'Hmm?'

'Well. Could it possibly be that they have somehow *eloped?*'

Oh, for shame and dear Lord, those poor girls had borne witness to all of it!

She must write to her husband at once.

CHAPTER XVI

The Atkinson Affair – as she would always privately refer to it – presented Fanny with the first major diplomatic and domestic challenge of her married life and, though it could not have been handled in any other way possible, there came in its wake a great deal of unpleasantness. For the following few weeks, everyone she cared about was thoroughly miserable, and they all laid the blame at her door.

Of course, the greatest casualty of all was poor Miss Atkinson herself, whose frequent letters, telling of heartbreak and wretchedness, punctuated Fanny's difficult days. It would be impossible not to have sympathy with the lady – her prospects were bleak in every direction. But on the other hand, it was not easy to quell one's profound irritation that she had been so weak as to get them all into this mess.

Sir Edward would insist on using the word 'scandal' – even though nobody knew of it apart from themselves. And even though it was he who had employed the governess in the first place, he was deeply displeased with everybody else. In particular, he seemed to be forming a strong aversion to the Knight boys in general, about whose moral rectitude he was developing doubts.

This grieved Fanny most terribly. Sir Edward had a brother in *gaol*, and yet he dared to find fault with her darling brothers? She might almost be minded to change the habits of her marriage, and speak up to her husband in their defence. However, her siblings had all taken William's side in the matter, and no one at Godmersham, apart from her father, would even see her. And from that she deduced all those many, past visits from her boys – the 'flocking' of which Fanny had been so very proud – had not been to see her but, in fact, the governess. That did rather hurt.

But worse than all that was the situation with Mary Dorothea. Before this unpleasantness, Fanny would have described her stepdaughter as an odd child, of almost tepid emotions. It was clear she was devoted to her father, and of Lady Banks she was, strangely, fond; then there was Mary's deep friendship with Cassy and her unlikely sympathy for her poor brother, Norton. Beyond all that, though, there had never been any discernible evidence of particular feeling. But when Miss A was dismissed, the shock of it seemed to unleash something within her. Mary Dorothea was suddenly become a creature of raging, ungovernable passion. Or so one was told. As the girl refused to come out of her room, Fanny could not confirm it.

Twice a day, this most diligent stepmother took herself off all that way to the children's wing, knocked on the door and begged – pleaded – for entry. Twice a day, Mary could be heard moving, sobbing – even issuing the occasional howl – but would not reply. Sir Edward was still in Town and the boys were all back at their schools by then, leaving only two people who were allowed in: Booker, the maid, and Cassy Knight.

Fanny let the situation continue for a while until one afternoon, at work in the sage-green peace of her dressing room, she took the opportunity to interrogate her younger sister.

'So,' she began brightly as she sat in the (unused) nursing chair and delved into the seemingly bottomless basket of mending. 'How is Mary today – any better? It has been a week . . .'

'Really, Fan!' Cassy looked up from the sock she was darning with a disappointed expression. 'Of course she is nowhere near *better*. What is a week in the context of *agony*? We have suffered the most *terrible* shock, Mary and I.'

Was the child becoming rather earnest? That did seem a shame.

'I, for one, am still *reeling*, and *my* grief is not even close to poor Mary's. She' – too emotional to work now, Cassy dropped the wool into her lap – '*she* says it has been as bad as *losing her mother.*'

Was that intended to wound her? Fanny dared not allow it. Desperately, she tried to move the conversation on. 'Well,' she said brightly, 'it might please you girls to know that, in Town, Sir Edward is even now looking for a replacement—'

'*A replacement?*' Cassy exclaimed in horror. 'Dear Fan, I do wish you would listen. Truly, you dare talk of *replacement*? I suppose you might equally talk so casually of *replacing a mother?*'

A chill fell on to the dressing room. The two sisters glared at one another.

At last, Fanny spoke: 'Then, perhaps,' she began, 'it might be a better idea to go forward without a new governess.'

The thought had not occurred to her before that moment, but she suddenly saw that there was no alternative. Indeed, that this was the only right course of action. While in London with Sir Edward, Fanny had suffered yet another of her unfortunate events, and Dr Maton had confessed that, in his medical view, a success now looked unlikely. Somehow – though, oh! how it grieved her to think it – she must accept the Lord's will and surrender the dream of her own darling baby. And to take her mind off the misery, she could now devote her life to the many motherless children already under her care.

'And *I* shall look after you both from now on.' There must be worse fates, she supposed – though the heart might not thrill at the prospect.

'Ah.' Cassy's eyes narrowed and her mouth set. 'So am I right in thinking that what you are saying is, in effect: we can now leave the schoolroom?' To Fanny's ears, she came across as a horse trader at the close of a deal.

'I do not see why not.' Fanny was starting to form the suspicion that she had walked into a trap. 'Indeed. Leave the schoolroom – do! – and start to accompany me around and about the place, and then deputise on all my various duties and calls . . . After all, you are both of an age . . . Then next year, we can start the whole process of you "coming out".'

'Fan, you do *mean* it? We *can* count on your word?' Cassy leaned forward. 'And you are *definitely* authorised to speak on Sir Edward's behalf?' Her blue eyes were alight, ringlets trembling with tension. 'We *must not* get left behind, Mary and I. Not like poor dear—'

Oh, *really*! All the younger girls seemed quite obsessed with Marianne, as if she were some *victim* rather than a lucky young lady with an extremely comfortable life. 'I shall write to Sir Edward this very afternoon and explain my decision.' She put her hand inside a sock and, addressing the hole in the toe, asked, 'Might this news please Mary, do you think? At least just a little.'

'Very much so,' Cassy began cheerfully, before she got that horse-trader look back and piped up again. 'But oh!

I nearly forgot. There is one other matter which causes her much *terrible* sadness.'

'I am sorry to hear that.' Fanny stifled a sigh. 'Pray, do go on.'

'Well, dear Miss Atkinson *had* promised to teach Mary to ride in their free time.' She looked up at Fanny. 'Do you know, up to now nobody ever has? *Poor* Mary, sometimes it is as if she just gets *forgotten*—'

'I see,' Fanny cut in. She was getting the hang of these negotiations: it was clear the girls had thrashed this all out between them, and now Cassy had come in with their list of demands. 'So she might also like her own pony, is that it?'

'Yes!' Cassy had the pleasure of a teacher whose struggling pupil had worked out a sum. 'I do believe she *would* like that, very much indeed.'

'It can be arranged, and I can ask one of the lads in the stables to offer instruction.'

'No need!' Cassy almost sang happily. 'The groom has already agreed it, and Papa has a horse for her over in Godmersham. Oh—' She realised her error.

Fanny started to pack up the work bag. 'Then that is most kind of him.' So yet again, they had all been talking behind her back. She felt a sharp twinge in the heart area. 'I do wish her the best with it.'

She rose, indicated the door and Cassy walked half through, then one more thought seemed to occur and she poked her head back around. 'It will be all right, Fan, if we both continue to write to Miss Atkinson? I am sure you cannot mind it? We have been so close, after all.'

'You may,' Fanny said wearily.

'Sir Edward will not object, I hope?'

'I am quite sure he will not.' Though it might be for the best if Sir Edward was not informed. 'And before you go, Cassy, I would like to make it quite plain that I thoroughly expect to see you *both* at breakfast tomorrow. Please do make sure that you pass *that* on to Mary.'

'But of course, Fanny dear!' Cassy tripped, cheerful now, towards the top of the stairs. 'Do you know, I think she may well feel better already.'

PART THREE

CHAPTER XVII

Mary stood alone at the window of Number 20 Great George Street, watched the sun trace its path above the grey houses opposite, and let out a sigh. It was the year 1824 and the start of yet another fine spring London day – set fair for a promenade, perhaps, or trip to the gallery. But, yet again, she would play little part in it.

She drifted back to the sofa, selected a stocking from the basket and then put it back. It was quite beyond all darning and, anyway, where was the virtue in work if 'the Mama' did not witness her doing it? So she reached behind the pillow, retrieved the Fanny Burney she had stashed away, and fell into the pages. But these days, the very act of reading took her mind not into the story, but instead into another world entirely: one in which Miss Atkinson had never been banished; a place of laughter and interest, possibility and promise. Wrenching herself back to disappointing reality, Mary instead reached back into the basket, and gave in to that which was expected.

The noise from the street – drivers and cabs; sellers competing; a riot of bells now chiming ten – came in sharp contrast to the quiet of the drawing room. Still – she found a suitable thread and cut it to length – Mary found she did not much mind the silence of solitude; indeed, she was getting quite used to it. And rather that than the silences which arose when one was in company: those she could hardly bear.

By 'company' of course, she was here referring to the Mother, Lady Knatchbull. With no more governess or lessons, Mary had been returned to her own family, and 'mama' and 'daughter' were now constant companions. This should have afforded them new opportunities to create some sort of alliance – nay, even friendship. No such miracle occurred.

It was now nearly four years since the fates had brought them together, but still they had not found a means by which to communicate. It was hardly as if Mary was taciturn by nature – with her friends, she was almost loquacious. Yet, somehow, when it came to her step-mother, she was selectively mute.

Being quite so disobliging did not bring her any particular pleasure – indeed, Mary was starting to dislike the person she became when the Mother was around, though she could see how her non-cooperation had come about. First born out of shyness, then – it was true – turned into protest, it was now no more than an unfortunate habit.

And yet Fanny made no sort of effort to make Mary break out of it. This supposed mama never dared stray on to any matter that might provoke true conversation. Instead, she merely stated the factual – the weather was fine, say, or Sir Edward stayed too long at the House – thus demanding only a nodding consent rather than com- mentary. It left Mary puzzled, and somewhat frustrated. After all, curing one's children of their very bad habits: was that not what parents were *for*? Truly, she thought, for the ten-thousandth time: her papa had chosen to marry the most curious creature that Kent had to offer.

But before her mood could descend any further, the door opened and there came into the drawing room a great draught of fresh air.

'Miss Cassy Knight,' the footman announced, and, after a moment's enquiry: 'With *Miss Austen.*'

∼

'What happy chance that we should come to call, Miss Knatchbull.' With a strong stride and air of great pur- pose, Miss Cassandra Austen led them across Grosvenor Square and on to New Bond Street. 'We dared hardly hope to find you, presuming you out with your fondest mama.' She held the girls back while a gig passed by, then hurried them over to the other side of the road. 'I am very sorry to hear our dear Lady Knatchbull is *ailing*.'

'Perhaps not ailing, exactly.' Mary almost ran to keep up. 'Sayce described her as "indifferent", if I remember correctly.'

'*Indifferent?*' Miss Austen stopped still on the pavement and issued Mary with a look of the beady variety. 'Indifferent, indeed.' The word seemed to ring with significance. 'Then that is most interesting.' She began striding again. 'In which case, you may well be in need of an alternative chaperone for the length of your stay.'

Giving no thought to the reasoning, only delighted with the outcome, Mary and Cassy beamed at each other and linked arms.

'Then how perfectly *lovely* it is, Aunt, to have you with us.' Cassy took a discreet little skip. 'I have been longing for you and Mary to meet. I am so pleased with Papa for bringing you here. It is a great sorrow to us all that we see you so rarely in Kent.'

'Ah.' Miss Austen spoke over her shoulder. 'My dear, I am rarely seen anywhere beyond Chawton these days. You see, Miss Knatchbull, I live with my mother and she does like to have me around the place.' With that, she stopped again. 'Pray, do not suspect me of any resentment. Far from it! She has been an exemplary parent, and though it may be a duty, it is also my pleasure.'

'Since my *other* aunt, Jane, *so* sadly died—' Cassy began. Miss Austen cut in with brisk force. 'My brothers are all busy men. Nevertheless, I remain secure in the belief that, *were* I to ask, they would make sure to assist.' She looked up then, and around her. 'Here we are. The Strand. Keep together as we cross, girls. Unless they have moved it since my last visit – and with the great Engine of Change, all things are possible – we will find our destination just to the south.'

Mary followed closely, and pondered. Since her father's marriage, she had discovered so many new people to whom she was now considered to be, in some vague way, related. This latest arrival merited some consideration. Miss Austen was tall, vigorous and still, somehow, erect. Though the poor creature seemed to have strayed into her *sixth decade* – was it not odd how single ladies seemed to live so very long, when the mamas rarely did? – there yet remained a few traces of earlier beauty. Her best features could be seen on others in the family: the high brow, for example, and aquiline nose. And like some, though not all by any means, a keen intelligence shone out from her eyes.

Theirs was but the briefest acquaintance, but Mary's mind was already made up. She decided she liked this Miss Austen very much indeed.

∿

Once at Somerset House, the two girls were astonished to find yet another delight waiting there.

'Good day, ladies.' George Knight was leaning against the wall. 'May I have the pleasure?'

'George, darling!' Cassy called, running to embrace him.

But, just like his brothers, this Mr Knight set great store by his manners. 'My dear Aunt.' He bowed, tipped his hat and then, with great fondness, kissed her.

'So you *could* find the time, dear. How splendid.' Though clearly thrilled to see him, Miss Austen's tone was quite dry. 'I wonder that *more* young men do not read for the law, affording as it does such a wide *opportunity* for the pursuit of pure *leisure*.'

Laughing, he greeted the girls. 'A fellow cannot win! A note came to chambers, and such was the command in the tone, I had not a thought but to obey it. What counts the law' – he took his aunt's arm – 'when compared to an outing with *you*, madam.'

Mary's new and high spirits rose further. She had enjoyed few previous dealings with this Mr Knight; until now, had only known him as one of the gaggle. Though he was not *much* younger than Ned – perhaps no more than a year – the difference was crucial. George could not expect to inherit but instead must make his own way in life, and so was most often in Town.

In pairs, they proceeded through the business of entry into the gallery, and without meaning to eavesdrop – such a thing was abhorrent! – Mary could not help overhearing the conversation ahead.

'I say, Aunt,' George was confiding, 'Miss Knatchbull is somewhat *altered* since the last time I saw her. I must confess to feeling quite disconcerted.'

'Ah, yes.' Miss Austen gave a light laugh. ''Tis always the height of a young lady's powers: when Beauty appears, but she has not known to expect it and is yet to hear it is come.'

They had come for the Stubbs room, but did not stay very long.

'What a relief,' Cassy declared as they emerged into the sunshine. 'I am quite done with horses and as for *execution* and *brush*, who gives a fig? All I could think of was the wretched beast, forced to stand still for hour upon *hour*. You don't have to *live* in a *field* to grasp how much the poor, noble darlings *loathe* such—'

'Knight!' The cry came from the street. 'Knight, my dear fellow.'

'I say, sir!' Mr Knight's fine blue eyes danced with delight. 'I must declare *this* a coincidence.'

The stranger – tall, dark and, Mary could hardly deny it, exceedingly handsome – crossed over to meet them with a quick, graceful step. The necessary introductions were made.

'. . . and, lastly, may I present my sister, Miss Knight.'

Naturally, Lord George Hill, for *this* was the stranger, acquitted himself admirably while addressing each of the ladies. Although was it Mary's imagining or did he indeed rather *linger* about Cassy?

The gentlemen proceeded to regale them then with the story of their acquaintance. Mary heard something about a regiment, a brother and a party; the inevitable slaughter of some unfortunate wild animals and the amusement it brought. But in truth, Mary's attention was a little diverted. For she could not help but notice that their party had undergone a slight, subtle change.

The compact, happy foursome which had emerged from the gallery was now broken up. During the course of telling their story, it appeared that both gentlemen had been on quiet manoeuvres, with the result that his lordship was now standing with Cassy, and Mr Knight by Mary's side.

Miss Austen, somewhere between the two couples but also distinctly alone, sucked at her cheeks, before raising an eyebrow and, finally, a smile.

'Well now,' she declared, 'is this not most pleasant?' She turned to the street then, and gasped. 'And do look: the first of the daffodils! What a glorious vision!

'When I left Hampshire, you know, the trees were quite brown and bare. One or two more weeks in the company of you dear young people, and I shall return to a new world of green.'

$$\approx$$

With hindsight, Mary's London spell of the year '24 now seemed no more than a dream.

After their trip to the gallery, George Knight had taken the girls under his wing. Miss Austen was correct: the law did provide him with ample free time. In consequence, Mary's own life became one long excitement. And during their subsequent outings to the opera and around the bazaars – their walks in the park – she had felt herself change. Of course, it would be quite wrong for *Mary* to describe her own bloom – may God strike her down! But it was the word Cassy used and, though Booker was very much *not* given to compliments, Mary could not miss the new look of approval when their eyes met in the glass.

So the traditional Easter return to Hatch, with only her parents for company, was for Mary a dismal enough prospect.

And when, in the wake of all that fun, she suddenly fell quite catastrophically ill, it was enough to crush her completely.

The first sign of her apocalypse came in mid-April. From the point of contracting only the mildest of colds, she was suddenly assaulted by symptoms, at once both confusing and yet clearly severe. A violent bleeding from the nose brought with it a fever which, in turn, set off an all-over agony. By the following morning, she was swinging – as if strung to the pendulum in a clock tower – between the horror of consciousness and hallucinatory ravings.

She was vaguely aware that the Mama found the nursing a strain – 'It is a terrible *pity*, but I am perfectly *shattered'* – and that poor Marianne Knight was brought in to take over. Mr Whitfield was called, prescribed leeches at her temples and all over arms. But then he came again, and again – morning *and* evening? And from that Mary knew that *this* was true danger. Determined, she fought; in terror, she struggled. But after three days, or four – she had lost all sense of time, now – Mary could bear it no longer. Her grip on reality started to slacken.

The tunnel was long, at its end was a light and within that, was a figure. *'Mama?'* In disbelief, she looked away; in new hope, she turned back. And – ah! – it was true! Her mother had come for her!

'I am ready!' Mary cried out. 'My few possessions are neatly assembled! Do call me, Mama, call me now! For I can quit in an instant.' But the vision turned its back then, started to fade and soon was quite vanished. In its place came an earthly commotion, and a voice in her ear.

'I have *cancelled* the *Yeomanry.*' The room shook as Sir Edward fell to his knees. 'Dear Lord,' she heard him intone. 'Thy will be done . . . Deliver her, I pray . . . My precious . . . my light . . . in Thy mercy . . . such a good Christian girl . . . If she has . . . then I beseech . . . and by Thy forgiveness . . . *The best that I have.'*

And who could resist such a declaration of love? Mary opened her eyes – reached out her hand – before, remembering her role, she strained for the means to offer him comfort. 'Poor, dear Papa.' Somehow, she summoned the strength for a whisper. 'Poor, dear Papa.'

'My dear, *darling* child.' He took her small hand in his, pressed it to his wet cheek. 'He heard me, He heard me. God's will be done.'

He lifted her from the pillow; caught her up in the most affectionate embrace that they had enjoyed for some long years. Mary breathed in the scent of cologne at his neck, thought: Here – *here* – is my distinguishing feature. My father loves *me* above any other.

She lifted her eyes to the room and noticed Fanny, standing close to the door – looking on, biting her lip – silently weeping.

CHAPTER XVIII

That summer, it was decreed the Knatchbulls would remove themselves to Hampshire to spend some time with the Knights. Mary was not sure how or why this decision was reached – it was her lot to be moved through life as a piece on a chess board – but still it delighted her. Almost anywhere was more amusing than Hatch with only her parents for company, but to be with dear friends was the best outcome of all.

She and Cassy travelled together, with Sir Edward and Lady Knatchbull following closely behind. Having been separated for some months, the girls passed the first part of the journey in play, gossip and shrieking, so that Booker was forced to issue sharp knocks on the window from her place on the back. But as they thundered through Surrey, travel fatigue overcame them – how Mary *hated* long journeys – and they slumped into quiet.

At last, the carriage turned off the turnpike, swung on to a lane and, as they came to the edge of the village, the horses fell from a gallop down into a trot.

'And so here we are,' Cassy announced. 'The mad, giddy heart of the village of Chawton!'

Mary, suddenly revived, pressed up to the window; she saw a singular street but of its population there was no obvious sign. To her right was an inn, though it was possibly closed, and beside that, a modest round duck pond. There were *some* signs of life – if one were to count the drake with its beak under its wing or the man stretched out on the grass, face obscured by his cap. But not enough to prevent Mary stating the obvious deficiencies from the girls' point of view. 'Not *quite* the Pleasure Gardens.'

'As if we would ever be allowed,' Cassy pointed out. 'I say. Imagine an evening *there* with *Lady Knatchbull*.' They collapsed into each other with a fit of the giggles. 'Dear oh dear.' Cassy collected herself. 'But all the boys will arrive soon and, as Cakey always tells us, we must make our own entertainment. Oh, before we turn off, one more great landmark.' She pulled Mary over and signalled to the left. 'That is where my grandmama lives.'

'Ah.' Mary sprang to attention. 'Then so does Miss Austen.' It was a neat brick house with a porch around the door; its garden a tangle of roses and foxgloves; the bough of a plum tree rich with new fruit: modest, yet with a certain dignity and an immediate charm. As the carriage took to the right, Mary craned her neck to study it further. She was undoubtedly struck. Though the building itself could have no particular importance, still it had in its possession some unmistakeable *air* . . .

'I must visit, of course,' said Cassy. 'Might you come with me, dearest? Would it be *too* dreary, after the dire year that you've had? The dear lady is *frightfully* old and—'

'But of course,' Mary cried. 'I should *love* to meet Mrs Austen and spend more time with your aunt.' Though they might joke about running wild in insalubrious places, in truth it was the last thing that either desired, being both sweet, good Christian girls. 'And anyway, I am your sister now, pray do remember – so surely that makes her *my* grandmother, too.'

They were now on a lane, going away from the village, with low, ancient cottages clinging to one side and vast, green, open parkland falling away from the other.

Mary felt her heart lift. 'But this is charming! I must fall ill more often, if this is the cure.'

'Don't you *ever* do that to me again.' Cassy flung an arm around her neck, and held tight. 'We cannot live without you and I hereby forbid it.' Then a smile came into her voice. 'Now, here we come . . . Wait and prepare . . .'

The carriage turned left from the lane, and Mary heard her own gasp. 'So *this* is it.'

They took to the long, straight drive, ancient oak

standing sentry; passed a small, pretty church nestled down in the dip. Their path rose up again; Mary saw barns and a stables. And then there, just below the hill's brow, proud in its green parkland as a jewel upon velvet, she beheld the glorious vision of the Great House.

'Oh, do look!' Cassy was squealing. 'Dear Ned is out there, awaiting us! How *handsome* he looks: soon to be master of all he surveys, with that *darling* hound there by his side. I rather think Chawton suits him completely.'

But Mary made no reply. What cared she for Ned, or even his dog in that moment? Her eyes were for the house only; the house alone. It was solid white stucco, softened by stone gables and harked back to the time of Elizabeth's reign. In her fond imaginings, she could see a fair lady, bedecked in a coif, gazing back through the mullion.

This was quite unlike Hatch, or Godmersham, or any other of the houses which Mary knew well. They were all modern affairs, created to feed a desire for ostentation and luxury. The Great House was born some centuries before, and from a more serious purpose: shelter for large, long generations; the manor upon which the entire village had cause to rely. Put beside this, the product of the mere present looked flimsy; inferior.

Mary was struck by the thought that to be mistress of Chawton would be something indeed.

∽

She looked forward to dinner with considerable interest and only some trepidation. After all, this was the first time that Sir Edward and young Mr Knight had been at the same table since that first, unfortunate occasion when her parents were newly engaged. Though a repeat of those fireworks would be more than diverting, Mary presumed that their host would be using this opportunity to make amends for the past. For surely Ned would now want to curry favour with her papa? Everyone else did, after all. By some power which she could not quite understand, Sir Edward Knatchbull was simply one of those men whom other men were desperate to please.

As they all took to their seats in the ancient, oak-panelled room, charged their plates and turned to their food, Ned began his remarks in expected fashion. 'It is an honour and a pleasure to have you all here at the Great House.'

Dull pleasantries were exchanged, Mary's interest in the diners started to wane, and she directed it instead at the cracked portraits in oil lining the walls. Who were all those subjects? Had they, too, once suffered tedium at this very table? If so, she wondered how they had borne it . . . And just then, Ned picked up all caution as if it were a cricket ball and hurled it away, high and long, into the close, dining room air.

'Indeed, Sir Edward, you were in my thoughts only last week when, strangely enough, I happened to find myself in your house on Great George Street.'

'What on *earth*—?' Fanny exclaimed, dropping her fork. 'But *we* have not been there for some months!'

Sir Edward said nothing, though Mary could not help but notice his face had turned purple.

'Did you not know, Fan?' Ned asked cheerily. 'Lord Byron was lying in state, as they rather grandly termed it, in your very drawing room!' Before adding, for clarity: 'The late, great poet that is – not my good friend.' He reached down to the dog – who, to popular surprise, was also invited to dinner – and stroked him. 'Imagine the loss of *this* noble beast! Too tragic to—'

'Sir *Edward*?' Fanny turned to her husband in shock. 'Surely *my brother* must be *mistaken*.'

'Forgive me, my dear.' Though he spoke to his wife with a voice under control, his eyes were on Ned. And Mary could see all the familiar signs of his fury. 'I felt no need to bother you with this most *trifling* affair. It was no more than a *commercial* arrangement made with a *highly* respectable contact of mine.'

'And one that stands greatly to your credit, Sir Edward.' Ned supped at his wine. 'In his lifetime, the famed nobleman was one of the most coveted guests in any society household. And to think: yours is the only one which can claim the great honour of having hosted the *corpse*.'

Fanny placed a hand on her bosom. 'I *shudder* to think . . .' She turned to Sir Edward. 'That *wicked* creature! And I take it that this is *common* knowledge?'

Ned answered for him. 'I should say so, old girl. You had half of London tramping through your front door. The queue snaked down right to the Park.'

Sir Edward glowered; Fanny paled. Mary and Cassy shared a look of astonishment. Of course they adored Lord Byron! How could they not? Dearest Miss Atkinson, their much-loved once-governess, had worshipped both the man and his verse. Naturally, the girls had no choice but to copy her.

'To think, darling!' Cassy whispered. '*We* have been in the *same room!*'

'I can hardly *believe* it.' A shiver shot down Mary's spine.

Unfortunately, their hushed words came at a time of no conversation and, instead of ignoring them, Ned chose to reply.

'And you may find, girls, that when you next go there, he is lingering still. After all, he died some months ago, then had to be carried by sea from Greece. So by the time he came to call at Number Twenty Great George Street' – Ned put a finger beneath his aquiline nose and burst into laughter – 'our national hero was not quite at his best.'

The next day, Sir Edward was, sadly, called away on some 'business' – though on the exact details of said business he was, oddly, vague. And whenever her husband was absent and she was back in the bosom of her own family, Fanny took the opportunity to relax her normally assiduous performance of the maternal role. All of which meant that Mary was able to run free, in the company of her Knight friends and within the confines of that lovely estate.

She and Cassy, her favourite playmate, were joined by George and William Knight. And her own brother, Norton, was out of school for the holidays, though the younger ones were off staying with cousins. Mary missed them, of course. She did not see them as often as she would like, but the Mother was known to find all five stepchildren together a little *de trop*.

For the whole time of their stay, Ned Knight was a whirlwind. If the weather was fine, he organised games and sports out in the grounds; when conditions allowed, he took all the brothers out with their guns. On top of all that, there was his duty of management of the land and the men. And, owing to some concern for the harvest, he was away from the house on this particularly dull morning in the first week of their stay, when the party of young people decided on a game of Hide and Seek.

George Knight, down in the hall, counting in his deep, lawyerly boom, made Mary smile. How men did like to be boys when they got half a chance! Apart from her own papa, of course . . . But there was no time to ponder that anomaly now. Instead, she scampered up the stairs, past the maid on her knees with the beeswax – slipped on the new gleam – and came out on the landing. Known to the family as the Haunted Gallery, it was not her preferred Chawton location. There had been verified *sightings*, they said . . . She quailed; dithered about which way to turn; heard George bellow: 'Coming!' and, in a panic, climbed on to the seat at the long mullioned window, drew the heavy crewel curtain and hid.

Hugging her knees, heart thumping at ribs, Mary tried to keep herself calm by gazing out at the vista. The little flint church of St Nicholas, squat in its graveyard, she decided must be among the most charming in England and thought that if one really must die – and she would much rather not – it would be a fine place to rest in eternity. Though, for the *living*, was it not a little *too* close to the house? Suppose one or two of the spirits were not peaceful but actually restless?

And just then, Mary heard footsteps – slow; tread heavy – cross the floor of the attic over her head. She shrank into the panelling. The boots descended the stairs, and began their slow plod along the – yes! – along the Haunted Gallery. She covered her face to stifle her screams. The curtain was torn back. She was exposed! Mary's heart stopped.

It was Ned. How shy she had been on their first solo encounter in Godmersham. Now, such was Mary's relief that he was not, after all, some unfortunate Tudor in want of a head, she simply laughed.

'Found her!' Ned called over his shoulder, while looking down upon her with a crinkling smile. 'Good work,

Miss Knatchbull. You discovered the best nook in the house – the one I always use, as it happens. The others are nowhere near brave enough. Now you have proved both your courage and skill, I shall be *honoured* to share it with *you* in the future.

'But for now' – he did not take her hand, but stepped back and gestured that she should come out – 'sad to say, your *revels* are *ended.*'

She stared up, wide-eyed.

'Lady Knatchbull awaits you down in the parlour.'

~

It was a relief to discover that the Mama only wanted Mary and Cassy to join her in paying a visit.

'Well, this *is* a pleasure.' Miss Cassandra Austen gathered up her darning, hid it under her armchair and rose up to greet them. 'You are so kind to call on we *poor* ladies, in our *little* cottage.'

She kissed Fanny and Cassy, and smiled upon Mary, who at once fell into her best curtsey.

'*Mother, dear?*' At the top of her voice, Miss Austen was addressing the sofa, upon which sat a bundle of black clothing with a white cap balanced on its top. Old Mrs Austen, whose hearing was obviously poor, jerked awake and gazed round. '*Do look who has come.*'

The grandmother accordingly looked. Though it was clear that she also had struggles with her sight, those clouded old eyes still had a twinkle. 'Well I never did! Lady Knatchbull come at last, is it? This is an honour, indeed. We barely see you these days, my dear.'

'Really, Mama,' Miss Austen chided, while straightening the older lady's cap. 'We can hardly expect it. Fanny is now a *married lady*, and to a gentleman of great *consequence*. She has her hands full.' And then raised her voice again: '*I said, her hands are quite*—'

'Oh, I do not doubt.' Mrs Austen gave a knowing smile, and patted the space by her side. 'Well, now you *are* here, do sit for a moment and tell me all about your new, *interesting* life.'

Mary was intrigued to observe Fanny obey with an impeccable politeness, combined with a marked reluctance. Why would she not be pleased to see her own grandmother? Mary was sure that if she had one of her own, she would thrill at the prospect. Meanwhile, Miss Austen went to the kitchen to order refreshments before settling down with the two girls. She quizzed them both on their stay – enjoyed the stories of fun and games – before becoming impatient at the maid's failure to appear with the tray.

'You stay here, Aunt.' Cassy grabbed Mary's hand and pulled her upstanding. 'Let us go and see.'

They helped the one maid in the clean, simple kitchen and were on their way back – in the little vestibule outside the parlour – when, as was their habit, the girls stopped to listen to the conversation inside.

'I *do* like your Mary, my dear.' Miss Austen was speaking to Fanny. '*I was just saying, Mother.*' Yet again, she was forced to raise her voice, which was becoming increasingly strained. '*I do like this little Mary Dorothea.*'

Cassy shot Mary a look of wide-eyed pride and delight. And Mary herself could not but feel pleased.

'*Do* you, Aunt?' they heard Fanny reply. Mary could tell from the note of surprise in her tone that her face had that familiar, quizzical expression. Cassy looked cross.

'Oh, very much indeed.' Miss Austen was emphatic. 'I was particularly struck by her instantaneous affinity with our beloved Chawton. It is not to everybody's taste. Indeed, I remember the first visit made by your beloved late mama, God rest her soul. Sad to say, the Great House was not to *her* liking, yet Miss Knatchbull loves it at once.'

'*Does* she?' Still, Fanny seemed rather puzzled.

Mary nodded at Cassy with vigour.

'And furthermore,' Miss Austen went on, 'she is so taken with our beloved Knights, which I do love to see. *Miss Knatchbull is very fond of your grandchildren, Mama!*'

Mary blew a silent kiss towards Cassy, who placed a hand to her own heart.

'And they her, if I am not mistaken. She certainly seems to have caught our George's eye. *George, Mother! I was just saying he SEEMS RATHER KEEN . . .*'

Cassy was now doubled up, and clutching her sides. Mary bade her hush, desperate to hear the Mother's reply:

'Aunt, pray forgive me.' Fanny sounded sharp now, and firm. 'But I think you must be mistaken. Mary is such a timid, plain little thing.'

Cassy clamped a hand to her mouth to stop the scream of amused outrage.

'The poor girl can hardly say boo to a goose, let alone *flirt* with a *gentleman*.' She gave a shrill, confident laugh. 'And as her *mama*, I do keep her under quite tight control.

'So no, my dear Aunt. There is nothing like *that* going on and nor will it ever. Of that I am *perfectly* sure.'

CHAPTER XIX

The Chawton visit was over, and Fanny felt a little bereft. Even after four years, she still found it unsettling to leave her dear family and return to the Knatchbulls and Hatch. And to make matters worse, Lady Banks had demanded Sir Edward's presence elsewhere. Fortunately, Fanny's favourite sister was kind enough to come and keep her company for those few, difficult days.

The first evening, they had dined out at the Finch-Hattons, and even taken the younger girls, Mary and Cassy, with them. On the second, though, they were home and alone and able to coze in the drawing room – which came as a relief to Fanny, who for some reason felt uncommonly tired.

'Your little Mary was a wild success last evening.'

Lizzie stretched out her long legs, placed her feet on the footstool, turned her elegant slippers this way and that and studied all angles with complete satisfaction. 'Do you have plans for her yet?'

'She did seem to go down rather well.' Fanny spoke into her sewing. 'No doubt we can put it down to the girl being a *novelty* . . .' She selected a new thread. 'We are such a small world here in Kent that the milieu is grateful for anyone new. I shall be launching her shortly.' She looked up then and added, in confidence: 'I must say I do rather dread it, but perhaps it will not, after all, be as quiet as one *fears*.'

With one eyebrow arched, Lizzie studied her sister in silence – opened her mouth, closed it, wriggled deeper into her armchair – and then spoke up again. 'Dearest, I do sometimes wonder if you have eyes in your head.'

Fanny dropped her embroidery into her lap and looked up in astonishment. 'What on *earth* do you mean?'

'For a start, are you the *only* person in all of Christendom *not* to have noticed that George is wild for the creature?'

'George . . .' Fanny repeated. 'George Knight? Our *brother*?' Her head felt strangely muddled. 'But this is getting ridiculous! Aunt *Cassandra*, of all people, was saying the same only last week.' She had that left-out feeling again. What was it they all knew which she did not? 'It is as if you have all created some *myth* in your heads. I mean, have you all asked yourselves *what* he might see in her?'

Lizzie just laughed. 'The age-old story, my darling. The girl is uncommonly pretty.'

This was getting too much. '*Surely* you *cannot* mean Mary?'

But instead of arguing her case, Lizzie just stared and stared until Fanny was forced to defend herself.

'But she has that unfortunate *sallow* complexion,' she began, and then conceded: 'Although I suppose it has become a little more pink since *I* found her a pony. And her figure is—' Well, that was rather graceful. She would give the girl that. 'But anyway,' she concluded with triumph, 'her hair is as straight as a plumb line!'

Lizzie smirked. 'And how would yours be if Hall didn't visit you weekly? You are her mother. If her hair is not good enough, it is up to you to do something about it. Not that anything is needed for, as I say, the child is a beauty. And it is high time that *someone* brought it to your attention, as any minute now your Sir Edward is in for a visit – if not from George, then some other poor swain.'

'You cannot be serious.' Fanny picked up her sewing again, while knowing full well that a stitch done in rage always needed unpicking. 'Apart from all the obvious problems' – to take just one example, Sir Edward would shoot any suitor on sight – 'George is nowhere near being established. There is no money and that is that.'

'Oh, *money*!' Lizzie scoffed. 'It's not *everything*, darling. You cannot keep putting an end to perfectly good matches just because of *that*. First, poor Marianne – I do fear she may never recover – then Will and the *dear* little teacher person . . . Darling, we are a family of eleven! None is in danger of starving, but not every *one* of us is going to die *rich*. It's simply not possible. And not *everyone*—'

Fanny's head was bent over her work, but she could still feel Lizzie's eyes, almost boring a hole in her head.

'Not everyone – if they *just* marry for *money* – is going to die *happy*.'

Fanny's whole being contracted as if she had been scorched. Was Lizzie referring to her? And if so, then how *dare* she? It was such an injustice that her siblings saw her own marriage as unhappy, when in fact she was *completely* content. But before Fanny could collect her riposte, Lizzie rose to her feet, gave a little stretch and then a yawn.

'Forgive me, dearest, if I have been a little *harsh* this evening, but I just felt it all there, on my tongue's end, as it were, and needed to say it.

'Besides which, I fear I have started yet another baby already. Dear me – how many is it now? I can hardly count the number of little darlings.'

Fanny, forced to surrender all hope of even one child, felt her heart drop in her breast.

'But you do know how I get with it in the beginning. *Cross* as a *cat*.' She bent and kissed Fanny's cheek. 'Do sleep well, dearest. I certainly shall.'

~

The Mary Problem, as Fanny privately referred to it, occupied her thoughts for the remainder of the week. The idea that the girl might be considered a beauty she would like to discount. The plain, thin little child whom she had first taken on had not markedly altered, as far as Fanny had noticed, but she was forced to concede that fashions did change and perhaps that rather ordinary, average look was now *comme il faut*. And anyway, if the public had somehow got it into its head that she was, in some vague way, attractive, then that was – most annoyingly – that.

On the other hand, looks were not everything and, surely, any suitor would, in the end, be quickly repelled by the girl's personality – or absence thereof. Put simply, Mary had nothing about her! No conversation, beyond the odd 'yes' or 'no', added to which was an unfortunate tendency to be rather sullen. And that was hardly a quality that any sensible man would desire in a wife.

However, if the girl should take it upon herself to pursue some unfortunate match – and, sadly, one could not put it past her – then that would greatly upset poor Sir Edward. And, more to the point, it would reflect badly on Fanny – unfairly, of course. But then, when did natural justice ever concern itself with the defence of the stepmother? Hers was a sorry position, indeed.

The only thing for it was for Fanny to concoct some strategy of preventive action. And, after long hours of plotting, she had it all clear in her mind just in time for her husband's return.

~

To the right of the fireplace, in a high, wing-backed chair of plum damask, Sir Edward sat behind the large, open pages of the *Kentish Gazette*; to the left, his wife was busy with an embroidered pillow she was working on for Lady Banks. Though it still should be the summer, the evening was cool and an early fire crackled between them; the clock ticked on the mantel above, and the vast acreage of the gilded drawing room hummed that near sonorous hum of domestic contentment.

Fanny pulled the silk through, reached for her scissors, stopped, thought, braced herself and then spoke: 'Dearest?'

The *Kentish Gazette* did not move.

'My dear?' Fanny put down her scissors and raised her voice. 'Sir Edward!'

'I am listening,' he said, while remaining invisible.

'Thank you. There's something on my mind, and I would just like to share it.' She selected a dark green, and paused while threading the needle.

'Share away, my dear.' He licked at a finger and turned a new page. 'Share away.'

'It is on the matter of Mary.' The silence seemed to suggest that further clarification would be welcome.

'Mary Dorothea,' she said, before adding, for good measure, 'your daughter.'

'Indeed?' He slapped the pages together and folded the paper on to his lap. If there was one subject with which Fanny could always get his attention, it was his precious only daughter.

'There has been the most *astonishing* development.' She put her embroidery back in its bag and leaned forward towards him. 'I cannot tell you how long it has been in the *brewing*, so to speak. The first *I* noticed was on – let me see – Monday, I believe?' She looked up at the ceiling while counting on her fingers. 'Yes, definitely last Monday. I had just come in from *relieving* the *poor* . . .'

Sir Edward stifled a yawn. Fanny had strayed from the subject. She sped up her delivery. 'Or could it have been the Indigent Blind?' She had invented all this for effect, of course, and was rather pleased by how well it was going. 'Anyway, I was just taking my bonnet off, when Mary came running down the stairs . . .' After such careful rehearsal, she could not edit it now or she might lose her thread, but she did need to get it all out before he was asleep altogether. 'And perhaps it was the way the light caught? Or just that I turned around at speed and caught *myself* unawares, so to speak. . . but, anyway. *There* it was! *Clear* as day!'

'What exactly was where, my dear?'

'The fact! The fact was there and *irrefutable*.' She clapped her hands as if the idea actually pleased her: 'Mary Dorothea has become . . . *rather a beauty!*'

'Become?' Sir Edward stretched out his legs and shuffled deeper into his chair. 'Was she not *always*?'

'Oh! Well, no.' Fanny now worried that she had misjudged it. 'I mean, of course, *sweet*.' Though Mary had never been sweet, in Fanny's opinion. 'But, as for *beauty*, I would say that is . . . quite new?'

'Good Lord!' He jolted back upright, suddenly some distance from sleep. 'Hmph.' Sir Edward, when discomfited, could become a little brusque. 'To my eyes, she was always the epitome of all that is good and pure . . . Perhaps, when one is father to a daughter, one simply rather *presumes* the presence of beauty . . .'

'Ah, yes.' Fanny had the horrible feeling she had rather spoiled things for him. 'I am sure it is so. But now,' she said brightly, 'you can do more than presume. Your daughter is suddenly thought to be lovely. Without wishing to blow one's own trumpet, I do like to think that the *riding* has rather helped. I hope you remember that *I* arranged the pony and lessons and so on? It has definitely had the desired effect on both complexion and posture.'

'I see.' He looked into the flames, pondered and then asked: 'And do we *want* her to be' – he circled his right hand as if it were rolling down a never-ending hill – '*lovely*, et cetera, et cetera? Is that altogether a *good* thing?'

Fanny spent much of her married life asking for Sir Edward's opinion, awaiting his divine judgement on any number of matters, so that, on the rare occasions that things coincided with her own areas of expertise, she did rather enjoy it. She could even become – and did have to check this, for Sir Edward would disapprove – a little *professorial* in her pronouncements.

'Funnily enough, I did wonder myself. It *can* sometimes present problems to keep under one's roof the local honey pot, and have to bear all the consequential buzzing about.' Fanny had learned that the summer Lizzie came out. Young men seemed to pick up her scent from several counties away. 'But I think with dear Mary that issue need not apply. The fact that she has always been rather – well – *others* might use the word *plain*, will have given her a good, sure foundation, I'm sure. She has built up great reserves of common sense and character.' If only Fanny could be sure that was true. 'Far too late now for her dear head to turn.'

'Indeed.' Sir Edward's brow started to furrow, and his teeth chewed at his lip – the signs, Fanny now knew, that her husband was on the brink of supplying an opinion. 'I have often worried that the marriage market has the potential to be an uncomfortable experience for the innocent young girl. And for Mary, in particular . . . Such a sensitive creature . . . I would not like to think of her becoming attached to some *stranger* . . .'

Fanny chose not to mention the yet greater threat posed by her own dear family. It was not only George, but all the Knight boys now came to Hatch rather often. The bad feeling occasioned by Miss Atkinson's dismissal was completely forgotten, Fanny was forgiven and they all *flocked* once again. She did not wish to ban them from visiting now, but she must protect Mary and at all costs.

'Perhaps it might help her if we were to narrow the choice, so to speak . . .' He looked up and across to his wife with a keen sort of gaze. 'My dear. Might you be so kind as to invite Dr Knatchbull to dine with us at his earliest convenience?'

'Oh, Sir Edward!' Fanny replied, touched. 'How clever you are!' The permission for a bit of controlled match-making was exactly her plan. 'Dr Knatchbull, I take it, has *a suitable friend* . . .'

'A *friend*?' Sir Edward looked utterly baffled. 'Wynd-ham?' His jowls shook along with his head. 'I would very much doubt it. We Knatchbulls tend not to go in for *friends*, as a rule.'

Fanny had that feeling one gets, when missing the last step on one's descent down the stairs. 'We *are* talking of the Dr Wyndham Knatchbull who is also your *brother*?'

'Only half-brother, my dear. We are not from the same mother.'

'Yes, yet—' Fanny stopped, before breaking her own iron rule of arguing with her husband. But surely he could not be serious?

'All well above board.' Sir Edward's patience was starting to fray. 'Intelligent sort of fellow. Can't stay at *Oxford* studying *Persians* and what-have-you for ever. Soon to take up the living at Smeeth – not too close, not too far, and a handsome house, too. Yes, good old Wyndham. Come the autumn, invite him to dine and I will explain the position. He'll see the wisdom of marrying *in* – an arrangement to suit the whole family. Can't have her yet, mind. He will have to wait a few years, but I doubt—'

And then he stopped, wincing with pain – screwed up his eyes and clutched at his jaw.

'My dear?' Fanny felt instant alarm. 'You are not well?'

Sir Edward suddenly wailed.

Fanny ran to the bell – rang for a servant – and back to his side. 'Sir Edward! What is it? Do say!'

'Mouth,' he spluttered. 'Tooth.' He rocked to and fro, and rubbed his face with his hands. '*All over agony.*'

Graves came in then, called other servants – summoned Dr Whitfield – and whisked his master to his bed.

'I shall follow you up shortly,' Fanny called after them and then sank into her chair as hope rose up within her and flooded her being. 'Ague of the face!' she whispered to herself. A warm feeling of happiness began in her toes. 'That is what ails him.' That feeling crept up and up, and sought out her heart. 'It is ague of the face.' Tooth, temperature, a shooting neuralgia: were these not the very symptoms from which he had suffered at Lady Banks's house, back in the year '21?

And if so, was that not extraordinary! For now Fanny

examined it, she had, of late, felt unusually tired. She was definitely a bit plumper. Certainly, her hair was thicker and of a particular shine – Sayce had commented on it only this evening as she was dressing for dinner. She stretched out her fingers and started to count . . . And – oh! Praise be to the Lord who is kind, and our God who is merciful. Fanny was having a baby and felt perfectly well.

CHAPTER XX

Mary waited to be announced, and then slipped into the bedchamber and clung close to its threshold.

'Ah, good morning, my dear.' Lady Knatchbull looked up from the tray on her bed, and dabbed at her lips with a square of monogrammed linen. The bright morning sun caught the wisps of new grey coming loose from her nightcap. 'Thank you *so* much for coming and – pray! – do not look so fearful. It is not my intention to *bite* you!' She gave an unnatural little laugh – one she had taken to using with her stepchildren as a signal that humour *had* been committed, and any consequent mirth would *not* be discouraged. In the silence that followed, Fanny laughed long and alone.

'Good morning,' Mary cut in at last to save any further embarrassment. Even so, her own custom dictated there must be a significant pause, and that be left to ring long and loud around the pale blue, silk bedchamber, before she pleasantly added: 'Ma-*ma*.'

Mary smiled to herself. They were entirely alone and yet still took care to put on their usual polished performance, so that even a maid would presume there was a fond friendship between them – as nearly all the world did. Over four, long, awkward years, both parties had somehow formed this unspoken agreement: the mutual *froideur* should remain a strictly private affair, of which Sir Edward, in particular, must never know.

Fanny let out a delicate sigh that screamed: *Is there no hope for us?* before collecting herself and beginning anew. 'Pray, do come in and sit for a while. We have been so very *busy* this summer – August already! Where *does* the time go? – that you and I have had too little time on our *own*. And we do like our little chats, do we not?'

'Oh, very much indeed, Mama,' replied Mary, who had memories of few such occasions, and none of them particularly pleasant.

'Quite so. And now here you are, suddenly seventeen years of age! I can hardly believe it. How you have come *on*, my dear child, since I first came to Hatch.' Again, to any outsider Fanny's look would appear as one of approval; only Mary saw the pity in her stepmother's eyes. 'From now on, you will join us to dine, and Sir Edward is agreed you shall come out at the Ashford Ball at the end of the month. There, is that not excellent news?'

Even in this company, Mary could not disguise her eager excitement. The Ashford Ball in August was said to be the best in the whole calendar. And, oh! – how she had longed for this moment.

Childhood had felt more like oppression, and did not merit a moment of mourning. Her own past was no more than a burden that had to be borne on the path to this door and, at last, here Mary stood: at the threshold of life. No one and nothing could stop her. She would throw herself forward—

'Now,' Fanny pressed on, as if delivering a speech already prepared. 'I can see that you may have some reason to doubt my own commitment to your launch, as I am soon to be somewhat preoccupied . . .' She started to stroke the growing curve of her stomach; at once, Mary studied the ceiling. 'And I wanted to reassure you on the matter, as well as issuing my personal guarantee that, for the rest of this year at least, you can expect my *fullest* attention. To that end, I have written to Hall, my hairdresser, to order you *curls*.'

With some caution, Mary brought her eyes down again. 'Curls, Mama?' Mercifully, the hands were now holding the tea dish.

'Yes, Mary. Curls. They are so *very* much of the hour, and as Nature has *not*—' Fanny stopped, momentarily flustered, then cleared her throat to continue. 'On your behalf, I have discussed it with Hall and he is of the *professional* opinion that your terrible illness has taken its *toll.* In consequence and as per the very latest in medical thinking, he recommends that we . . .' At which point, her voice dipped into a mumble and the words ran out at speed.

'Forgive me' – a quick rest – 'Ma-*ma*, I could not quite catch—'

'Ah. Indeed.' Fanny's eyes froze wide in pure panic. 'Yes. I was saying.' The same voice now rose up to a squeak. '*Shaving* the *head* . . . can bring on a *miracle* . . . Or so it is said.'

For a long moment, Mary stood still by the bed, stared at its occupant and thought, not for the first time, that she might be a lunatic. Then, as if back in the schoolroom trying to grasp the subjunctive, she slowly repeated that which she thought she had heard. 'You have *kindly* arranged for *my* head to be *shaved.*'

'Correct!' Fanny exclaimed, in seeming relief that her message had landed so well. 'My dear, please believe that your father and I want *only* the best for you. Since the moment we met, my *dedication* to your improvement has been unfaltering, as I am sure you have noticed?'

'Thank you, Mama.'

'The dancing masters, the music teachers – the pony *I personally* found: all these things were arranged by your loving mama in the interest of your future; the improvement of your *chances.* My dear, do believe me when I say that – though you may well struggle to believe it – you

are, actually, really, one of the fortunate. But if I may –
there has always been this one *tiny* matter crying *out* for
improvement.'

'And here you speak of my hair.' Mary had a moment-
ary vision of Booker's likely reaction.

'Precisely. You know, Mary, your papa does have the
very *highest* hopes of your *eventual* success. *Dear* man.'
She smiled and shook her head as if almost in sorrow.
'Such a *fond* parent . . . Surely it is in both of our interests
to at least *try* to ensure his wishes are met?'

'Forgive me, Mama.' Mary's icy calm tone belied the
wild storm in her breast, 'but I feel it important to establish I have quite understood. So my first ball is in a fortnight, I shall present with no hair and you do not expect
any adverse effect on my "chances"?'

'Well, I too had worried a little, but am newly convinced that all will be well!' Fanny returned, smiling
brightly. 'We have two weeks after all, during which we
may see *some* growth and – let us hope! – a new, shall
we say, *richness* in texture. Furthermore . . .' She leaned
forward then, and put on the expression of a happy conspirator. 'I have consumed *all* the reports of the London
season and can you guess what I learned?'

Mary looked back at her blankly.

'Our luck is in, Mary! *Turbans* are quite *à la mode.*'

∿

A half-hour had passed since the hairdresser's departure. The sun was now meeting its zenith; the swallows were diving; somewhere out on the lawn, willow struck leather with metronomic precision. But still, Mary sat where Hall had left her: in her room, at her dressing table, in front of the glass, where she came slowly to terms with her new reflection.

Actually, Mary remembered it now: had she not grown up assuming herself to be plain? After all, no one about her had ever said otherwise and she had somehow gathered, from novels and so on, that when Beauty was evident people did tend to remark it. And so imbued had she been with religious principle – the rigorous catechism and bible study; church twice on a Sunday – that she had learned not to much mind. Was not the soul worth more than the flesh? Of course, the recent talk of her 'bloom' had been rather pleasant, but then she had never quite believed it: just one look from her stepmother had been quite sufficient to return her to earth. No, plain had she been; it now seemed plain she would always be. One must simply get used to it.

Mary blinked slowly and looked back into her own eyes. The naked scalp was now hidden by her white cotton cap. Beneath it was hidden a band, to which the new hair was attached, but that was a secret known only to her and her maid. All the world could see was that around her face hung a crop of rich, chestnut ringlets which rightly belonged to some other girl. She sighed.

Imagine being so poor as to be forced to sell one's own hair. Mary fell into wondering how she might cope with such a forced deprivation, before realising that she would not have that option. Who on earth would buy *hers* when it 'cried out for improvement'? It was a testament to her good, Christian optimism that the thought made her burst into laughter.

'Have you gone mad, child?' Booker lifted her face from the handkerchief in which she had buried it. 'You've got nothing to laugh at, believe you me.' The sobbing resumed. 'We won't forgive her for this in a hurry and that much is certain.' She gulped, somewhat damply. 'Quite tempted to—'

A maid popped her head around the door. 'Lady Banks waiting down in the drawing room, miss.'

'And here, let me correct you. Lady Banks is *very* much not.' The familiar, short, untidy figure pushed through and barrelled into the bedroom. 'My *opinions* on *waiting* are more than well known.' Shooing Booker out of the armchair, she sat down with some heaviness. 'My dear, I am come to celebrate your significant— Oh my good Lord, what on earth have they done to you?'

Mary recited the facts of the morning, while expressing no comment.

'Well, I have not heard such nonsense in all of my days. And where is her *ladyship* now, pray?' She thumped her cane on the carpet. 'I demand her presence at once!'

'Pray, Aunt, I beg you do not.' Mary rose and went to

her side, bent to kiss her dry cheek. ''Tis done now and I believe her intentions were perfectly good.' The last thing they needed was a conflict over which her papa was made to rule, for he would never upset the Wife in her interesting condition. 'And, anyway, what does it matter?'

'Oh, you naïve little creature.' Such a fine day, yet Lady Banks's voice rolled like incoming thunder. 'It matters a great deal, or why would it have happened? I must express my *pr-r-rofound* disappointment, after all that I said to her. And when you were becoming so *lovely* . . . Bah! Second wives, Mary.' Her jowls shook with dismay. '*Second wives.* Will the good Lord not spare us from . . .'

She let the mysterious thought hang, then rose to her full height, which these days did not quite meet Mary's shoulder. 'Ah, I must away to your father before he takes offence – never takes much with *him*, as we have all found to our cost. But first let me say this.' She took both hands in hers. 'If there is ever – and I stress *ever* – a time when you need my support, then please *promise* you come to me. No matter how major, or trivial. I married a Man of *Science*, remember. Nothing can shock me. I remain where I have always been: right on your side.' Lady Banks shot a look towards Booker. '*Somebody* has to be, is that not so?'

She moved to the exit but, on reaching the door, something else struck her. 'Why on *earth* do they still stick you out here in the nursery? Yet another indignity! You are now a young lady and I expect you to be treated as such. Where *is* Sir Edward?

'He shall get a piece of my mind.'

~

Mary and Cassy sat down on the bench at the edge of the field and prepared to watch play.

'How *lucky* you are.' Cassy sighed heavily. 'Your very own cricket pitch! My dear brothers are near *demented* with envy.'

'Ah, the poor Knights of Godmersham.' When Mary laughed, the ridiculous ringlets bounced on her face. She brushed them away. 'So deprived of amenities. Can we not start a fund?'

But Cassy's interest had now swung to the Greek gods striding out in their whites. 'Here they come! Now, who have we here?' Under cover of their charming, straw brims the girls studied the players. 'I *say*, what a spread. A Finch-Hatton, a couple of Darnleys – don't get your hopes up. Too grand for *our* sort – and all those Wykeham-Martins. *Six* sons in that family, plenty to choose from. Any take your fancy?'

Mary smiled in reply. Perhaps it was down to the year's difference between them, but she did not yet share Cassy's obsession with gentlemen. And, anyway, there was nothing like a shaved head for the quelling of romantic notions. With all *that* now behind her, Mary could only look on objectively; cast a purely dispassionate eye. In which case, it then became perfectly obvious all were mere shadows set next to Ned Knight. That charming chaos of hair, the joy on that face – even those close-cut, white britches were oddly . . . Mary turned quickly away, twisted her parasol and, instead, took to the study of the other spectators.

'And *whom* do we have here?' Mary tilted her head to an unknown group near the pavilion and, in particular, the cynosure in pale lemon muslin. The lady was vibrant; her many gentlemen friends were enraptured. Even with the distance between them, Mary could still come to judgement. 'She has one of those *musical* laughs, don't you think? You don't even have to hear it, to tell.'

'Without doubt. How does one learn it, I wonder? It's definitely the type of thing we *ought* to be practising . . . Watch them all dance on attendance.'

'Slaves, to a man.' Mary was riveted. 'Another capital flirt, I should say.'

'Lucky her. I bet *she* will never have her heart broken. Gosh, I do *still* mourn Miss Atkinson, don't you?'

Mary sighed. 'Poor, *dear* Miss A. Nothing's the same, now she has left us.'

'*She* would have shown us the ropes. I doubt poor Fan knows the first thing about it. Dear sister and all that, could not be *sweeter*, yet I fear there are some crucial areas in which we are being most frightfully let down.'

At that moment, one of the slaves stood, waved to the girls and strode over to join them.

Cassy sang out: 'George, darling! Are you not playing?'

'Waiting to go in,' George Knight replied, with a quick swing of his bat. 'Something up with your voice, Cass? You sound awful peculiar.'

Both girls fell into unladylike giggles. 'Oh, *Georgy*. We *so* long to flirt, but we don't have a *clue*! Will *you* be our teacher? One couldn't help but notice you there, at the feet of an *expert*. Who is she, by the way? Do we *know* her at all?'

'That' – he flicked one eye back to the pavilion – 'is Lady Elizabeth Bligh, Lord Darnley's girl. The family keeps her well under wraps as a rule.'

'Hard to blame them,' Cassy retorted.

'Now, now.' George sounded quite stern. 'First rule of flirting: don't be a cat about your own sex. A fellow can't bear all that stuff.'

'*Really?* How more than extraordinary. Are not men odd, Mary?'

'For what is left then to talk about?' Mary replied.

'There!' George smiled down at Mary. 'More like it – the old witty riposte, eh? Good dash of humour. Nothing outrageous, mind.' He shot Cassy a look. 'Just a quick line, the odd joke: raise a smile. Chaps rather go for it.'

'Not all of them, surely, Mr Knight?' Mary was considering her father. Did he laugh? She could not now recall.

'The *modern* chap, I mean.' He leaned on his bat as if upon a lectern, clearly enjoying the professorial role. 'We're a quite different breed from our forebears, you know. And it's us you should be aiming for, after all.'

'Oh, darling, you are marvellous!' Cassy clapped her hands with great glee. 'What else, what *more*?'

'Heaven's sake, you are my sister! Flirting with you – ugh! It's almost unseemly.' George sounded quite cross. 'But if you *insist* upon forcing my hand, I shall flirt with Miss Knatchbull and *you* shall watch on.' He cleared his throat, dropped his eyes, pressed bat into turf and looked up with a smile. 'And what brings you to our little match today, madam?'

'She lives here, you fool!'

'Cassandra!' George admonished her, then turned back to Mary.

'Oh, *sir*,' Mary said sweetly, getting into her part. 'To my enormous regret, I must confess that my knowledge of cricket is quite pitiful. And yet, and yet' – she looked into his eyes – 'I find myself *deeply* intrigued. What I lack is a *master* – one with the patience to explain *all* and in *full*. I wonder, can I ever hope to find such a one?'

In an instant, George appeared to forget their charade, sat down by her side, and began to explain. 'So we call that the *wicket*.'

'How perfectly charming!' Mary cried. 'Is that with an "h" or without it? I shall write it all down in my journal this evening.'

Thus encouraged, he continued to outline the details for some minutes more. Mary was increasingly baffled. There seemed to be a great stress on *refreshments* for something she had thought of as sport. Was that why they liked it? 'Chaps' were fond of their food, that much she did know.

A call came from the field, and he suddenly stood. 'I'm in.' With new purpose, he strode towards the field, then stopped and turned. 'You will watch, madam?'

'Oh, Mr Knight!' She made a stab at a musical laugh. 'I am already entranced.'

With a broad smile aimed solely at Mary, he walked backwards the rest of the way.

～

It was a good ball at Ashford that August. A crowd of 250 gathered to mark the end of the summer and, did they but know it, the debut of Miss Mary Dorothea Knatchbull.

A large party, made up of her own family, the Knights and a few respectable neighbours, had gathered at Hatch before it. With so many in the house, the mad hour of preparations had come close to a riot: maids running hither and thither with hot water for bathing and irons for pressing; doors slamming, men shouting, ladies shrieking. And then, at last, all were assembled, each in their splendour, awaiting their carriages and, at once, the panic became joy and excitement. Mary thrilled at it – was *this* really her own sombre home? So delightful was the moment, she had concerns that it might prove the best part of the evening.

But now here she stood, at the edge of the dance floor, one of the crowd and her heart nearly burst with delight.

'Darling!' Cassy came from behind her and shrieked into her ear. 'You are simply *superb!*' She fingered a corner of Mary's dress – blonde net over satin – and mock-swooned at the turban of silver and pink. 'The success of the night! See how they stare.'

The girls got quickly to work: those long, youthful hours spent in social dissection now serving them well. Two pairs of expert eyes swept rapidly around the candle-lit ballroom and considered the assembly. Mary gasped. Was not every lady simply magnificent? Of course, she herself could not even begin to compete – still, no matter. She was just grateful to be here, and that was enough.

But, to her utmost astonishment, George Knight approached, putting himself down for two dances, which struck Mary as uncommonly kind of him. Then, Dr Knatchbull, apparently one of her uncles, booked her for three – sadly, she could hardly refuse. A Finch-Hatton, no less, asked for a waltz; *even* a *Darnley* requested! And within minutes, her card was filled right through to supper.

'At last!' Mary smiled to herself as she spun round the floor. 'I am living at last and no one can stop me!' Not even a sad, shaven head could hold her back now. Was it not odd, but all that doom when it happened, and yet no one remarked that she had sprouted a thick fringe of curls out of nowhere. It was almost as if humans only truly examined their own selves, and took little to no notice of others.

She left one set of arms and was claimed by another. The bonnets had stayed on since the shaving and as for this turban, well: it was, in fact, rather fetching. So much so that the Mother, whose idea it had been after all, seemed almost shocked when first she beheld it. 'Well, well!' She had affected a slightly pained smile, and: 'Are *we* not the vision?'

While she danced, Mary practised her flirting. She made George Knight laugh – it did not take very much; let Mr Finch-Hatton discover her deep passion for cricket; and, in response to her avowed fascination, Dr Knatch-bull could have lectured on Arabic for some hours, had he not stood on her foot and so disrupted his monologue. Such was her success, her card was soon booked after supper and beyond to the end of the night.

Several friends were kind enough to say that Mary was glowing as George Knight escorted her through to take soup. The sitting-out room was heaving, and they were late to get a good table. For a moment they stood, trying to see a spare place. And then they were hailed.

'Brother!'

Mary swung round and was astonished to see Ned

Knight – in the best possible position – rising out of his seat. But he was not of their party! She had not seen him all evening. With whom had he come? While he crossed over towards them, she caught a glimpse of the partner he had left at the table; blonde net over satin, a head full of curls. Was that not Lady Elizabeth Bligh?

'Dear boy.' He pumped George's hand, gave a few pats to the shoulder, then turned to Mary. 'Madam.' Mr Knight bowed, smiled and waited – as if to be introduced – before looking again, with a queer sort of expression. 'Is it – *is* it – *Miss Knatchbull?*'

Mary fell into a deep curtsey, all over confusion. Such an extraordinary reaction! What on earth could account for it? And how could she rise now and face him anew? But one could hardly stay down there forever, eyes to the floor . . . And so, with great dread and reluctance, Mary finally stood. To find that he stared at her still.

The Knight brothers fell into discussing arrangements. Mary pretended to listen, head tilted towards George, but she could sense, throughout it, Ned studying her profile. Again, what on *earth*—? And then – oh the horror! The thought struck like electricity. There could be but one explanation: he had *noticed* the *hair*. Of all of the people she had mixed with this whole glorious summer . . . he alone . . . only *he* . . .

Mary blushed to the edge of her turban.

It was agreed that the carriages should come after two, and Ned finally left them. Mary kept her eyes keen on his back as he returned to his place, to ensure that he would not return. She watched as he sat, discerned him regale his friends with something amusing.

George looked on too, then whispered to Mary: 'Ned has asked for her hand, don't you know? Lady Elizabeth, that is. Can't fault my brother's ambition!'

At which moment, Mary found the heat of the room had become a little too much for her. She begged George take her outside for a breath of fresh air, turned for the door and heard a musical laugh cut through the air.

CHAPTER XXI

Over the following autumn and into the long, bitter winter, Mary became increasingly conscious of change, in both herself and her life. She had dined, she had danced and, to her own great astonishment, been decreed a success – by all but *one* gentleman, anyway. She was out of the nursery and into her very own apartment in the main part of Hatch. And there Mary now sat, on the last day of January in the year 1825, looking into the new glass on her new walnut table, from which a new, proper, young lady smiled back.

The Mother had vanished into confinement soon after Christmas. Of course, the child was a *girl* (Mary knew He would punish her eventually), and also called Fanny (an absurd act of vanity even if it did follow a long Knight tradition). And though it might not look very much – not to Mary, at least – this baby had somehow contrived to upend the whole household and in myriad ways. One was that the Knight siblings suddenly flocked about Hatch to care for their sister. The place was a-buzz! Another was that Mary did not have the time to truly enjoy the pleasure of their company. Indeed, so busy were her days, there was barely a moment even to even flirt with dear George – which did seem a shame, with him so very convinced she still needed more practice.

Instead, she was now expected to take on her stepmother's duties while the lady was absent, some of which proved to be more enjoyable than others. For instance, Mary was delighted to take charge of her own brothers and sure they were all five Knatchbulls much the better for it. She loved visiting the village children down at the school and was diligent in getting aid to the poor; could hardly believe herself trusted with that weightiest of issues: the Indigent Blind – Fanny's particular project – and threw herself in.

But while accompanying her dear papa on business and visits *should* have been pleasurable, it turned out to be somewhat less so. Mary did take care to remember how her own, girlish self would have thrilled at such precious access. But as Sir Edward had disappointed her then, so he disappointed her still. Though once he had talked of his own, unending misery, now he spoke only, at some length, of his happiness: his wife's 'excellent feelings'; the baby's 'utter perfection'; his 'extraordinary good fortune' that the Almighty should so bless him again. And Mary – returned to her old, childhood pattern – sat, ramrod and decorous; listened politely; hoped he might notice her goodness and be minded to love her.

That sadness apart, she was, on balance, more happy than not. Her days were at least full of purpose, rather than indolence and flirting which were, anyway, only more wickedness. And at last, she could see life – *real* life, not that previous, poor approximation – spread out before her. A banquet yet to be tasted; the dawn of a bright, clear, new day.

'Thank you, Booker.' Mary looked into the glass again, and did not even pretend to be displeased with the vision before her.

The maid met the bright eyes and gave one, final pat to the hair she had just dressed. 'Just look at those curls.' She chuckled. 'Not that there was much wrong before, mind, nor will I ever forgive what she did to you. Still, *eel foe soof rear*, that's what my last lady used to say, though the Lord only knows what she was on about.'

'I think it's French, dearest.'

'Hmph. Shame. Well, I'll still say it anyway.' She tucked one, last stray wisp into the chignon. '*Eel foe soof rear* and will you not look at it. Bet Madam's pleased with herself.'

'Oh, Books, darling.' Mary laughed up at her. 'She has not said a word, of course. Doesn't notice a *thing* which isn't to do with that baby.'

'Now, now, miss.' Booker struck Mary's exposed

bosom with the back of the brush. 'Off you go and behave yourself.'

Mary tripped down to dinner as the gong was being struck and that evening's diners were already in their places. At some point in the day, dear Marianne had left – so another friend lost – and been replaced by Mrs Rice, the Married Sister – the one they called Lizzie. Mary issued a curtsey and sat down beside her. Sir Edward, who famously preferred earliness over mere punctuality, raised one baleful eye but, for once, did not issue a reprimand. All of which gave the impression of something important being under discussion. How very tantalising. What on earth could it be?

In the end, Mary's curiosity proved too great for her manners. 'Pray do excuse me, but of what do we speak?' It was quite the boldest beginning, but surely they were all only family and she must be permitted the odd little query, just now and again. After all, had she not dined, had she not danced: was she not *out*?

Fanny, with her vacant new-mother air, looked over, blinked, seemed to consider a frown, but then only sighed. 'We are today in receipt of the most terrible news.'

'Come, come, my dear.' Her father, hard at work on a dark slab of liver, seemed significantly more cheerful than the ladies. 'It is hardly *that,* to my mind.' He settled to chewing.

'Sir Edward!' Lizzie dropped her fork to her plate. '*Really,* how *could* you?' She was always the most forthright in her address to all gentlemen. Mary could only put it down to her extraordinary beauty. 'Everyone *knows* he had *proposed* to that wretched creature. The entire *world* is simply *consumed*.'

There came a mirthless laugh from the head of the table. 'My dear madam. Speaking as a *Member* of His *Majesty's* Parliament . . .' He paused while a footman charged his glass with good claret. '. . . I can assure you that the world is, in fact, consumed by the Catholic Question; not *your brother* or Lady Elizabeth Bligh.'

'Pray, husband.' Fanny began to tremble with some violence, and raised a handkerchief to a damp eye. 'I beg you, never mention that name again in my presence.'

'Nor politics at the table, if you so please. One has no wish to hear another thing about *Catholics*, whatever their *query*.' Lizzie put down her spoon. 'They quite ruin the appetite. Of a piece with the *daughters* of *earls*, if you want my opinion. All simply *live* to upset one.'

Mary felt suddenly cheerful. Since her launch, every dinner she had attended was, frankly, dull – much dressing required for very little amusement – so that she had rather given up looking forward to them. *This*, though, was splendid! Frank conversation, open dispute – discreetly, she tucked into the pudding – even the food was particularly pleasant. While she ate, Mary longed to hear more. For why *had* Lady Elizabeth – why would any lady, indeed – refuse young Mr Knight? And when there had been such a clear attraction between the couple. Of course, having pushed her luck once, Mary dared not ask anything of anyone ever again. Thanks to the Married One, there was no need.

'So it transpires' – Lizzie turned and bestowed upon Mary the honour of speaking as if to an equal – 'while *she* had accepted *him* in the moment, the *parents* then swanned in and squashed it. As if *Ned* was not good enough! The heir – the *sole heir* – of Chawton *and* God-mersham did not meet their *requirements?*' She placed a hand on her pretty bosom. 'I have thought so for some time, though good manners prevented me mentioning: the Blighs, as a family, are quite perfectly *ghastly*.'

'Enough, madam!' Sir Edward slapped his hand down on the table and wrenched the napkin out from his dress shirt. 'I shall *not* have a peer of the realm maligned in my house. His lordship acted perfectly properly and arrived at the only possible outcome. We have a hierarchy in this country, *Mrs Rice*, and we must take care to protect it. A title – even the humblest baronetcy such as my own – is a matter of some consequence.'

Mary could sense that her papa was building up to a roar. The earlier mild disposition was gone; a storm was incoming. She studied her plate and braced for it.

'*Furthermore*.' Half the candles spluttered then died. The table grew dim. 'Thus far, I have restrained myself but can do so no longer.' A servant rushed in with a taper. 'It falls to *me* to point out that your brother has – as per his *regrettable* nature – behaved in the most *reckless* manner.

To propose to the lady at all was quite foolish. To ask the *woman* herself before approaching the *father* – whose business this is, may I point out – is the act of *a scoundrel.*'

Fanny let out a cry of almost physical pain.

'Forgive me, my dear.' He placed a hand upon his wife's shoulder and tempered his tone. 'But henceforth, it is vital that we *all* be more vigilant. In some ways, I must confess to having harboured a certain admiration for young Mr Knight's extraordinary self-confidence. No doubt he enjoys it as a God-given blessing, but is it not in fact more of a curse? Surely it has brought him consider-able embarrassment in *this* matter and I fear it could yet again. I must say' – he shook his heavy head and picked up his glass – 'I dread it, for then what will become of us? And to that end, I must issue this warning – here and right now, before his two loving sisters.

'I will not – I repeat *not* – have one whiff of scandal attached to my excellent name.'

CHAPTER XXII

Having been lucky enough to enjoy a few winters in Town, Mary now understood that numbers worked a little differently in Kent. In her first winter in London, the short month of February had sped past in a flash, a whirl of arcades and outings. This year, all thanks to that new baby, she was stuck out at Hatch and the same twenty-eight days dragged like a decade. No doubt even the thought would be taken as yet further evidence against her true piety, yet Mary was convinced of it: God created the Capital to spare one the trials of an over-long winter.

To add to the misery, it seemed that everyone was up *there* while Mary was not. Kind Mr Austen Knight had taken his three unmarried daughters to an hotel, from which Cassy wrote often. She reported that Ned had, typically, emerged unscathed from recent events;

George was also often around, despite the great pressure of Chambers; and with the House now in session, even Sir Edward was enjoying himself in Portland Place with dear Lady Banks. Meanwhile, Mary stayed alone, with the Mother, her child and multiple nurses. Could life get any worse?

Apparently so. For, as a bluebottle drawn to the fresh corpse of poor Mary's joy, Dr Knatchbull landed at Hatch.

~

One afternoon, somewhere in the long middle of that eternal, short month, Mary returned from a solitary walk to find the new guest was arrived.

'Sir.' She dropped into a modest curtsey, and made for a chair in the hope of being ignored. Only to find that he leaped to his feet, grasped her cold hand and, rather dramatically, kissed it.

'Madam.' The bow was extreme: too long and too low. 'I had very much hoped to find you in residence, having wished to deepen our acquaintance since that dance in Ashford. Was it not the most pleasant of evenings?'

There was something a little over-moist about the mouth when he spoke. A certain dampness hung in the air between them. Mary waited politely, issued a suggestive stare at the hand still trapped in his. At last, she was free to sit down and take tea.

'Dr Knatchbull was just saying that he hopes to stay

with us through to the summer, while works are done on his rectory at Smeeth.' Fanny fussed around with a teapot and cakes. 'Is that not excellent news? I fear poor Mary has found it very quiet here lately, sir, with no other *young . . .*'

Mary looked across at the tall, sombre, learned clergyman and tried to guess at his age, but it was not obvious. Though he might still be young, he could just as equally pass as a septuagenarian. She put him down as one of those poor unfortunates, rather like the Mama, who had simply been old since the womb.

'Then perhaps *I* might try to entertain you a little?' the gentleman simpered. 'I was most *encouraged* by the interest you showed in my subject – the *Ancients* and *Arabic*, as I am sure you recall. It is my dearest hope that these long months together will afford much opportunity for us to *explore* things in greater *depth*. I hereby attest there is nothing else in the world that could bring me such intense *pleasure*.'

Mary stared at her plate in horror. This was all her own fault. That minor flirtation had been taken as major encouragement. And now . . . was there not something unseemly about his delivery? The man was Sir Edward's half-brother. *He was her very own uncle!* Surely, the Mama must be shocked and appalled. Someone must put a stop to it.

Instead: 'What a splendid idea,' Fanny exclaimed. '*Exactly* the diversion required!'

~

Though Mary still felt every right to expect some sort of protection from this awful oppressor, it gradually dawned that he and Fanny had in fact formed some alliance. What on earth could explain it? Mary had no idea. But it was clear that the next weeks would be very delicate.

When not under attack from one quarter – 'Now *this,* though perhaps a bit long, I accept, should have all you need to know on Ptolemy. If you find it a struggle, then pray, do call for guidance. I should be only too happy' – Mary was in skirmish with the other. Biographical facts struck her like bullets: 'Though he *did* have an arrangement with a lady, that *is* in the past and, one gathers, *all* to the best,' Fanny explained, ever helpful. 'There was even a rumour she hailed from *Surrey*, but that may have been malice. People can be so cruel, Mary.'

Details of Dr Knatchbull's property rained down on her head: 'It is, as I say, an exceptional house of its *type*. Do you think you might *like* a rectory, dear? It appeals to me as a rather *romantic* life. Do you know, my own grandfather was also a Man of the Church? Of course, one *might* lose in comfort, yet there is also so much to be said for good, plain *respectability*.'

Though her arsenal was limited and weapons but few, Mary employed all she could in self-protection. Good works got her out of the house, although the wretched short days of darkness meant she could not stay out late. On the other hand, the season did bring with it an excellent array of possible illnesses, and she claimed to fall victim to one after the other. In some other household, this poor pattern of health might have raised some suspicion. After all, did not Mary ail only when Dr Knatchbull was in residence? When he was called to Oxford or Smeeth, was she not, by some miracle, suddenly well? It went without notice, and Mary stayed, calm but alone, in her room. Even the leeches seemed but a small price to pay. Better to lose blood than the soul.

Of course, there were still dinners – terrible dinners *à trois* – which she simply had to attend, but there she drew her smallest stiletto. Mary had discovered, quite by chance, that if she addressed *him* as '*My uncle*', then both enemies flinched. It was as devastating as the pause on '. . . *Mama.*' Once learned, she pursued it with vigour.

And come the day when she simply had to break free or risk losing her sanity, Mary slipped through the front door, crawled beneath all the windows and dashed to the stables.

'Af'noon, miss.' Daniel the coachman was scrubbing her father's large bay. 'But if you're after a ride, I'm afeared you're to be disappointed.' He cocked his head at the shining, huge carriage which had been rashly purchased without the requisite increase of staff to support it. 'Be no more time for trotting out with you, miss.'

'Then I could go alone . . .'

'And have Sir Edward find out?' He shook his head, and went back to the flank. 'More than my life's worth.'

'And more than mine's worth to stay.' Mary grabbed at his sleeve. 'Daniel, I *beg* you . . . Or I shall simply die of the *boredom*.'

Within minutes, she was out and alone in quite open country. For the first time in weeks, a sense of living returned to her, thrumming through her limbs. And did not Nature feel the same way? Locked away in her apartment, Mary had no notion of spring, but now she saw hedgerows heavy with catkins, shining primrose beneath. She smiled, turned her face to the watery light and relished the prospect of the happiness ahead. Soon her friends would return. The Knight boys would flock back for the summer. How had Miss Cassandra Austen put it? *A new world of green.*

The pale sun was now slipping; the horizon glowed pink. With a start, Mary realised the hour, looked around to see where she was. And – oh! – was not that the castle at Chilham? The crenellations, the flagpole . . . Then, quite without meaning it – by no sort of design – had she not travelled almost to Godmersham . . . ?

With a pull on the reins, she brought the horse to a stop before heading home; she raised her eyes to the vista: saw the silhouette of a dog on the brow of the hill. One could not mistake it: that was Lord Byron! And only then did she notice the human figure beside him. How very odd of young Mr Knight to be here now, when he could be in London. So, still the singular kingfisher, then.

Mary smiled to herself, heard the dog bark, as if calling her name. And, with her heart in her throat, turned the horse around and rode back to Hatch at great speed.

∾

Cassy returned to Kent the following week, and rode over to Hatch at the first opportunity.

'*Darling!*' she shrieked as the two girls embraced. 'I came the minute I could. Did you near die without me?'

'Oh, it has been perfectly hideous. You can have no idea, how—' Mary pulled back and took a good look at her friend. 'I can see London agreed with *you*, madam.' Ever a pretty girl, Cassy was suddenly a young woman at the peak of her bloom.

'Not *without* its diversions, I must confess. So much to *share*—'

With his own, impeccable timing, Dr Knatchbull came into the drawing room and launched into a detailed report of the improvements at Smeeth. 'Though the addition of an orangery may *seem* an expense, however—'

'Sir, do forgive me but I feel rather faint. Do you mind—?' Mary grabbed Cassy's hand and pulled her out of the house to the air.

'Phew.' Her whole being seemed to sigh with relief. 'Here at least *we* can talk. Catholics have the confessional; Knatchbulls the gravel. This is where my parents come when there are *things* to discuss.'

They linked arms and began a tour of the circle.

'And so who was *that*, pray?'

'Oh, *Cass*. Where to begin?' Mary had not dared to mention Dr Knatchbull in her letters – suppose Fanny had learned of it? Only now could she recount the whole, hideous saga. 'And the worst thing is – really, I struggle but I swear it is true – I believe they mean me to *marry him. Uncle* as *husband*! Is that not a scandal?'

But to Mary's astonishment, Cassy showed no surprise. Instead, she said simply: 'So that is the gentleman. In which case, oh dear.'

'You *knew*?'

'Don't shriek! They'll hear.' Cass looked at the house and dragged Mary away from it. 'I shall tell all, but in turn you must *promise* me not to hate Fan. She's a good sort deep down, you know, and wants only the best for you.'

So even a friendship such as theirs could not compete with the Family. In that moment, Mary was returned to her childhood. Once again, she was completely alone.

'I *gather* it's come out of all that flirting with George. I mean, dear sister and all that but she does rather *err* on the side of the cautious. Seems she was watching – eyes in the back of her head, Cakey says – and rather took fright. Scared you might turn into one of those *dangerous women*.'

'Me?' Mary was stunned. 'She cannot possibly think . . . We heard her say it ourselves: I have not once in her hearing said boo to a goose.'

'Darling, you are positively *angelic*. But the poor

woman lives in terror of that husband of hers – forgive me, your dearest papa and all that, but still – she just wants you all tucked up and settled, out of harm's way.'

Mary stopped walking and stared at her friend. 'This is pure insanity and yet you report it as a matter of fact. Am I to think you approve?'

Cassy cried out with a smile: 'Pray, allow me to finish!' and grabbed Mary's arm as she took back to walking. 'Having now *met* said Romeo, I quite accept your learned opinion that good Lady Knatchbull has gone quite staring mad. Of *course* you cannot marry *him*! Heaven forfend! I hereby forbid it. We pledged once, remember? I shall carry you off with me to Ireland, if I must.'

'Ireland? Well, that would be drastic.' Mary laughed, faith returned. 'You are funny, dear.' Then she stopped again, and turned with eyes stretched to their limits. 'Ireland . . . Lord George Hill lives in . . . *Cassy?*'

'He asked! Darling, he actually *asked*. And Papa has consented.'

Reunited in happiness, they clung to each other and sobbed.

∼

In the highest of spirits, Mary swung down to breakfast. 'Good morning, Mama,' she trilled.

Lady Knatchbull sighed into the letter she was reading. 'I am glad *someone* is cheerful.'

After two excellent weeks of parties and sport, Mary was very cheerful indeed. Dr Knatchbull had gone away, fun was returned and with the start of yet another fine day, she was at the top of her tree. Still, one moment with the Mother and she was now thoroughly squashed.

'It seems you are not.' She went to the side and filled up her plate. 'I am sorry to hear it – Ma-*ma*.'

Fanny emitted a longer, even heavier sigh, dropped the paper and turned to her tea. 'More bad news, I'm afraid. Still, I will not blame myself. My father was in charge, after all. No doubt, *had* I been there, this might not have happened but one cannot do *everything*, Mary. Not with a *baby*. The precious *must* be my priority. One's hands are quite full enough.'

'May I ask—'

'Hmm?' Fanny met her eyes for the first time that morning. 'I suppose you shall hear, in the end. The arrangement between Cassy and Lord George Hill. It's all over. Not *our* side, of course. Oh, no! Yet again, we Knights are found wanting. "All charms, and no money," or so says *his mother*. Though it pains me to admit, the fear begins to take root: we are struggling to marry even one of them off. At this rate—'

But she was addressing a quite empty room.

Daniel did not even argue it now. One glance at Mary and he handed over the horse; watched with some horror as they bolted out of the stable.

Once clear of the house, she stopped to bunch up her

skirts. There was no time for side-saddle. She must get to her friend. Oh, poor darling Cassy! That sweet heart must surely break now.

She flew over hedges, thundered across fields and fury – burning, white hot – built in her chest. The names of other such ladies swam into her mind. A roll call of war dead: Marianne, Miss Atkinson; even, there was cause to suspect, Lady Elizabeth Bligh. All of them bewitched and then thwarted. So then can none ever hope to marry for love? Or must they all just surrender to duty, like Fanny?

Iron now entered into her soul.

Mary came to the castle but sailed on straight past. The same silhouette appeared on the brow of the hill at the limit of the Knight estate. Again, he had seen her. Again, he waved and Lord Byron barked out her name.

And this time, she charged straight towards them.

CHAPTER XXIII

'Miss Knatchbull, by what happy chance.' Young Mr Knight lifted his hat; sunbeams danced through that hair as they might dance through a light summer cloud. 'For I was coming for you.' The dear dog bounded around her, expressing his joy.

'Sir.' Mary, close to breathless from the speed of her journey, gasped as she drew up beside him. 'Your sister – how fares your—' With one, practised, dainty manoeuvre designed to protect her own modesty, she swung a leg over the saddle while gripping her skirt and came gently to earth.

'Then I can take it the news has already reached Hatch.'

Even as torment raged through her breast, Mary found, to her shame, that she could still enjoy the display of balletic grace with which he dismounted. In those britches— She cleared her throat, fixed her eyes firmly forward. Each with one hand on their reins, they fell into step and started to walk in the direction of the house. 'Sad to report, Cassy has not left her room since the letter arrived late yesterday evening.' Ned's shoulders drooped, as if he alone bore the weight of the Godmersham world.

'Oh, Mr Knight.' In that moment, his sympathy appeared to her so deep, so true, so tangible almost, that Mary was moved to reach out and stroke it. She took the reins into both hands with a furious grip. 'And when they were both so exceedingly happy . . .'

Ned's demeanour was grim. 'Lord George Hill's fond mother has, I am sure, acted with great sense and pragmatism, but I suspect rather overreacted. While the couple might not have much in the immediate, still they did not face starvation and there remains every reasonable hope that, once the gentleman does inherit, they should live in some style.' He looked up and into the rich blue above, traced the swoop of a hawk on a field yellow with corn. 'Tale old as time. A good parent cares only for status and comfort, with the result that two dearly loved children are condemned into suffering.' He shook his fine head. ''Tis cruel, Miss Knatchbull. Unnecessarily cruel, and I am sorry for it.'

This passionate outburst left Mary astonished, so marked was the contrast with Fanny's response. She was all irritation, he only excellent feeling: so a very *good* sort of gentleman, then. Ah, but had he not also been the victim of an equivalent rejection, and so very recently? Perhaps it was more that the wound smarted him still. She must take pains to remember it.

'And so we find ourselves back once again in the sad but inevitable process of supporting another unfortunate sibling.'

They had arrived at the temple, high on the hill. Beneath was the Godmersham house in its own parkland. In more ordinary times, Mary saw it as a symbol of safety and solidity; now she could think only of the distressed women within it, and was desperate to get to them. But here, quite unaccountably, Ned chose to stop.

'Miss Knatchbull, do look!' he exclaimed in a quite different tone. 'And is that not wonderful? I was here but a half-hour ago, and am sure there was no sign at all. Now—'

Mary followed the lead of his gaze, and saw they were standing hard on the edge of a riot of poppies. '. . . a whole new world of red!' she supplied, though of course he could not know the reference. 'They are right by us, yet I had not even noticed.'

'To them, 'tis but the work of a morning. Madam, one can only marvel at what Nature achieves in the time that Man wantonly squanders.' He took a step forward, bent to peer into a bloom the colour of fresh blood. 'And as you so cleverly put it, the world is painted anew.' A bee hummed as it foraged deep in the petals. 'You immediately came into our minds' – he gave every appearance of addressing the insect – 'as the best person to call on.'

With a start, Mary realised the words might be for her. 'That *I*, sir—'

'Yes, madam.' Coming back to his full height, Ned turned the full force of his blue eyes upon her. 'My father, Marianne and I are all in agreement on the matter. Without your support – your kind friendship – we should find it hard to continue.'

'Indeed?' That Marianne might suggest it came as no sort of surprise; that either Ned or his father would ever think of Mary at all, in any possible connection, was astonishing. 'Well, of course you can count on it. Though it cannot compare to the love of an excellent family, I do like to think of your sister Cassy as my *particular* friend.' Her tone was casual – dismissive – and deliberately so.

For this encounter had come about with such ease, only now could she grasp its full import. The simple fact was that Mary had never – not once in her life – been *alone* with a *gentleman*. And for it to happen right there – on the top of a hill, no other being in sight . . . Her papa would go into conniptions.

And yet, as Ned continued to gaze at her in an intense sort of fashion, Mary felt a strange calm. She had not even blushed, though, of course, she might yet. In the interests of safety, she turned towards Godmersham, clicked her tongue at the horse and resumed her journey.

Later that afternoon, Mary rode gently back home, past the castle at Chilham. Though the sun was now slipping and Mary would be expected at Hatch, the air was too stifling for any great exertion. Anyway, there was much to reflect on and reflection required peace, and she could expect none of that once she was home with the Mother.

Poor Lady Knatchbull. Fanny had been rather satisfied with Cassy's match – to the degree that she could almost ignore the fact that Lord George Hill was Irish. Well, she might have sighed once or twice in Mary's hearing. But it was quite clear that the title more than made up for it. This fresh disappointment was bound to have an adverse effect upon the maternal nerves. Mary's smile turned to a grimace. For when Fanny's equilibrium was disturbed, the whole household knew of it. She slowed the horse even more, and turned her thoughts back to her sad Godmersham friend.

Cassy had still been in her bed when Mary arrived. Pale, of course; pink at the eyes, puffy of cheek. But even while sobbing, she could give a flash of that spirit. 'At least we now know I *have* charms, darling.' She choked into a wet handkerchief. 'Put *that* on my gravestone once I've *died* of my *poverty*.'

Curiously, it was her sister's suffering that seemed to be greater. Marianne's own failed engagement, those long years ago, she had come to accept with a quiet, noble calm. From that day on, she had given every appearance of contentment with her role of dear daughter, sister and aunt upon whom all could rely. So that she should only now show the signs of a true, deep distress—

'Miss Knatchbull!' The deep voice came from behind her. Lord Byron bounced up to her side.

'Oh!' Mary jumped, and then turned. 'Oh, Mr Knight! Oh, do forgive me.' She laid a hand to her breast, hoping to steady her heart. 'You gave me a shock.'

'Then, madam, 'tis for *you* to forgive *me*.' Ned drew up beside her, saw that she trembled and took hold of her reins. 'How foolish – to startle a rider – what on earth was I thinking?' His habitually blithe countenance was shot through with alarm. 'That *I* might ever put you in danger – the idea—'

Such was his agony, Mary cried out to appease him: 'Pray, sir, you are blameless.' Calmer, she smiled. 'I was in my own thoughts – "away in my head" as my great-aunt likes to put it. A bad habit, I fear, formed back in my schooldays.'

'Interesting,' he murmured. 'I did not know—' as if this small fact could be a missing part of some greater collection. He then returned to the moment. 'If you would prefer to be alone on your way back to Hatch, then of course—'

'Mr Knight.' Mary tilted the brim of her straw. 'I would welcome the company.'

And so they proceeded. He maintained control of her horse as well as his own and, with meticulous steering, enabled their riders to travel but inches apart. Such proximity was irregular – Mary had not been led in this fashion since the days of her girlhood – but somehow not exactly objectionable.

An easy silence settled between them. He did not ask for a report on the state of his sisters, nor did she supply one. To even suggest at some superior intimacy would be to stray over her remit. A Knatchbull could never be considered the equal of a Knight, however much their stories might be entwined. At the same time, it would be heartless to speak of anything else. So they simply sank into the heady beauty of a fine summer's evening – drank in the pungent flavours of the nicely warmed hedgerows – and said nothing at all.

They reached the great yew that stood at the edge of the Knatchbull estate and slowed down by the hawthorn.

'And here, madam, we must part.' Mr Knight stopped, as if at the gates of some Forbidden City.

The ride was so lovely that she was already close to intoxicated. Then Ned passed over the reins. His hand touched hers – skin colliding with skin; nerve striking a nerve – and in less than an instant, Mary was completely undone. The spark of connection fired deep in her core. Sensation – strange and unnatural – coursed through her being and beyond all control.

Powerless, she clung to her horse and cast her eyes to the path. Mr Knight spoke again, though the words came to her as from some distant planet. He announced he would leave in the morning, not return before autumn, beseeched that she look after his sister.

In her turn, Mary made a mumbled farewell, tapped the flank of her horse. And cantered towards the safety of home.

CHAPTER XXIV

That summer – the first since her launch – was one long disappointment. It rained for the races. The ball was a poor one. Cassy was darling and brave but, quite understandably, in no sort of mood to have fun; the Knight boys all chose to join their brother in Chawton. Mary went through the motions of the Kent social season, but her mind was brimful of one person alone. And, at last, she understood her own purpose. She had been born to love young Mr Knight. But would he distinguish her by loving her in return? She had left him too suddenly to form any idea. And so by her own cowardice, she was condemned unto turmoil.

Clearly, the stench of distress rose up as a cloud which drifted to Smeeth, for the bluebottle had returned in mid-August. Mary had suspected he might. The Mama still bore the wounds of the Lord George debacle, and it seemed that the only cure she could possibly think of was another match. Nothing too ambitious, mind; no need to frighten the horses. Just a sensible arrangement between two reliable parties. To that end, Fanny returned to Dr Knatchbull's cause with renewed vigour, and took the added precaution of recruiting Sir Edward.

'My dear child,' her father announced at the end of dinner one evening. 'Let us talk.'

When Mary found herself led not into the drawing room as was traditional, but out on to the gravel, she sensed it was ominous. This was very much the parents' preserve.

'It occurs that I have lately omitted to say how very proud of you I am, Mary.'

'Thank you, Papa.'

'A young lady's life is not always easy, I know. Temptations abound; pitfalls lurk in your path. Your dear mother and I are most encouraged to see that you conduct yourself still, as you did as a child, with fine, Christian excellence.'

'I do try, Papa.' So Fanny had not mentioned the flirting, then. That he might ever hear of it! Or discover that she went riding alone, brushed her bare hand against . . . Mary felt herself blush.

'We see it, my dear, and we are pleased. Indeed, if I may for one moment put aside all humility, I feel I can now congratulate myself. Did I not always, from your very first days, stress the importance of your goodness to me?'

'Oh, yes, Papa. You were so clear on the matter that I could never forget it.' They turned once again. Mary was close to dizzy. 'Strait is the gate, and narrow the way . . . The prouder I made you, the better you would love me. That was the gist, I believe.'

'Mary Dorothea!' He stopped and stared at her. 'I never— You are my firstborn! My treasure! You are everything to—'

'Thank you, Papa.' If only he had said that at the time, then how different their histories would have been. With a tight, hidden sigh, Mary led him to walking again.

'To return to my point. It is a comfort to me to know that you have grown into a woman whose head cannot be turned.' And out of nowhere, as if he could not help himself, the roar came upon him. 'One to hold *friendship* higher than *passion*. To favour the *familiar* over the *foreign* . . .' This went on for some time until, seemingly spent, Sir Edward fell into silence and the pair turned yet again.

At last, as if starting a quite different subject, he spoke up. 'Our guest, Dr Knatchbull.'

'My *uncle*, Papa?' she asked, quite demure.

'Come, come. Only a pedant would address him so, surely. We are not of the same *mother*! One must not be *enslaved* to *formality*.'

Mary raised a brow at the gravel. Over the years, she had somehow formed the impression that Sir Edward was formality's friend.

'The gentleman has asked that he might drive you to

Sandgate one day this week. The *seaside*, my dear. A little *excursion*. Such a pleasant idea – I am minded to permit it.' He squeezed her arm with his own. 'It would do you some good.'

There was nothing for it but that Mary should fall victim to another mysterious illness. She kept to her room, doctors were called and leeches applied yet again. From her place on the pillow, she studied the clear, summer skies and, for the first time in her life, longed for the autumn – half agony; half hope.

~

At last, on 11 October 1825, life started anew. More than that, when Mary looked back on it later, she saw it was the day her life truly began.

She had already heard that the Knight family was recently returned to Godmersham, but had no idea if Ned was of the party or if he had remained in Chawton. Mary could hardly ask Fanny, though she might die of not knowing.

So when she went down to dinner that evening, Mary was quite unprepared.

'Ah, my dear.' Fanny was gleaming with pleasure. 'You remember *this* Mr Knight? I am sure you *must* have met at some point, though one could forgive you for struggling to keep track of us all.'

Ned rose and bowed; Mary curtseyed then, rather

shakily, sat. While Sir Edward said grace, she bent her head low and gave every impression of harking his words with the piety of a nun, newly professed. But for once, the prayer was a short one and, before she had truly collected herself, dinner began.

'Something of a red-letter day for us, Mary,' the Mother went on, 'for my brother is come for a dine-and-sleep. Have you ever done so before, Ned? I do believe this is the first. Darling, do say.' Fanny put a hand on his arm. 'What can I possibly have done to *merit* such an *honour?*'

Ned flicked open his napkin and smiled into his wine glass. 'Nothing in particular, Fan. Other than I have decided to stay in Kent from now through to Christmas – the odd matter to *pursue* – *leads* to be followed – and thought it might be my opportunity to enjoy these pleasant surroundings at last.'

Mary's heart danced in her breast as she studied her lap. He had come – might she hope? – could it be that he had come here to court her?

Firmly, he turned to the head of the table. 'Though, sir, I should hate to impose, but my brothers do speak most highly of the shoot you have grown since taking over the estate.'

Sir Edward's enormous capacity for taking offence was outweighed only by his weakness for flattery. And any compliment to his estate in particular had the potential to quite alter his mood. So now, seemingly to his own great surprise as well as that of the company, he went into some detail about drives and stocks and, at the end, appeared almost stunned to hear himself extend a warm welcome.

'Then I look forward to it,' Ned replied earnestly. 'Furthermore, I was wondering – though do say if it is inconvenient – might I accompany you to the Quarter Sessions – watch you at work? As I have hopes of having a similar role soon, in my own county, the opportunity of observing such an *experienced* . . .'

It seemed that he was, in fact, courting her father! Too astonished to eat, Mary put down her fork and returned her gaze to her lap. The two previous dinners these men shared had ended in warfare. Yet this time – she stole a glance from under her lashes – her father was positively purring with pleasure.

'And *Miss* Knatchbull.'

She had no choice but to look up.

'I hope you are well.' His wide eyes met hers, but if there was a message within them she could not read it. 'And have you been able to ride out at all? The weather has not been much on our side.'

Fanny cut in. 'I have secured Mary a rather good *grey*, Ned. And, at my suggestion – I *do* think it *good* for our girls – she rides out, with Daniel of course, early most mornings.' To the table: 'My brother is quite an *exceptional* horseman, you know . . .'

The evening ended early – Sir Edward was tired. And for Mary, the night stretched eternal. The thought of that gentleman under her roof was hardly conducive to rest. Did the Mother say the Green Room? But that was just over the landing! So only two walls between them . . . She was up and dressed soon after eight.

'You *are* better, then,' Booker approved. 'Will you look at that bloom?'

And well before nine, she was saddled up and quite ready. But where should she head?

At a loss for any other alternative, Mary innocently trotted towards the place where they had parted, all those long months ago. Coming now to the limits of the property, she slowed down at the hedgerow now heavy with dark fruit: looked over to the yew at the edge of the property.

And saw, from behind its great boughs, the dear person of Lord Byron emerge.

CHAPTER XXV

That autumn of 1825 was especially clement, as if the weather were blessing them, so that each day, before breakfast, Mary was able to ride out of the stables, cross the low fields still shrouded with mist, head for the high ground of the vast Kentish Downs and trust there to find a sharp, blue-golden morning, full sparkling with promise.

In the first week or two, she had taken good care to stick to the paths around the Knatchbull estate – the edge of the woods or the far side of the lake: the places where she might reasonably expect to be found, should some-one come looking. But as that someone did come, every day – without failing her once – Mary grew ever more daring. Her routes became random, confusing: a puzzle to solve, the course of a hunt. But, though she might cast herself as the quarry, still – oh! – how she longed every day to be caught.

One Thursday, towards the close of October, Mary was halfway to Brabourne and beginning to worry that, this time, she might have gone just a little too far. But Ned Knight was a true sportsman and Lord Byron a fine hound. They would brook no defeat and suddenly – from a soundless approach – he was right there beside her, tilting his hat while the dog barked out their victory. Though she concealed it, joy flooded her breast; pleasure danced in his eyes, but he made no pretty speech. Instead, as they did every morning, both of them laughed: he at his triumph in finding her, she with the pleasure of being, once again, found.

Without any discussion, they turned away from the busy village towards wide, empty country, settled into an easy pace and a comfortable silence. This was not unusual. Some mornings they talked, joked, amused one another with foolish games – for all his masculine swagger, Mr Knight could be as restlessly playful as a seven-year-old boy. On others, though, barely a word was exchanged and, curiously, Mary treasured the quiet encounters as much as the other. Having become so used to forced, social intercourse and stupid flirtation, she found the release from those evils a revelation indeed. They were now climbing to the ridge, where the pale moon weakly loitered as a marmalade sun rose. And while her companion hummed with a peaceful contentment, Mary marvelled at how composed she could be while in his dear company.

Of course, she well understood that it was all due to Mr Knight's extraordinary confidence. That quality, lately despised by Sir Edward, was what Mary so richly admired. And such was its strength, was it not even contagious? Up to this moment, she had been too easily influenced by the behaviour of others: allowed the edges of her character to be buffeted by the strong winds of personalities bigger than her own. So she could be quietly pious when met by her father, plain sullen when Fanny was present, frankly silly with Cassy – when, in truth, she was none of those things. Now at last, out in the country with Ned by her side – whether they spoke perfectly frankly or spoke not at all – Mary Knatchbull could take her first, hesitant steps on the path to discovery of her own natural self.

'Oh, do look!' she exclaimed now as they came to an old beech upon which was stretched a great canopy of lace from the bough to the trunk. Shafts of sun turned the dewdrops to diamonds. 'I know we must love the summer, but is not this in fact the loveliest season of them all?'

'A pretty enough sight, I will grant you. But as for the autumn, I cannot agree.' Already he was riding on past it, head set firmly forward. The air was quite still, yet about him was turbulence. Mary studied his back, mystified. Surely her observation was perfectly harmless. How could Ned, of all people, have taken offence?

In the past, or if out with another, Mary might have held back, stewed in mortification and let the incident go unremarked. This time, she galloped to reach him and demanded he explain.

'Forgive me.' He sighed. 'I am not, as I hope you now know, one troubled by mere *mood*. Emotion, on the other hand . . .' He slackened the reins then, and fixed his eyes on the distance. '*Emotion* I am slave to. It was in this very month, back in 1808, that our dear mother was taken and, though it does not speak well of me, I find myself unable to forgive it. That October still dares to flaunt itself, year upon year – revive its great beauty while hers remains lost – strikes me as a heartless parade of—'

'I quite understand,' Mary cut in and, without any rehearsal, heard herself add: 'I do wish I had known the pleasure of meeting your mother, sir.'

Ned stopped his horse then. Mary, a few paces ahead, did the same, turned and saw that he stared at her now with a new depth of expression. In fact, was that a tear in his eye?

'What a – that is—' He gathered himself, cleared his throat and began anew. 'I am so moved to hear it, Miss Knatchbull. And may I ask why?'

This time, Mary thought before speaking; she wondered, had she plunged in too far? Perhaps there were still places their conversation was not ready to go. Well, if so, then when better to test it? 'I think of her sometimes,' she said simply. 'I did not know the lady, have heard little about her and yet she does come into my mind.' She gave

a small shrug. 'I suppose there can be but one explanation. That is: she brought into the world many excellent
children whom I now hold very dear.'

He raised his brows in enquiry; Mary dropped her eyes
to the saddle, felt herself blush. This could only end in
something close to flirtation, which she had vowed to
avoid. So instead, she mumbled about Cassy, Marianne
and George; even – this *was* desperation! – Fanny's name
found its way on to the list. And when finally she faced
Ned again, she was blessed with the sweet, crooked smile
that reached into her heart.

⁓

Not a soul knew of these morning meetings, save Daniel
the coachman and he could be trusted – were Sir Edward
even to suspect any collusion, the poor man would face
certain dismissal. Fanny was entirely taken up with her
precious firstborn and had already started another. The
stepchildren, whom she had always found to be more
trial than pleasure, were now almost forgotten. So when
Mary breezed down to the hall early on the following
Tuesday, it was a shock to find Lady Knatchbull up,
dressed and firmly positioned in front of the door.

'Good morning . . .' In her absolute fury, Mary hit out
with a rest the entire length of a semibreve in the slowest
pavane. '. . . Ma-*ma*.'

'There will be no riding today.' Fanny was pale, plump

and thoroughly bad-tempered. 'It is truly outrageous to take up all Daniel's time. He has plenty of work with the new coach-and-four which, *as you well know*, is your dear father's proudest possession. It must not be compromised, Mary. I shall not have it.'

'But of course,' Mary replied, without any edge of apology. 'The *conveyance* must come first at all times, I completely agree.' She moved as if to take off her cloak, and sighed. 'And pray do not worry, Mama. I am quite sure my health will not suffer unduly. Perhaps you have noticed that I have not taken ill even once this autumn? Booker puts it entirely down to the riding . . . Still, we will just have to trust it to continue, I suppose. Certainly, it would pain me to cause *you* any more inconvenience, dearest Mama, with you being *indifferent*—'

'Oh very well.' Lady Knatchbull was starting to look rather green. 'See if Norton will take you. I am returning to bed.'

'I say, but you ladies have the hell of a life,' Norton grumbled, quite amiably, as they trotted towards Brook a half-hour later. 'It's quite the revelation. All these years of hateful separation and it turns out I don't know the first thing about you, old girl. Look at the seat on you! Had no idea. Is this what you were doing all day, while I was locked up in that prison in fear of my life?'

'Come, come, dear,' Mary laughed. 'I refuse to believe that Winchester College was so very bad. You seem to have survived it.'

'By the skin of my teeth. Thank God it's now over. Enemies the lot of them – boys on the one flank, dons on the other. They were all out to get me, you know.'

'*Really?* Yet, at the same time, they seemed quite keen to see the back of you. Did not the Master write to Papa and *beg* that you not be returned?'

Norton roared at her then – he was turning into Sir Edward – lunged at her shoulder and made her horse bolt. Screaming with laughter, Mary charged around the wood with her brother in hot pursuit. At which point, Ned made his appearance.

'Good morning, sir!' Norton sharply drew up his horse. 'A *pleasure* and, what's more, a coincidence! You are some miles from Godmersham. Might you be calling on our mother? I fear she is not at her best . . .'

Mr Knight had kept the promise he had made to Mary all those long years ago, and kept a kindly eye on her brother throughout his unhappy schooldays. His reward was that Norton now worshipped him as a hero, and in meeting him now could hardly contain himself. He started to jabber, nineteen to the dozen, about shooting and hunting and his new glorious freedom, until Mary felt it only humane to put the boy out of his misery. Politely, she cleared her throat.

'Do forgive me!' Norton finally collected himself. 'I am

sure, sir, you must know my sister – but of course you must – what can I be thinking?'

There was nothing else for it, so the couple just laughed.

'Oh!' said Norton; then, as he looked from one to the other: '*Oh?*' he repeated, before letting his mouth hang wide open.

'Why don't you take out that new gun of yours, old chap?' Ned put a friendly hand on his arm. 'I was just over at Hinxhill. Knee deep in rabbits. Excellent practice.'

Norton hesitated; turned back to his sister.

'Darling, don't look so worried!' Mary reassured him with a smile. 'This isn't a kidnapping. Mr Knight has very kindly been – er – *helping* with my riding. But still, Norton, you wouldn't . . . ?'

'What, tell 'em?' Norton retorted. 'Course not.' And with a comradely wink to the gentleman, he rode away and they were alone.

∽

Since the subject was first breached, their late mothers came often into their conversation and – as if the poor ladies themselves were the keys to two secret chambers – their relationship deepened accordingly. That morning – prompted by the appearance of Norton, and Ned's concerned enquiries for how he had suffered back in his boyhood – they at last came to discuss the awesome moments of loss.

At several intervals, Mr Knight's voice broke as he

described how he was at Winchester when the tragedy occurred. That he had entirely missed his precious mother's last month on this earth was still the cause of great bitterness. And as for the moment at which an uncle appeared to deliver the news: the reins trembled in his hands as he recalled it.

Mary, whose own experience was quite strikingly similar, could not help but be deeply moved. 'And then you were brought back to Godmersham.' This was more statement than question, for surely a family such as his must have done the right thing.

'At the time, that was not thought to be practical and, in fact, for *that* I can hold no resentment. Instead, I had the great fortune of being taken in for some days by my Grandmother Austen and younger aunt. I shall never forget the sympathy, love . . . and really rather remarkable intelligence they brought to the awkward business of my terrible grief.'

'Ah,' Mary exclaimed, with something quite close to envy, though that was hardly appropriate. 'Fortune indeed! Having met one of those ladies, I can imagine no better company in circumstances so vile. As for the other, I presume here you talk of your late aunt – she who wrote the delightful novels?'

Thus far – despite the beauty of the Weald all about them; the crisp clarity of that particular day – they had proceeded buried beneath a cloak of dull and dark misery. Now, as if the identity of Jane Austen were the spell in a magic trick, that was quite ripped away.

'You are an admirer then, madam?' Ned turned to her sharply, damp eyes now bright, face pink with pleasure.

'But of course!' Mary laughed, for who on this earth would not be? 'I have read every one and return to them often. It was my old governess who first introduced me – perhaps you remember Miss Atkinson?'

'Ah, yes.' Ned shook his head. 'Poor Miss Atkinson. That was another bad business. I remember thinking at the time that had my Aunt Jane been still with us then, she might have shown the lady a little more sympathy than our combined families . . .' He sighed, paused – as if in solemn remembrance of the fallen – before, with the ease of one so at home in his own present, snapping back into life. 'And I can have no doubt that Lady Knatchbull, too, has encouraged that particular literary interest?'

'Oh.' How very odd. 'In fact, she has not.' The omission had not struck Mary before. 'Indeed, I had no idea of any connection between you until Cassy claimed the lady as your own.'

Ned stopped his horse and seemed stunned, in sheer disbelief. '*Fanny* had no cause to *mention* it? That I struggle to— Of course, you speak only the truth, but then is that not *bizarre*? I have a very clear memory that she and my aunt were particularly close.'

Now, Mary too was surprised. Having formed such a strong image of the *writer*, it was hard to imagine that she might find much in Lady Knatchbull to please her.

'Your mother does read with you, though, surely?' He

started to ride again. 'By the fireside, in the evening – the family circle: that is an established Austen tradition.'

'Oh, yes!' Mary conceded, while her eyes followed the sway of the horse. 'I cannot say that many *novels* could ever meet with my dear *father's* approval, but in his long absences, then your *sister*' – the word 'mother' felt quite inappropriate, in so many ways – 'then your sister will reach for a book. Lately, we have been enjoying *Discipline* – do not laugh! It is not quite as dull as it sounds. Otherwise, she is *particularly* fond of the works of Sir Walter Scott.'

'Humph,' Ned expostulated, before adding, 'well, *well*. Scott above Austen, eh? That is not without its significance.' He turned around a sapling bent down by the breeze. 'Marriage, Miss Knatchbull, 'tis an extraordinary stuff. Some thrive within it completely intact, while others are utterly changed. We must take good care, you and I both. Good care, indeed.'

They had begun their descent back to Hatch and their breakfast.

'We must not have that happening to *us* when it is our turn to be settled.'

~

Norton relished his part in the young couple's secret. He thought of Hatch not as a home – he had spent too little time there for that – but rather as the scene of an unending battle between children and parents. So on those

terms, when he escorted his sister out every morning –
enabling her escape – he was in his mind engaged in some
great act of valour.

Some days her brother stayed with them; their outings
were vigorous and sporting and amused them all equally.
For the rest, though, he was content to politely withdraw
and then, in relief, they were free to talk more.

'So you, too, were at school when your own mother
was taken? And yet so many years younger than I!' Ned
ran an agitated hand through his already wild hair and
ruffled it yet further. 'Then, madam, your suffering
was more acute still . . . I take it, though, that *you* were
brought home at once?'

Mary had to think deeply before she replied. It was
vital that she present the facts in the best possible light –
not only to save her good father from any unfair opprobrium, but also to spare herself. She had only rarely
before discussed the subject, and each time the listener's
pity had made her feel oddly pathetic – as if she were no
more than a victim of Sir Edward's cruelty, rather than
the great light of his life, which was the image she rather
preferred.

So she proceeded to convey, with the most earnest
sympathy, her father's great love for her mother and the
difficulties he faced, with six, then sadly five, motherless
infants, and – unlike the Austens – no loving family to help
and support him. 'He would have thought me to be safe
there at school, with its solid routine and my sweet little

friends . . .' Now almost adrift from the truth, Mary found she could no longer continue and took refuge in silence.

A fine rain started falling; dark clouds threatened worse. For protection, Ned guided her into the woods where once-bright morning was now gloaming like dusk.

'You are very loyal to Sir Edward.' Hooves clipped over acorns which cracked furiously at their weight, but Ned's voice was gentle.

'He is my only parent! How could I be otherwise?' Mary refused to be pitied! She would not allow it! 'It is *my duty* to love and support him.'

'And his to you, I dare say?' Ned plucked the fruit from a horse chestnut and lobbed it into a far bough. A twig fell to the ground.

'But of course. I am his firstborn! His only daught—' She shrugged then, suddenly helpless. 'That is, I *was* for many long years.'

'He is clearly a gentleman who *demands* – no, that is unfair – perhaps *inspires* loyalty in others. We have all noticed *that* with our dear Lady Knatchbull. Mind you, Fan always did have it in her – the best of us, in her way – but still, it does sometimes occur to one she can be loyal to a fault.'

Mary was tiring of this conversation. Defending herself was one thing; to mount a defence of the Mother was a whole new experience. Still, she was out on a limb now, and so she said wearily: 'He is her husband! What would you expect?'

Though the trees were still dripping, it seemed that the rain had abated. They started to head through the wood to the village beyond.

'I think,' Ned announced as they came to the clearing, 'when *I* am wed, I should prefer to aim for something more like equality.'

'Oh, Mr Knight!' All discomfort forgotten, Mary now laughed aloud. She might be bedazzled, but she was far from a fool. 'A fine word, that: *equality*. I have heard gentlemen use it before even at my own father's table. But how can he or you – or any man of *your* sex and *your* class – even *begin* to imagine what it might entail?' Ned began to protest, but she held up her hand to forbid it. 'We ladies talk of it too, by the way. Are we not the ones who might have more to gain? Yet, for us as for you, we might as well be discussing the topography of the Heavenly Kingdom itself . . . We have no earthly idea.'

'Still,' Ned insisted. For all the talk of equality, Mary saw that he did not enjoy being challenged. 'I should like to think that I might be permitted the *ambition* at least. To be a fair husband and a kind, loving father: these are not trifles, Miss Knatchbull, whatever experience may have taught you. To my mind, *there* is the very foundation of a good Christian life. The qualities by which Our Lord Almighty will one day come to judge us, when we reach that very place.'

They had emerged by the blacksmith's and it was time now to part. Despite the tone of their meeting – their first almost-dispute – Mary found she was smiling as she rode back to the stables. For was it her own, soft imagining or had his words not sounded almost as if he was drafting a contract?

If only she had thought to bring with her a pen.

CHAPTER XXVI

With both Daniel and Norton in on the secret – and Booker, too, having formed some idea – Mary felt horribly guilty that Cassy was still in the dark.

Of course, Mary could hardly tell her. Supposing, just supposing, it was all in her mind? For even as the weeks went on, and their ritual continued, still she must question it. After all, Ned *did* like to ride and was famously fond of the country about Hatch. He craved company in general, and she was always available while others were busy . . . But then, she would catch him studying her at dinner while her father opined, and see the warmth of his eyes in the candlelight . . .

It was to Mary's benefit, if not her dear friend's, that Cassy was often preoccupied. Since the moment of the Lord George disaster, Fanny had at once cast the poor girl into the role of useful spinster and set her to work, so that when Mary did visit Godmersham, she would most likely find Cassy sorting the china cupboard or up to her elbows in linen or away altogether, helping out in the Married One's nursery. Come Christmas, however, the Knights and the Knatchbulls were often combined. And it was then that Cassy started to guess that something was afoot.

On 29 December, as they were dressing together for the Ashford Ball, she mused into the glass, as if they had been mid-conversation: 'My point is, Mary, though you have *long* been pretty enough to be almost *annoying*, I have found it in my heart to forgive you, for *I* am essentially *kind*. But I must say – thank you, Lane' – Cassy tipped her head to the side to examine the chignon – 'I suppose I shall *do*.' She turned to the bed upon which Mary sat, ready. 'I must say that, all of a sudden, you are starting to take things to a somewhat unfortunate *extreme*. Stand up! Let me look at you.'

Mary obeyed, smoothed down the white Chantilly on her skirt, and issued a twirl.

'Well, quite. Absolutely outrageous. I shall not be standing anywhere near *you*, that you can count on.' Cassy rose up to standing, a sweet vision in pink. 'It is simply not *fair*.'

'You are divine, darling.' Mary gave her a tentative hug – neither girl wanted to disturb her own dress – and Cassy softened at once.

'Of course, it is love,' Cassy began, almost casually, as she gathered her fan and squashed a scent bottle into her reticule. 'That is what *everyone* says, and one is forced to agree. There is not a lady on *earth* who can look quite so *enchanting* without an *ardent* admirer as the cause of it. It is just nature's way. No need to speak!' She flounced a little too dramatically. 'I know you shan't tell me. I must discover it myself.'

~

The ball was a late one – they were out till past three – so the next day, both families laid low in their own houses. It was New Year's Eve when Mary was brought back to Godmersham. She went at once to find Cassy up in her room. The gentlemen were out shooting and the girls had agreed to start work on their costumes for the Twelfth Night Masquerade. Mary was much looking forward to it and keen to share her ideas.

'I rather think we should try the Tudor style,' she began in her excitement, even as she walked through the door. '*You* in a crimson and – Cass! Is something the matter?'

Cassy stayed in the armchair, hands in her lap, and raised one pretty, dark eyebrow. 'I *know*.'

Mary tried to dissemble. 'Know what, dearest? I can't think what you mean.'

'We will have no more of that, thank you. I fear you are *rumbled*. Do you think I learned *nothing* from all those romances we used to devour? Excuse *me*, but *I* am an expert. I knew what to look for and saw it at once. You danced with George for half of the night!'

'*George?*' Mary fell on the bed and burst into laughter. 'Of course he is a darling but I *promise* you, Cass' – she made the sign of the cross – 'I am *not* in love with George!'

'I know that, you fool.' Cassy laughed then, too, and went over to embrace her. 'There is nothing between you two, as there is nothing between you and any of the other poor swains who took you on to the floor. There was just one who did not even dare ask. Who kept well away . . . And *that* gentleman is—'

A knock came on the door, and Marianne put her head round. 'Ah, there you are, Mary. I thought I should find you here. I come with a message.' Her expression was puzzled. 'Our brother has asked if you might meet him down in the orangery?'

Cassy gave a great whoop of triumph; Mary became flustered.

'There must be some mistake, Marianne. They are all out on the shoot . . .'

'Ned stayed behind,' Marianne explained, matter-of-fact. 'Most unlike him to miss it, I completely agree. Yet miss it he has . . . Shall you go to him or shall I—'

But with a loud cry of 'Happy New Year, darling!' Cassy had already pushed her out through the door.

~

Mary found Ned pacing across the black-and-white chequered floor. Candlelight danced in the mirrors. A fine fire roared in the grate. He turned as she slipped through the long door – that smooth, lovely face contorted with agony. She walked slowly towards him.

'You came,' he sighed, and his whole being relaxed.

So somehow he had doubted her? He too had suffered uncertainty? The insight astonished her. So, in this, they *were* equals!

'It is time that I spoke. Our – this – *friendship* between us has become something more to me, and it would be unfair to continue it further without my declaration.

'Miss Knatchbull – my dear, *dearest* friend – you have become, quite without any design on my own part, most precious to me. Should you not feel the same, pray believe I shall at once go back into Hampshire and bother you no longer.

'But first I must say that I love you, most deeply – have loved you, I think, since the spring.'

How long had Mary waited! How much could her heart take? And yet, e'en still, her wretched mind could only be rational: was that not indecently soon after Lady Elizabeth Bligh turned him down?

'Dare I now ask if you might feel the same?'

Mary wanted to laugh. How could he not know! 'Oh, yes, sir. I do. I love you completely. And if you would like me, too, to declare for exactly how long, well then.' She looked up at him, beaming. 'I do believe I can date it back to that day in the summer but last. When I first laid my poor eyes upon the glories of Chawton.'

'You beast!' He grabbed at her wrists then. The first time they had touched since his hand had brushed hers. She shivered. 'You wretch! I don't know whether to marry you or box your ears.'

'On balance, sir,' she replied prettily, 'I think I might opt for the former.'

'Then marry me, I pray you! Put us both out of this misery!'

And there, it was done. Mary had defied the rules of all romantic novels! She had found the love of her life, her heart was intact and no obstacles stood in her path! The future lay out before them, bright as a midsummer day. They both laughed in their joy. His hands moved to her waist; sweet lips then found hers. A great heat – a wildfire – shot through to her core. Fireworks exploded through her mind and her soul.

And though now she should be somewhere far, far beyond any form of rational thought, still the words came to her:

So this was it. *This* was electricity!

CHAPTER XXVII

Fanny sat, content and alone, in the Godmersham library, secure in the knowledge that all of her loved ones were in pursuit of good, wholesome interests elsewhere. Sir Edward and Mr Austen Knight were in Canterbury for a Church meeting, the boys off with their guns and the girls at work on their costumes. What a splendid feeling it was to have all of one's ducks in a row, for a change! Oh, no doubt they would all reappear soon, as the light started to wane and the temperature dropped, and bring in their noise and their antics. But for now, she intended to relish her peace and indulge in a moment's reflection on the year they were now leaving behind them.

All told, 1825 had been rather an odd one, bringing as it had both extraordinary joy as well as worry and considerable unease. And now, as she looked back, Fanny could not say she had borne it all as well as she might have. Of course, most of her energies had been consumed by her first, darling baby – the light of her life; the saving grace. Perhaps it was simply the inevitable exhaustion that made her so cross about everything else?

For instance, that ghastly business of Lady Elizabeth Bligh refusing dear Ned: why had Fanny made such a fuss about that? It was her brother's embarrassment, surely, not hers. But of course, as was her way, she had felt somehow responsible, and let herself in for unnecessary upset.

And then William's marriage to the Portal girl – that too had gone badly, but why? After all, the boy *was* told to drop the governess and go off and find a rich girl. Yet, as soon as he did so, the Knatchbulls suddenly decided they could not approve her. Had she and Sir Edward behaved poorly? Might others perhaps have seen them as snobbish? After all, the Knights found no quarrel with the lady. Fanny paused for a moment to allow a brisk frisson of guilt.

Furthermore, in the privacy of that armchair, Fanny did have to admit that, while embracing her new role as a mother, she might have *slightly* neglected her younger stepsons. Were they happy at school? Did they mind frightfully when, in the holidays, they were packed off to relations? She could not rightly say, but made a mental note to kindly enquire the next time she saw them.

Fortunately, when it came to Mary Dorothea, Fanny need have no such concerns. The girl had been with them in Hatch for some months and conducted herself well:

calling on all the right people, doing good works in the village . . . Although Fanny must admit her monitoring might not err on the side of *obsessive*, she had the comfort of knowing there was no need for it. Whatever others might say to the contrary, Fanny knew, in her heart, that poor Mary was essentially a bland, good little creature. And one who would be, soon enough, tucked away with Dr Knatchbull in Smeeth – an excellent arrangement that would, in time, relieve Fanny of much effort and worry.

The sound of a carriage at the front door interrupted her thoughts. Ah, that must be the menfolk returning from their meeting. Give them a moment to change out of their things before calling for tea . . . Until then, Fanny would resume her review.

After one health issue, then another – the boy was uncommonly prone to accidents – poor Norton had left school altogether, returning to Hatch and his role as yet another cross for Fanny to bear. Dear oh dear, where would *that* saga end? she wondered. He was simply one of those *difficult* creatures. Might he take after Sir Edward's father? She shuddered, sighed and treated herself to a change of subject.

The weather in the autumn had been uncommonly wet—

There suddenly came the most terrible roar. Fanny tilted her head. Could that be *Sir Edward*? She supposed that it must. Her papa almost never raised his dear voice. *Now* what had happened? She sat up, preparing to rise and go and investigate. Then, with equal suddenness, peace reigned once more.

Fanny sat back, and considered the unfortunate mortality rate among sheep and oxen. And it had been a bad year for hops too, had it not? As for the banking system—

The door was flung open and banged back against the wall.

'*Lady Knatchbull!*' This was loud even by Sir Edward's own, very high standards.

'My dear?' Fanny was up and out of her seat. 'You are upset! What on earth is the matter?'

'Collect your things and bring Mary Dorothea. We are returning to Hatch this very instant. Daniel is waiting. There is not a minute to waste.'

'But why, dearest . . . ?' She rushed to his side and took his hand. 'Pray, surely, you owe me a reason . . .' And she had been so looking forward to a Godmersham family dinner.

Sir Edward staggered to the nearest chair, fell into it and buried his face in his arms. All strength seemed to have left his excellent body.

'My dear.' Sir Edward looked up at his wife. 'I beg you.' His dear face was collapsed into itself with sorrow. 'Now. Let us go.'

~

By the time their wheels cut the gravel, the day was well into its twilight. With a gloved finger, Fanny peeled back a corner of damask curtain and saw fields glistening with cold; a new surface of ice at the edge of the river; a white moon rising in a navy blue sky. The atmosphere inside the carriage was colder still.

Fanny studied the girl sitting opposite. Although Mary had a right to feel put out, or shocked, at being forced to leave Godmersham early – she should even now be preparing for yet another party that evening; Fanny could see through the gap in her cloak that she was already dressed in her gown – in fact Mary seemed not entirely unhappy. Was she blushing indeed? Surely not. Anyway the light was going, so Fanny could not rightly decide.

Her husband's mood, on the other hand, was quite easy to read. He was breathing loudly and heavily, shoulders rising and falling with each long respiration: a bull in the ring. Occasionally, a growl was emitted, with the shake of a head. To sum up, the demeanours of her fellow passengers could not be more different. But still, neither was speaking. Fanny could bear it no longer.

'My dears,' she began. 'I fear I am at a considerable disadvantage. Clearly something has occurred, and only *I* know not what. Might *one* of you be so kind as to shed light on the mystery?'

'Your *brother*.' Sir Edward almost spat the word – sent it out drenched with contempt.

'Oh dear.' Fanny felt suddenly sick. 'Which . . . ?' she asked, nervously. There were six, after all, and, in truth, her kindest of husbands did not have a good word for any.

Sir Edward tried to reply, but Fanny could not quite hear him. He tried again: still indistinct. So she put her head close to his mouth – as if hoping for the last words from one on his deathbed – and caught something that sounded a little like '*Ned*'.

But that could not be correct . . .

'Husband.' She put a hand on his forehead to check for a fever, and spoke with a soothing tone. '*Ned* cannot have been getting into *mischief*! He has been the whole day with the shoot.'

At that, Sir Edward lifted his face and looked at his wife with an expression of pure misery. 'No. No, he has not, my dear, I am sorry to tell you. The shoot was no more than a vile deceit.

'Your other brothers were out, certainly. *They* can be trusted, on this matter at least. But that rogue' – he clenched both his fists – 'the absolute *villain* . . .' He was looking out of the window now, and into the distance. 'Oh, yes. *He* had lined up for himself another, better amusement . . .

'. . . in the *orangery*, if you please.' His voice rose up to its strongest roar possible. '*Asking Mary Dorothea for her hand.*'

Fanny stared at her husband: open-mouthed; stunned. She knew nothing – absolutely nothing at all – of even a friendship between them.

She turned to face Mary. 'And, pray, what was your answer?'

The girl merely sat, immobile, and stared into her lap.

'*What was her answer?*' Sir Edward repeated, contemptuous. Both ladies flinched. Fanny had never previously known him quite so excitable. 'What does *that* matter? *Her answer, indeed.* It is what *I* say that counts. And *I* say—'

Fanny put a hand on his arm to stop him. 'I think we can all gather, my dear. But still, if you don't mind – and though they may be purely academic – I would like to hear our daughter's thoughts, too.'

Mary did lift her eyes then and seemed to be forming some sort of reply, but Sir Edward was having none of it.

'Lady Knatchbull!' her husband demanded. 'I pray you *desist!*'

And they were all silent for the rest of the journey.

Once back at Hatch, Fanny rushed like a madwoman straight to the children's wing; ran down the passage to the door of the nursery; then slowed and, holding her breath, approached the cradle and feasted her eyes.

As ever, her darling Fanny Elizabeth – the name was Sir Edward's suggestion; she had been so very touched – slept like an angel: a perfect rosebud embedded in lace. Just the sight of her, after one night away, was enough to bring tears to the bewitched mother's eyes. Lady Knatchbull was fond of all of her stepchildren, of course she was. Even though they brought with them no end of problems and caused so much concern, she loved them. She was sure of it.

But somehow, she could not help but love her own just that little bit more.

~

It was not until late in the evening that Sir Edward was, at last, able to speak and inform Fanny of what had transpired. Though it hardly seemed credible, it appeared that her dear husband had returned from his meeting, no doubt exhausted – his many great duties did *drain* the poor man to the most *dreadful* degree. And, at the very moment of his return, he had been met by a clearly deranged Ned and his extraordinary request.

Although her husband had already turned her brother down flat and the matter was over, still he wanted to discuss it with – or rather vent his feelings to – Fanny on their return home. So, of course, it was late when at last he took to his own room, in which he continued to audibly rage through what remained of the night. And by that point, Fanny's distress was so great that there was not a wink of sleep to be had.

Once alone and able to think a little more clearly, Fanny had come to the uncomfortable conclusion that there were but two explanations for this highest of dramas: either her brother was, as Sir Edward suggested, stark, staring mad, or she – who had certainly *endeavoured* to be the most assiduous of mothers – had somehow managed to miss a brewing affair. And, though one should generally guard against being too solipsistic, it must still be acknowledged that neither boded well for Fanny herself.

After all, her whole world revolved around two immoveable features: the Knights and the Knatchbulls; her two guiding stars. It was essential to her own happiness that harmony between them was maintained. But could that now be flung into jeopardy?

On the one hand, Sir Edward, though so loving to his own wife, certainly – and regrettably – had doubts about her many siblings and might easily blame them for this unaccountable change in his own daughter's character. On the other, whether Ned was a lunatic or pursuing a love match, she could quite see her brothers taking his side. In which case, the relationship between the families would quickly degenerate, leaving Fanny on bad terms with each. It really did have the potential to be most disagreeable.

What an unfortunate start to the New Year. She could only pray that the worst was behind her.

CHAPTER XXVIII

The next morning, the first day of January 1826, Fanny was alone in the breakfast room when the footman announced 'Mr Austen Knight'.

'Oh, *dear* good Papa.' With a clatter, Fanny dropped dish upon saucer. 'As you might well expect, you find us all in a deep state of shock and the most terrible *anguish*. My poor husband is suffering acutely, and I might add that I too feel more than a little *aggrieved*. What on this *earth* can have *given* Ned *such* a *dreadful* idea – mere *folly*, would you say, or has my brother quite lost his senses?' She shook her head in despair. 'Though, of course, it is Ned himself who should be *begging* forgiveness, I very much doubt that Sir Edward would see him. Still – he is out walking at the moment – my husband will take some comfort from knowing that *you*, dearest, have come in his place.'

She issued a kind smile – for Fanny had long held the role of family pacifist – signalled the muffins and passed the preserves. But her father, never before known to refuse any sweetmeat, refused this with a show of the flat of his hand.

'My dear Fan,' he began, more puzzled than stern, 'we seem to be speaking somewhat at cross purposes. I am not here to apologise, rather to make the case for the match.'

'The *case*?' Fanny felt the first stirrings of fear.

But her father's attention had turned back to the breakfast. 'Oh, perhaps I might indulge in a morsel. A crisis always gives one an appetite, do you not find?' All comforts established, Mr Austen Knight sat back in his chair, took a mouthful and stared out of the window. 'Fanny.' He coughed. 'My *dear*.' He put down the plate and gathered his strength. 'Clearly, the manner of last evening's proposal did not go as well as it ought. It seems Sir Edward feels very strongly that Ned should have sought his permission first. Ned now sees that, regrets it and has, quite rightly, apologised.'

'Well, that is *something*,' Fanny had to concede. 'Though I still cannot quite understand what exactly—'

But her papa was not listening, appearing intent on his own speech rather than any discussion. 'However, to deprive this good couple of happiness on a mere point of formality would be an injustice.'

Couple? Happiness? Then – oh – may the Good Lord

protect her! Fanny had quite settled on lunacy as her preferred explanation. After all, one had recourse to doctors
and treatments. But *love* – especially that of the wild and
romantic variety . . . Here, love was the much greater
evil. Cold dread ran through her veins.

Her father pressed on. 'We in Godmersham – Ned's
side, so to speak – find the Hatch view a little short-
sighted and hard to comprehend. If you will indulge
me for a moment, let us examine it, minutely. In Ned' –
he pointed to a large ginger jar on the side table, most
likely Ming – 'we have a good-looking gentleman from
an impeccable family, heir to an *excellent* estate – who, up
to this instance, has charmed every parent in every fine
drawing room up and down this great land.'

Fanny could hardly quarrel with that. She adored her
dear brother and took great pride in her own, happy
heritage; some of the things her husband had said last
evening – well, she had found them rather hurtful. Of
course, she had said nothing then, and she would say
nothing now.

In the uncomfortable silence, her father helped himself to a second muffin, dabbed with a napkin, and then
resumed.

'And in Mary Dorothea' – signalling a fruit dish of
rich coloured glass; possibly Venetian – 'we have a good-
looking lady from a . . . a . . . *good* family, brought up to
live as the chatelaine of an excellent estate.'

Fanny bridled. That was hardly a generous comparison.

She had no memory of any such slight when her father was marrying *her* off to the Knatchbulls. Had she really been such a poor, desperate case? Once again, her feelings were hurt.

'I must say, were they characters in a novel by your dear Aunt Jane . . . In fact, no! Your Aunt Jane would not have troubled herself to invent such a couple. For so impossible is it to think of any objection that they would be wed by page two and that would be that.'

Now, argue she must. This nonsense had to be stopped. 'If I may, Papa, you seem to be forgetting one rather salient point. And that is there is no relationship between them to speak of! Ned and Mary *may* have seen each other about the place, certainly. Indeed, as you know, he has stayed with *me* a lot, of late.' Or had he not been there for Fanny at all? It could not be true! She would not allow it! 'However, they have shared no conversation, spent no hours alone . . . They are effectively strangers!'

Yet even as she spoke so very emphatically, Fanny could quite see the reverse might be true. It had been a difficult few months. Had she not been closeted away with her own darling baby? Had one's *hands* not been unusually *full*?

'Well, this is peculiar.' Her father now looked quite bemused. 'Ned has assured me of a very deep friendship. And your sisters have all confirmed it to be genuine.'

The couple was in love . . . the girls were all in on the secret . . . and she had been excluded. It was as if Fanny were caught in a nightmare. She fought back the tears, gathered herself, sighed – and stared at the ceiling. The new gilding really was very successful. How lucky she was to live in a house with such perfect features. She really must make an effort to *look* at them more.

'And Mary herself accepted him at once! How do we explain that?'

This was enough to bring Fanny out of self-pity and into a state of cold fury. 'I can only presume that, in the moment, Ned turned the silly girl's head.' She brought her gaze back to her father and adopted a brisk tone. 'But whatever her reasoning, 'tis of no matter. Sir Edward simply cannot approve any immediate match. Mary is simply too young.'

'Ned is prepared to wait,' her father shot back.

'That is *too* kind.' She smiled tightly. 'Yet still immaterial. Sir Edward is particularly sensitive on the subject of *scandal*, and the mere thought that it might, once again, attach itself to his family upsets him greatly. Apart from all the other objections, he is *very* much of the view that Ned is, in effect, Mary Dorothea's uncle and—'

'Yet, my dear, he is *not!*' Mr Knight thumped his fist on the table, giving Fanny rather a shock. 'That is what is so hard to comprehend! There is no scandal here. Especially when all the world knows he is indeed plotting for the girl to marry his own brother.'

Fanny took a deep breath, determined to maintain her poise. There was, she must grant, some slight inconsistency in her husband's argument. In fact, no – that was not quite true. Last night, when Sir Edward was with her and – even in his fury – able to carefully *explain*, in that excellent way of his, his position had seemed to make perfect sense. It was afterwards, in the solitary small hours, that the reasoning seemed rather to fall apart in her hands. So it was fortunate, really, that she would only ever allow herself one way to turn.

'Papa,' she began, keeping her voice as steady as she was able. 'I shall not go against my husband on this matter – or any other, come to that. Nor, I know, would you expect me to. I have given you Sir Edward's opinion, and I do not expect him to change it. Especially as Mary has not asked that he might. She did not utter a word on the subject last evening!

'I repeat, once again, that, whatever you have heard to the contrary, *we* have seen *no* evidence of a serious attachment on *her* part. Nor, indeed, has she given any indication that her estimation of Dr Knatchbull is in any way altered.' And, with a great, final flourish of maternal authority, she declared: 'We are her parents! *Who* could know better than *we*?'

And though she might doubt her own words – had every reason to suspect, indeed, that they could even be fraudulent – her father was left with no choice. With a sad sort of shrug that caused Fanny to wince, Mr Austen Knight surrendered at once.

'Ned is a good man, Fan.' He rose, gave a shake of his

head and prepared to depart. 'A fine man, indeed. You know it as well as I. If there is no chance with Mary, then he will be sure to accept it.' He frowned. 'What has led to this unfortunate misunderstanding, I cannot fathom. But of course, if the young lady herself has no interest, I shall not wait for Sir Edward. We have no more to discuss.'

CHAPTER XXIX

'Good afternoon, Papa.' Mary dropped into a deep curt-sey, eyes to the Aubusson. 'Thank you for seeing me.'

'My dear child.' Sir Edward rose from his seat at the desk. 'However *busy* one's day and *onerous* one's duties, there must still some time for one's *children*. I hope you would agree that I have not once given you cause to find me anything less than the most *approachable* parent?'

Mary started to tremble, kept her head still averted while her unrested mind spun out of control. For what fresh hell was this? Last night had been terrible: Sir Edward's wrath more extreme than she had ever before known – almost enough to shake the carriage clear of its wheel shaft. The intervening hours had been spent in steeling herself against more of the same. And so now to be met by such underhand tactics! For in the hands of one so swift to anger, sweet reason was a sharp weapon indeed.

'But of course not, Papa.' At last, she dared lift her gaze up to his and was met by a smile, though from a face puffy and pale. 'Indeed, quite the kindest.'

He reached out to embrace her. 'Now, how can I help you this morning?'

All through her life, and certainly since the loss of her mother, Mary had loved this man deeply. Even when that love had been challenged – and oh! how legion the challenges brought by his behaviour and temperament – she had fought to maintain it, with a dogged persistence. As she had so often reminded herself, whom else did she have? And now, though they might stand at a precipice – for this would, in all likelihood, be the most difficult interview – still, she was determined to ward against any ill feeling.

Sir Edward returned to the authority of his desk chair and signalled that she sit low on the sofa.

'I would be grateful, Papa, if you might find it within you to discuss the events of yesterday evening?'

'Events?' he asked pleasantly, as one raking his memory.

'Yes, Papa.' If this was his game, then she would play it. 'Events. In fact, I request that we speak of one in particular.' Mary was ever polite. 'That being the moment you learned that Mr Knight has asked for my hand.'

'Ah, *that*.' Stretching out his short legs, knitting his fingers around the girth of his stomach, he added complacently: 'High spirits, I gather – all brought about by the gaiety of the season. Though, as you would expect, I must mark the gentleman down for yet *another* impetuous performance, still – to respect good Lady Knatchbull's desire for family unity – I am minded this time to ignore it.' He turned back to his papers. 'Pray, do not punish yourself, Mary. I am settled in my mind that you did nothing to deserve such an insult and we shall not speak of it again. The *subject* is *closed*. Now' – he lifted a document to his face and spoke into it – 'unless there is anything else?'

Mary drew back her shoulders and retrieved her earlier steel. Her life hung in the balance. She must not be thwarted. 'There is, Papa, yes – if you would be so kind as to indulge it. I would like – be most grateful indeed, if – well – that is—' She gulped. 'I politely request that the subject stay open.'

Slowly, he turned back towards her, eyes of ice blue stretched wide in amused disbelief.

'Furthermore' – she gripped one hand in the other to steady them both – 'I would be grateful if you might allow me the opportunity to declare my own feelings on the matter.'

'Your *feelings*,' he cut in, affecting astonishment – as if they were now in some new realm of fantasy. '*You* are proposing that *I* am to *consider* your *feelings*.'

'If you would be so kind, Papa.' Her own nerve astonished her.

'*MARY DOROTHEA KNATCHBULL.*' His fist slammed down on the desktop; the many gentleman's trinkets leaped up as salmon en route to the sea. 'What is this impudence? I have issued sound judgement – one taken with care and informed by the great wisdom of years – and you dare to contest it with your *girlish feelings*?'

'But, Papa! I beg you that you hear me.' All air left the room. 'It can no longer be hidden.' She felt all over strange, and light-headed. 'For Mr Knight and I are in love.'

And with that, Mary fell back and cowered in the depths of the sofa – arms by her head; hands to her ears – and awaited the thunderclap.

'*In love?*' It came out more like a jeer than the customary roar. '*You*, still fresh from the nursery – where *I* had you raised to my own impeccable standards – you dare speak already of *love*? Then, child, I despair. You can know *nothing* of love and little of this – this – *person*. He is no more than a stranger to you! And may I remind you that you speak of your *uncle*—'

'Papa!' Mary felt she had to cut in then, for he was now drifting, rudderless, towards the absurd. 'We are not related by blood.' She thought it best not to bring up Dr Knatchbull's name here. That would only inflame him. One suitor at a time . . . 'Mr Knight has been under this roof for much of the season. He has dined with us often.'

'And *thus* he repays my kind hospitality?' At last, the roar found its voice. 'In refining his dark arts of seduction, even *at my own table*?'

'He did not, sir – as you were his witness.' As she happened to be the one with Right on her side, Mary could keep her voice measured: 'But, as you are also aware, our families are often together. We are the closest of neighbours. It is a connection, as I understood it, most warmly encouraged by both you and my mother, and one that has afforded us many, quite natural opportunities to deepen our friendship.'

The response was entirely impetuous. 'Then if so, I regret them! I regret every moment of freedom we have ever allowed you. It has all come upon you too soon and, with the folly of youth, you – yes, even *you* of whom I was till recently proud – have conducted yourself ill. Strait is the gate, Mary! Strait is the gate—'

'—and narrow the way,' Mary finished for him, by rote. 'I have not forgotten it, Father. Nor do I believe myself to have strayed very far.'

He looked at her now with contempt. 'And yet you come here to tell me of your friendship with a *gentleman*, while you are a *child*?'

'A child, sir? And yet, as I remember it, one thought sufficiently competent to consider an arrangement with Dr Knatchbull . . .' There. How did she dare it?

'Bah! You make the suggestion of paradox, where in fact there is none. When *I*, in my role as kind *parent*, make the case for a suitor, then it behoves *you* to consider him. Our roles in that process cannot be reversed! You have not the sufficient maturity for freedom of choice.

A mere eighteen years on this earth is . . .' He paused, lost for words.

In furious desperation, Mary pounced to supply them, though of course only in the mildest of tones: '. . . the same age as my own mother, when she chose you, sir?'

'And she was too young!' Sir Edward cried out, as if in agony. He rose, crossed the room, loomed over as if he might strike her. 'Far, far too young. Have you understood nothing? Did you merely watch on in ignorance all those years that I suffered? I loved her. Oh, how I loved her – truly, profoundly. Yet still I can only regret it.'

This was too far. He had taken them both to a moment most terrible. There was no turning away now. Half awed, half greatly outraged, Mary stood to confront it.

'Regret, Papa?' she asked carefully. 'You speak of *regret* that you loved my mama?'

He began to shake with some violence. 'I regret that she left me too soon.' Purple veins stood out on his forehead. 'I regret my own lot in having to raise our infants *alone*. Can you begin to imagine it? Demented with grief, yet shackled by duty?' He choked at the memory. 'God's will be done, and 'tis not my place to question, but He shall not take you, Mary.' Tears sprang from his eyes now. 'While there is breath in my body, He shall not take you from me. *Not* into the arms of that *scoundrel*.'

But she could give no thought to his message, for now the sound of his sobbing was piercing her heart. All steel left her young body; her spirit was dust. She was six years of age again: returned to Mrs Grant's parlour in Albion Place.

Taking him into her arms, she pressed her own face to his. 'There, there, Papa.' Mary could do nothing but comfort him now. She knew no other way. 'There, there, dear Papa.'

But even as she repeated the well-practised mantra, her poor mind was consumed with the import of that which she had heard: he had regretted her whole existence; he had regretted the lives of her brothers.

Her own father wished his own children had not been born.

~

For the whole month of January 1826, a great cloud of bitterness hung over Mersham-le-Hatch.

Sir Edward's fury showed no sign of abatement. Though he had broken two hearts, crushed two lovers' dreams and triumphed completely, he could only brood over the fact that he had been wronged in the first place. Even the ludicrous conviction that he had Right on his side – mentioned daily at breakfast *and* over dinner – did not seem enough to placate him.

Lady Knatchbull, the most obedient of wives and yet devoted of sisters, seemed to be in dismay at the position in which she now found herself. She would not quarrel with Sir Edward, of course, but nor could she join in his hatred of her own brother, so instead she blamed Mary. Any maternal warmth she had previously mustered – and it had never reached higher than tepid – was turned unto frost.

And clearly, one parent or other must have conducted an enquiry into Mary's past movements for – to her absolute horror – Daniel the coachman was suddenly dismissed! Without even a day's notice! The guilt of it almost defeated her; so deep was her despair that Mary would not even contest her father's new strictures. How could she care about being forbidden from riding alone, from mixing with Godmersham – or missing out on Twelfth Night – when she had ruined the livelihood of an excellent man? While the parties went on without her, Mary stayed in her room and wept at her wickedness.

But on the 23rd day of January, she had no choice but to emerge. It was the Mother's birthday, and Lady Knatchbull was very much one of those people who liked the day to be marked. So she went in to breakfast, extended her wishes – was met with little beyond the tilt of a head – and after a silent half-hour, took her leave.

Though she had checked once already, again Mary went through the letters on the hall table . . . Of course there was nothing. She was no longer surprised by it, but could not help but be pained. Three weeks since the proposal, yet already she was forsaken. Of course, Ned's life would go on without her. He was not made to look back, only forward; he was never known to be still. A solitary tear splashed on to the pewter.

She was halfway up the stairs to her room, where she might cry unobserved, when a large, hairy boulder crashed into her legs and nearly felled her.

'Lord Byron?' she cried as she clung to the banister. 'Lord Byron, you *dear*!' Two great paws were pinned to her shoulders; his tongue licked the tears from her cheeks. 'How – Where – Then is your master—?' Heart now flooding with hope, she spun wildly about. Her eyes were met, as they were met once before, by a great halo of light. The sharp white winter's morning came in at the doorway. A tall, dark figure strode through it with purpose.

'Darling!' he cried out at the sight of her. This was not a gentleman to be constrained by the presence of a footman. 'Oh, to get even a glimpse!' The commotion brought out the butler; Ned paid him no heed. 'I have suffered such agonies! Pray will you come to me—' He moved fast, intent on embracing her! Already, he was at the foot of the stairway!

'No further!' Mary called out in alarm. 'My parents are *there*,' she hissed, signalling at a solid oak door, 'still at breakfast.'

He stopped as she bade. 'Then let me speak quickly.' At least he too now lowered his voice. 'I am come here to speak to your father, in the belief that he must now be calmer, more rational. This time, he *will* hear me.'

'So you have not given me up?' Mary sank to the floor, weak with relief. The dog climbed into her lap.

'Give *up*?' He rubbed both hands through his hair and stared, all astonishment. 'What can you mean? Every day, all hours, I have been out in search – Lord Byron is run ragged – I thought – I feared—'

'Oh, dearest. They have not treated me ill.' She froze as the door to the breakfast room opened; breathed again at the sight of a maid. 'But they are taking me to London next week, intent on keeping us apart. I fear you will find my father's mind is unchanged.'

'Then it must fall to *me* to persuade that mind otherwise.' The lopsided grin proved he still brimmed with self-confidence. He began to bounce on his heels, buoyant as if at the start of a game or a hunt. The very idea of defeat was to him an anathema. That he might find his match in the short, stocky person of Sir Edward Knatchbull was not a thought one such as Ned could begin to entertain.

Mary gazed down upon him – drank in his presence while she still had it before her – marvelled at his spirit, and loved him completely.

CHAPTER XXX

'Well, at last and thank goodness,' exclaimed Lady Banks from the depths of her armchair as the footman announced Mary's name. 'I know you have been in Town for three weeks and had started to think you have forgotten me. Indeed, I'd surrendered all hope.'

'Dear Aunt.' Mary traversed the gloom of the great Portland Place drawing room and planted a kiss on a cheek heavy with rouge. 'Here you are, snug in your mansion, yet speaking as one who has dropped down a well and is waiting for rescue.'

'My dear girl, you have quite put your finger on it.' She tossed aside her embroidery ring which had not, Mary noticed, moved forward in more than a year. 'Summed up old age. Half deaf, half blind: praying for release. Now.' Lady Banks put both hands in Mary's and squinted up. 'Let me look at you. Ah, yes. Peak perfection, I'd call it. A remarkable specimen. If my husband – God rest his soul – were still with us, he'd put pins in both hands and frame you in glass. Is my god-daughter not lovely, Miss Fairfax?'

Mary had not before noticed the grey, almost elderly lady asleep by the fire. She was clearly the latest in a long line of companions; none was yet to find favour.

'Miss Fairfax!' This met no reaction. 'The Lord only knows why one bothers. Now, tell me your news.'

Mary presented a careful, anodyne account of the last turbulent weeks.

'Very good.' Lady Banks pursed her lips and raised one emphatic brow, artlessly blackened with coal dust. 'Thank you for that, dear. Now, why don't you sit down and pay me the compliment of speaking the *tr-r-ruth*?'

Mary sat, all astonishment. 'Lady Banks, I cannot believe that my father would relate . . .'

'Of course he did not! I gather that temper of his won out yet again. Your dear late mama could always control him, you know. This *new* one, though – simply not up to the job. He is become quite incor-r-rigible.'

But then, how had Lady Banks heard? Mary started to panic. It had not previously occurred to her that the fact of Ned's proposal was known even in East Kent. That it had somehow reached London was mortifying enough; that she might now be the subject of gossip would drive her father demented!

Lady Banks continued as if Mary had spoken aloud. 'Never mind how I heard it. Let us say one has one's sources and leave it at that. What I want to hear are your own feelings on the matter.' She sat back, preparing to listen, then noticed Mary's reluctance. 'Ah. Miss Fairfax? *FAIRFAX!* Yes, thank you for joining us and I *do* hope you sufficiently rested. Now, off you trot to your room, dear, there's a good thing . . .' She watched with contempt as her companion grabbed her knitting and scuttled away, then turned back to Mary.

'I love him, Aunt,' Mary said then, perfectly simply. 'I have for some time and am secure in the belief that he loves me.' And then, to her horror, she started to cry. 'He is such a good man with so much to recommend him. But my father is set dead against. He has turned us down twice! And now they have forced us apart and brought me to Town . . .'

'My dear girl.' Lady Banks rummaged and produced a clean handkerchief. 'London is hardly a *haystack*. If this gentleman wants you, then he will find you. Let it be his first test. And as for meeting, in *private* . . .' She looked into the fire, seeming to consult with the flames.

'A few years ago, I promised you my help if it were needed. Now' – she looked stern for a moment – 'I shall not, I *cannot* go against Sir Edward's express wishes. My views on rank disobedience are more than well known.'

'Yes, Aunt, and nor would I expect—' Mary sniffed and gulped at the same time.

'*However,*' Lady Banks declared to the room as if to some vast assembly. The grandeur of manner brought Sir Edward alive in Mary's mind. 'It would be perfectly natural for this Mr Knight to call on me one afternoon – our families are closely connected, after all. And it would be equally natural for you, my dear, to be here when this visit occurred. And, if I happen to like him – *Will* I like him?'

'Oh, very much so, dear Aunt. Everyone does! Other than my father, that is, and none of us can quite understand it.'

'If that proves to be so, well . . .' Her ladyship was starting to enjoy herself. There was an unmistakeable twinkle in her old eye. 'Who could deny the odd *nap* in a *chair* to one of my advancing years? I shall oblige you by coming over all Fairfax, and afford you some privacy.' The mention of her companion's name seemed to darken her mood again. 'Wretched woman. She will have to go.'

~

Cheered though she was by this scheme, Mary could not see a way of getting word through to Ned. Though she did not believe herself to be under arrest, still she could be sure that Fanny was monitoring her letters, because that had gone on for some years. And while she suspected that Cassy would come to her aid, still Mary was loath to ask her. There was now so much friction between the

Knights and the Knatchbulls and it would be wrong to create more. Mary felt awkward enough as it was.

The following day was the last of the holidays for the younger boys before their new term in Winchester, and Fanny had granted them one, last, special outing. She could not herself go, being both loath to leave her first baby and made to feel exceedingly indifferent by the next. But a manservant was commissioned to provide a suitable escort, with Mary and Booker in strong support.

When the party arrived at the Exeter Exchange, the boys were in a state of advanced excitement, but Mary was in no sort of mood for it. While they admired the yeoman on guard at the entrance, loudly wishing one day to be him, she heard them with bitterness. The dear little fools: they still lived under the illusion that adulthood was all choice and potential, while she knew it brought only laws and denial.

Nor, once they had fought their way through the multitudes and queued up the stairs for something close to eternity, could she like what she found. Gawping at wild animals trapped behind bars in close, airless rooms was very much not her idea of a treat. Of course, the boys were transported, one moment teasing an old lion with mange; the next throwing peel, stolen from Cook for the purpose, at the monkeys. And Booker was having the time of her life. Mary kept a large handkerchief over her face – the smell was appalling – and longed for it all to be over.

But at the final exhibit – the menagerie's *pièce de résistance* – even she could not look away. The sight of an elephant in the small upper chamber of a building just off the Strand was, obviously, somewhat out of the ordinary. Mary pushed with the rest of the crowd, was buffeted, bruised – at one point, lifted clear from the ground – until at last she found herself pressed to the cage. And there her eyes met with those of not only the largest, nor just the most magnificent, but also the unhappiest creature she had ever beheld.

While he thrashed with his trunk and bellowed out his frustration, Mary's heart spilled over with a feeling of fellowship. He, too, was trapped. He, too, was the victim of a malign higher force. He, too, was destined to live in eternal—

Suddenly, Booker's elbow dug into her ribs. 'Quick, miss! There – over there, by the back wall! Hurry, while they're all still occupied.'

What could it— Surely not – he could not be here? Pulse throbbing at her throat, Mary turned, pushed. The crowds parted before her. And there, indeed, leaning quite happily, as if idly waiting for no one in particular – with his feet crossed at the ankle and dear head tilted in greeting – stood Mr Knight.

'How did you—' she began.

'No time for all that. We only have minutes. It has been almost insufferable – merely to glimpse you—'

She dropped her handkerchief, took a step forward

and each stared at the other. Discreetly, he picked up the bait and stretched out a hand. While his eye scanned the room, he found, with his fingertip, the space on her wrist at the hem of her glove: flesh met with flesh. Mary shuddered with longing and feared she might faint.

Instead, quickly she gathered herself and spoke in a rush. 'My aunt, Lady Banks, is happy to receive us. Together. In Portland Place. We can be alone!'

'Then God bless the lady,' he said, though with a look quite as sad as the elephant's. 'And how much do I long for it. Sadly, I must quit Town tonight. It will be mid-March, I fear, before I can come here again. My darling! ' He bit his lip then, looked quite close to fearful. 'I hardly dare ask, but do you still wait for me? *Will* you still wait for me?'

'Oh, my dear sir!' The idea she might not made her smile. 'I will *never—*'

But her speech was interrupted. The chime of the hour brought with it a surge of incomers. The mass moved like an organ in the throes of convulsion. The boys were spewed out from their places, fetched up beside Mary.

And Ned was nowhere to be seen.

~

'Honour thy father and mother;' Sir Edward intoned, *'which is the first commandment with promise; That it may be well with thee, and thou mayest live long on the earth.'*

Mary kept her head bent over the tapestry on which she was working and blinked back her tears of frustration.

'Servants, be obedient to them that are your masters according to the flesh, with fear and trembling.'

There had been no reading of novels for weeks now. And, though he might still be popular on Drury Lane, in Number 20 Great George Street even Shakespeare had fallen from favour. Instead, she was expected to perform to her parents – sing prettily through her great misery – until the Bible came out every evening. It seemed that her father, always God-fearing, was now close to petrified. Mary could not decide whether the current craze for religiosity was to be put down to his wife's condition – with this second baby, the doctor came every day – or if it was all part of a programme to subjugate Mary.

The month had dragged on, a sequence of lessons and visits – church twice on a Sunday – and all of it played out against a background of hopelessness. Would March never come? If her parents had thought that, by this deprivation, Mary might forget Ned, or look again at Dr Knatchbull – or be somehow reborn as a quite different person – then they were to be disappointed. With each passing, tedious day, her heart hardened against them. Each night was passed in a state of delirium – neither conscious, nor sleeping – at the edge of her nerves, until Booker came in and roused her.

'They killed him then,' the maid announced with great satisfaction one morning, as she swept back the curtains.

'Who?' Mary sat upright. 'Dearest!' Being so obsessed with her own private drama, her mind went at once to the one person who mattered. '*Whom did they kill?*'

'Chunee,' Booker replied merrily. 'The elephant.' She went to the fireplace, picked up the poker and added, with relish: 'Shot him. Point blank.'

'But that is an outrage! How dare they? And *why?*'

'Went for the keeper, according to Cook. She heard from the milkman—'

'But he was not a *bad* animal! Merely unhappy. They should never have trapped him. What else would he do but strike back at his captors? What would any of us do if our freedom were taken away? Oh, if only he had found some means of escape.'

'Lower your voice, if you please. There's no use getting at me, madam!' The fire now built – coals starting to catch – Booker turned to the wardrobe. 'I ain't been killing no elephants.'

Mary collapsed on to the bolster; let the hot tears fall unabated; considered the fates of Marianne Knight and poor, dear Miss A.

And began to think the completely unthinkable.

~

At last, the trees in the park became bridal with blossom. The daffodils smiled. The air lifted and sharpened. The world was not turned yet, but still Mary could feel it: the green was upon them. And Mr Knight would return.

Furtive, she started to plot how and when they might meet. With the Mother's mind so much on her health, Mary had gained slightly more freedom. She was now allowed to move around Town with only Booker for company. The situation was promising.

But then, just as Ned's arrival was imminent, Fanny brought her sister Marianne up to town. And suddenly, Mary was never alone.

Every morning of the season, she was engaged to take lessons at the fashionable stables of Mr Allen in Bryanston Square. Riding was thought to be beneficial for the health of the body, as well as the more *difficult* mind. An hour out with a horse, and a troop of young ladies of her age and class, would be all to the good. And Mary enjoyed it, in fact. It was the only pleasure she knew.

But when Marianne was also signed up to the course, her suspicions were heightened. The lady was a Knight! *They* needed no lessons. And now at twenty-four years of age, would she not, in that company, look rather odd?

The one explanation Mary could come up with was that Marianne was employed as her gaoler, and it left her dismayed. Not only was it irksome to be spied upon, it was most disappointing to think that Marianne, of all people, had agreed to act as the spy. For had not she too been thwarted in the fulfilment of her ideal match? And yet now she betrayed Mary! Was there no sisterhood?

While being only ever polite, Mary now held back from treating this Miss Knight as a friend. On their outings together, she listened impassively while Marianne's tongue tripped on with news of nieces and nephews, of her dear father's gout, as if she had no other life of her own.

Until, one day after their lesson, as Mary and Booker were exiting the stables, Marianne cried out that she had somehow forgotten her bonnet. It must be retrieved. She begged that they saunter on, and promised to catch up.

'Ah, a moment of peace,' Mary began, rather uncharitably, as she took Booker's arm. 'If I hear one more word about *teething*, I do believe I shall—'

'Ooh, well I never!' Booker squealed as they turned on to Montague Square. Before adding mysteriously: 'I've got a stone in my boot, so if you'll pardon me, miss.'

And there was Ned, rushing towards her with the wind at his back.

'You!' was all Mary could manage. She had to grab at the railings to hold herself up. 'You have come.'

'You cannot have doubted me?' With one hand, he lifted his hat; the other worried his hair. 'I have been counting the days . . .'

'But are you quite well, sir? You seem somewhat different.' Though never pale after a season out hunting, still there was a tinge of grey to his face, which lurked 'neath the bronze. He was not quite his full self, away from the country and apart from his dog.

'Nothing ails me, as such.' His demeanour was grim. 'But the past weeks have come at a cost, madam!'

'Oh, unendurable!' she gasped. 'The atmosphere at home with my parents . . . Mr Knight, I can bear it no longer.'

'And I fervently hope you will not have to.'

He was so close to her now, she caught the scent of cologne on his neck. Did he wear it for Mary? The idea of him picturing her as he dabbed at his own skin brought with it a shivering thrill.

'There is a new plan.'

'Yes!' Mary exclaimed, all at once presuming his mind to be at one with her own. Sensing then Booker's approach from behind, she dropped her voice low and spoke urgently. 'I, too, am *convinced* of it. If we simply keep going to my father with the same question, we will hear only the same answer. Present him with a fait accompli, though, and he will be left with no choice but to accept it. It is time! Darling.' She looked into his face; felt tears brim at her eyes. 'My dearest.' It was the most auspicious moment. The bravest, most noble action of Mary's short, timid life. 'I am willing, *for* you – *with* you by my side – to settle this forever. Let us take the ultimate step.'

He fell back, astonished. 'By God, madam! You mean – you *cannot* mean – *Scotland*?' He was aghast. 'Pray believe I care nothing for my own name, but to have yours, my love, mired in the dark pit of some *scandal*—'

'But you must *see!*' How could he be so obtuse when her own mind was clear? 'There is no other solution.'

'If you would but listen,' he shot back, 'I have formed a new plan.' Ned stretched out a hand to her; then, recalling their situation, cast about himself wildly and wrenched it back down to his side. 'Forgive me,' he whispered, looking over her shoulder. 'My sister will not be long.' He brought a finger to his lips to instruct her to be quiet. 'At my entreaties, my father has agreed to act for us. It might just make the difference. Sir Edward will hear from him tomorrow. Our case will be made for us in a calm, sensible manner which—' He started. 'She is coming! It is for the best that she is not made into a witness.'

And with a tip of his hat, he was gone.

CHAPTER XXXI

The next morning, Mary was still in her room dressing for breakfast when the air was filled with a roar of such volume that she immediately thought of that elephant. Had it escaped after all? Was it even now marauding through Mayfair? She rushed to the window and looked down on a street where all proceeded quite as it should. Then, without even a knock, Booker put her head round the door.

'Hope you brought your armour, miss.' The maid was uncommonly cheerful. 'You'll need it for this one.' She signalled downstairs with her chin. 'You're wanted. Down in the study.'

She found Sir Edward pacing the floor and brandishing the letter. 'Well, *madam*?' He had clearly decided on a more forthright approach than the one he had used at the start of the year. 'An explanation, if you please.' He took a seat at his desk and drummed his plump fingers upon it. 'The very least I deserve.'

'Good morning, Papa.' Mary curtseyed, remained standing and affected concern. 'You seem a little upset. I do hope you have not had bad news?'

'The worst!' The force of his fury brought him back to his feet. 'For I have had the misfortune to learn that you, my own daughter, are no more than a . . . a . . . *Jezebel!*'

Mary froze. She could not chastise him, but nor would she tolerate any more of his nonsense. Instead, she appeared rational. 'I cannot think what you mean, sir.'

It was the perfect response, for even he seemed abashed – though, of course, he gave no apology. 'Mr Austen Knight informs me' – he held up the paper and sat himself down again – 'that you have met with that *person.*'

'With *young* Mr Knight?' she asked pleasantly. 'That is correct, sir. I was coming out of the stables, and he happened to be passing. It could not have been helped. I might have mentioned it last evening, but you were so late at the House.' She thought for a moment: 'I do wonder, Papa, if these night sittings are not taking too much of a toll? You seem rather strained.'

Sir Edward glowered. 'And he writes – quite how he dares is completely beyond me but somehow he man-ages. *Really,* that *family* – he actually writes that you still have *feelings* for the—' He stopped, veering from slander.

'*Feelings* which I have *forbidden!*' With that he rose and returned to his pacing. 'He is even so bold as to make the case for the match.'

The rest of his speech was addressed to the carpet. 'I know that, were I to permit it, you might now speak of Mr Knight's qualities, his estate and his worth . . . Believe me, I hear enough on that subject from Lady Knatchbull herself and consider it no longer relevant.

'I issued my decision on the day I was asked and will not change my mind, Mary. I will not; I cannot. That is the *command* of your *father* – to you, the highest power on this earth, beneath only Him who sits as our Ultimate Arbiter.

'You cannot challenge me now, for that I can never forgive.' Did his voice crack then with emotion, or just ugly, hot rage? 'This family would fall into chaos. You are the eldest – *remember it!* The first of you all to face this decision, and as such *must* tread with good care, ever mindful of the example that you set for your siblings.' He flung down the pages and balled his fists in aggression. '*In particular, the example you set for your sister!*'

'But—' Mary was about to protest that she had not a sister, and then she remembered. Was she seriously expected to put the moral interests of that baby above her own happiness? Would he truly throw over Mary for *her*? She refused to believe it.

'Father, all my life I have honoured you.' Her words

were carefully chosen. 'Though it may, at times, have felt like a challenge, I have tried desperately to obey your every stricture and I have done so with love.' Her message acute. 'So now, pray, I beg that you hear and believe it when I tell you that any action by me in defiance of your wishes will cause me great pain and regret. I have never wanted to hurt you, and nor do I now.'

It was a forewarning of her coming apostasy. Of course, he heard only compliance. She had deliberately eschewed any use of the conditional; yet he, in his arrogance, chose to presume it was there.

'Thank you, my dear.' Her father patted her arm, complacent; sent Mary off on her way.

And there the interview ended, with each party convinced that its own case had been clearly made.

～

Mary was in her room and still trembling when Marianne came up to find her.

'Dear girl, do not take on so.' Miss Knight rushed to the bed to embrace her. 'All will be well in the end, I am sure of it.' She kissed Mary's head and clasped her hands. 'I just came to ask when you might next visit your aunt, Lady Banks? She sounds a most interesting lady and I should so like to meet her.'

'Oh.' Mary sniffed. 'Yes, of course. She expects me on Thursday about three after noon.'

'Excellent!' Marianne exclaimed, satisfied. 'But what a shame, I shall not be free.'

~

It was only on entering the Portland Place drawing room that Mary realised Marianne Knight was not, after all, in the employ of her parents but was, in fact, in alliance with Ned. For there he was, long legs stretched out from the chair by the fire, with Lady Banks sitting across from him, enthralled.

'Welcome, my precious!' Her great-aunt trilled in a manner quite close to coquettish. 'Do come in and join us.'

Mary sat, as she was bidden, in the place beside Ned while their hostess remained at some distance.

'I have been *regaled* by tales of the exploits of the God-mersham family. How we have *laughed*, have we not, Mr Knight?' Lady Banks was chuckling still. 'Highland jigs in costume! Governesses – of all people – putting on unsuit-able plays and getting dismissed for it! I must say it sounds like a permanent *r-r-riot*. How on earth our good Lady Knatchbull came out quite so very *pious* must remain one of the great mysteries.

'Dear, oh dear.' She dabbed at her eyes and, in so doing, smeared coal around her forehead. 'You are naughty, sir, for a lady of my years cannot take *too* much diversion. One is simply not used to it.'

And with no further discussion, Lady Banks sank down, as if into a sleep.

'Good afternoon, Mr Knight.' Mary spoke softly and smiled. 'This is most odd, for when were we last able to speak freely indoors?'

'Ha! You make a fair point, madam. There was that one occasion, on New Year's Eve, *if* I recall . . .' Ned gave that dear crooked grin and, with an eye on their chaperone, took her hand in his.

The sensation was delicious. Mary felt her breath start to quaver.

'But otherwise, never. Indeed, there is due cause for concern,' he went on, quite smoothly, while tracing a circle on her wrist with his finger, 'that our relationship might be like one of those species – a philadelphus, or some such – that thrives in the garden but once transplanted indoors, wilts and collapses.'

Mary could quite see herself wilting – could imagine the many ways in which he might cause her to do it, though such wickedness should be resisted. But the collapse of a passion such as theirs? It was surely impossible.

'The first time I entered the Great House at Chawton, I at once felt it had a particularly' – she searched for the word – '*fertile* sort of air.'

'Is that so, madam?' Now, the tip of that finger was slowly drawing a line to the inside of her elbow. 'A theory that must be tested, I think. It is many years since it has been home to a young married couple.'

Lady Banks stirred in her sleep then. Alarmed at her own wanton behaviour – for somehow she was leaning towards him, face close to his – Mary wrenched her hand away and so shattered the spell.

'Now, to serious business, for we have not much time.' Ned's words came rapidly, his voice at last hushed. 'The latest entreaty found no favour with Sir Edward. The reply was unfriendly, that avenue now closed. Since then, I have thought long and hard about that which is, in all senses, our last resort. And, not without some great trepidation, I hereby conclude that – if *your* feelings do match my own – there is no other option.'

Mary sank back in her chair, stared at this perfect gentleman and let herself be overwhelmed by the moment. He was willing to do *this* and for *her*! And so they were soon to be married! Their love *had* been challenged and yet it had survived. Furthermore, in one mental footnote, Mary acknowledged that, to safeguard her reputation, Ned was now gallantly claiming her audacious plan as his own. She could leap into his lap, dance around the drawing room – rush into the street and shout to the world! – but Ned had still more to say.

'This morning, I conferred with my father and, though I made no confession and kept the matter vague rather than specific, he gave me every impression that we would be forgiven by *him*, at least. It is hardly surprising. After all, what good, loving parent would cast out his own child? The thought is fantastic. So one question remains, though still it pains me to ask it. My darling, are you truly willing to take all the many, great risks that elopement entails?'

The dread word was now spoken. Mary quailed at its awe. 'Yes . . .' she began, but there was a new note to her voice.

And Ned, of course, caught it. 'I shall not – never will – pressure you!' he insisted at once. 'This is no minor matter and, I must warn you, to some it will appear as an enormity. We must be braced for vile gossip and loathsome attention. There may even be a risk of a few months' estrangement between you and your family. To think of your dear younger brothers, the precious bond between siblings . . . Madam, I beseech you, if you now fear it too much—'

'Ha! You imagine I fear *this*?' Mary burst out in protest. 'Oh, Mr Knight! Do you not *see* the alternative? It is to watch as my future burns bright on the altar of my father's whim.' Her voice caught. She plunged on. 'And then what would become of us? You – oh, *you* would still know your freedoms. But I beg you think now of *my* life. What then is left to me?

'*That*, sir, is something to fear!'

The very idea of that future brought tears to her eyes. Blinking, she saw they were matched by his own.

'Oh, my dear one,' she said then, with new tenderness. 'If *I* can have *you* . . . If *we* can, at last—'

But there was no going on. Ned was out of his seat.

His lips were on hers. And Mary felt it again – the great heat! Those fireworks! Then Lady Banks let out a loud snore and, with a laugh and a grimace, he shot back to his seat.

Gasping, Mary fell back against hers, closed her eyes – caught her breath – until something quite close to calm was restored to her being and she could finally speak again.

'I can assure you,' she began, with her palm to her breast. Though her voice was now steady, her heart was not yet. 'I am decided and, sir, I too have thought deeply about what this entails. My brothers are growing and have no great need of me now. And their love is secure – there is no fear on *that* score. But, alas, my poor father . . . still – *still* – I can do nothing but care for his feelings.' She felt no need to pretend in this company. Ned was a good man. He understood her. 'So often in my life, since I was a small child, my father has spoken and acted in ways that should be repellent. And yet—'

'*Honour thy father and mother,*' he said, '*which is the first commandment and promise . . .*'

'So ingrained in us all!' She smiled then, but was now forlorn. 'I fear it is no coincidence that, lately, Sir Edward has taken to reading that passage every night after dinner.'

'And does he break off then?' Lady Banks was, all of a sudden, sharp and awake. 'Or does he run on? Oh, I may be the widow of a Man of Science, my dear, but still I know the Good Book as well as any fine parson.

And, ye fathers – that's how it continues – *And, ye fathers, pr-r-rovoke not your children to wrath.*

'The Lord can speak unto us of *honour* as much as He likes. But then, the *Lord* has never had to suffer Sir *Edward* when his temper is up.'

CHAPTER XXXII

What Fanny found so splendid about that particular spring of 1826 was that the very best of Kent appeared to be gathered in Town, so that one could almost ignore all the tiresome, latest distractions – the cream of society – and fancy oneself still in the country. Lady Banks, always a generous hostess and amusing companion, was, as usual, ensconced in Portland Place. Several other kind neighbours were scattered about, but a short walk away. And, now May was almost upon them, a portion of the Godmersham family was due to arrive and join the good Kentish throng. Mr Knight was bringing George, William and Cassy and they would put up at the Brunswick Hotel – though, of course, the families would combine whenever possible. Would they not?

For all the pleasure with which she looked forward to

the rest of the season, Fanny did have to own to some minor trepidation. Though Marianne was with her – the dear girl was proving to be *such* a treasure – she had not seen her father or siblings since her own arrival in London. There had been letters between them all, of course, but none of an intimate nature. And, in the odd, uncertain moment, Fanny did wonder if there was not a certain *froideur* between the Knights and the Knatchbulls. Though still hoping to soon be proved wrong, she was already sure in her mind that, if there were indeed any unpleasantness, there was no question whatsoever upon whom the blame could be laid.

Ned was not due to appear this time, thank goodness – business in Hampshire was to keep him safely away. Nevertheless, Fanny hardly dared relax, for it seemed he had lately developed a skill for creating disturbance even from afar. What on earth had possessed him to prevail on their father to write to Sir Edward – and why the good man had even *thought* to comply – Fanny could not at all fathom. Her husband had only just recovered from the affront of the proposal, and then she had had to deal with all *that*. Oh, the slurs he had flung at her own flesh and blood! Much as she tried to pretend otherwise, they did strike at her heart. The whole episode had caused such an upset that Fanny could not forgive it – especially as Mary herself had assured her father that, in her own mind, nothing had changed.

She sighed deeply, rested her hands on her growing

stomach and then suddenly smiled. Oddly enough – the thought only then just occurred – the person who gave Fanny the *least* worry these days was Mary Dorothea. Though the irony was glaring, it was simply a fact: since their arrival in Town, Mary's conduct had been pleasingly faultless. And when Fanny thought of the terrible saga of Sir Edward's own lovelorn sister, who had had to be imprisoned in her room by day and by night, she could only count her own blessings.

Of course, Fanny had made perfectly sure that Mary Dorothea was never alone for a second. Dear Booker was with her at all times, and Marianne too, when she could be spared from the nursery. But Mary could enjoy the freedom of taking a chaperone to her cousins or Lady Banks whenever she liked. And, at Fanny's careful insistence, the girl did still pursue her ladylike interests – *refine* her *accomplishments*. So she rode almost daily; took lessons in singing at the same time every morning from Mr Crepaldi in his studio. And after a few months of a good, wholesome routine, the change wrought was remarkable. From the pale, miserable creature of the start of the year, Mary Dorothea was quite transformed. Pink, bright-eyed and strong again. And for that, Fanny felt entitled to take much of the credit.

Her ruminations were disturbed by the appearance of the footman.

'Mr Austen Knight, madam.'

And so natural was her delight at the sound of her

dear father's name, Fanny quite forgot to prepare for any possible unpleasantness.

Their greeting was as warm as ever and – first things first – Fanny at once took him up to the uppermost floor to admire her baby. The darling was, like an angel, soundly asleep – she was an *excellent* sleeper. They were, truly, *so* blessed – and therefore unable to display her latest accomplishments. But still, they stood by the crib for some time, while the devoted mother described, in a whisper, how the baby could *not only point* but *also clap* and, according to others, was already displaying the signs of a remarkable intelligence.

But, as they walked down the stairs to the parlour, and Fanny was about to embark on a report into newly cut teeth, her papa launched his assault.

'I suppose the child shall be reared to the high, modern standards,' he began in a benign enough manner. 'The fashions have changed, I have noticed. It is not like one's day, under the old King, may God rest his soul.' They had reached the ground floor. 'No doubt you now judge me, as a parent, to have erred on the side of the *liberal*. I am quite sure that Sir Edward disapproves of my approach.'

'Good heavens, Papa!' Fanny, leading the way, nearly missed the next step. 'What on earth makes you say such a thing?' It was almost uncanny – as if he had *lurked* in the *wainscot* and heard Sir Edward's declamations on that very subject.

Her father did not acknowledge the question, but

instead he went on: 'I hope, though, that you think of and will remember me as an affectionate one.'

'Oh, the kindest, dearest of fathers!' Fanny exclaimed as they reached the parlour. 'It has been our greatest good fortune—'

'Thank you, my dear,' Mr Austen Knight cut her off briskly, sitting down to inspect the refreshments. 'And as such, I feel it deeply when my children are suffering unhappiness.'

'I am sure it must be pure agony,' Fanny agreed earnestly. Already, even the thought that her daughter might one day encounter real pain or distress could bring her to tears.

'Hard though it may be for you to believe, caring for an infant is much the easiest stage of parenthood. And one imagines, at the time, that one will use all the powers in one's gift to shield them from life's many great evils.'

Fanny took this as a plea that she would hereby devote all her energies to the protection of his grandchild, and was suitably touched. 'Oh, Papa! As long as I have *breath* in my *body*—'

'But one simply cannot, Fan!'

This took her aback. Fanny felt rather at sea, but had to wait while he made a performance of swallowing the shortbread – which was suitably moist – before, at last, he explained.

'It is my firm belief that the more we *ban* and *forbid* and *control*, the more trouble we make for ourselves and our offspring. Instead, should we not *trust* to their judgement? Allow them the freedom – limited, admittedly, but nonetheless – *freedom* to deal with their own problems as they see fit?'

Was this all an obscure attack on her husband? Fanny's hand started to tremble to such an extent that she was in danger of spilling her cordial.

'Of course,' he rambled on as if entirely amiably, 'Mary Dorothea is not *my* daughter . . . And there is no doubt in my mind that you, Fanny – her *mother* – have talked to her in some *depth* on the subject of Ned and her feelings.'

Fanny stared into her lap, held her drink tightly and felt the first flush to her throat. Of course she had done no such thing – and perfectly properly! Sir Edward dealt with his child, he reported back to his wife – and, quite frankly, that had proved wearing enough.

'In which case, you can have no fear for the girl's virtue, or need to lock her away from us all.' And, at this point, as ever, her dear father softened. 'Poor Fan!' He reached over and patted her knee. 'To be both Knatchbull *and* Knight, with all this' – he lifted his hand, waved another sweetmeat about – 'going on. It cannot be easy to manage.'

'Thank you for that, Papa.' With careful control, Fanny placed her glass back on the chinoiserie tray. 'Both your advice, and also those last kind words. Now.' She looked up and across at him brightly, hoping her complexion had suitably paled. 'Do tell me: what news from Kent? It seems an *age* since we first came away.'

~

While Fanny would prefer to forget her father's words, they rather stayed with her and, when alone with the space for reflection, she found it hard to deny that there might be contained within them a kernel of wisdom.

She *was* a Knight after all, and could testify that their father had never once failed to hear his children's opinions or treat them with kindness. On the other hand, it was hardly unfair to point out that the Knatchbulls tended to be rather more *strict*. And, though Fanny did try to turn a blind eye, one could hardly not notice. So did *their* way work well? She counted the many expulsions from school, the endless disputes – the *brother* in *gaol*! – and concluded that there may well be room for some doubt.

And, once she had thought all this through to her own satisfaction, Fanny determined to allow herself one small – entirely private and safe – act of rebellion.

The following week, the Knights had an outing planned to Lambeth Gardens. Having previously decreed that Mary should be kept away from any such nonsense – surely the girl should be better employed in something *worthwhile*? – now Fanny relented. Of course one should have fun in one's youth! And it was perfectly natural that

Mary should spend time with her own mother's family. With Ned out of the way, what possible harm could befall her?

Fanny went too, of course – she was nothing if not vigilant. The gardens were verdant: the air heavy with scent rising up from the flower beds. It was a perfect day in late spring. And when they encountered the rest of the party, the reunion was joyful.

Cassy was the first to see them approach and, with a skip and a squeal, she came trotting over.

'Dearest!' Her younger sister first issued a brisk kiss to Fanny's cheek and then swept Mary into her arms. 'Oh, darling,' she cried in her unrestrained fashion.

Fanny prickled. It was high time that Cassy adopted a more ladylike air.

'I have missed you so much that it gave me a *pain*. Cakey had to take me into her lap while I sucked my own thumb, which, of course, we both loved to *absolute* bits. Why must one *ever* leave the nursery?' They linked arms and walked a little ahead. 'Being a grown-up is so *frightfully* hard.'

And when the breeze carried back Mary's earnest reply – 'This year, in particular' – Fanny felt a frisson of guilt. The poor girl had lived the whole of the year with only her parents for company. How lonely she must have found it! And why had Fanny and Sir Edward chosen to punish her so?

After all, it was perfectly obvious that Mary had no

feelings for Ned. When the girl was upset, she did not bother to hide it, as Fanny had learned to her cost during that other ghastly affair with the governess. No, Fanny was clear in her mind: there was no further evidence that Mary had done much beyond drive Ned stark, staring mad. And that was hardly her fault . . .

'Oh, do look!' Cassy was now squealing. 'A *dear* little man with a shy! Boys,' she shouted out to her brothers, 'do win us a coconut! Mary needs all the strength she can get.'

'Papa,' Fanny said then, 'I have been thinking . . .' She took his arm and guided him away from her siblings. 'About your advice of last week, that is.'

Mr Austen Knight slowed his pace, turned to the side and studied her, expectant.

'And perhaps there is *some* sense in your methods,' she said with a shrug. 'I can see that Ned, in his current, regrettable condition, is unlikely to take Sir Edward's word on this difficult matter – or any other, come to think of it.'

Fanny had not acknowledged it before, but now she could see that not one of her siblings had ever been prepared to give her husband a fair hearing. The realisation brought with it a great sense of injustice.

She stopped walking, stood with her father and watched her brothers in their latest antics. They had now taken a boat out on the pond. William was standing and rocking it sideways, threatening George with a dunking. The girls on the bank, clutching their coconuts – the

Knight boys were all *excellent* shots – were both hooting with laughter. They must be the noisiest family in the whole park.

What fun they all used to have, Fanny thought, with a pang. And what fun they all still had, without her. Why had she let herself become so very separate?

'And so . . . ?' Her father gave a gentle nudge to her arm and brought Fanny back to the moment.

They started walking again while she got up her nerve.

'And so I am willing to allow them a short interview alone.' Fanny gulped and felt rather faint. What on earth was she doing?

'My dear, you *are* sure?' Mr Austen Knight could not hide his surprise.

'No more than ten minutes, mind!' she added in a panic. 'And *I* shall be in the next room throughout it. Pray, make that clear.'

But, as soon as the promise was made, Fanny felt unusually resolute. After all, her logic was faultless. Had not Sir Edward assured her, on numerous occasions, of Mary's disinterest? Would not this concession play well with the Knights? They must surely appreciate that she had now done *something* for Ned, and was no longer the *enemy*.

'It is the only way I can see that we bring this whole thing to a close, and return to normality. I just want our families to return to the way we once were!' Oh, how she yearned for that! She led her father back to the party. 'So yes, Papa. I am perfectly sure.'

And, though it sounded somewhat absurd even to her own ears, she then whispered: 'I shall send word when the plans have been laid.'

~

At a quarter to eleven on the morning of the following Sunday, Fanny paced the long, narrow hallway and rubbed at her side. She had a strange sort of pain in the rib area. Was it caused by the baby? Or the fact that she was about to commit a transgression for the first time in her married life – and possibly ever?

Her spirit started to tremble. She could not do it! She *would* not do it! But then the party descended the stairs, dressed and ready for church and, somehow, she did.

'Not this morning, my dear.' Fanny put a hand on Mary's shoulder, like a constable. 'Sir Edward, would you mind *terribly* if Mary and I stayed back this morning? There is so much to do – the Indigent Blind, for my sins. The demands are unending!'

Mary stared at her with a puzzled expression, as well she might. Fanny had not mentioned the poor blind, nor given them a thought, since her baby was born.

'We shall go to the service this evening,' she ran on before the blush took her into its grip. 'Marianne will accompany you now. Thank you so much, my dear.'

And when her sweet, caring husband – whom the

world thought so difficult – went off like a lamb, Fanny could almost feel the fresh stain seep into her soul.

She ushered Mary into the parlour, retrieved the work basket which she had so long ignored and together the two ladies sat and arranged their materials. The atmosphere between them was unchanged from that when they first met. Not icy, exactly – to be fair to the girl, never that – but a cool sort of politeness which Fanny loathed. She listened to herself gabble – the weather; the likely congregation at church; her own father's gout – and despaired as conversation eluded them both. Once the morning's ordeal was behind them, she must somehow establish an intimacy.

At last, as arranged, at one minute past the hour – just as the vicar ascended the pulpit and worship began – there came a sharp rap of the knocker, the creak of the heavy front door. Voices in the hallway.

And Ned strode in.

'Dear Fan,' he declared as he kissed her cheek with a warmth he had not shown for some years. 'I will forever be grateful.'

'Ten minutes, mind.' Fanny felt rather like Nanny. 'Dear boy,' she whispered only to him, 'I implore you to not make a scene.' And with that, she withdrew to the breakfast room and left them alone.

Fanny did not try to return to her work; she could hardly sit still. Those minutes lay out before her as an eternity. For, having been so sure in her mind that she was doing the right thing, doubt now assaulted her. She was hardly a natural conspirator – her devotions to the Good Lord had, happily, bent her mind towards Truth and Honesty. But now she must admit to a possible flaw in her plan. For could she trust that *Ned* was equally truthful? She had to hope so. But what about Mary? She had not the first clue as to what went on in the girl's head. Surely, Fanny should have spoken to her first? Mary might be terrified – trapped, as she was, with a possible madman. Or equally she could be unleashed, and . . . Oh, dear Heavenly Father!

Fanny sat down on the nearest chair with an unlady-like thump. Images came to her mind of what the couple might now be doing, cloistered in there alone. She rose and found herself leaning against the wall – ear pressed to silk. And only when she heard the unmistakeable hum of rational, businesslike conversation was she, at last, calm.

And with one minute to spare before their time was up – an encouraging sign in itself – the couple emerged from the parlour and Fanny joined them in the hall. She watched as they bade each other farewell in a respect-able fashion: judged Mary demure and Ned, curiously, unruffled.

And, just to make sure, when he finally left, Fanny stood at the window and studied her brother as he walked down the street. Ned moved at a speed and had a bounce in his step, but that was no cause for concern. For did he not always, and was that not men in a nutshell? Though they might claim to know heartbreak, the *masculine* heart seemed to mend with remarkable ease.

There, Fanny thought to herself and returned to her work and her chair – this time sedately – where she proceeded to reflect on an extraordinary morning. So she had put all her faith in the word of her husband, and been proved right so to do. Was that not a fine lesson for every good, Christian wife?

It was most satisfactory all round. They could finally put the whole troublesome affair behind them, and no Knight had cause to resent Fanny, or attach any blame to her darling husband. And, as he had done already before and no doubt would soon do again, Ned was already moving on to his next entertainment.

CHAPTER XXXIII

In such an establishment as Number 20 Great George Street, there could be no secrets. So no sooner had young Mr Knight left than word quickly spread: the mistress was calm; the crisis now over. And at once, the household sank back into mundanity – placid and insular.

So great was the general relief, for the matter had cast quite a cloud, that no one even suspected Mary – cheerful, polite; prettier yet than before – was host to an interior turmoil; that while she played her part to perfection, she was, in fact, consumed with both longing and dread. They never could have imagined that she might be thinking of Ned – their impending union and all that would entail. That her flesh would then tingle with the most delicious sensation, which she could neither identify nor wanted ever to end. And they had no idea that she was, just as often, assailed by the most terrible visions: presentiments of her father's near future, which then revealed to her the true meaning of agony.

And at last, the great moment was come. After the longest week of her young, difficult life, the night of Saturday 13th was finally upon her. In just a few hours, little Mary Dorothea – that good, Christian child – would take to the stage in a drama set to shock the whole Knatchbull world. But first – for every climax must have its foil – she must somehow endure a few hours of the entirely banal.

Mary's last family dinner, at a quarter to six of that evening, was all set to be a modest, rather humdrum affair. Sir Edward was out at a long-arranged engagement and, as was their custom – Lady Knatchbull never ordered a hot dinner when menfolk were absent. It seemed to her quite *de trop* – Mary and Fanny took a simple cold supper in the parlour and talked of nothing that mattered.

'That was a most pleasant day, Mary dear.' The Mother dabbed at her lips with her napkin, sat back in her chair and rang for a servant. 'Thank you for your company.'

'Thank *you*, Mama,' Mary replied, marvelling at her feigned air of serenity. How could she pretend so? Oh, but when they discovered the truth, they would think her so wicked! Mary silently pledged that – once this one, last, heinous act was behind her – she would never dissemble again.

Mary laid down her cutlery, stole a glance at the clock

on the mantelshelf and brought a hand to her mouth as if to stifle a yawn.

'If you do not mind it, Mama' – a final, petty falsehood. Where was the harm? – 'I am most frightfully tired. I may withdraw to my bed early—'

But Fanny paid her no heed. Instead, 'Dear Mary,' she began, leaning back while a servant cleared all the dishes, 'with my husband so *very* busy, I am often alone and *you* are my great *consolation*. I shall miss it, my dear, once you are married and settled, and no longer to hand.'

Mary was stunned. She had always presumed herself to be an encumbrance. That Fanny should at last suggest otherwise, and on this very night! She thought of her trunk, nicely packed; Booker, no doubt with her cloak on already, fretting upstairs. She tried to picture the house in the wake of her flight, but it was almost impossible: like imagining one's own death. 'Thank you, Mama,' Mary repeated. As she twisted with guilt, there came a new surge of sympathy. 'Though if you sometimes feel lonely, then I am sorry for it.'

Fanny sipped her tisane, thought for a little; replaced her cup in its saucer and then replied. 'Not that, exactly. Not loneliness. Of course, I am no *stranger* to that evil. When I lived in Godmersham, even though my dear family was always about me, I did suffer, on occasion. Curious, is it not? We were such a crowd, yet I did sometimes feel a little at odds. But *since . . .*' She studied the ceiling and seemed to choose her next words with care.

'It was the good fortune of my life that your father chose me, my dear. I do know – we *both* know – that there are many in our circle who do not find him easy. He *can* show – shall we say – a certain *harshness* of feeling. He does not suffer fools!' Fanny gave a fond laugh. 'And I do believe there are *people* – just one or two, mind – who take *him* at surface and feel sorry for *me*. Well, they could not be more wrong, Mary.'

'Indeed, Mama,' Mary said fervently. And as it seemed that they were now to share a new candour, she went further: 'My papa is a very good man. And yet, from time to time—'

Fanny held up her hand. 'As we are both well aware, and do not need to discuss.' She returned to her theme. 'I suppose what I am wanting to say is that no one, outside of a marriage, can judge what goes on within it. Of course, there are some who make a great show of happiness – though who can ever know what really goes on? Apart from the servants, that is.' She gave a little laugh. 'But in truth, I once used to look upon others with pity. Now I despair at my ignorance.

'My own marriage is a blessing, whatever the world may think of it. To be the one, particular light in the life of another – especially one so *very* distinguished as my darling husband – is both a privilege and the ultimate comfort. I fervently hope that – whether it be with Dr Knatchbull or another, equally good gentleman – in but a few years, you too will know such a happiness.'

Mary smiled, and affected an innocent air. Journey permitting, she could expect to know happiness by some time on Monday. Her flesh tingled again.

'My dear child,' Fanny continued. Having finally embarked on the act of confiding, she seemed unable to stop. 'It has not escaped my notice that you have endured a . . . *troubling* few months, and I would like to take this opportunity to give credit for the manner with which you have conducted yourself. Though it cannot have been without its challenges, you have behaved perfectly properly throughout.'

'Thank you, Mama.' Fanny might have embarked on a mystifying new intimacy, but Mary's own script was unchanged.

'It has been an unpleasant business. Such a *pity* that my dear brother had to take on so, but there – we can now put it behind us. Though you have been the primary victim, I must say that it has not been easy for me. I have been—'

'—in a difficult position, Mama,' Mary finished for her. 'Oh, I have seen that.'

'That is *most* kind. Entirely between us, I am not sure your father has fully appreciated the fact. But I am *slightly* concerned that while my energies have lately been taken up with *his* feelings, I *may* have neglected your own.'

'I bear you no resentment, Mama,' Mary replied, at last in all honesty.

Fanny acknowledged her with a tilt of the head. 'But

I fear it *was* remiss not to talk to you directly and that troubles me still.' She lapsed into silence for a moment, studied the flames in the fire, stroked her expanding girth and then went further. 'For the record, I would like it to be known that – once I had got over the *shock*, that is – I was never *overtly* hostile.' Fanny gave a sad sort of smile. 'Actually, it might have been rather *cosy* – another secure tie between our two families.'

Sudden hope rose in Mary's breast. She turned her head, studied her mother. Could she be brought on side after all? Should Mary confess even now, plead for a blessing? She chose her next words with care. 'It *is* a pretty thought, Mama . . .'

But, of course, Fanny took it no further. 'Sadly, your father could not be convinced of the same.' She sighed. 'And once he had hit on the idea of my brother being your uncle—'

Mary had to speak up then, and did so in earnest. 'I never have seen him that way, Mama.' It was important that she, too, went on the record. 'As you know, I have become deeply fond of all the Godmersham family, and to my mind they are not quite relations, but rather dear friends.'

'Speaking perfectly frankly, Mary, I am delighted to hear it, and completely agree. But when your father's mind is set . . . Ah, well.'

For where was the merit in discussing Sir Edward's opinions when they could not be altered? Neither lady could ever hope to know that sort of power. And so, they instead both surrendered and lapsed into a silence that came close to companionable.

After some minutes, Fanny finally rose, a little unsteadily. 'Now, if you will excuse me, I am all over fatigue.'

She then bent to kiss Mary's cheek with a tenderness she had never before shown. 'I do not expect your papa home until the small hours. I pray he does not disturb you on his return.

'Good night, my dear child,' Fanny said softly. 'May the Lord bless you.'

And then she withdrew.

Mary reeled in her wake. She could not have imagined her mother would ever reveal herself so – and that she should do so just now . . . Already this was proving to be the most astonishing evening, and the real drama was yet to begin. She waited a while, listening; caught the sound of the latch on Fanny's door, and began her own, slow ascent up the stairs.

But despite the self-possession she had shown over dinner – and, indeed, throughout the previous week – Mary was surprised to find that she was shaking all over. And more troubling still, she knew why. This was not *doubt*. She could not change course now. No, this was her conscience – wounded enough by the treachery she was to inflict upon one parent, under new attack from the other.

All these past weeks, Mary had lived under the shadow

of her father's imminent misery. And had she thought to consider the effect upon anyone else? Not once. As Sir Edward dominated the lives of all in the family, so he dominated all of their thoughts and concerns. Such was his tyranny, only now could she see it. Mary paused, tried to grip on the banister with a trembling hand; started to climb again; tripped on the step and was forced to stop by the window at the first landing.

And there – the point at which she could see both upstairs and down – her mind was assaulted by images of what was to come. She pictured the morrow: the discovery of her own disappearance. The household in uproar. Doors flying open; servants searching the house. Sir Edward's inevitable, stupendous fury that could rock the foundations.

But though she would be its cause, Mary would not be its witness. By then, she would be well clear of London, halfway to the North. It would be down to Fanny – good, decent Fanny, who preferred peace over passion – to deal with the fallout. And oh! – that *poor* lady. She did not deserve any of it.

CHAPTER XXXIV

Booker was, indeed, in high agitation and already dressed in her cloak. When Mary entered the bedroom, she sprang up in alarm.

'Oh, it's you, thank the Lord.' Booker sank back into her chair, with a hand on her heart. 'I've been that worried about a maid coming in and seeing the place . . .'

Two sealed trunks stood against the wall, screaming intention. The wardrobe was emptied; the washstand was cleared.

'And how was the mistress then?'

'Oh, *Books*.' Mary staggered across the room, fell on to the bed and curled up like an infant. 'She was . . . kind. Charming and honest and really – yes! – very *kind*.'

'Humph.' The maid shrugged. Once effort had been spent in coming to judgement, she would not go to the trouble of revising it. 'All put on, I don't doubt. Well, she picked a fine time to start . . .'

Mary gave a sad shake of her head. 'Booker, you are a darling. But sometimes, you come across like my father . . .' She sat up and hugged her knees. 'It did not feel like pretence. Indeed, I truly believe that, for the very first time, she was at last being frank. It led me to wonder—'

'There's no time for wondering, miss.' Booker rose, grabbed her hat and marched to the mirror, armed with a pin. 'We've got a coach to catch.'

'Oh, do sit down! We still have a whole, interminable *hour* and you are making me anxious.' Mary needed to talk. 'It led me to wonder how things might have been different. We could have had a better relationship, my mother and I. And perhaps I am to blame as much as she.' Mary stared at the ceiling. 'She must have viewed these five, motherless children as objects of terror. And we did not make it easy for her, that I confess. It was not as if we *asked* for a *stepmother* – who on earth ever would? We resented the *role* she was to play in our lives but, in so doing, did we ever *consider* the nature of the woman herself?'

'Well, I've never heard such nonsense in all of my days.' Booker stabbed pin into hat with some violence. '*She* was the adult, and *she* is to blame. And that reminds me . . .'

She strode back to the chair and, sitting erect,

addressed the drawn curtains. 'While we're on the subject of *mothers* . . . There are things *she* should have told
you, if you were doing all this the *proper* way – though
I doubt even then that she would've, as your class never
does right by its children if it can help it.' Booker cleared
her throat and adjusted her bonnet. 'On a gentleman's
wedding night, he likes to expect—'

'Oh, *dearest* Books!' Mary collapsed back on the bed
with the giggles. 'Spare yourself, do! Remember, they
sent me to school, and for year upon year. What do you
think genteel young ladies discuss after lights out – the
catechism? There is no need to give me the Talk: I have
heard it all backwards. Though if by, say, Newark we're
half dead of boredom, you could test me and Mr Knight
on our knowledge? You remember, like Miss Atkinson
used to do with French verbs and tenses . . .'

Booker now stared directly at Mary, jaw open, eyes
stretched. 'Well, I never did! Little Miss Butter-Wouldn't-
Melt . . .' And once she had got over the shock of it, rose
to reassert her authority. 'Well, that's enough of all that.
Now, down to business!' She marched to the desk and
slammed a hand down on the writing paper. 'You've put
it off long enough.'

Mary covered her eyes then and let out a groan. She
had planned to leave a few, brief words propped up on
her dressing table, but Ned had counselled against. A
note in the house could be discovered by chance before
morning. If Sir Edward was alerted, he would send out

a party to hunt them down. Instead, Mary must write a good letter to her father, Ned to his own and they would post them en route, well after midnight. By the time they were delivered, then it would be too late for her papa to obstruct them.

But the task was not easy. Mary sat down at the table, picked up her pen – stared into the vellum – summoned the words, but they did not hear her call. Booker paced, scoffed and chided. Mary wrote a few lines, scratched them out: started again. The clock ticked on the mantel and the long hand marched resolute up to the hour. Mary let out a cry of frustration, threw aside one sheet and reached for another. Until, suddenly, there were but minutes until the point of departure. The matter was urgent and she could only dash out an inadequate message:

My dearest Papa,

I am gone to Scotland with Mr Knight and beg that you not try to follow us, for it would be to no purpose.

I am sure I do feel so much the <u>wickedness</u> of what I have done and that nothing can alter the disgrace which I am bringing myself. I have no doubt that you will think me deserving of every cruel punishment. But, Father, I pray – do not withdraw your love from me. Anything but that evil, for I could never cease loving <u>you</u> – deeply and dearly.

To maintain your affection would bring me such happiness that there is almost nothing I would not sacrifice to effect it. But I <u>cannot</u> give up Mr Knight. As I have tried to tell you on several *occasions, we are deeply in love. I only wish that you had troubled to hear me.*

Forgive me, Papa. Dear, dear Papa, I <u>beg</u> you forgive me.

Your devoted daughter,
Mary Dorothea

'There. 'Tis done.' Mary sat back in her chair, stunned at her own audacity. Through hot tears, she watched as Booker snatched up the letter and packed it into her valise.

'Right then.' Booker came over, mopped at her face, then reached for her cloak and held it out like a matador.

Mary rose and let the maid dress her before glancing at the clock. 'Three minutes to go . . .'

And together, they stood to hand in hand, stared at the slow progress of time. Until: 'Lord above, what a spectacle!' Booker burst out. 'What on earth are we doing? This is madness. Careering off to the ends of the earth . . .'

Though the tension was close to unbearable, Mary could not help but smile. 'Scotland, darling,' she reproached, with an encouraging nudge and a smile. 'We are only going to Scotland.'

'*Scotland.*' Booker shuddered. 'The North Pole, Timbuctoo . . . They're all one and the same to me, and that's the absolute back of beyond of the ends of the earth, if I know my geography.'

But of course: she was terrified! Again, Mary twisted with guilt, for here was another good woman who did not deserve it. She put an arm around Booker's broad shoulders. 'You are so brave, dearest.' She kissed the maid's cheek. 'So wonderfully brave and I thank you – *thank you* – for agreeing to come with me. I could not even think of doing this without you.'

'As if I had a choice,' Booker retorted. 'You can't do a blind thing without me.'

Mary moved to gather her in a proper embrace. And then it came: the chime of the bells of neighbouring churches. They both froze – counted each strike. And on the ninth, Booker crept to the door – listened to the slumbering silence – and each grabbed their valise.

The maid cast one lingering look at their trunks: 'You really do trust *that mistress* to send our things on?'

Mary reassured her again. 'After this evening, I am convinced of it.'

And, hands enjoined, they tiptoed down the stairs.

∼

It was still only the middle of May, and though the days were now fine, the night was a cold one. Brisk air slapped Mary's face; her lungs felt close to splitting. Still holding hands, they ran down Great George Street towards St James's Park, where, at last, Mary pulled Booker in.

'Here,' she gasped. 'Storey's Gate.' She clutched at the railings. 'He definitely said "Storey's Gate".'

They hid beneath the branches of a budding magnolia,

and peered out. The odd conveyance came trundling past, but all were unhurried and none stopped for them.

'So where he is then?' Booker said, as if hopeful. 'That great lover of yours has changed his mind, has he?'

'He will come.' Mary smiled back. She now had her breath back and her spirits were rising. 'There are still a few minutes to go 'til our rendezvous.'

'And just suppose he does not, eh?' Now, she was close to triumphant.

Oh, Mary thought, how you long for that! 'Then we shall take to our beds and I hereby pledge to unpack *both* of our trunks before breakfast,' she replied briskly.

Mary's faith was unwavering. Ned would not desert her. No plan of his could ever fail. There was but one, last, small piece of business which still troubled her. 'Books dear, where will *you* be sitting on the journey, do you suppose?'

She had long dreamed of being alone in that carriage with her future husband: thundering north in his arms. The stuff of romance! A memory to share through a long, married lifetime! An outspoken maid with a loathing of travel might prove somewhat *dampening*. On the other hand, two days on the back with the boxman did seem rather cruel . . .

Booker shot her a look of pure outrage. 'I shall be right in the middle of you two, thank you very much. You are still an unmarried lady, madam, may I remind you? It falls to *me* – and me alone – to protect *your* good reputation.'

'I fear it is a bit late for that!' Mary laughed and shivered with delight at her new wickedness.

She looked up Horse Guards and down Birdcage Walk, while her mind did the arithmetic. It must by now be four after nine . . . So one minute to go until the time he had promised her . . . Silently, Mary counted the seconds . . . reached five . . . He could not – he would not – let her down now . . .

And, at that very moment – as if out of nowhere – a coach-and-six came suddenly careering towards them. The two women froze; each groped for the hand of the other and squeezed it.

'Is it *him*?' Booker whispered.

'Surely—' Mary could barely breathe.

'Good heaven above – do you not see? It could be *anyone* – lover *or* bandit!'

And there they were, two ladies at night – alone and unguarded.

'Oh, Lord,' the maid muttered, in terror. 'Oh, foolish child, *what have you done to us*?'

The driver pulled on the reins, drew up, jumped down to the pavement: raised his hat in respect.

'*Daniel*?' Mary fell back in astonishment. '*Is* it?' She gasped. 'It is! Dear *Daniel*, of Mersham-le Hatch!'

'Daniel of Chawton now, my love.' Ned was beside her, taking her hand from her maid's. 'He was not easy to find. But I am delighted to report that Daniel has kindly agreed to work for us from now on.'

Us . . . They were now *us* . . . And *he* had gone to all that trouble on *her* behalf . . . Oh, Mary could swoon into this fine gentleman's arms.

But he was holding out the door, ushering the ladies into their seats. Booker took up her position in the middle – solid as a brick wall. Ned slapped on the carriage, cried: 'Gretna Green!' and they set off in haste.

CHAPTER XXXV

That night, Fanny slept remarkably well. It was gone eight o'clock when a shaft of golden spring sunlight fell on her pillow and roused her. She opened her eyes, noted that she felt quite refreshed and recalled the events of the previous evening.

What a success! She wriggled her toes with great satisfaction and allowed herself a short moment to bask in the glow of it. Mary had been *such* a dear that Fanny could not think why she had not tried earlier to form a rapport. After all, every girl needed a mother, as she herself knew. Well, it was never too late . . . Now Mary had that particular confidante, she might *finally* flourish and find her way.

There then came a scream from the floor above. The crash of a tray. Running of footsteps. The bedroom door was flung open.

'Madam!'

'Sayce!' Fanny scolded. '*Really.*' She pulled her bed jacket around her. 'What on *earth* is the matter?'

'She's gone, ma'am!'

Fanny let out a cry, became all over cold. She leaped out of bed but her legs would not carry her.

'*My baby!*' She fell to the floor. 'My baby,' she gasped. 'My baby is gone!'

'Madam!' Sayce crossed the room in a flash, flung open the drawer of the bedside cabinet and found the salts. 'The baby is upstairs having breakfast with Nurse.' She held the vial beneath Fanny's nose. 'And we need to pull ourselves together. There's trouble afoot.' Gently, she drew her mistress up and then lowered her into a chair, placing a hand on her forehead.

'Trouble?' Fanny repeated, feeble. 'But if not the *baby*, then what . . . Even so – dear, oh dear – that *is* a pity. Sir Edward does not like *trouble.*'

'He certainly doesn't and he's not going to like this.' The maid swept her mistress's hair back and took her face in her hands. 'It's Miss Mary, ma'am. Looks like she scarpered.'

'*Scarpered?*' Fanny was not entirely familiar with the word or its usage, yet still she knew fear.

'Gone,' Sayce said, impatient now. 'Left in the night.'

No! Fanny would not believe it. She cast about, frantic: found one, last straw of hope and grabbed at it. 'Then she must have been *taken*! Taken by *someone – against* her *will*! The child is surely in terror!'

Sayce rolled her eyes in a somewhat impertinent fashion that Fanny did not care for one little bit.

'Well, if she was, he made a nice job of it. Chamber's all cleared . . .'

Fanny listened to the litany of evidence, and then said quietly: 'I see.' She tilted her head back and closed her eyes. 'Thank you, Sayce, for that detailed report.'

So there it was. Ned had – as ever – got his own way. They were now all in disgrace. The servants knew everything . . . And this was a moment of peril.

She thought quickly. Mary Dorothea – weak, silly creature! – might choose to destroy her *own* reputation, but she would *not* take her family down with her. The next hours were crucial. Sir Edward and Lady Knatchbull must be sure to mark their own conduct, or the household would gossip and hell be let loose.

Fanny paused to collect herself and adopted what she liked to call her Voice of Authority. 'Sayce, I fear I was woken too early. Perhaps you would be kind enough to see that I am not *further* disturbed, till I have caught up on my sleep.'

And as the maid made to leave, she casually added: 'Oh, one *small,* further matter. Might I ask if my husband has yet been informed?'

'No, ma'am.' Sayce, suitably subordinate now, bobbed into a curtsey. 'Thought it best *you* heard before *him.*'

'Quite so.' Fanny nodded. 'Thank you then, Sayce. I think that will be all.'

Fanny climbed back into bed – reached out a limp arm for another dose of salts – then, once revived, pulled the coverlet up to her chin, as her mama had once done when tucking her in as a child. And with a new clarity of thought she set out to assess the grim situation.

But of *course* the maids would choose to tell Fanny first; no one was brave enough to beard Sir Edward with a crisis first thing in the morning. And no doubt – for was it not simply the Way of the World? – they would anyway class this as the mistress's fault and the mistress's business. The Mother was always to blame.

On the first point, she decided firmly against. She would *not* be the one to go to her husband. The rage would be such that he would inevitably lash out, say hurtful things – make wild accusations – which Fanny could then never forget. Better leave it to the valet, or the butler – or even the chimney sweep, should he be so unlucky. The kind wife would emerge at midday.

Meanwhile to the matter of her own guilt: Fanny plunged into a period of deep self-reflection and then surfaced almost at once. She had done nothing wrong! Sir Edward had dealt with all this alone, since the moment of the first proposal. It was *he* who had talked to his own daughter; *he* who had claimed that the girl had no feelings . . . Throughout, Fanny had stayed at a distance – to the extent that she had not even seen *her own brother*, whom she adored. Or had done, until ten minutes ago.

Indeed, had they not – all three of them – in some way

betrayed *Fanny*? She had taken her husband's reports in good faith. She had complimented Mary on her behaviour. Outrage rose in her breast. She had *trusted* Ned to come into *her home* . . .

And the next thought struck like an arrow. Of course, it explained their businesslike conversation. How else could Ned have communicated his plans? They had hatched their plot on that last Sunday morning, while she had stood by in the very next room.

Then could it even be said that Fanny had been in some way *complicit*? Surely not that! She had been entirely unwitting. Played for a fool. Had she not?

Although, were she perhaps to dig deep into the far chambers of her feminine mind – that place which she generally liked to avoid at all costs – might Fanny then discover that she had somehow known, all along?

She buried her face into the pillow and started to cry.

～

Though she was never to know who did the deed, Sir Edward's unmistakeable roar rang through the house soon after nine. Sayce came in shortly after; Fanny affected deep sleep. But soon the noise of his grief, from the study directly below, pulled at her good, wifely nature. He was her husband! He needed her comfort! She rang the bell, called for Sayce and got dressed.

'Oh my dear! The dreadful news has only just reached me,' Fanny cried as she rushed into the study.

Sir Edward was bent over his desk, face sunk into arms. That full, solid form – which she had always found such a comfort – was racked with his sobbing.

'I am so sorry, my darling. So very sorry.' Fanny curled herself around him, leaned her head on his shoulder. 'Still.' She stroked his dear head in a gesture of soothing. 'What's done is done and, somehow, we must find it in our hearts to forgive them—'

Sir Edward wrenched himself up then, turned and stared at his wife with pure fury. '*FORGIVE THEM?*' He stood, fists balled. 'You expect *me* to *forgive* that which I had expressly *forbidden?*' He shook his head violently. 'Oh, no. They shall not get away with this!'

Fanny recoiled, took a few paces back to the plush armchair away from the desk, settled herself and chose her next words with care. 'Husband,' she beseeched him. 'Pray, dearest, do *think* on it. They have been gone for some hours . . . By tomorrow, they will no doubt be wed and then' – she held out both hands – 'there is nothing that anyone can do.'

He looked back at her with contempt. 'You must forgive *me*, madam, but that is naïve. What *matters* a *marriage* in *Scotland?* Bah! My lawyers will unpick *that* in an instant. I have summoned them already.'

'But then, if they seek sanctification in a *proper*

church – in *England,* I mean?' Ned never did things by halves, as she well knew.

'Trust me, that will not happen.' He started to pace. 'I intend to write to the Archbishop this very day and, *by my word*, he will instruct the whole clergy to turn them away.' Sir Edward turned back then, in full pomp. 'No priest will marry them!'

Fanny studied her lap. There was a whole other layer to this calumny which she had not yet considered. Her brother William was now ordained . . . he adored Ned and would never refuse him . . . Her throat became hot. The flush rose on her face. Were *all* the Knights in on the conspiracy? Even her father had seemed to warn her of *something* . . . That left-out feeling came back, sharper than ever: pierced through her good, loving heart. She suddenly felt entirely alone.

They both fell into silence – he now brooding; she urgently groping for a way through. For if the two families should be cast asunder by this, then Fanny could never know contentment again . . .

'Dear husband.' She tried once again to make him see sense. 'I feel your grief and – believe me! – I share it. They have inflicted on you – on us *all* – the most grave injustice. They have wounded your pride. Yet still, for all that, nothing can change the fact that Mary Dorothea is *your daughter*. You *cannot* simply *reject* her!'

'Madam, believe *me!*' Though he still spoke in rage, hot tears of true grief now spilled from his eyes. 'I *can* and I *must*! How can you, of all people, expect otherwise? I forbade, I forewarned – I made it *abundantly clear* that I would never forgive. And I did so for the sake of *our family* – for the rest of *our children*. So what choice am I left with?' His substantial being seemed suddenly small. 'My hands are quite tied.'

'But – *sir* – you love her! You love her *deeply* and *honourably*. You are the most *excellent* parent!'

'No more, madam.' Sir Edward presented his palm as if swearing an oath. 'I am her father no more.'

'Oh, dear good Sir Edward.' Fanny fell to her knees, clasped her hands as if in supplication. 'Oh, *excellent* man! Cast your mind back to that Easter, two years ago – when Mary was so ill that we feared for her life. You *wept*, you *implored* the Good Lord that He spare her. I am your witness.'

Fanny could never forget it. Such was his passion, she – then childless and bitter at it – had felt a horrible jealousy. It had been a moment of great personal shame.

'Better He had taken her then!' Sir Edward burst out.

'No!' Fanny leaped to her feet in sheer horror. 'Husband, I *pray* you remain mindful of your good, *Christian* feelings! What is left for us all if we do not suffer the Good Lord and His influence?'

Sir Edward's countenance darkened. Even his piercing blue eyes appeared to turn black. 'May He forgive me, but in this I am sure.

'*'Twould be easier for me now if my daughter were dead.*'

CHAPTER XXXVI

At ten o'clock in the morning of Tuesday 16th May, in the very best chamber of Gretna Hall, Mary awoke. She opened her eyes, studied the heavy oak in the ceiling, the curtains framing the bed – noted the tartan festoons – and started to smile.

So she had done it. Little Mary Dorothea had actually done it, and – oh! – was it not bliss? Turning on to her back, she ran through that roll call: those familiar names of poor ladies bewitched and then thwarted – sent up a prayer for their futures – and then rejoiced in her own triumph. For had not she, too, faced every obstacle? Had not she too been expressly forbidden? Yet she alone, only Mary, knew victory.

Her *husband* moved in the depths of the bed, then.

Mary propped herself up to study the manner in which he slowly reached consciousness: saw that, even in sleep, his face crinkled with happiness. She kissed his dear lips before he had quite come to.

'Ah.' Blindly, Ned reached out a hand. 'That's right,' he murmured; pulled back, beholding her now. He stretched first, then smoothed the wild curls from her forehead. 'You came after all.'

'You cannot have doubted.' She nestled into his shoulder, looked about and drank in the sight of him, bare-chested beside her – as if witness to a miracle.

'But of course!' Suddenly, he was all matter-of-fact. 'Every second of the journey: had you asked to turn back – though my heart would have been broken – I should have obliged.' He ran a hand through her hair. 'It felt, always, almost too much to ask of you. Now, having got my own way in it—'

'Which you, sir, are well used to!'

'That may be true.' He shrugged and smiled down at her. 'Nevertheless, I hereby pledge that I will always be grateful.'

'Even when we are long married, and I am no more in your eyes than a good piece of furniture?' Mary was sceptical. 'Men do rather tend to fall into that sort of indifference.'

'Not this one.' Ned turned on to his side, extended a forefinger, touched under her chin and slowly – so slowly – began to draw a line down to her breast bone and then – ah! – even beyond. 'I shall never not feel gratitude for this.'

She gasped as he stroked her.

'Good morning, Mrs Knight.' He spoke softly.

'Husband,' Mary returned, though she could hardly speak for the heat of her skin.

'I hope you slept the sound sleep of the respectably married woman?' He was whispering now in her ear.

She shivered – 'Not exactly' – and started to wilt.

'Even after a journey such as that one!' Ned was up on his elbow. 'Forty hours or more in a coach not enough for you? For one who presents as a rosebud, you are made of some steel, madam.'

Mary giggled. 'Oh, I confess to being perfectly shattered, sir – what with *one* thing and *another* – if the thought of *that* pleases you. I meant more that I do not feel quite respectable.' She sat up too and, though it was a bit late for modesty, pulled at her nightgown, which had drifted way past her shoulders. 'Can it really be true' – she fiddled with the ribbon up close to her throat – 'that all it takes is for that peculiar blacksmith to bang at some metal and—'

Ned tipped his head back and guffawed. 'What a ridiculous nonsense it was! And how very pleased the man was with his own great performance.'

'He might have washed his hands first,' Mary grumbled. 'Of course, I chose to wear my best pink for "my wedding" – such as it was – and now it's covered in smuts and my gloves are quite ruined.'

'Oh, my love, what have we done?' Though the facts of the past days were frankly appalling, still he was only amused. 'Can you believe it? Running away in the night! Careering by coach to this wild, foreign country! Do you know, I do believe I have actually slept with *your maid* . . .'

Mary shrieked. 'She guards me like Cerberus!'

'And to top it all off, we said our vows *in a forge*, of all things.' At last, he became serious. 'I am sorry, my darling. You deserve so much more.'

'Believe me, I want for nothing.' She sighed happily as she laid her head on his chest. 'For I am now Mrs Ned Knight of Chawton Great House! And I cannot wait until we at last cross that threshold.'

'One other stop first, my love.'

Mary flung her head round and stared at him. Though she could envisage a time at which his habit of scheming without previously sharing the details might yet prove irksome, now she could only marvel. This expedition must already have taken some weeks in the planning, and there was more?

'My brother William has agreed to marry us properly – in the Steventon church where my dear Grandfather Austen was once the well-beloved rector. So much of our history has been played out in that dear place. My Aunt Jane was baptised in its font.'

'A credential indeed!' And how delightful the thought that Mary was now a part of such an extraordinary family.

'So, charming though this sojourn may be' – he waved his arm around the dark, gloomy room – 'we must get there post-haste. Your father is quite likely to attempt some legal challenge to a Scottish marriage – do not worry!' He pressed a finger to her lips before she could protest. 'He cannot. But still, knowing him, he might try.

'I shall not rest until the moment when we can repeat our vows before God – whom even *Sir Edward* must accept as a much higher power.'

Mary struggled to imagine her father conceding to any being at all, temporal or celestial. With Right always on *his* side, there was never a need for it.

'In short, we must linger no more.' Ned rose and, with his long stride, crossed over the room. 'You must write another note to your father, and I to his wife.' He pulled on his undershirt. 'Inform them of the fact of our marriage. Beg their forgiveness again.'

He wrenched open the curtains and set about collecting the clothes that had been cast off without care the previous evening. Once again and already, Ned was returned to himself: restless and active.

Meanwhile, Mary stayed just where he had left her: leaning back on the bolster; staring at the pale, northern sky; watching the tops of the trees sway in high winds – and felt her heart sink. From the warmth of that bed – host to such joy – the world looked irresolute, and so very cold. And now heavenly fantasy must make way for more awkward reality.

What sort of welcome could they expect to receive? She thought of her father and mother – they would need time to recover from the shock; her brothers, who, though they might pretend otherwise to their parents, would be secretly thrilled. They had always loved Ned.

But there were so many others besides: friends of both families; neighbours in Kent who had once thought her demure. The villagers of Chawton, whom she must somehow befriend even as they learned of her shame. And – but of course! – she must soon face Miss Austen: dear Aunt Cassandra, in her sweet corner cottage. How Mary had once thrilled at that good, Christian lady's approval! How she would loathe her disapprobation. E'en still, she must prepare for it.

And – oh! – Mary thought, for the first time since the adventure began. *Oh, what have I done?*

PART FOUR

CHAPTER XXXVII

On the 25th day of May 1826, Miss Cassandra Austen swept in from the sun into the gloam of the wood-panelled drawing room of the Great House, crying, 'Good day, Mrs Knight,' and 'Welcome to Chawton!' with a blithe and carefree good cheer.

On the whole, Cassandra was not much given to sweeping in anywhere – those days were behind her, if, indeed, they had ever been known. Now perching somewhere between her fiftieth and sixtieth year (she had dispensed with precision. It was no longer of interest), she was naturally inclined to conserve her own energies. And as for a carefree, cheerful demeanour, well . . . Though there certainly was such a side to her character, it had been a while since she had known cause to display it, nor did she feel entirely at home while so doing.

So this was hardly her typical method of entry and it left both parties equally taken aback.

'Miss Austen?' The words emerged as more question than greeting. Their speaker – flushed, nervous, self-conscious – dared not meet her guest's eye.

On instinct, Cassandra crossed the carpet, stepped forward, took the young hands in her own and pecked the pink, downy cheek. 'My dear, I cannot tell you with what eagerness I have been awaiting your arrival.' She was all too aware that she was starting to gabble, but sensed that the situation demanded it. 'There are so many blessings to my situation, living as I do in the dear cottage up there, on the corner.' Idle chatter was, in her view, the very best sort of weapon in the face of great awkwardness. 'There are windows on both sides – I do not know if you have ever noticed that charming feature? – thus putting me in a position of enormous advantage. I am always the first to know who comes into the village and I was *determined* to be the first to call upon you.'

She finished with a flash of the social smile of the everyday morning visitor; she received a disarming, level and serious gaze. In the silence which accompanied it, Cassandra studied her hostess.

The last time she had laid eyes upon Mary Dorothea Knatchbull, which was not so long ago, she had been a sweet, pretty girl of quite obvious innocence who seemed ever eager to please. So that when the shock news of the elopement first reached her, Cassandra had struggled to believe it to be true.

The creature before her now was quite different: much closer to being a woman and, of course, at the peak of her beauty. A lilac silk gown, cut low at the bosom, showed off her figure: that tiny waist was close to unnatural; rich, chestnut curls were piled high on her head; the chiselled little chin – said to come from her mother – was sharp as a bevel on a fine diamond. So her attractions were manifest. But though her clear, hazel eyes had not lost their shine, grey shadows had moved in beneath them. And while she blushed in the manner befitting a newlywed, her still lovely countenance was pinched in with pain.

This was no gay, light-hearted bride, then; more one riven with contradiction and conflict, and, it was clear, in no sort of mood to join in her visitor's mindless prattle. Instead, Mary responded with frankness. 'Miss Austen, you are most kind to call when, as I understand it, many condemn me. This is an honour which I, a pariah, had not dared to expect.' She then shied like a miscreant under threat of a whipping. 'Unless you are come to express your great disapproval . . .'

Surely the girl had never known any mistreatment? In her surprise, Cassandra did raise a brow then – that could not be helped; it had seemingly lifted entirely of its own accord – before responding to the question in appropriate terms: meet like with like, as was her way. 'May I?' She signalled the sofa – a deep, red damask, worn with the neglect of long generations. It could do with replacing.

'Miss Austen, forgive me,' Mary gasped. She was clearly unused to the position of hostess. How could it be otherwise? She was still only eighteen years of age. 'Pray, do.' Mary lowered herself to the edge of a chair, as might an unwelcome visitor who could not hope to belong.

'My dear Mrs Knight.' Cassandra made herself comfortable and adopted a new, firmer tone. 'No doubt I appear to you as a relic of some bygone age. Indeed, no doubt I *am* such a thing.' Despite her best efforts, a weary sigh escaped. 'But I do like to think – and very much hope that your dear husband will testify – that I *try* to tend *not* to the *pompous*. And though I may be that stock comic creation, an *aunt* of significant *years*, we do not all *disapprove* just for the sake of it. I certainly feel no sort of disapproval towards you, my dear.'

Mary was all relief and surprise. 'Then I thank you for saying so.' Though that sadness still lingered. 'But I fear the rest of the world feels very differently.'

'The *world*?' Cassandra gave a small laugh, as if at the follies of youth. 'I regret to inform you that the world does not think of any of us as much as we all like to think.' It was at least true that at her own time of life, it did not give a jot. 'As for the *minuscule* circles in which we both live . . . It may be true that you have created a *minor* diversion. But for what do we live but to create sport for our neighbours?'

Mary gave a tight smile to acknowledge the Jane Austen reference and Cassandra was pleased.

'I assure you, it will not last for long.'

This was a severe understatement of recent events. In the two weeks since the couple's elopement, they had been roundly condemned and abused by all the usual, more prurient suspects – *tricoteuses* at the guillotine. Each age has its own. Cassandra found it distasteful and quickly determined to set up in opposition. She would act as the young lovers' ally.

'People move on, Mrs Knight! Indeed, I suspect that process is already begun.' Though there was still, inevitably, the odd sister-in-law who was enjoying it too much to let go in a hurry. 'I have lived long enough to witness many such – well – little *disruptions*.' She refused the word scandal, though others did insist upon using it. 'Of course, opprobrium might flare up in the *moment*, but it cannot be sustained. Soon enough, you will find it has dimmed to mere ember and, before you expect it, is turned unto ashes.' Cassandra issued an encouraging smile. 'This too shall pass, my dear. This too shall pass.'

'Oh, Miss Austen.' Mary twisted her hands in her lap, gazed down at the new, narrow gold band on her finger. 'You cannot know my father.'

In fact, Cassandra had had that misfortune, but chose not to mention it. 'I do have some knowledge of fathers in general, and in particular those who abide within the strictures of good, Christian values. Though the Lord may allow us to give vent to the darker emotions – even towards the members of our own families! – He has blessed us with the gift of unwavering love and the capacity for forgiveness. And in the end, we must trust in Him to steer us all back to our one, rightful path.'

Still, Mary did not seem convinced. 'I *do* hope you are right.'

'I can assure you, I am,' Cassandra replied happily, before it occurred to her that she might be coming across as, well, rather pompous. Slightly alarmed, she moved on. 'It is a warm day, is it not? I confess I developed a thirst on my walk up the long drive. You may not yet have had the pleasure, but the Cook here – a good enough soul and no need to fear her – is famed for her ginger beer. Might . . . ?'

Mary leaped up in agitation. 'Pray, forgive me *again*. I fear I am not yet used to—' She looked wildly about her.

'You will find the bell just there, by the fireplace,' Cassandra pointed out, ever useful, while thinking: the girl is nowhere near prepared for all this, and already at a loss. To find herself suddenly the mistress of an estate such as Chawton, with no mother or sister of her own to support her, was a burden indeed. So how very fortunate that she, Miss Austen, would be ever close by to assist her. The thought brought with it a thrill.

The door opened at once and, as well as a servant, Lord Byron – that famous stranger to discipline – bounded in and over to Mary, the herald of his master.

'Aunt Cass!' Ned did come in with a sweep, but then he was naturally one of life's sweepers. 'You are here!'

He took her up and into his arms – the only person left on this earth who still chose so to do.

'But of course.' Cassandra spoke into his frock coat and feared she might have turned pink. This nephew always did have that effect on her, though it seemed almost unseemly now, in front of his wife.

'You are not appalled then?' He pulled back to study her, with a very faint touch of nerves. 'I should hate—'

'My dear boy.' She smoothed down her dark dress and corrected her plain, simple bonnet. 'I was a *little* surprised, I confess. But there, 'tis done and, once a couple has been joined before God, it behoves all of society to respect and support them. I wish you both every happiness.'

'By heavens, you're splendid!' Ned kissed her again, laughed, ran a hand through his hair until it stood on its ends and spoke over her shoulder: 'Did I not say my aunt is quite splendid? I do believe she will be our particular friend.'

'I should like that, very much.' Now with her husband – the muzzle of his dog deep in her lap – Mary's demeanour was utterly transformed. 'Miss Austen has been very kind.' For the first time she smiled. Her dimples appeared. And at last, she looked like a bride.

The ginger beer was delivered and the unlikely threesome settled down to discuss the intricacies of the journey to Scotland. Miss Austen was not much entertained – the travels of others could only ever be of limited interest – but preferred it to tales of the behaviour of Sir Edward Knatchbull. She had read more than enough in her many letters from Kent.

Within a half-hour, Cassandra began to sense that she might be a little *de trop*. What did a young couple on the first day in their new home – and so obviously wildly in love – want with a dusty old relative? She prepared to return to her quiet cottage; rose, took her leave. And was surprised and delighted to be invited to dine that very night.

'My wife's aunt, Lady Banks, is to join us,' said Ned.

'She meets with my father this morning,' Mary said quietly, 'and will bring her report.'

Tension returned to the room; Ned chose to ignore it.

'And I cannot think of a finer first party, can you, my love? Two of our favourite people!' His enthusiasm seemed entirely genuine. 'What is the collective term for aunts, do you suppose?'

Cassandra braced herself for a joke that might feel to her more like an insult.

But at once, Mary – cheerful again – leaped in with: 'An *excellence*?'

And Miss Austen felt happier – more necessary somehow – than she had felt for some months.

CHAPTER XXXVIII

They all left the mansion together – out through the great, thick oak door, down the flagstone steps worn to a shine by the forebears of centuries – then the couple bade Cassandra goodbye and took the path to the stables. She allowed herself a small moment to stand in the carriage sweep with the Great House to her back, the green glory of Hampshire around her, and watch them go.

As usual, Ned moved at the pace of one in competition with time. Mary, her hand in his, skipped along by his side. Was she yet fully aware that she had married a man who could not sit still? Cassandra smiled as she wondered. Even as their distance increased, their laughter could still clearly be heard. This evident companionship – nay, intimacy – was not unintriguing. The family reports and, in particular, the letters from Fanny had given Cassandra the impression that the couple were virtually strangers; that their declarations, and certainly their marriage, were somehow unserious; that this was no more than a manifestation of Ned's sorry, impetuous nature.

Yet to look on them now was to witness a love not only deep, but longstanding and tested. How could that be? How could two dutiful parents have missed that which was right under their noses? Cassandra shook her head, proceeded down the slope to the church and, instead of coming to judgement, allowed herself a frisson of pleasure at how the morning had passed.

Thank heavens she had chosen to take the friendly approach! Had she joined in with the mass disapprobation, then how much would she have lost? At the start of the year, her mother had suffered an unfortunate episode that had left her quite bedridden. The doctors agreed that she was not long for this world and so, after many long years of daughterly devotion, Cassandra would soon be alone. Some kind friends did try to suggest that, when the sad moment finally came, her daughter would at last know freedom: a life untrammelled by duty! In her own mind, it loomed more like a demotion.

She had been dreading the want of a purpose. So how very kind of the Good Lord to deliver her this: a nephew close by who loved her – she was perfectly aware that most struggled to go beyond merest respect – with a dear wife who showed every promise of becoming a friend; a house in need of attention. And might one entertain the hope of the arrival of babies? There was certainly a large nursery to fill.

Cassandra came to the small, parish church in the dip between hills; stopped at the white fence and looked over the graveyard. On an ordinary day, she might approach it and pay her respects to forebears and friends, but on this, she resisted. Scent wafted up from the camomile lawn; a cuckoo cried out its delight from the heights of an old elm. Preferring to dwell on her pleasure, she began her ascent through the park.

Cassandra was rather looking forward to the evening. It was her experience that, having attained some significant years, ladies could always find plenty to talk about. Life had thrown down its challenges; they had been met with and survived and, suddenly, one's station and origins diminished in consequence. Age was a leveller.

So when she happened to catch the sight of the liveried coach on its way to the manor – not that she was glued to that particular window; merely that it offered the best light for her mending – she was not unduly put off. What mattered a gold crest on the door – and goodness – was that really *six* horses? Her thought still held true: once nearer to the end, we can only have more in common than not.

But the evening was set to begin in the most curious

fashion. It was clear that the august visitor had not expected Miss Austen's presence, nor did she welcome it. And it seemed that Lady Banks saw this as no ordinary dinner, but instead more a contest of aunts in which she was determined upon her own victory.

On being introduced, she was politely unfriendly. Though the taller by far, Cassandra formed the distinct impression that she was being looked down upon. But what bothered her more was the evidence that, despite the grandeur of her conveyance, Lady Banks could not afford the right clothes to fit her. The strain in the stitches was enough to cause her to wince. Were they better acquainted, she might offer to let out the seams.

'My attachment to Mary is more than well known.' Lady Banks issued her first challenge over the soup. 'I may be but a *gr-r-reat*-aunt, but I am also her *godmother*.'

'Then that is a position of great honour,' Cassandra conceded at once. 'And one that brings even more weight to your already gracious decision to bless this young couple with your presence, so soon after the shock of—'

'Ha!' Sharp eyes, buried like pins in the vast, plump cushion of face, flashed then with triumph. Victory was already hers. 'Oh, *Miss* Austen.' Her jowls shook with the pity of the conqueror for the recently conquered. 'It was no shock to *me*, I assure you. For I knew all about it!'

'Indeed?' Cassandra tried to hide her surprise. Acceptance was one thing – she herself had found it with remarkable ease – but collusion another matter entirely.

'You knew of the plan?' Her manner remained mild, as if she sought only to clarify, and not to accuse.

'Not quite!' Ned cut in gallantly. He had the sense to see that, by her boasting, the lady could bring damage to her own reputation. 'But as for the *principle* – Lady Banks was aware that we were considering the possibility, and was kind enough not to *discourage* us. And for that' – he bestowed a smile of the particular sort that was a crest-holder's due – 'we will forever be grateful.'

Lady Banks purred and preened, while Cassandra's mind boggled at all this intelligence. Again, Fanny had given the impression of a young couple taking sudden leave of their senses and Mary, in particular, acting quite out of character. Either the Knatchbulls did not know the half, or those letters were not worth the paper they were written on.

In contrast to the visitor, Cassandra held no power whatsoever and had long ago learned that any criticism from her would only be heard if it came dressed as a compliment. 'Then, Lady Banks, allow me to commend you for your courageous position. It cannot have been easy for – as with so many others – are you not also *famously* close to Sir Edward?'

'Quite so!' Lady Banks exclaimed, as if her position brought with it no moral conflict. 'Since the moment he lost his own mother, back in his boyhood, I have devoted myself to his welfare and, even as a man, he has had the good fortune to live much under my influence.'

'Ah,' said Cassandra. 'I see.'

She spoke with a great sense of meaning, which Lady Banks quite misunderstood.

'But I did not begrudge it!' she cried. 'We *aunts*, Miss Austen, must never shy at our duties! My reward has been to watch his continued success. And in his *first* wife – Mary's dear late mama – I had a fine ally. Oh, she was a *fine* person, whose skill for controlling his extremes of emotion equalled even my own. We agreed on most everything. But since the arrival of the *other* . . .' Suddenly mindful of the company, she let the thought trail away.

'So I did *try* at the time to convince him to accept the excellent offer from this most *estimable* gentleman.' Though she had no real lashes to speak of, she batted the few stubs that remained towards Ned.

In that moment, Cassandra saw that she had once been a beautiful woman, sure of her powers, and had yet to catch up with the fact that she now was very much not.

'But would he heed me? *R-r-really*,' Lady Banks declared, with some considerable pomp, 'he can be so *pompous*.'

'Although, of course, a father must do his duty as he thinks fit,' Cassandra mused. 'And the law as it currently stands puts its trust in *his* opinion over the—'

'But *this* father is *mistaken!*' Lady Banks seemed to erupt. It was almost as if the unfortunate temperament was a family condition. 'And *I* took the opinion – based on *my* own sound judgement and the wisdom of years – that it was high time someone taught him a lesson!' Her voice was a roar. 'Only when faced with a fait accompli could one such as Sir Edward be made to accept that he has committed an injustice.' She brought the flat of her hand down on the table.

Cassandra jumped half out of her chair, but both Mary and Ned sat up to attention. After all, the whole point of this visit was to report on Sir Edward's current position, and only now did it seem they were near.

Mary reached out to her husband, gripped his hand and – sweet almond eyes full of hope – asked in a trembling voice: 'Pray tell us, dear Aunt, how did you find him? Has my father come close to acceptance?'

Lady Banks seemed to deflate, as if all that hot air had suddenly flown out from her person. She shuffled in her seat, sunk into despondence, and was forced then to admit that – *despite* all her strong words and wisest *possible* counsel – Sir Edward's position remained completely unchanged.

CHAPTER XXXIX

To watch a large, affectionate family at play is to gaze upon beauty, and by the summer of the year 1834, the Knights of Chawton were approaching peak glory. Mary had produced first two charming boys – Lewknor and Wyndham – and then two pretty girls – Annabella and Georgina. And on that July afternoon, they were all out on the lawn in the sunshine and thriving. Miss Cassandra Austen, from her favoured position in the shade of a cypress, looked on with great satisfaction.

After all, so deprived of her own happy childhood – growing up with no model to learn from – what Mary had achieved was close to miraculous. Having once had to skip to keep up with her husband, she now matched him in energy. Since arriving in Chawton, she had transformed the Great House into something it had not been for decades, and that was a home. On top of that, she had established a smallholding right there in the grounds; and her work with the local women and children was of such a standard as to merit even Cassandra's approval. And all this Mary had accomplished while raising her offspring to be good, loving Christians. She had every right to feel proud.

And though she would say this to no one, so too did Cassandra. For if the Knights were a masterpiece, then could it not be said that she played the part of the master's apprentice? The hours she spent picking up Spillikins or soothing tantrums seemed not unlike the work of those minor artists who toiled unheroically, filling in the deep background so vital to the whole. No doubt, her services would be required again at any moment – peace never reigned for too long. In the meantime, she was content to sit quietly, and enjoy the fetching tableau.

With one small child wrapped about his neck, Ned stood over Lewknor and guided his bat; the good Reverend William Knight, there for the day with a selection of his own seven fine offspring, was the bowler – though he played with the handicap of a tiny daughter attached to each leg.

'Shot, sir!' Ned cried as, by his force alone, the ball soared up into the infinite blue and away. 'Now, run! Run for your life!'

Lewknor squinted into the sunlight – unsure whether he had indeed scored a hit – set off in a slow, gentle amble across the back lawn, then stopped to examine an ant hill.

'Fielders!' called William. 'Where are my—? Dash it!

Gertie, how many more times? There is no scientific value in testing a chin with a buttercup! And how can you catch, Dickie, when you're cuddling a kitten?' He flung out his arms in exasperation. 'Brother, what is wrong with our children?'

'I fear they're all duds,' Ned roared back, in laughter. 'When we were that age, we were playing at Lords, if I remember correctly.' Pausing the game, he strode towards the table beneath the rose arbour where the lemonade waited. 'Is that not right, Aunt Cass? Were we not already feted as sporting heroes?'

From her wicker chair, Cassandra called out that they had both been the most horrible ruffians and the despair of all nurses; received a volley of cheerful abuse for her excellent memory. Then the riotous party returned to the pitch, and she fell back into contented reflection.

For was she not, in that period, the most fortunate creature? This family had been delivered unto her as a gift: a gift from the Lord, made even more precious by its time of arrival. She had once expected to spend the autumn of her life dwindling away in quiet solitude; thanks to the Knights, it was all busyness, amusement and constant diversion. Having once kept their distance, now all of her nieces and nephews flocked about Chawton – dear Ned drew everyone in. So their old aunt now saw them all often; knew every offspring. How many single ladies could boast of such a position at the centre of the great family whirligig? What she had possibly done to deserve such an honour, she could not quite say. But she would forever be grateful.

The arrival of a goose, swaggering on to the scene, leading a fine flock of bantams, was the sign that Mary approached. As Lord Byron had once been his master's herald – the poor dog now snored by Miss Austen's feet, too old even to run for the ball – so domestic fowl performed the same role for the mistress. They came with her everywhere.

'My dear wife!' Ned greeted her as she came round the corner. 'Pray be so kind as to remove your menagerie from the pitch. How can we breed sportsmen in such conditions? Off with you!'

The goose turned and hissed, and continued.

'Excuse me, but you are addressing our next Christmas feast,' Mary scolded. 'Show some respect, sir, or you will be dining on string.'

Would their parents have addressed each other in similar terms? Cassandra very much doubted it – their mothers were, typically, much more subservient. This amiable frankness struck her as progress.

'But Mr Goose is my very best friend.' Lewknor began then to wail, as he so often did. Fat tears rolled down his cheeks; the younger ones joined in and soon the entire crowd of children was consumed with despair.

Mary picked up each one in its turn, wiped every face, pledged to let the bird live in conditions of comfort into old age, before marching towards Cassandra, the calm and the shade.

'The Lord give me strength!' she exclaimed, fanning her face with a quick, pretty flick.

'It seems He has already given you plenty,' Miss Austen replied. 'But perhaps it may be wise not to lift them all, in your condition? They are no longer babies, my dear, but sizeable children.'

'I can hardly reach down, as I have no waist left to bend.' Mary sat back complacently, and rubbed at the shape of the next baby, due in a matter of months. 'And I refuse to leave them to cry! I know all too well what that is like for a little one.'

'You must be the judge. Forgive me for fussing.' Cassandra gave in at once, and chided herself. Mary had got off to a difficult start: Lewknor had been born prematurely and was still worryingly delicate; the next child born still. It had been a very dark time for them all and, though the fond aunt had issued her comfort, still she could not shake her concern.

But then had not Mary simply sailed through her past three confinements? She now presented as a strong and healthy young woman – as was so often the way. Look at Fanny, for example. Having endured nearly five years of misery, she was now the proud mother of seven, with one more on the way. The thought occurred that it was rather like a sailor getting his sea legs, and caused Miss Austen to chuckle.

'It seems to be a pleasant enough afternoon.' Mary caught her husband's eye, sent over a sweet smile and a wave. When she turned back to Cassandra, she was all over pink – as if still in the first days of new love. 'Dear Ned – never happier than when a brother is with him. Is not sibling affection a wonderful thing? I do hope my own children grow up to enjoy it.'

'You sound wistful, my dear.' Cassandra reached for Mary's hand and took it into her lap, before daring to remark: 'I am conscious that your life now is very much more Knight than Knatchbull . . .' With Lady Banks dead, Mary had no visitors of her own. 'Might there one day be an opportunity for your own brothers to visit?'

Mary turned her head towards the walled garden. 'I should love it, of course. I miss them, quite horribly. They do *write*, at least!' The boast came out as pathetic. 'Ah, dear. The thought simply never occurred . . .' Her narrow shoulders drooped as she sighed. 'But my father . . .'

As ever, the very thought of Sir Edward cast its own pall. How Cassandra resented his corruption of this couple's happiness.

'It wounds me that none of my family has yet met my children. Who could have ever imagined such an estrangement would come to pass? I put all my trust in his fatherly love for me, but I fear that trust was misplaced. It appears that to disobey *him* is the ultimate sin.'

'For which you have paid ample penance!' Cassandra exclaimed in high passion. 'And now *he* offends God by refusing forgiveness!'

But still, even after all these years of Sir Edward's wilful mistreatment, Mary would not condemn him. Instead, she turned her head back towards the game on the lawn, and smiled. 'Oh, do look at them, Aunt! Sinner I may be, but I can never repent, for how much have I gained?

She paused to applaud Wyndham's first cartwheel. 'I regret, very much, that my father forced me to into a choice. But I can *never* regret choosing Ned.'

~

That August, the family whirligig took on a new vigour, when – with no more than a day's notice – Cassy Knight came to stay at the Great House.

Her presence was not, in itself, unusual. She and Mary had retained their deep friendship and, when one saw them together – witnessed their shared understanding and affection – it was easy to mistake them for sisters. But this time, she brought with her new drama. For Cassy was now in disgrace.

As they sat in the drawing room awaiting the visitor's arrival – one eye on their stitching, the other on the drive – Mary caught her aunt up on all that she knew.

'So it seems she has engaged herself to a Reverend Musgrave Harris . . .' Mary fiddled with her thimble.

'Then is that not excellent news?' Having finished one shift to her own satisfaction, Miss Austen pressed on to the next.

'No! For she still loves Lord George Hill!'

Cassandra thought back to that long ago day in London, when she had witnessed the two lovers meeting; remembered the conviction she had felt at the time: *there* was a match.

'But she could not *have* Lord George Hill.' Though more was the pity. 'And if she has now found a replacement, then I am delighted to hear it.'

'Well, no one else is,' Mary said darkly. 'Fanny, in particular, is set madly against and has turned all of Godmersham around to her view.'

And here we go, again: another poor woman to be forced out of her choice. 'For any particular reason?' Cassandra enquired, with more mildness than she felt on the subject.

'She simply does not approve it.' Mary shrugged as she snipped at her thread.

'He is a man of the Church, though!'

'And of a very good family,' Mary agreed. 'But he spent some years in India, where he fell sick with the cholera—'

'Then he merits our sympathy,' Cassandra replied firmly. 'And that is not reason enough to bar him from matrimony.'

'Apparently, it has left him rather *weak*. And on top of that, he is not, according to Fanny at least, *one of the illuminé.*'

'Again, I see no obstruction. If a man comes from *money*, he can be as *dull* as he chooses. The world shall not mind it.' After all, Cassy herself had always been higher in spirits than intellect. 'Surely, if she has accepted him, then we must support her?' Miss Austen was forced to stop and unpick a stitch. All this aggravation was making her sloppy.

'It seems not. We have our instructions from Godmersham: we are to persuade her against it. The Lord only knows how, as she is so perfectly stubborn.' Mary let her work fall into her lap. 'Why do you laugh, Aunt?' she asked sternly.

'You do not see the irony? *You,* of all people, accusing another of stubbornness? *You* persuading *her* out of her choice? Now, let us cast our minds back . . .'

'You make a fair point.' Mary smiled too then, abashed. 'I was not to be argued with. Still, there is no *love* there, or so they say, and we must do what we can. I shall not go against the Knights – the one family who has offered me acceptance. But, my dear, *dearest* Aunt, I beg that you help me.' She screwed up her sweet face. 'I cannot hope to succeed without your assistance.'

'*My*—?' Cassandra was aghast. 'May I remind you that I am naught but a spinster, and one of some significant years? Hardly the best counsellor on matters matrimonial.' She refused to be part of this. 'I have nothing to say!'

'Oh, *Aunt!*' Mary scolded. 'You are wise and all-knowing, and you *shall* do your – Hark!' At the sound of wheels upon gravel, she leaped out of her seat. 'She is here!'

CHAPTER XL

It was not until the afternoon of the third day of the visit that the issue was broached. The children were all at rest in the nursery; Ned was out in the woods with his gun: it was a rare moment of peace in that busy household, relished by Mary and Miss Austen in the cool of the parlour. Until Cassy marched in.

'So this is where you are *hiding*!' she said crossly. Cassy had been cross since the moment she arrived. 'I know you're avoiding me. Pray, do not argue!' She held up one delicate hand while lowering herself, prettily, on to the chair. 'Poor darlings – if only you could see your own faces! Honestly, it is the same wherever I go. The company *droops* when I heave into view. It is *utterly* humiliating.' A dish of tea was placed on the table beside her, but she ignored it. 'I was the gay young thing once, if you remember?' Cassy twisted her fingers and stared into her lap. 'All of a sudden, I am twenty-seven years of age, and the Family Problem.'

'You are hardly a problem, my dear,' her aunt replied smoothly. 'Shall we *work* while we chat?' Conversation flowed so much more easily when conjoined with mutual manual endeavour. Miss Austen rose and collected the poor basket.

But Cassy refused. 'Thank you, but I find my own *perpetual misery* occupation enough.'

'Misery, my dear?' Her aunt gathered her patience and began yet another new hem. 'Whoever suffered the melancholies when newly engaged?'

'Ah. Cleverly done, Aunt!' Cassy said, with great bitterness. 'At last, we are on to the Great Subject. Pray, do continue! Delight me with *your* sermon. I have heard all the others.'

'I shall do nothing of the sort!' Miss Austen replied calmly, and ignored Mary's meaningful looks. 'You are perfectly old enough to make up your own mind. Who am *I* to judge *you*, my dear?'

Cassy, flummoxed, dropped her belligerence.

But Mary, it seemed, had spied an opportunity. 'Then perhaps, instead, you might tell us what your sister would say, had God chosen to spare her and she were here?'

'Jane, too, was unmarried,' Cassandra retorted.

'Yet not short on advice or opinion . . .' Cassy smiled with the memory.

'That much is true.' The aunt chuckled, and a new harmony reigned in the room. 'Now, let me think . . .' She had already finished one hem and was selecting another. 'I remember when Fanny was wrestling with a decision herself, in her much younger days.'

'Ooh!' The two women squealed like young girls. 'Who *was* he? *Do* tell!'

'I fear the name is quite lost to me. All I can say is that *she*, too, asked for Jane's guidance and my sister and I worked on the letter together.' She stopped stitching to gaze out of the window, with the hint of a smile, remembering how very convivial their dear cottage was once. 'There were two salient points to it, as I recall. The first being: *never to marry where there is not yet affection . . .*'

'Which Fanny then did, may I point out?' Cassy responded. 'And I do not believe that *she* harbours any regret . . .'

'Affection can grow over time, it is true.' The hemming continued. 'Though one cannot count on it.

'But perhaps, more pertinent to your case' – Miss Austen buried her head, fussed in her work bag in search of the scissors and to hide her own face – 'was the second. I cannot recall the exact phrasing, but believe it was something along the lines of: *Do not marry one man while your heart belongs to another.*'

That seemed to have an effect. Cassy studied her lap, and fell into silence. Mary's eyes flashed with approval.

And having scored one success, Miss Austen was

emboldened to go further. 'To that, I can add very little.' Using both thumbs, she evened the space between stitches, and spoke as if in idle chatter. 'But if you seek any more of my *sister's* great wisdom, all I suggest is that you return to her novels. That is what *I* do, when I crave her advice. I am sure, in those pages, you will find something to guide you.

'There!' She lifted the new, finished product – an apron made from old curtains – and looked upon it with some satisfaction. 'All done! I think that is enough for one afternoon, do not you?'

But Cassy remained silent, and Mary had already put down her work and hurried out of the room. Miss Austen listened to her quick footsteps, noted with pleasure that they seemed to stop at the library. And thought: now, let her find the appropriate book . . .

~

And so it was that, on 21 October 1834 – a mere two months after that afternoon – Cassy Knight was married to her best beloved, Lord George Hill.

It promised to be the grandest affair, and something of a departure for the Austens and Knights: a smart London church; half of society expected to attend – and, surely, the guest list must be enormous. For even Miss Austen received an invitation, and she had not been at a family wedding for decades.

A fleet of carriages carried the family from breakfast to the ceremony and, purely by chance, Aunt Cassandra was put in one with only Fanny for company.

'My dear, we have not been together for ever so long!' she began happily. It had sometimes felt that Fanny now avoided her, which was a trifle upsetting. Aunt and niece had once been so close. 'It seems I have barely seen you since – oh – since you were married yourself.' One of the many weddings to which she had not been invited.

'Were you there?' Fanny – suddenly very much Lady Knatchbull – replied haughtily. 'I do not remember it. Ours was both modest and intimate, which I must say is more to *my* taste.' She peered out of the window, then fell back into the corner. 'Do look at the horrible *crowds*! Simply frightful. What on earth can they *want* from us?'

'Is it not marvellous?' Cassandra pressed her face to the window – she saw no benefit in hiding – and studied the multitudes lining the streets. 'Just listen to the roar! All these kind people, cheering the couple. Desperate for a glimpse of the future Lady George Hill.'

'Poor little creature.' Fanny shuddered, with a hand to her face to obscure public view. 'I cannot imagine *she* wanted something so vulgar.'

'Possibly not,' Cassandra conceded. 'But she is happy with her match, and that is all that matters.'

'I still do not *quite* understand how it all came about so very suddenly,' Fanny declared as she fiddled with her reticule. 'We sent her to Chawton to get rid of *one* fiancé, only to find her return with another.' She shuddered. 'Of course, one must blame oneself – as usual. I should never have let her go off to *Hampshire* alone. It all seems to have got rather *giddy*.'

It was only then that Cassandra understood Fanny's nose to be quite out of joint – after all, a lord was one up from a baronet. 'We have Mary to thank for it all,' she explained – as if to be helpful, while knowing that she was, in fact, adding further insult. 'As soon as Cassy gave up the *first* gentleman, Mary did her research – discovered his *lordship* still single – and invited him down to Chawton. Was that not inspired? The whole business was settled in a matter of days.'

They were now on the approach into Hanover Square; the procession had slowed – they were caught in a queue of conveyances – and the cheering had grown even louder.

'So very *clever* of her,' Cassandra went on. 'Do you not agree?'

Fanny stared straight ahead at the back of the coachman. The air in the carriage became frigid, until Fanny finally spoke.

'I hear you and Mary are now rather *close*?' She sighed. 'I confess, I am happy for it. As the years go on and the horrible *shock* of her *departure* fades in the memory, I find myself—' She started to stutter. 'I cannot *escape* the *suspicion*—' The words were not coming easily until, at last, she exclaimed: 'As a *mother*, I failed her.'

'Oh, dear Fan.' Cassandra reached for a hand and patted it. It felt like a return to their intimacy of old. 'Mary has never accused you in *my* hearing. Nor does she speak ill of her father.'

But at mention of Sir Edward, Fanny became Lady Knatchbull once more. 'My husband is a *good man*, Aunt Cassandra.' She withdrew her hand from her aunt's reach. 'A *great* man of high *virtue*.'

'I have no doubt.' Cassandra had met him but briefly, and only had hearsay to judge, though that seemed conclusive. She returned to the window, and the gaiety of the sightseers. She really would rather be delighting in the day.

'Yes, he is *proud*,' Fanny was continuing. 'And with more than good reason, I might add. But when his own daughter betrayed him, his *pride* was *wounded*!'

And that was reason enough to destroy his own family, Cassandra thought with contempt. But she said only: 'I see.' And then: 'Such a pity he could not be with us today. I was so looking forward to furthering our slight acquaintance.'

'Heavens above!' Fanny exclaimed. 'I fear you have no real idea of the Ways of the World. Sir Edward is *far* too *busy* for this sort of thing.'

'But of course!' Cassandra returned. Though they both knew he was avoiding Mary and Ned.

'Oh, Aunt!' The Fanny of old had returned. 'Who could have foreseen that this battle would go on for so long?' Again, they held hands.

Cassandra said carefully: 'There is always that risk: when a bond has been broken with violence, it requires some hard work to repair. Without, it is only too easy to let the weeks drift into months and then years. Until that which was once unimaginable has, all of a sudden, become completely the norm.'

'My only ambition was to raise a good, Christian family.' Fanny sighed. 'I am sure I set out to try my *absolute* best. I now fear this – this – *rupture* has become a stain upon all of us.'

'There is still time to cleanse it!' Cassandra said urgently. 'Fanny, dear: there have been ample opportunities to set everything right again – not least, the birth of five babies. They are such a sweet family and, in refusing to know them, your husband only denies his own pleasure . . .' Tis a *shame* he had no time to spare us today, but I beg you: when the next chance presents, then *you* must act.'

Suddenly, they drew up at the steps of the church. 'Ah, our turn at last,' Fanny said with relief. 'Thank heavens *that's* over.'

And Cassandra – who had been more outspoken than she would have believed herself capable – could not agree more.

Once in the family pew, the two women took equal pleasure in the spectacle of the large congregation. Cassandra only had eyes for the Godmersham servants, fine in their livery. 'Oh, do look,' she whispered, 'there is dear Cakey!' The fond nanny was already wiping her tears.

However, Fanny's attention was all on the array of nobility. 'Lady *Salisbury*, I see. So *gracious* that *she* should turn out for *this.*'

How marriage had changed her, the once-fond aunt thought sadly. The husband's character had infected her own. Though always regrettable, it was not uncommon. Some couples brought out the worst in each other; others, like Ned and Mary – thank goodness – brought out the best. And, though she had not known the gentleman long, Miss Austen had no fears for the two lovers approaching the altar. They had been tested; endured opposition; forced to wait for so long. This love was true.

And, at last, there they were, at the sacred moment of union: Cassy resplendent in white lace; Lord George a fine figure in uniform. The vows were spoken with proper solemnity; the families moved through to the vestry, whereupon the entire assembly seemed to burst open with joy.

CHAPTER XLI

The measles ripped through the Great House at Chawton in the spring of 1837 and, with now six children in the nursery – not to mention a household of twenty – it was a terrifying time. Indeed, it seemed to Miss Austen, as she ran between sick beds, not unlike a cramped, medieval city when hit by the plague. There were so many patients; no one was safe.

Cassandra did not fear for herself. Though it was half a century since her own bout, she must still be immune – and anyway, what mattered *her* health compared to that of the babies? She could vouch too, for Ned, as she had once been his nurse, decades before. But when it came to the facts of her own medical history, poor Mary was ignorant. No mother to ask; no father to speak to; in fact, precious little memory of her childhood at all. It was as if she had wiped it all from her mind to spare her own pain.

The mystery was solved in the third week of the outbreak, when Mary succumbed. By that time, the children were all – by God's grace – on their way back to full health. Ned remained well; Nurse and Booker – that redoubtable workhorse – had the attic nursery under control, which left Cassandra in charge of Mary. But when the rash crept up from the limbs, spread to the face and so threatened her sight, the young mother's state came quite close to perilous. And Cassandra had no other option but to send to Godmersham for assistance.

The following day, Mary was subdued with a tincture, and Cassandra dozing on a hard chair by her bedside, when there came a tap on the door.

'Aunt Cass?' It was only a whisper, but still clear enough.

Cassandra jumped to her feet, fixed the curtains against the glare of that May afternoon – Mary must not look upon light! – and went out on to the landing.

'My dear.' The aunt embraced her sweet niece with natural affection. The ancient oak floorboards squeaked out their protest. 'They have sent you to nurse?'

'That is my lot, it appears.' Marianne shrugged, with no evident pleasure. She was now approaching her thirty-sixth year and still bore the traces of beauty, though the joyous spirit had flown.

'There are worse!' Cassandra adopted a brightness

which she did not quite feel. 'And with a family of our size, there must always be one good woman to rely on.'

Marianne raised one delicate eyebrow, said: 'And *I* am now *she*.' Adding: 'Tell me, what can I do?'

For a full week, they shared the duties of care, together fought back the fever and at last returned the sad patient back to something like life. Still, Cassandra could not shake her concern. Mary's eyes were restored, but her complexion had suffered and it seemed doubtful that she would ever recover her previous bloom. More than that though, her entire system had been weakened severely. She had little to no energy and the strength of a newly born lamb. It would be some time before she could return to the full duties of mother-of-six and mistress of the household. A long convalescence would be required. Cassandra would need to be firm.

And, throughout the month of June – as the sun bestowed a kind warmth and the grounds burst into splendour – the devoted nurse got her own way. It was not long before Mary could walk out unaided – fill her lungs with great draughts of green air – and take pleasure in her family again, though still she tired very easily. There was every hope of a full recovery, and Cassandra was able to return to her own bed at night now, catch up on missed sleep and find enjoyment at the Great House once more.

~

Serious illness is a trauma for every household; the blessed relief of its passing brings with it a new and sharp pleasure in the banality of the mere everyday. And so, on a glorious Thursday morning in the third week of July, it was a very cheerful Miss Austen who tripped down the drive to take tea with Mrs Knight in her chamber. As was their habit, they would sit for a while in the pink, airy bedroom – discuss the plans for the nursery; the news from the village – until Mary was ready to rise. There was no reason to suspect that day would be any different, and she approached it with pleasure.

'Good morning, Booker,' she chirruped as the maid opened the door.

'Oh, no it's not, madam,' came the gruff reply. 'See if you can knock some sense into that head. I give up.' And she stomped out of the room.

Cassandra found Mary in a state of high agitation: sitting up straight against the bolster; wild curls springing out of her nightcap. The mahogany writing box was balanced on her lap and she was frantically engaged in the act of composition – like Beethoven at the height of his madness.

'What on earth—?'

Mary looked up, almost unseeing. It was a moment before she registered the visitor. 'Ah! Yes. There has been a development.' Her scarred face was pink with excitement. 'I have today heard from my mother.' She rooted in the counterpane, found the letter in Fanny's hand

and tossed it across for Cassandra to read. 'My father is sick and – oh, Aunt! – Fanny has seized upon that as her opportunity . . . My mother is so good . . . kinder than I ever deserved . . . And at last, he is persuaded to see me! I am writing to him now.' She put down her pen. 'Pray, listen and tell me what you think.'

She picked up the paper and started to read: '*Hearing of your illness and the possibility of you dying without me seeing you and you forgiving me, causes—*'

'Dying, Mary?' Cassandra cut in with alarm. 'Sir Edward is in danger?'

Mary looked up from her writing. 'My mother suggests that *he* feels he is in danger, hence him agreeing to meet. He has always harboured great fear for his *own* health, but somehow, from her words, I did not get the impression that *she* was over-concerned. Oh dear!' She looked suddenly stricken. '*Could* it be serious? I *believe* my mother said he was suffering something called *trigeminal neuralgia?*'

Cassandra gritted her teeth. For was this not the great inequality? His daughter risks her own life with every confinement; Sir Edward gives every appearance of being entirely unmoved. And yet what was no doubt unpleasant but essentially trivial provokes a great, mortal terror. 'I am sorry to hear it,' she replied. 'But Mary dear – though I am no physician – I do not think one *dies* from the face ache.'

'That is a relief, and much as I suspected.' Mary cheered up at once. 'Still, if he *feels* at death's door, then that is useful for me. Ned and I shall set off in the morning.'

'My dear girl!' Cassandra was horrified. 'Do you not see? *You* are still convalescent! This comes *too soon*. The journey into Kent is long and, it seems, not at all urgent. I *beg* you put it off a few weeks at least.'

'Oh, Aunt Cass. You do not know my father. When sick, he is vulnerable. But, once he is well again, he will go straight back to his old ways.

'My mind is made up.' Mary picked up her pen again. 'This is my chance, and I must seize it.'

Cassandra left the room in surrender and found Booker waiting out on the gallery. 'Madam?'

'No luck, I fear,' Cassandra said, simply. 'Mrs Knight is determined.'

The maid let out all the breath she had been holding in. 'Then mark my words: this is a calamity.'

'Dear Booker,' Cassandra said, soothing, 'I cannot endorse the idea, but it should not prove *dangerous*. We can trust that her husband will take no unnecessary risks.'

The maid guided Miss Austen on to the window seat that looked over the park. Panelled in dark oak, cut deep into the stone wall, it had been a favourite hiding place of the Knight children for two generations. Oddly, Cassandra had never sat there before. She made herself comfortable among the crewel work, glanced out of the mullioned window and sensed the ghosts of the ages.

'This is not *un*charming,' she remarked in her dry way. 'I can now see—' But she was interrupted.

'There is more to this than the measles,' Booker

whispered, fast. 'I have no right to say it . . .' She looked back, checked the gallery for spies. 'Not sure if the mistress knows yet herself.' She leaned in conspiratorially. 'I have every reason to suspect that she's back in the family way.'

Cassandra was stunned. The past months had been nothing but chaos and crisis. The thought that – well – how could? – and when? Seven in one decade! Still, it must be the truth. There could be no better informant on matters . . . *biological* . . . than a lady's own maid.

'And yet she is still feeble . . .'

'All those hours in a coach . . .'

But the plans were all set. The couple set off early the next morning. And Miss Austen waited in Chawton, and fretted.

Of course, she kept herself busy. However heavy one's burdens or troubled the mind, the fruit must be picked and preserved or what would become of us? So it was that Cassandra was selecting the best plums from the tree in her garden when, three weeks later, the coach sped past the cottage and turned right for the Great House. In the shock of relief, Cassandra dropped her basket, leaned against the bough to steady her old heart and watched as the late-summer dust settled back down on the road.

Mary was safe; the couple was home: Chawton life could now resume. The thought set off within her the most curious sensation: blood flowing back in to a limb.

Having allowed sufficient time for the family's joyful reunion, Miss Austen walked down the lane, past the shorn fields brown with stubble and up to the mansion. Ned was already out in the woods with his guns and his boys – a long journey for him was akin to a sentence in gaol. They could meet later. First, she must see Mary in order to settle her own mind.

With the grudging permission of Booker, Cassandra put her head round the door to the mistress's chamber. 'May I disturb?'

'My dear aunt.' Mary gave a wan smile from the pillow and lifted a pale hand. 'Forgive me. I felt the need to lie down. The little darlings have left me quite spent!'

'They have missed their mama.' Cassandra moved to the bedside and planted a kiss. 'Still, we have managed plenty of sport in your absence and, as you now see, all is well. I shall not stay long, but – pray! – do tell me your news. How did you find the Godmersham family?' Though her curiosity was all for the subject of Sir Edward.

'They are all well and our time there was as pleasant as ever,' Mary replied flatly. 'As for Hatch – it was a joy to see that dear place again, and Fanny – my mother – was exceedingly kind. My father, however . . .' A tear dropped on to her cheek. 'Sad to report, we were alone together for a very short time . . .' She spoke through her sobs. 'No more than ten minutes.'

Cassandra felt utter dismay. All the way into Kent, and for *that*? She took Mary into her arms and let her weep on her shoulder. 'Well, it is a *beginning* at least, is it not? You must try and take hope from it. Reconciliation is, in itself, a profound Christian act.'

Mary bit her lip, took back to the pillow and admitted defeat. 'I fear we remain at some distance from being *reconciled*. My father wanted only to report that he still feels the *offence* of my actions, very deeply indeed.'

'*Even now?*' Cassandra could hardly believe it. 'More than a whole decade on?'

'From the way he behaved, you would think it all happened yesterday. The fury, the grief . . . It did not make for a comfortable interview, to that I can testify. There were moments when the distress became almost too much to bear . . .' Again, Mary cried.

That he should put his daughter through such an ordeal, when she had been so lately unwell! Cassandra gathered Mary into her arms again and said, rather archly: 'I am surprised that he should be so careless as to upset *himself* when so *dangerously* ill . . .'

'Oh,' Mary sniffed, 'he is very much better. Almost himself.'

'Then is that not a miracle?' Cassandra raised a brow, pulled back, peered into Mary's sweet face and thought: But you, my dear, are thoroughly spent.

'Thank you, Aunt Cass.' Mary gave a wan smile. 'You are such a comfort to us in our various dramas. And, pray, do not worry yourself on my account. I now hold every hope that my father and I *shall* meet again. And something tells me that it will not be long till we do.'

CHAPTER XLII

Autumn at the Great House was hardly conducive to proper recovery. Like the beat in a fast-moving melody – a polka, say, or a jig – the rhythm of annual events propelled the family along. From the excitement of Harvest Supper, then nutting and shoots; through Rent Day, the great lunch for the tenants, and so on to Christmas. And all the while, Mary – the fond wife and mother – performed all her duties with charm, while growing greater with child. But to Cassandra's sharp eyes, she appeared thinner, more depleted in energy.

Though the confinement approached, neither Mary nor Ned were parents who would countenance any stinting on the Christmas festivities. Equal in their devotion to their children – determined to satisfy the excitement engulfing the household – they threw themselves in.

And Cassandra was delighted to see how they followed deep family traditions at every stage. The games that the Austens had once played in their rectory all those long years ago were brought out again – enjoyed anew by this young generation. And the Masquerade on Twelfth Night – the King, the Queen; costumes and processions – was quite *à la Godmersham*. Such continuity came as a balm to Cassandra's soul. Her beloved, large family now had its own folk memory.

And whatever fate might have in store, she could have faith that the indomitable spirit of the Austens of Steventon would live on through the ages.

~

Miss Cassandra Austen could not remember a January as harsh in all her long days. Snow fell day after day, frosted then froze, and she was trapped in her cottage. The poor of the village would, of course, be in the most dreadful distress, but such were the drifts, how could she go out? For an always capable woman, impotence at a time of great community crisis was a trial indeed. At last, she and her maid hit upon something useful to do: producing vats of good broth, which a few able menfolk – shod in their old pattens as had not been seen for some years – came daily to collect and then distribute. To be so useful and busy was, at least, of some comfort. Still, Cassandra could not shake her feelings of foreboding for dear Mary.

Towards the end of that long January, the skies finally cleared, and though there was still ice on the roads, a few hardy souls now passed by her windows in wagons. And on the 28th day of that month, when Daniel appeared, without prior notice, at the door of her cottage to take her down to the mansion, Cassandra presumed the hour of Mary's confinement had come.

Only to find the couple both preparing to dine.

'This is to be our last evening in Chawton for a while, Aunt,' Ned explained as he led her to table. 'And we wanted you with us.'

Cassandra noticed at once that his demeanour was altered. That breezy optimism upon which her nephew had floated through life had suddenly flown. Having so often counselled against an ever-cheerful approach – was it quite wise to expect only the best when the worst could so easily happen? – she now found that she missed it acutely.

Ned sat, recited the grace and charged his wife's plate with the beef he had grown.

Mary paled, averted her eyes from the rich food and rested her hands on her stomach. 'My dear husband has got himself into a lather.' She smiled. 'He is insisting we go off to London tomorrow. It seems I am now grown so grand that only some fashionable surgeon will do.'

'Dr Stone comes with high recommendations,' he insisted.

'And with so much expense that I do not deserve!'

Mary declared. 'I must confess to feeling quite mortified by all this attention. Still, I shall argue no longer. And when we are home again, it will be for Mr Knight to be embarrassed for having made such a fuss.'

Cassandra felt numb. She cast her eyes down to her dinner plate – blood oozed out of rare meat; formed a thick, dark pool – while her head thrummed with the sad echoes of history.

'Ned, dear.' Somehow she managed to speak. 'Are you quite confident that—?'

'Ah, madam!' Mary cut in. 'Surely you must know by now that *confidence* is my dear husband's greatest strength. It is one of the many reasons to love him.' She reached out her hand across the starched linen.

He took it – planted a kiss on her fingers – and pressed it into his cheek. The affection between them had never once dimmed. The couple still seemed like newly-weds. While his eyes locked on his wife's, Ned addressed his aunt. 'Only the best . . .'

And what could Cassandra say to dissuade them? Only that she had once thought the same, twenty-odd years ago. With every faith, she had carried her ailing sister away from this very village and into a city. She too had hoped to find superior methods – was promised that Jane would be cured! Instead, she denied that dear home-bird of life's ultimate comfort: a peaceful death, with her loving family about her, and in her own bed.

'You must trust your instincts, and I know all will be

well,' she said now, as if calm. 'Pray, do not worry about the children. I shall keep an eye.'

'I thank you for that.' Ned turned to face her. 'But – I almost hesitate to ask it, for the journey is arduous and this winter is cruel – you will come to us, should we feel need of you?'

Cassandra smiled. 'But of course. Just send the word.'

~

Miss Austen arrived, as bidden, at the rented house in South Audley Street, Mayfair, on the 4th day of February, bringing the fresh blizzard with her into the dark, narrow hallway.

'I came as soon as I could,' she told Booker as she peeled off her gloves. 'The weather . . .'

The maid took her cloak and bonnet – iced in the time it had taken to run from coach to door – and, with sudden emotion, flung her arms around Cassandra.

This was so out of character that Miss Austen's first thought was that she was already too late. 'Tell me.' She pulled back and spoke urgently.

'The mistress was delivered this morning.' Booker blinked back the tears. 'Dr Stone was by her side all the while. She is tired but – thanks be to God – entirely herself.'

'Then what fools we have been.' Cassandra smiled out her happiness, turned and took to the stairs. 'Might I be allowed just a peek?'

Booker followed behind her. 'She has been asking for you . . .'

'And the baby?' She paused at the half-landing and looked back at the maid.

'A fine specimen.' Booker held out her hands in amazement at this unexpected development, before adding: 'Though of course they've only gone and given him one of their funny names again. William Brodnax, if you've yet heard the like? Poor little mite.'

Miss Austen stopped, stared at Booker and raised an eyebrow. Had they not already used William for Wyndham? Then he must be known only as *Brodnax* . . . The two shared their amusement – they were of the same mind on most matters – and pressed on to the chamber.

∾

The next week passed perfectly peacefully. The nanny had charge of the baby; Nurse and Booker each took their turn to tend to the mother. Cassandra read aloud at Mary's bedside – *Pride and Prejudice*, naturally. What better restorative? – each afternoon. And every night, as she tried to get comfortable on the narrow bed on the top floor, Cassandra longed for her cottage, where she hoped soon to be.

But on 15th February, Mary started a fever. Dr Stone came at once, administered potions – saw no cause for concern. Mary rallied at once, to great, general rejoicing.

By the 20th, though, it returned with some force. And the following day, relieved from her stint in the chamber where she had passed some long troubled hours, Cassandra went slowly – sorrowfully – down to the drawing room, and Ned in his misery.

At the sight of his aunt, he leaped out of his chair. Ran a hand through his hair. 'Well?' he demanded.

Suddenly aware of a bone-crunching weariness, Cassandra fell into a chair and felt shame at her weakness. 'My dear.' She spoke carefully. 'Might I suggest that you now send for her father? Of course, he may well refuse . . . and one could reasonably argue that such a privilege is beyond his deserts . . . Yet we both know that Mary would – would have – hoped . . . nay, *expected* . . .'

For one long, quiet moment, Ned sat with his face in his hands. Then he sprang into action, and out of the room.

At eight o'clock in the evening, Sir Edward Knatchbull arrived, was met by the son-in-law whom he had sworn never to meet, and ushered into the bedroom, alone. It was the concession that Mary had longed for: the occasion of intimacy – demonstration of love from a parent – for which she had yearned. But by then she was beyond any knowing that her prayers had been answered; or that, at the bell's final toll, she had at last been forgiven.

And at two o'clock in the morning of the 22nd day of the month – with only her beloved husband beside her – Mary Dorothea Knight née Knatchbull drew her last breath.

Throughout the dark hours, Cassandra issued comfort to Ned. Then, as dawn broke, she stole one last, private visit with the dearly departed.

A strange magic occurs, soon after death. Cassandra had seen it before, with her own dear Jane. When the contortions of pain are no more – the cruel symptoms of sickness no longer required – so then the face of the corpse seems to settle and recover the beauty of the once-living self. It must be counted as but one of God's many blessings. He does it that we may be spared the memory of the suffering, and reminded of the one we have lost.

But Cassandra had no need of such kindness. She had never once lost the image of Jane in her prime. How could she? Every day since her death, her sister had walked – she walked still – beside her: whispered in her ear, shared her best thoughts. Still her favourite company; still the greatest of friends.

And so it would be again. In the faces of her children – the perfect, enclosed world of Chawton built by her love – Cassandra would see Mary always.

And miss the dear lady for the rest of her days.

EPILOGUE

Sir Edward Knatchbull arrived at Chawton Great House on the 17th day of March in the year 1838: a date almost perfectly judged to inflict not one, but two evils upon Mary's grief-stricken family. For it came well before they were ready, while also being twelve years too late.

The visit presented as a harrowing prospect for the young widower, still raw in his sorrow. Ned had begged Cassandra be there to support him and, though diminished in strength and with little to no appetite for any further distress, she could only agree.

Sir Edward had sent no hint of a time of his arrival, so they waited in the library together all morning – one at work on her patchwork; the other too over-wrought to be still. The clock ticked; the sun passed its zenith; the tension came close to unbearable. Having paced long enough, Ned could bear it no more. With a great cry of 'Dash it!' and *'Devil!'* he assembled two boys and three guns, and carried them off into the park. So when the carriage finally drew up at the door, at two after noon, it fell to Miss Austen alone to welcome the visitor.

If he was insulted by his lowly reception, Sir Edward was too careful to show it. And if Cassandra had expected an awkward exchange, she was to be more than a little surprised. Once tea had been brought and the weather discussed, he went straight to the heart of the matter.

'It is gracious of Mr Knight to allow me to come. After all that has passed' – he looked down at his hands, cleared his throat and collected himself – 'it would be within his rights to refuse me.'

From all she had heard of Sir Edward, Cassandra knew how much those words must cost. 'There was no question of that, sir. Such opposition is not in his nature. Moreover, in his mind – in all of our minds – this is still very much the home of your daughter. Mary wished you be made welcome. Indeed, she once longed for this moment – spoke of it sometimes, with hope.'

He bowed his head for some time, rubbed at the black band on his arm. 'In the days since . . . since . . . I am haunted by how little I know of my daughter's life.' He looked up, brow furrowed. 'I do try to imagine . . . trace her past . . . but the pictures are blurred and unformed. I lack—' He stopped and looked utterly lost.

Though she struggled to find sympathy, Cassandra

saw his predicament. He had no knowledge of – no reference for – his daughter as wife, as mother – nor even as woman. The Mary he had long ago chosen to cast out of his life had been but a young girl, whose only crime was to fall hopelessly, madly in love.

'Then come, sir.' Cassandra rose and extended her hand. 'Pray, come with me.'

~

'So Mary slept here?' Sir Edward stood, frowning and mournful, in the centre of the Rose Room, and looked around. The soft, pink curtains – framing a pale, wintery sky – still hung in their place. But the dressing table had lately been taken elsewhere and a chintz sofa stood facing the fire, in place of the bed.

'This was very much the mistress's chamber,' Cassandra explained, 'but it was lately decided it would be better used as a sitting room. Since the sad day, the family has taken to gathering here each afternoon. They say they still feel the fond presence, and find some comfort in that. But, of course, it is a little easier for the children if they do *not* have to see all her personal things about them.'

'Indeed,' the bereft father said gruffly. It seemed that he, too, had a sense of Mary still being there.

'It has a symmetry for me, one which Lady Knatchbull will, I think, understand, for it was a sitting room once before, in the old days. Indeed, I remember my sister in here, reading *Pride and Prejudice* to Fanny for the first time!'

Cassandra turned to him, hoping for some expression of recognition. None was returned. She was irked, but hardly surprised.

'And there' – Cassandra pointed to the oil on the wall, which he had not yet registered – 'my nephew has put up her portrait.'

Sir Edward looked up and studied the likeness in silence. Mary – full curls; bright, hazel eyes; sharp chin turned up in confidence – smiled down upon him. 'Ah.' He cleared his throat. 'And that was done when?'

'I cannot say exactly.' Cassandra did want to be helpful, but the years skipped about in her memory and she struggled to catch hold. 'It is certainly recent.'

'It must be. She looks quite altered from how I remember her . . .'

Cassandra was mystified. 'Yet, sir, did you and Mary not meet, only last summer?'

He started at that, and turned away from the picture. 'Ah, indeed. I forgot for a moment, but you are entirely correct, madam. We did meet, that once. Very briefly.' It seemed then that he blushed. 'Little knowing at the time it would be our last opportunity.' He walked to the window and spoke to the parkland. 'God's will be done.'

Silence fell upon the room until, at last, Ned strode in and broke it.

Of course, the meeting was bound to be awkward.

Too much had passed and, anyway, God could not have created two men more diverse in their characters. Still, it had been made in good faith, and with a great deal of effort . . . Cassandra stood back, heart full of hope.

'Sir Edward!' Ned crossed the room; shook his father-in-law's hand in hearty fashion. 'How passed your journey?'

Cassandra watched on with dismay. So they were on the wrong foot at once. Both men were at fault: each was misjudging the other. Ned – whose grief had been manifest – was now presenting the brave face that, he presumed, his adversary expected. 'And where did you break it? To my mind, the best table is to be found at the George in East Grinstead.'

In turn, Sir Edward interpreted this display as an absence of feeling, and did not trouble to hide his resentment. 'So *oppressed* was *I* by its sad *purpose* that I fear, sir, I failed to take *notice*.'

To her tremendous relief, the day was suddenly saved by the arrival of the six dear children. They came armed with their beauty, good manners – their favourite toys – and within moments, all that had been strange was suddenly natural.

Cassandra sank into the low armchair with the wild-flower sprigs and watched fresh affections spring into life; listened to laughter and prattle – all hope restored. Until, exhausted by their play, Sir Edward came over to join her.

'I must confess', he said in a low voice, 'that I find it quite overwhelming.'

'Oh, they are lively enough! Some nights I leave here thoroughly worn out. But are they not charming with it?' Cassandra could not hide her pride. 'And a credit to their mother, of course.'

'Oh yes, all that,' Sir Edward conceded, with no particular grace. 'But I talk more of their high spirits. How is it that children can have such *forgetfulness* – such want of recollection – at a time of the most profound sorrow?'

Cassandra turned to him, outraged. He, too, had lost his mother in boyhood, yet he could find no fellow feeling? Though he had failed as a father to Mary, he was being given a second chance with her offspring – and he now dared to find fault with their *manner of suffering*? The late Lady Banks had been right: Sir Edward was a man in need of firm guidance.

She realised, then, that it fell to her to put him right. 'I cannot say,' Cassandra replied crisply. 'But is it not a merciful dispensation of Providence that it should be so?'

Suitably humbled, Sir Edward rose, returned to a kneeling position down on the floor and resumed play with a wooden farm. The new baby was sent for, brought in by his nurse and warmly admired.

And so it was that this beautiful, unfortunate family started to settle into its strange and new shape, and take the first, hesitant steps towards a quite different future.

~

As dusk started to fall, Cassandra made her excuses and took her leave. She yearned for the quiet of her cottage and felt strongly that the two men should dine alone. She was now an elderly lady and would not always be there to bridge the great gulf between them. They must find the way through on their own.

The evening was pleasant, and she dismissed Daniel's offers and set off on the walk past the sweet, little church where young Mary now lay, close to Cassandra's own dear mother. It was too late to call on them now, but she would do so on the morrow. So much to report! Such a day!

The hill rose ahead of her; its brow fringed with a red-golden light. She stopped to take a deep breath and saw, at the edge of the field, the thrust of a first daffodil – radiant in a great clump of green. She smiled. So nature was turning once more: taking that which is dead and creating new life from its goodness. Binding the past in with the future.

And, with a strange sense of ease as she had not known for some months, Miss Cassandra Austen resumed her long, slow ascent through the park, to the eternal comfort of home.

AUTHOR'S NOTE

Fanny Knight kept a daily journal from 1804, when she was eleven years old, until she was eighty. And, though I have taken one liberty – Cassandra was not at Mary's death-bed, but anxiously waiting for news back in Chawton – the narrative of this novel exactly follows her record of events. However, though the diaries are detailed – who, what, where and how was the weather? – they are hardly confessional. Feelings and attitudes are only mentioned at times of some crisis and the rest I have imagined.

The pocketbooks in which Fanny wrote are very small and she tended to use a thick nib, so they are not always easy to decipher. Still, it is possible to read between the lines of what she chooses to say. For example, whenever she mentions her spouse, he is always 'My darling husband' or 'Sir Edward' – even though she's so short on space. And all of her family – father and siblings – get a 'darling' or 'dearest' before their names. Her stepchildren, however, do not. Indeed, Mary does not become 'dear Mary' until after she has betrayed her own parents. But by then, of course, she has become a Knight.

Although Fanny was only writing for her own interest and perhaps for her children to read after her death, the pocketbooks now have a whole other value which she can scarcely have imagined, for they are our principal source of Austen chronology. It is from their pages that scholars have managed to piece together many blanks in her Aunt Jane's life and chart the full history of the extraordinary Austen family.

We see fortunes rise and then fall; hopes being crushed; love starting to blossom. But most striking of all, to the modern reader, is to witness the perilous nature of the lives of the married women. The birth of every child is a moment of danger. The loved ones of expectant mothers are on high alert. As well as her own mother, who died after her eleventh baby, Fanny lost two Austen aunts in the same way and later, one sister and a few sisters-in-law. If you married young and were happily fertile, then it was a game of Russian roulette, year after year.

Of course, there were some who seemed to sail through. Old Mrs Austen, Jane's mother, produced eight children and was still fit enough to run the busy household in Steventon, as well as the smallholding. After five years of mysterious 'unfortunate events', Fanny herself ended up a mother of nine – on top of Sir Edward's first family – and lived until she was nearly ninety. Most remarkable of all was her sister Lizzie: 'the Married One'. Having taken the great risk of marrying at eighteen, she gave birth to fifteen living children, and enjoyed a long and happy old age. Were they particularly robust, or was poor Mary Dorothea simply unlucky?

Edward Knight – Ned – mourned his lovely young wife for the standard two years after her death and then, of course, began to look around for a successor. After all, he was still only in his forties, had a large, very young family to raise and, by then, his Aunt Cassandra was an elderly lady who could hardly be expected to dance in constant attendance. So no one was surprised or affronted when he married again. Some, though, did argue with his choice of bride.

Adela Portal was young, cheerful and home-loving; nevertheless, Ned's eldest sisters thought her nowhere near good enough. Lizzie refused even to attend the wedding: *Any set of people where Portals are the finest must be at a lowish ebb.* And Fanny was witnessed, at a later occasion, clearly *hating them all.* Though both ladies had snobbish tendencies, they may perhaps have had a point.

Adela was a flamboyant figure, according to Marianne Knight: *very smart in strong pink flounced silk and yellow tussore with lilac – very fat.* She dabbled in mesmerism and phrenology, of which some disapproved. She had an uneasy relationship with her motherless stepchildren, overtly favouring her own. And though, generally, the Austens and Knights were never that imaginative when it came to naming their offspring – just look at all the Edwards – Adela took that to extremes. She called each of her five daughters after herself.

But every Sunday morning of her married life, as she paraded into Chawton church wearing her finery, leading her enormous brood – as she took her rightful place in the family pew beside Mr Knight of the Great House – her eye must have strayed to the plaque on the wall. And she would have read, as we can still read to this day:

MARY DOROTHEA, WIFE OF
EDWARD KNIGHT ESQ[RE]

HER AFFLICTED HUSBAND CAUSED
THIS TABLET TO BE ERECTED,
TO RECORD HIS IRREPARABLE LOSS,
AND IN THE HOPE THAT HER CHILDREN
WHEN THEY READ THESE LINES,
MAY CALL TO MIND, AND ENDEAVOUR
TO IMITATE THE VIRTUES
OF A GOOD AND AFFECTIONATE MOTHER.

'THE LORD GAVE, AND THE LORD
HAS TAKEN AWAY.
BLESSED BE THE NAME OF THE LORD.'

ACKNOWLEDGEMENTS

I could not have written this book, or its two predecessors, without access to the impeccable research of the many excellent Austen scholars and enthusiasts – all of whom have been so generous with their time and their knowledge, and seem ever eager to help.

Of course, the late Deirdre Le Faye laid the foundations for all Jane Austen studies. Her *Chronology* is fixed to my desk, and I think of her daily with fond admiration. Grateful thanks, also, to Hazel Jones, Maggie Lane, Sophia Hillan and Margaret Wilson, who have all produced wonderful books about the various members of the Knight family. And to the estimable Helena Kelly, who was kind enough to read this work in manuscript form and catch a few howlers.

But, most of all, I am completely indebted to Margaret

Smyth. Not only was she so kind as to share all that she already knew on the subject of Fanny and the Knatchbulls, but Margaret also threw herself into the quest of discovering yet more. Though I may, somehow, have written *The Elopement* without her, it would have taken years longer and been a much lonelier experience. I am so lucky to have found such a formidable fellow traveller and also, I hope, a good friend.

In Kent, the staff at the Maidstone Records Office were ever efficient and helpful, and Fiona Sunley and Rochelle Godden were both gracious with their homes and their time. And I have learned so much from my many happy visits to Chawton over the years.

Once more, I have had the great good fortune to work with Selina Walker and, yet again, she has proved herself to be the perfect editor. My thanks go to her and the formidable Cornerstone team. Venetia Butterfield, Laura Brooke, Sophie Shaw, Laurie Ip Fung Chun and Emma Grey Gelder. And as ever, to my brilliant agent, Caroline Wood.

Finally, all my love and gratitude to my husband, Robert Harris – first reader and soulmate – and, of course, my girls, Holly and Matilda. But this one is dedicated to my sons, Charlie and Sam Harris, and my darling new grandson, little George Harris Parr.